THE BOOKWORM

More praise for Charles Durham
and
THE LAST EXILE

"Well-researched, expansive . . . Durham's tale warmly embraces old-fashioned values and morals."
Publishers Weekly

"An interesting romp through regions, cultures, and events few readers will have the opportunity to sample elsewhere."

Booklist

"When the author writes with such attention to detail and sensitivity as Kansan Charles Durham has done with THE LAST EXILE, then the reader can walk away after reading it as if he has traveled into the distant lives of the characters."

The Wichita Eagle-Beacon

THE
LAST
EXILE

Charles Durham

BALLANTINE BOOKS • NEW YORK

Copyright © 1989 by Charles Durham

All rights reserved under International and Pan-American Copyright Conventions. Published in the United States of America by Ballantine Books, a division of Random House, Inc., New York, and simultaneously in Canada by Random House of Canada Limited, Toronto.

Grateful acknowledgment is made to McGraw-Hill, Inc. for permission to reprint a map drawing from *Frontiers of Fortune* by Donald Honig. Copyright © 1967 by Donald Honig. Reprinted by permission.

Library of Congress Catalog Card Number: 88-92229

ISBN 0-345-37382-0

Manufactured in the United States of America

First Trade Edition: July 1989
First Mass Market Edition: February 1992

This book is for Linda, who, in one form or another, appears on so many of its pages.

ACKNOWLEDGMENTS

I wish to express my great appreciation to Toni Simmons for her enthusiastic acceptance of *The Last Exile* and for her invaluable guidance. It was Toni who opened that indispensable door.

I wish also to thank Jean Dawson, whose excellent understanding of the French language and culture was a great help to me.

CONTENTS

PART ONE 1715–1746   1

 1 The Warrior Angel   3
 2 An Awakening   10
 3 Michel Lebrun   24
 4 The Uninvited Guest   37
 5 Farewell to a Friend   46
 6 The Girl from Rouen   54
 7 On Horseback to the River   61
 8 The Change   71
 9 Looking for a Way Out   81
10 The Passage   92
11 The Island City   100
12 The Girl from Trinidad   108
13 The Night of Discovery   116
14 The Escape   125

PART TWO 1746–1747   137

15 Toward the Unknown   139
16 Over the Edge   145
17 Beyond the Height of Land   156
18 Huntermark's Lodge   166
19 The Boulder   174
20 The Outcast   188

PART THREE 1747–1748   193

21 Along the Ottertrack   195
22 Wind Lake   203
23 The Priest and the Dreamer   211
24 Among the Spontaneous People   220
25 The Girl from Wind Lake   232
26 The Winter Encampment   239
27 A Bruised Reed   246
28 The Island   254

PART FOUR 1748–1759   265

29   The Road of Souls   267
30   The Bramble Briar Lodge   273
31   The Letter   286
32   Reunion   293
33   On the Plains of Abraham   303

PART FIVE 1760   319

34   The Fruit of My Body   321

Author's Afterword   333

"FOR THE WRATH OF MAN
WORKETH NOT
THE RIGHTEOUSNESS OF GOD."

James 1:20

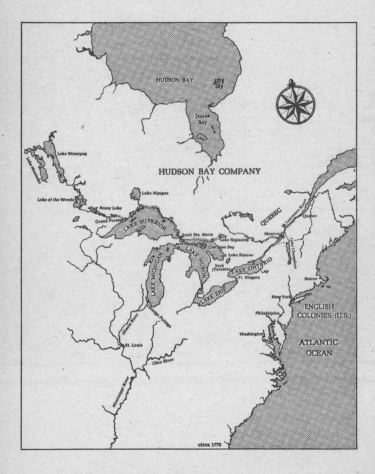

HUDSON BAY

James
Bay

Lake Winnipeg

HUDSON BAY COMPANY

Lake of the Woods

Lake Nipigon

Rainy Lake

QUEBEC

St. Lawrence River

Québec

Grand Portage

LAKE SUPERIOR

Sault Ste. Marie

Montreal

Lake Nipissing

Georgian Bay

Lake Simcoe

LAKE HURON

LAKE MICHIGAN

York
(Toronto)

LAKE ONTARIO

Lake Champlain

Ft. Niagara

Boston

LAKE ERIE

Chicago Portage

New York

ENGLISH
COLONIES (U.S.)

Philadelphia

Illinois River

St. Louis

Washington

ATLANTIC
OCEAN

Ohio River

Mississippi River

circa 1770

PART ONE

1715–1746

CHAPTER 1

The Warrior Angel

CATHERINE DUBLANCHE, barely twenty years old, lay pale and exhausted among the coarse rumpled sheets that in untidy folds rippled loosely over the wide hewn-oak bedframe and spilled down its sides to brush the old plank floor.

The hour was midmorning on a day in late June 1715. The Norman countryside was alive with new green, and the clear sweet songs of larks and doves bathed the hilltop in pleasantness. Last night an early summer storm had cleansed the atmosphere. The air smelled sweet. The sky was a marvelous blue. Over Catherine's bed, clear gold light poured through the crystal panes of a great bay window.

After the night's rain, the air of the room was damply chill, so chill that her husband and the two women who attended her had picked up Catherine's bed—with Catherine in it—and set it full in the rays of the warming sun. The sun's richness illuminated her pale, translucent skin so that the light seemed not to come from the sun at all, but from somewhere inside of Catherine. It glistened in the delicate drops of perspiration that beaded on her upper lip and in the faintly visible golden down on her arms.

Her long blond hair, thrown across her pillow, was damp with tossing exertion. With both hands she gripped the mattress fiercely at its edges.

The thin, coarsely woven cotton chemise—the only thing she wore—also wet with her struggles, had ridden up and left her long graceful legs bare to midthigh. Her soft blue eyes closed in weariness, then opened again. She rolled her head about, searching nervously for the face of her tall young husband. "Abel?" she said weakly.

"He's just outside the door, Catherine." It was her mother's calm voice. Annette Degrave stood looking down at her daughter

3

from above the headboard's right-hand corner. "He's nearby if you need him."

Catherine tossed her head from side to side. A long husky whine rose in her throat and ended in "Oh Abel! Abel!"

At the side of Catherine's bed sat a woman older than Annette. She was looking intently at Catherine's face, and her left hand gently bathed her forehead with a cool, wet cloth. With her right she held tightly to Catherine's wrist.

"Bear down, Catherine," she said in strong, kind tones. "Bear down! That's it. Hold on. Hold on now. All right. Now rest."

She was Jeanne Marie Lemaître, the most skilled *sage-femme* in Avranches. Jeanne Marie was sixty-one years old today, June 23. She was a woman of medium height and thick waistline, whose strong, pleasant face reflected her skill and confidence.

Catherine's most recent contraction subsided. Jeanne Marie distracted her by saying, "Everything's coming along, Catherine. You're doing well. Your baby will be here before noon."

Abel Dublanche had slipped into the room unnoticed, and for several minutes had been standing just inside the door, listening. At the midwife's words he looked sharply at the massive clock standing in the corner. It was ten-thirty. He took a deep breath and wondered how his wife could suffer like this for another hour and a half.

"Catherine"—Jeanne Marie's voice cut in brightly—"have I thanked you for calling me in the daytime? Much better than the middle of the night. Much better. And this is my birthday. You didn't ask me if I'd share it with a Dublanche."

Catherine turned her head toward Madame Lemaître, half opened her eyes, and managed a weak smile. Abruptly, convulsively, against her will, Catherine's shoulders lifted from the bed and the muscles of her swollen abdomen gripped at its contents like a vise. Jeanne Marie urged, "Now! Come on. Bear down again."

Catherine let go of the mattress and grabbed the woman's hand, gripping it so hard that Madame Lemaître sang out with surprise. "That's it, Catherine. That's *it*!"

She rolled her head back, and again her shoulders left the bed. She bit her lower lip until red blood trickled in a thin stream down her jaw. From between her clenched teeth came sounds that began in high compressed squeaks and ended in full-throated roars of pain.

Beneath him, Abel Dublanche's knees went weak. He muttered some sort of confused apology, walked quickly past the *sage-femme*, and bolted out the front door.

Like cold water, the fresh, clean air hit his face. He gasped down whole lungfuls, and leaned helplessly against the big trunk of the ancient oak that grew in the middle of the front lawn. The bark was rough against the palm of his hand. His head cleared. New strength flowed in, coming perhaps from the fresh air, or perhaps from this oak planted by his great-great-grandfather when generations ago he had cleared this hilltop and built the old Norman half-timber home.

For a while he stood in the great tree's shade. The light breeze from the sea turned the cold perspiration on his face yet colder. Suddenly he heard it; a sharp, thin, quavering cry.

At full noon Catherine Dublanche had borne a son, and she called him Gabriel.

Catherine Dublanche came of peasant stock, descended directly from the ancient Celts and from Viking invaders. She and the earth were the same, each a part of the other. Catherine knew the feel of soil sliced and turned by the shovel's blade, the pungent sweet smell of new hay hefted aloft from ground to stack. She knew the gathering of eggs and the soft yielding of the cow's teat in her strong hand, the sharp, rhythmic ring of the ivory-white stream hitting the side of the bucket or swishing through thick surface foam. She knew what it was to plant her feet hard on freshly turned clods, to seize with her hands the smooth grip-worn handles, to loop the reins about her neck and command a great Percheron's way as he pulled the plow's point through the rich, black sod.

Yet for all of that, Catherine was different. Toil had not dulled her mind and she searched hard for answers to questions that others never thought to ask. As she watched thunderclouds gather, she thought aloud to Abel, "When the rains come, smoke from our chimney ascends, then bends back to the earth again. Why?" And on another day, "How is it the snow goose finds its lonely way across the sea?" In a troubled mood she mused, "Abel, they say God damns the pagans who haven't heard. Can it be true?"

Abel would laugh sympathetically and say, "Catherine, only God knows. Don't worry yourself so," for Abel was a practical man.

Once on a warm late summer's afternoon, at the upper end of the pasture that sloped away from the house to the river, Catherine sat on the wide stone wall at the pasture's edge with her childhood friend Marie Lebrun. Marie, a smallish, dark girl with a pretty face, had grown up Marie Brunetière, the daughter of miller Paul Brunetière, who had met his death six years ago when a flash flood carried away both him and his mill. The year after her father's death, Marie had married Daniel Lebrun, and they now had a child, a boy born in autumn of the very year Catherine had given birth to Gabriel. Marie and Catherine often met here to talk, and to let their sons play together.

Today as the boys ran and tumbled in the pasture below the rock wall, Catherine suddenly broke off in midsentence— something about a fresh cutting of clover soon to be ready— and leaned down to gaze at a vine attached to the bare stones of the wall by tendrils that grew out like little feet stepping from stone to stone. A large praying mantis, just emerged from among the dark, heart-shaped leaves, clung to the vine near its very tip.

The mantis looked like a collection of oddly joined twigs, all a pale green, with two great, bulging red eyes. As Catherine leaned down and her face came close, it seemed to meet her gaze and quivered violently, as though about to lose its grip and fall.

"I wonder, Marie," Catherine said softly, "if he knows."

"Knows what?" Marie responded, puzzled.

"Knows he's there," Catherine answered, "as you and I know we are here. What do you think? Does he know it?"

Marie's bright, incredulous laughter bubbled out. "Catherine! Such a question! Only you would think it. Why don't you just ask the mantis?"

"Oh, how I wish I could," Catherine answered, undistracted by her friend's laughter. "Then I would know the answer to so many other questions."

Marie knew her friend well, and loved her well, yet she had never understood the curious turns of Catherine's mind. But curiosity gave zest to Catherine's life, and the taste of truth was sweet on her tongue.

Abel Dublanche had married Catherine Degrave when he was twenty-three. She had been only eighteen, the most beautiful girl in the Norman countryside. Her long blond hair reflected the sunlight as her deep blue eyes reflected the sky, and the soft lines of her pleasant Nordic face had told him she was as compassionate as she was kind. The lilt in her voice and the way she carried her lovely body had drawn him powerfully to her.

So he loved her, and he brought her home to live in the house his great-great-grandfather had built, the kind of half-timber dwelling common throughout the duchy of Normandy. The house was framed with massive timbers hewn square, mortised and locked to stand heat and cold, wet and dry, still and storm. Its roof was steeply sloped, thatched thick and tight with long tan grasses to turn the winds and rains that swept violently in from the great ocean to the west. The dark exposed timber frame, filled with native rock, then plastered over and painted white, somehow put one in mind of a ship at sea, its glistening sails filled with wind and crossed with sturdy masts and yardarms, under way, confident, and free. Yet the old house was anchored firmly to ground worked by generations of Abel's forefathers.

The house had come to Abel through his mother's side of the family. Abel's father—originally from the city of Rouen northeast across the base of Normandy's peninsula, and a night's passage upriver on a rising tide—was descended from the Romans rather than the Celts or Norsemen, and the olive hue of the Mediterranean was evident in his face and hands.

Abel's father once told him that an ever-so-great-grandfather, three hundred years ago, had watched the oily gray smoke of Joan of Arc's body drifting across the Seine.

Abel, who followed his father's trade, was a blacksmith. With the house he had inherited the smithy his father had built, a stone building that lay just fifty yards west, downhill, this side of the barn and nearer the road.

Abel's father had died three days before Abel's sixteenth birthday, and his mother just a year later, but the big house was filled with their memory. The hinges on the doors, the andirons and spits, the kettles and the iron trivets that hung on the walls—all were the fruit of his father's skill and labor.

So Abel followed his father, learned the business well, and by the time he was twenty had established his own reputation. He pumped the great bellows and hammered the red-hot iron into shoes for horses' feet and scythes for farmers' hands. He shaped new plowshares and on his massive anvil welded the ones that were broken.

But the work Abel loved most was everywhere up and down

the streets of Avranches. It decorated the iron gates, hung on mantelpieces, on kitchen walls, and over the doors of shops. From his forge and anvil he brought intricate, skillfully executed gates, andirons, and decorative ram's heads. He hammered graceful scrollwork for fences, made weather vanes with grand ships under sail, gray iron roosters that welcomed the morning, and shining black stallions that galloped into the wind.

Abel was a sensitive man who found pleasure in graceful curves and lines, a good man who loved his work and believed a day spent in toil and execution of honest labor was a day redeemed.

Gabriel Dublanche was endowed with his mother's mind. He was eight years old now, and had a wide streak of rambunctious curiosity.

An uncontrollable shock of dark hair fell across his forehead. His large brown eyes glistened in the firelight on winter evenings while Catherine told him stories of the distant past: how for twenty-five hundred years, his fair-haired, strong-bodied ancestors had lived in these forests, how with energetic minds they invented the plow, and created art of unsurpassed beauty, and established the first civilization this side of the Alps. It was they who had given to all the great rivers of Europe their names: Thames, Shannon, Rhine, Danube, and Seine. It was they, she said, who had founded London, Bonn, Geneva, Belgrade, and Paris.

Catherine told him stories of men down from the north, the land of fjords, gigantic men who swept the coastlands in fury, like wind-ripped froth on a driving sea, falling on towns and lone houses, even on abbeys where holy men prayed in terror. *"A furore Normanorum libera nos Domine."* "From the fury of the Northmen, deliver us, O Lord."

Gabriel thought his mother's voice sounded like sea waves washing the beaches. She told him of big ruddy men standing tall in the bows of dragon ships, men with names like Ulf the Red, Smoothing Stroke, and Hrolf the Walker—a man so big no horse could carry him.

One such night she dared tell the boy how the Northmen captured King Ella. "They broke open his back," she said, "and pulled his lungs out into the air. While they laughed and watched, the king breathed his last breaths and the naked pink lobes of his lungs rose and fell like wings. 'Carving the blood eagle,' they said."

Gabriel's eyes grew big and he drew into himself as though trying to hide. At the other side of the hearth, Abel took the clay pipe from his mouth and shook his head slowly at Catherine.

"But," she pushed on, "when the prows of the great dragon ships emerged from the mists of the sea and sailed up the Seine, their Viking days were over. They fell in love with this rich, green land, and with the girls who lived here. The big men with the ruddy skin married the girls with the golden hair, and . . . well, here we are."

And she laughed a laugh like the tinkle of glass bells and smiled mischievously at her bemused husband.

You must not think Catherine Dublanche crude or violent. She was not, and neither was her son. Gabriel was adventurous, curious, full of play, but he had his father's nature as well; a serious side, quiet, introspective, and for a man, unusually tender.

Sometimes the two parts wrestled within him; sometimes he was one thing, sometimes another. But more and more his quiet side was taking the ascendancy. From both Abel and Catherine he had learned—or inherited—a devotion to God. This devotion was keen and genuine, deepening as he grew. Perhaps it was the angel, the angel who was always there. From atop the hill where the old Norman half-timber stood, Gabriel gazed away across the sea to where the granite cone of Mont-Saint-Michel reached up from the water, where Saint Michel—the legendary Warrior Angel—presided over the toiling sea. Even on days when dense gray fog mantled the coast, Gabriel felt the great angel's brooding presence.

In mid-July of Gabriel's tenth year, when the spring storms had settled, the family took a week's holiday, the first Gabriel could remember. In a light open carriage they drove south and then west on an undulating road that ran along the coast between beach sand and forests. The Normandy hills fell behind, and the Brittany mountains rose ahead.

They did not hurry, so it was after dark on the second day when they stopped to sleep in a wide, grassy meadow that lay below the tall forest and above the open sea.

Gabriel bedded down in the back of the carriage. In a thick, soft quilt sewn by the grandmother he never knew, he wrapped himself against the cool night's sea breezes and nestled down among the baggage. For themselves, between the carriage and the sea, near the back right wheel, Abel and Catherine prepared a bed of boughs and blankets on the ground.

The night was black. A vastness of stars spread overhead. The invisible sea lapped against the sand, and they slept. After midnight, from somewhere nearby in the forest, a feral dog howled mournfully. Gabriel awoke, and the dog howled again. In spite of his warmth, shivers ran down Gabriel's spine. His eyes opened wide, and he dared not move.

While he had slept, the moon had risen, now three days past full and very bright. Its deceptive light made him wonder whether what he saw was real or an illusion. Gabriel gathered courage, rose on his elbow, and looked out toward the sea. His lungs filled sharply and his breathing stopped.

A deep mist, coated with silver by the moonlight, lay on the face of the sea. No air stirred. Big curling wisps of fog rose slowly upward, like fingers beckoning, and then fell again into the sea-bound cloud. Up from the floating whiteness pushed the mountain, silent as the mist, bathed in moonlight, girt by cloud, seeming to rise from another world, without earthly foundations. Massive fortress walls rimmed with battlements sat below a great pyramid of houses and cloisters. A vast cathedral crowned its peak, and over it all stood the angel. The boy gazed in wonder, his soul wholly absorbed in this mountain so mysteriously inhabited by the archangel of God.

But after a while, sleep once more pulled Gabriel's eyes closed. As he drifted off, the angel turned toward him and lifted his sword high over the place where Gabriel lay. And in his dreams, it seemed to the child a gesture of peace and benediction.

CHAPTER 2

An Awakening

IN 1727, when Gabriel was twelve, Abel's older brother, Joseph François Dublanche, came home from Paris. Joseph had left Avranches at the age of fourteen to study at Louis-le-Grand, the

Jesuit college on Paris' Left Bank. Five years later he graduated, and then stayed on at the college to teach. In twenty-three years he had come home less than a dozen times.

The Dublanche family was proud of Joseph François. "How wonderful," they said, "that a Dublanche, a man of our own blood, nourished in our soil, has risen so high." Gabriel, too, was in awe of his uncle.

But this time, having resigned his place at Louis-le-Grand in the early fall, and having taken a new appointment at the Hotel de Ville in Avranches as curator of the ancient illuminated manuscripts from the abbey at Mont-Saint-Michel, Uncle Joseph was home to stay. Now he would divide his time between work and his long-neglected family.

Joseph was a pleasant man, taller than his brother, handsome, dignified, warm, and open. In order to give himself entirely to study and work, he had never married, and had written often to Abel, his only brother, to whom he felt especially close.

Since his return, Joseph and Abel had spent many winter evenings together. Catherine was Joseph's supreme favorite among women, and Joseph doted on Gabriel as shamelessly as a grandfather. These times did nothing to diminish Gabriel's admiration for the man. The more he saw of Uncle Joseph, the more nearly he worshiped him.

One evening in early March, a warm south night wind blew. It touched the foot of late snow on the roof, dissolving it slowly, and the melt dripped pleasantly from the eaves. Within, Abel, Catherine, and Gabriel, with Joseph and Marie Lebrun's son Michel—now Gabriel's closest friend—sat together around the big open hearth of the old family dwelling. Joseph sat as usual, looking the part of the learned elder statesman, with his lean legs crossed at the ankles, gazing over the smoking bowl of his long-stemmed, white clay pipe into the glowing red logs. On the backs of his hands grew a thick mat of black hair that continued up his arms and disappeared under white sleeves turned up at the elbows. Joseph's fingers were not thickened by hard labor. Even so, he remained a man of the country, and had a special dislike for ostentation. Though it was fashionable for men of his rank to wear powdered white wigs, he did not. His long, dark hair swelled to tasteful fullness in the front, and was swept back to a single neat queue that lay on his neck. Gabriel so admired his uncle that, in imitation, he had combed and tied his own hair in the same manner.

A white collar banded Uncle Joseph's throat and met in a ruffled bunch of lace under his chin. His knee breeches were black and trim, the identical color of the thin, tightly fitting hose that spanned the long distance between his knees and shoes. The shoes themselves were faced with large silver buckles, buckles he kept polished to a mirror shine.

On this winter night, as on many others, Gabriel and Michel sat nearest the fire, on the warm flagstones, rubbing the fur of the gray, black-striped family cat, feeling the subtle vibration of its purr. Occasionally one or the other of the boys tossed a kernel of corn into the fire, listened for the pop, and watched to see its white flower burst from the coals.

The curved shining buckles of his uncle's shoes had caught Gabriel's attention, so that he sat marveling at the distorted reflection of the open fireplace in the bright metal. The orange-red glow in their center contrasted dramatically with their borders' silver-edged blackness.

Conversation drifted pleasantly through the standard repertoire of subjects—spring's nearness, the abundant moisture that boded well for crops soon to be put into the ground, the health of this relative and that—when out of the blue, Joseph François, his eyes fixed on Gabriel, said, "Catherine, I've been thinking." He paused in a relaxed way to let her curiosity build, then continued, "I've been thinking the time has come for Gabriel to go to Louis-le-Grand."

The responding silence was sudden and total. Joseph François felt the silence, took his eyes from the boy, and turned them toward his brother and Catherine. There was a mildly clever pursed smile on his lips. Catherine and Abel looked at him wonderingly, their eyes round. Their faces were as blank as if he had said, "Tomorrow the earth will collide with the moon."

It was Gabriel who finally broke the silence. "Louis-le-Grand?" he asked excitedly. "I, Uncle . . . I go to Louis-le-Grand?" His eyes glittered and his heart beat fast.

"Certainly," Joseph returned. "You'd like that, wouldn't you, Gabriel?" Obviously the boy was as eager as a racehorse waiting for the gun.

"Just as you did? Live near the river, see the palace Versailles?

Yes, I want to go. But . . .'' and he looked longingly at his mother and father.

"But Joseph—'' As Catherine leaned forward, the silver crucifix about her neck swung free from her bodice and shone orange in the firelight. "We've no plans to send Gabriel away.'' The proposal had taken her breath. "The parish school is quite good, and Gabriel's our only child.'' She paused, her cheeks flushed. "Joseph, I'm surprised you would suggest such a thing in front of Gabriel without saying something to us first.''

The hurt in Catherine's face set Joseph back. His voice softened, but the determination in his eyes shone brightly. "I know he's young, Catherine, and you're right; I should've spoken to you first.'' He looked directly into the boy's glowing eyes. "But many boys younger than Gabriel go, and he is at an impressionable age. Besides, Gabriel is a born thinker. You can't imagine what the Jesuit fathers could do with his mind.''

Abel broke in. "Joseph,'' he said evenly, "I'm as surprised as Catherine that you said nothing of this to us first, but what's done is done. I feel as she feels; he's too young. He's being well educated right here, and I need him to help me—already he's quite a good smith—and besides all of that, we haven't the money to send him.'' Abel looked tenderly at his son. Disappointment had dimmed the glow in Gabriel's eyes. Michel's face revealed nothing of his thoughts, but within he felt relief that his friend would not soon go away.

Joseph François did not give up easily. "The forge or the priesthood is the way I see it, Abel. The boy has a sensitive spirit. Unless I've missed the mark, he'll be a priest one day.''

Abel and Catherine looked at each other in silence. Tears glimmered in Catherine's eyes. "We'll see, Joseph,'' Abel said, opening the door ever so slightly to the possibility, looking first at Gabriel and then into his brother's eyes. "When he's a little older, we'll see.''

Avranches was a long way from Paris, bound to soil and sea, to family and to old values that made life orderly and predictable. In the middle of town, the highest point of the highest hill overlooking the estuary of the River See, stood the Cathedral of Avranches, its great iron spire pointing a slender finger to the clear blue heavens—the very cathedral on whose steps three centuries ago Henry received absolution for the death of à Becket.

The cathedral was the center of village life, its priest an honest man who shared the burdens of his flock, christened their infants, taught their young, married them, and buried their dead. Within the cut stone walls—walls built at great sacrifice by the hands of their fathers before them—the people entered into spiritual life through baptism and confession of sins. The great bells that rang in the cathedral tower pealed the townspeople's finest music; the Church's feasts marked their holidays, and its teaching gave meaning to their menial, weary lives.

The Church's morals governed their every act. In Avranches few men took mistresses, and when one did, he kept his infidelity the strictest of secrets. Only the most driven of women took lovers, and then painfully, against conscience's sharp goad.

Both in distance and manner, Paris was far from Avranches. Abel and Catherine Dublanche believed their son would grow up here, that he would live much as they had lived, that he would be like his father—a good man, a light among his own people, living and dying in the place where he was born.

But Joseph François remembered with fondness Louis-le-Grand and its Jesuit fathers. They had taught him to think, had opened the world to him, and given his intellect clarity and order. He was intensely grateful and stubbornly unwilling to let the matter rest. Again and again, until Abel nearly lost patience, Joseph said to him, "Abel, don't let your boy waste his mind."

So at last, at noon on the tenth of August, a month and eighteen days after his fourteenth birthday, a year later than Joseph had wished, Gabriel climbed into a sleek black phaeton drawn by a spirited horse the color of midnight, said good-bye to his parents and to Michel, and rode away with Joseph François, destined for Paris' Left Bank and Louis-le-Grand.

On a side street in Paris where homes and shops shouldered against each other and leaned out across the narrow cobblestones like two gentlemen bowing simultaneously, the crests of their gables almost touching, Jean Montaign sat and talked with his son Louis in an upstairs room over his linen shop. Suddenly a scream sliced through the late-afternoon air. In spite of his seventy years, Montaign jumped to his feet, bolted to the dark stairway, and with Louis close on his heels, their boots clambering on the worn pine stairs, plunged into the unlighted lower room.

At the foot of the stairs, Jean's wife stood facing him. Her hands quivered violently in front of her. Horror was painted like a white mask on the skin of her contorted face, and still she screamed. She fell convulsively into his embrace, her hands gripping his bare forearms like tongs of ice.

"Margaret! What's wrong?" he said in terror. "Tell me. What is it?"

A terrible wail tore from her throat. Her eyes rolled upward and she turned toward the shop's main room. Jean's eyes followed.

The room was growing dark. Its shadowy shelves, stacked with bolts of linen, surrounded a wide work counter above which hung an unlighted lamp. The rays of the setting sun were blocked by the houses across the narrow cobblestones and denied further entrance by heavy curtains drawn across the store windows.

Jean Montaign's eyes adjusted to the dim light. A dark column that did not belong in the familiar room swung heavily from the beams. For an uncertain instant, Montaign was absolutely puzzled as to what the strange thing might be.

Then awareness struck. He shouted with horror, "No!" Then louder, "No! No!" And he lunged forward, flung his arms around the swinging form and lifted upward. Louis sprang to the counter for a knife, reached high, and with a rapid sawing motion cut the length of rope that held his brother suspended in the semidarkness.

They could not revive Paul Montaign. He was dead.

While his mother and father reeled in the first shock of Paul's death, while neighbors who had heard the screams gathered at the door, while they waited for an officer to come, a new terror struck.

There was a law in Paris, strictly enforced, that any man, woman, or child who took his own life must be made an example of, that the body must be stripped naked and dragged by horses through the streets while passersby pelted it with mud and stones. Then the corpse must be hanged by its neck from a public gibbet and all the suicide's property forfeited to the state.

Jean loved his son. He could not bear to see Paul's dead body suffer this final indignity, and he whispered, "Margaret, we can't let it happen. Even if we must lie to prevent it, we can't let it happen." He was desperate. He knew only one thing, that he must not let them desecrate the body of his son.

She whispered, "But if they find out, what will become of us?"

He said with finality, "It doesn't matter what becomes of us."

At that moment the officer arrived. He saw the dark purple burn of the rope on the youth's neck.

"Suicide," he said flatly.

"No, not suicide," they answered breathlessly, almost in chorus.

"Then what?" the officer asked. He searched each frightened face in turn, trying to penetrate the secret behind their eyes.

What? There had been no time to think of what.

The officer arrested all of them and put them in keep, each in a different cell to await trial.

Jean and Margaret Montaign were Huguenots—that is to say, French Calvinists—a religious sect illegal in France. Marriage among the Huguenots was not recognized; their wives were considered concubines and their children bastards. If a man was caught worshiping in Huguenot meetings, he was swept away to the galleys, his wife went to prison, and their children were sent to be raised by a Catholic family. Forty thousand Huguenots had fled France for Switzerland and England; the rest worshiped underground. Of the Montaign children, one, Donat, their youngest son, had converted to the Catholic Church, but the other children, three boys and a girl, had followed their parents' example.

The dead son, Paul, had studied law, but when he had tried to enter practice, he found the profession closed to him. He must either publicly renounce his beliefs or let his years of study go to nothing.

Torn with indecision, he had become moody, had begun to brood and to drink, and finally, in total loss of hope, he had taken his own life.

The king's prosecutor charged Jean, Margaret, and their son Louis with murder. What was the motive? Why would parents conspire to hang their son? The prosecutor stood before twelve white-wigged judges and answered the burning question. It was obvious, he said. "To a Huguenot family, it is better for a son to die than convert."

Paul Montaign's body was not dragged through the streets. Instead, he was given a martyr's funeral and buried in one of the city's most prestigious cathedrals.

Then the officials brought the dead boy's father before them to wring out a confession. That he was an old man did not matter.

They put him on the rack and pulled his arms and legs from their sockets.

"Confess," they said.

"I did not kill my son," he replied.

"Confess," they said, and poured fifteen pints of water down his throat.

"I am not guilty of my son's death," he said. And they poured down fifteen pints more.

Gabriel Dublanche was now seventeen. He had grown tall, though not quite so tall as his uncle, nor even as tall as his father. His dark brown hair had grown thick and the unruly wave fell handsomely across his forehead. His shoulders were broad, his waist lean, and he had a quick smile that made him easy to like. Generally Gabriel was outgoing, sometimes quiet, on rare occasions withdrawn, and unfailingly polite.

With a mind keen as a razor's edge, he grasped facts and concepts quickly, and so had gotten on well at Louis-le-Grand. Current Newtonian physics and mathematics came to him easily. He read philosophy ravenously, was devoted to Aristotle, and in writing expressed himself brilliantly. But Gabriel had more than academic knowledge, for, like his mother, everything interested him; facts passed into his mind the way nutrients from the soil pass into the microscopic roots of a tree or flower.

Of tender sensitivity he had more than a very good man could use wisely. He was touched to see any living thing in pain; a terrapin on its back, a lost calf, or a bird with a broken wing distressed him. Human suffering tore mightily at his heart, so much so that he sometimes avoided the poorer sections of the city.

As they had done for his uncle before him, the Jesuit fathers taught Gabriel to think. He learned to take every proposition apart piece by piece. He no longer accepted unsubstantiated statements of supposed authority. Truth and fairness were of one bolt of cloth; they were the most important virtues of all. Yet, true to his youthful understanding, Gabriel did not know many things. The Jesuit fathers of Louis-le-Grand lived lives of frugality, industry, and deep faith. But the school was large, two thousand students in all, many of whom had abandoned all faith, aristocratic young men of wit and perception whose arguments against the existence of God stunned Gabriel and left him reeling with doubt.

* * *

Uncle Joseph had helped Gabriel with the problem of money. This he had done in two ways. Insisting that Gabriel not hire himself out to work, that he devote full time to study, Joseph had dipped into his own substantial reserves to pay for Gabriel's tuition and books. For Gabriel's lodging and food, Joseph looked to a friend, Jean de Sismonde, a government official who had a pleasant house less than a mile from the college.

De Sismonde, a mildly effeminate man nearing forty, and his wife Emilie, who was several years younger, had no children of their own. De Sismonde himself was often away on business and was glad to have a young man about the house to assist and protect his wife.

This was an exceptionally good arrangement at the beginning, but as Gabriel grew older he began to feel the magnetism of Emilie de Sismonde's strong sexuality. Yet, in an innocence of mind born of strong spiritual devotion, he did not imagine that she looked upon him with other than the eyes of a kind benefactress.

By the time he was seventeen, Gabriel could also feel the strong erotic atmosphere of the seething city about him. On the evening of September 2, 1732, he sat down at the table that stood before the curtained windows of his upstairs room and wrote a letter to his one close friend, Michel Lebrun.

My dear friend:
Uncle Joseph was wrong. At the moment I have grave doubts I will ever take the vows of priesthood, for though I love God with all my heart, He has not given me the gift of celibacy. Michel, if the girls of Avranches are lovely, the girls and women of Paris are twice so, and with young blood running hot in my veins, it seems imperative that I marry before being consumed with the spirit I feel in the very air of the streets.
No, I have not succumbed to it, but it pulls at me constantly. How could it be otherwise in a city where every man thinks it his right to have a mistress and every woman wishes to be one, where women are the life of every gathering, where their full, soft bosoms are displayed in dresses cut low to prove their softness, and their legs are so *deliciously* free in those great airy farthingales that to think of them drives one to the very rim of distraction? These women

tune their graces until sexuality flows from them like music. They highlight every bodily charm until no warm-blooded man can see one pass by without his heart tripping.

Here men adore beautiful women, they worship beautiful, *intelligent* women, for the ladies have doubled their charms by training their minds in matters that once belonged only to us men; worlds of astronomy and chemistry, mathematics, biology, even the political sciences, and especially philosophy. In the presence of such loveliness the philosophers sharpen their styles, simplify their explanations, and become more convincing than ever.

With their minds, their beauty, and their beds, the women of Paris have attained great influence in private and public affairs.

Having seen it, I am powerfully lured, yet I wish to yield only within the boundaries set by God. I laugh as I say it, yet I say it seriously, "My friend, pray for me."

On the fourth of October of the same year, Gabriel, in a pensive mood, rose, left the house early, and walked aimlessly through the ancient medieval streets, streets narrow and somber, strangely named: Street of the Fishing Cat, Street of the Hermit's Well, Street of the Wooden Sword. He passed ragpickers, beggars, and tattered dirty children who with sleep-filled eyes had just emerged yawning and scratching from the sewers and quarries of the underground city. With a solemn, hollow edge, the bells sounded, calling monks to morning prayers.

In the dark hours before dawn there had been showers. The entire sky was still overcast; the gray-blue cloud, still dropping its wide sheet of rain, now hung over the east quarter of the city.

The varicolored street stones, paste white, earth brown, dull red, worn smooth by centuries of passing feet and rolling wheels, were shiny-wet and slick, generally with rain, often with night soil thrown from upper windows. The smells of human waste rose from the pavement and mingled with ancient odors, subterranean winds from the sewers, the dust of the street, the aroma of early-morning cooking, and the sweetness of new rain.

At last Gabriel came to Rue Saint Jacques, climbed hill Sainte Genevieve, passed the Sorbonne on his right and the familiar church that entombed the body of Cardinal Richelieu. He turned north to the river, crossed by bridge to the island that sits like a vast ship eternally plowing the waters of the Seine, and threaded his way through a jumble of houses near which stood the great Cathedral of Notre Dame.

It came to Gabriel's mind that he would enter the cathedral's nave and pray. But as he approached, the clamor of a growing crowd reached his ears. The closer he came to the cathedral, the louder the sound. At last he rounded the final corner and found himself on the edge of a vast mob gathered in the cathedral's open square.

On the far side of the crowd, the ornate stone towers of the five-hundred-year-old church reached magnificently up into the gray clouds.

The mob was composed of every kind of person: young and old, men and women, children, students, beggars, pickpockets, vendors, gypsies, gentry, the ragged, the resplendent—and all surged as one toward a central point in front of the cathedral's Portal of Judgment. Yet no one entered the church. Its massive oaken doors were closed, barred and guarded by men who stood rigid with upright halberds in their hands.

The point toward which the crowd actually moved, which everyone stood on tiptoe and craned his neck to see, was a sturdy platform of heavy wood beams and planks that stood two feet above the heads of the tallest men. At Gabriel's side, a well-dressed man carried a child on his shoulder, the better for the child to see the events on the platform. Gabriel laid his hand on the man's arm. "Excuse me," Gabriel said. But in the jostling, yammering crowd the man did not notice. "Excuse me," Gabriel repeated in a raised voice, and he gripped the man's arm tighter. The man turned and the child tightened his arms about his head to keep from falling. "What's happening here?" Gabriel asked.

"Execution," the man answered, straining to be heard above the talk and shouting.

"An execution? Who?"

"Huguenot, murderer, Montaign. Killed his son. Tried to make it look like suicide."

"*Montaign,*" Gabriel said as the light of recognition dawned, for he had heard often of the imprisoned man. Immediately he set himself to burrow through the crowd toward the platform. It was hard going, but after many glaring looks, having been sharply cursed three or four times, once pressed hard between a solid man and a smiling girl of ample proportions in front of him, and once kicked hard on the shin by a small boy on whose foot he had stepped, Gabriel stood at last at the scaffold's edge. Now only a line of armed men separated him from the structure. On the gibbet's elevated plain stood three men—two executioners and the old Huguenot, Montaign.

Montaign was gaunt. Knotted blue veins stood out on his age-spotted face, pulsing rapidly with fear—not the fear of death, but the fear of pain. His face was clean-shaven, slick and red, as though the razor had come too close. Under his deep blue eyes dark purple sacks fell in puffy wrinkles on his upper cheeks. His chin trembled, and in the shelves of his sagging lower eyelids, clear bright tears were building.

His white hair, cropped short as a precaution against prison lice, now stood out in every direction as though an electrical charge were being passed through it. The old man's arms trembled, but he kept his chin and eyes high, ignoring the crowd, absorbed in his own last thoughts. Thus he stood, except for one moment when he looked down to his left past the platform's end. Gabriel followed the old man's gaze to the place where his frantic wife and children stood weeping and wringing their hands.

The chief executioner motioned for quiet. The sea of humanity complied, and a wave of silence moved outward from the platform to the crowd's farthest edge. As he stretched the old man gently on a supine cross, the executioner's movements slowed, burdened with a reluctance that Gabriel took to be pity. "Kindness in the strangest places," Gabriel said aloud.

The two powerful men raised the cross and set its foot into a loose-fitting socket. The old man stretched and strained at the agony, and the cross lurched and swayed. Each sudden stop added to his torture and strained his brittle bones, pulling his old tendons and abrading the skin of his bare back. He hung there, sometimes against the rough wood, sometimes dangling away from it, but always like a slaughtered beef in open market.

A murmur ran through the throng. The executioner raised his hand again and loud enough for all to hear said, "Monsieur Jean Montaign, this is your final opportunity, before God and man, to confess your crime. Did you on Sunday, the second of June last, strangle to death your own son, Monsieur Paul Montaign?"

Without hesitation and in a voice startling for its strength, Montaign cried loud enough for everyone to hear, "No. I did not." Three times his voice echoed through the wrought-iron grillwork of the great cathedral and from the stone walls and recesses of its facade.

The executioner took from his assistant a heavy iron bar, swung it hard, and broke the old man's lower right leg, then repeated the question. "No. No," the old man fairly screamed. "I did not kill my son." The executioner lay on with all his strength and broke the old man's right thigh. The questions and blows went on, alternating with his desperate denials, until each arm and leg was broken in two places.

"Dear God," Gabriel prayed in a loud whisper. "Can't he *see* it? The old man's telling the truth!" Gabriel broke the breathless silence. "Executioner," he yelled, "under God that's enough. Have mercy on the old man!" On every side the crowd stepped away from this brash young fool. The executioner, a huge, bear-chested man with a shaved head, turned and found Gabriel standing alone. Behind the executioner the old man screamed and wept with pain. At the platform's south end, Montaign's wife tried to look away, only to have a soldier grab her face and turn it in her husband's direction. She squeezed her eyes tightly shut and shouted, "No! No!" Another soldier pried her lids open and she rolled her eyes upward until only the whites could be seen. Tomorrow she would die in the same way.

For a time the old man hung there, molested no further. The crazed mob railed at Gabriel and cheered the executioner. Gabriel looked about in astounded wonder. "Are they insane?" he asked aloud of anyone who would listen. Then he turned and pushed toward the man's family, but the soldiers flung him to the ground and ordered him to keep his distance.

At last the men on the gibbet took down the cross—the old man was yet alive—and the chief executioner laid his iron bar across the prisoner's throat. When Gabriel saw what he was about, he lunged toward the platform steps, shouting, "No! In the name of God, no!" He managed to get halfway up before two guards caught him, picked him up bodily, and threw him through the air, back into the crowd. He landed hard against a well-dressed middle-aged man of strong build. The man caught Gabriel, held his shoulders tightly, and whispered in his ear, "Settle down, son. There's nothing you can do."

With a foot on each end of the bar, the executioner rocked back and forth. The crowd was silent. The old man's windpipe cracked and snapped. He rasped and gasped for breath, then died.

Gabriel heard muffled sobbing to his left and turned to see the tearstained face of a lovely blond girl not much younger than himself. She looked directly into his eyes, struggling hard for composure, then said to him earnestly, "You tried. It was a foolish, brave thing, but you tried." She touched his hand, then kissed his cheek.

The soldiers carried the cross from the platform, inserted it in a hole in the ground, piled wood around it, and set it afire. In time the flames ate through the ropes around the old man's wrists and his remains dropped into the burning wood. It was a long while before he disappeared into ash. The stench was terrible beyond words.

That evening Gabriel penned another letter to his lifelong friend, Michel Lebrun.

My very dear friend:

I did not expect to write to you tonight. Examinations are on top of me, and I need every scrap of time in order to be ready.

But I saw something today. I cannot tell you what it did to me, except to say that even now as I recall it, I am sick— sick to the very pit of my stomach. I am revolted! I am tired, so agitated I cannot think. I tremble all over.

There was a man in this city accused of murdering his son. For weeks he has been the talk of Paris. Some believed he was guilty, but a friend of mine who knew him says the man was not capable of murder. And after what I saw today, I, too, believe him to be innocent. This morning I was walking near the Cathedral of Notre Dame when I heard the clamor of a crowd. As I rounded the corner and came into the public square, I saw this man about to be tortured and murdered in the name of God and justice.

Gabriel related in detail what he had seen, and concluded:

I doubt I'll sleep tonight, but under God I will never forget what I saw today. It is burned into my memory like a brand burned into wood.

Can you imagine it, Michel? In Paris, the most civilized city in the world? God have mercy on the world if it's true.

What *is* civilization? Whatever it is, I pray God it is not this.

And the Church. Is there no middle ground between blind obedience—belief without question—and total apostasy? Forgive me if I blaspheme, but I am wounded. May God forgive me if ever I cease to bleed.

Pray for me, my friend. And write if you can.

As always, Gabriel.

CHAPTER 3

Michel Lebrun

GABRIEL was seventeen, and nearly through his third year at Louis-le-Grand, when one night in the black hours before dawn he packed his things and left Paris for home. He made the entire distance on foot and reached Avranches in four days. When he walked through the gate, Abel and Catherine were stunned.

His mother threw her arms around him, then drew back, looked her son directly in the eyes, and asked, "Gabriel, why?" He averted his face. "Tell us," his father urged. But a steely distance in his eyes spoke of Gabriel's determination to remain silent.

The evening of Gabriel's return, Joseph François said to Abel, "Try to forget anything's wrong. Whatever it is, he doesn't want to talk about it now. Just be glad he's home."

Michel Lebrun, his skin dark—dark as French skin is ever likely to be—and his hair black as coal, was like his name, Michel the Brown. As it turned out, like Gabriel, he was his mother's only child. When he was sixteen he already stood a half head taller than any other man in Avranches, and his large hands grew larger with each summer's work in his father's hay fields. Michel was imbued with enormous strength—Gabriel had once seen him single-handedly pick up a wagon bed, lift it over a rail fence, and set it on the other side—and had a reputation as a gentle giant of a boy. Like Gabriel, his heart was tender toward every living thing. His pleasant, even temper was rarely provoked, and he was almost always happy. No one could remember ever seeing him depressed, except when his father died.

It had been in early July, on a Tuesday. No one had seen it happen, but in the evening a neighbor had found Michel's father, Daniel Lebrun, lying facedown in the half-plowed field, his legs on the unturned grass, his body and face in the newly cut ground. When they turned him over, his left hand was clutched to his breastbone. Bits of the freshly turned, moist black earth clung to his ash-colored face. Michel was there, and even yet he could remember the sweet smell of the clean earth and its terrible incongruity with death and with the emptiness he felt in his heart.

His father's team of Percherons had done a few steps beyond their fallen master and stopped, patiently waiting for him to get up. As the evening sun was going down, they were still standing silently when the neighbor saw them and came to find why they stood alone. Daniel had been forty-four years old.

Michel, just fifteen at the time, but strong and capable, took over his father's farm. It was all the boy knew. It was simple, satisfying work, and hard, but there was no time for discontent, and Michel did not think to look for a way out. Escape from the rigors of labor was reserved for the hereafter.

So Michel carried on where his father left off, doing what he had always done, but doing more of it. He was up before dawn to milk. He wrestled the plow through the sod. With scythe and pitchfork he labored in the lush hay fields under the midday sun, all without complaint, understanding that good, hard labor was not curse but consolation.

Today was a day in early autumn after Gabriel's unexpected return from Louis-le-Grand. Gabriel and Michel rode out together into the crispness of dawn. Michel had freed himself for the day from the labors of the farm, and Abel had released Gabriel from the smithy where he had begun working again upon his return from Paris.

It was an uncommonly fine morning. The sunlight slipped easily through the thin air and cast a faint golden vapor about everything it touched. A haze lay over the tan and wine pasture grasses. The forest trees were dressed in full fall regalia, and small clouds of fine dust stirred from the cool ground by the feet of the meandering horses, ascended from the roadway that ran along the forest's edge.

The joy of life was upon them as they urged their horses to a full gallop over the sandy red road. After a while they drew in to a slower pace, talking, laughing, reminiscing over the days before Gabriel went away.

By noon they were fifteen miles or more from town. The forest of oak and hickory lay to their left, and the wide, level prairie to their right. The midday sun shone from directly behind them and warmed their backs. With almost no direction from their riders, the horses ambled slowly, even stopping now and again to crop dry grass that grew in tufts along the road's edge.

Michel held the reins slack in both hands at his saddle's pommel. His mare swung her head to the right, toward the prairie side of the road, to reach a new tuft of grass. A strong quiver ran through her neck; she tossed her head from side to side, and then settled down to eat contentedly, cropping the grass with clean, crisp bites. The conversation had lulled. A small, startled rabbit dashed in a gray, kicking streak across the road into the shelter of the forest.

Michel, sensing that Gabriel had mellowed into the proper mood, posed the inevitable question. Quietly, but directly, he asked "Gabriel, why *did* you come home?"

At first Gabriel said nothing. He shook his head slightly and looked at the ground between his horse and Michel's. Several moments passed. At last he took a deep breath, and let it all out in something like a sigh.

"I don't mind telling you," he said. "In fact, I want to tell you. I need to talk about it. I just don't quite know where to begin."

"Take your time," Michel answered kindly. His voice was young, but resonant and clear.

"Well," Gabriel began, "two things made me decide to come home. I'd thought for months that it might be best. But it took something extraordinary to set me off in the middle of the night."

"I guessed that." Michel chuckled.

Suddenly, as if he had gathered courage to dive from a dangerous height, Gabriel blurted, "How can I say it? I . . . well, I lost my innocence!"

"Some woman seduced you!" Michel shot back. "Now I really am surprised."

"No. That's not what I mean." Gabriel paused again, and then said pensively, "But that's close to the truth. It's another kind of innocence that I mean."

"What other kind is there?" Michel asked.

"The innocence of belief . . . the innocence of trust," Gabriel answered. "At Louis-le-Grand I learned to think. That's good. I'm not sorry. Yet it's a burden to feel I must question everything." Gabriel looked tired. "The meaning of life," he went on, "the existence of God. How can a man be happy when he must have everything of value proved to him?"

Michel did not answer. After moments of silence, Gabriel went on, "And the cruelty! I had never seen it before, did not know it *existed*—not here, not in the center of civilization. I can still hear that old man screaming to God for help. I can still see his wife trying to look away, and the soldiers taking her head in their hands and forcing her to look. She tried to close her eyes, but the soldiers took their fingers and pried them open." He paused, then went on, "And there was more. It wasn't just that day. I saw other executions.

"The first time I was so revolted I couldn't sleep. The second didn't bother me quite so much. But the last time . . . the last time I felt a little pleasure in it. That jolted me. When I realized that what a man can see or think without revulsion, he might someday *do*, I turned around and fought my way out of the crowd and found someplace where I could think . . . and pray. Oh, how I prayed that day."

Gabriel took another deep breath, stood high in the stirrups, and looked out across the prairie. "But the last thing," he said, "the event that set me packing my bag in the middle of the night . . . well, you're right, it *was* a woman. She was older, fifteen years older. I lived in her house, which was perfectly all right, of course, but for the fact that her husband was always away at Versailles on government business.

"Emilie was a beautiful woman." Gabriel gazed northward into the hard pale blue sky as though he could actually see her face suspended there and, seeing her, could not turn away. "*Is* a beautiful woman," he corrected himself. "Her throat is smooth as silk, slender, full of grace. Her eyes—you could get lost in them. Her body is beautiful, shapely, sleek as a young deer . . . and she has a laugh that made my heart sing."

"You tumbled for a woman fifteen years older than you?" Michel asked, amazed.

"Not at first, no. At the beginning I was only fourteen. I trusted her. It didn't occur to me that . . . I didn't realize that a woman might ever be interested in a boy. But after a while I began to feel warm when she was near. Even then I didn't realize what I was feeling, much less what *she* felt.

"From the first she would come into my room at night and sit close while I studied—trying to help me, I thought. Wanting to be a mother to me. But I would look around to make a point, to ask a question. Her eyes were big and deep, and she would look directly into mine. The bosom of her dress was cut low, and her perfume made my head swim.

"It went on like that for a long time, but that last night she came into my room in a diaphanous gown, stood between the lamp light and me, and told me she had waited so long for me to come to full manhood, for me to see her as she had always seen me. And of course I did see.

"Under God, to this day I can't tell you what gave me the strength to say no. She was hurt, said that I didn't love her—though I haven't any idea what love had to do with it—and said that I must find her miserably unattractive to reject her. I told her that wasn't it at all, that I found her terribly attractive. That was the wrong thing to say, it just set her running again. I told her that I just could not, that it was wrong. She said, 'Not today. It isn't wrong today. God wills our pleasure. The old ideas are disproved.' I said that I thought they were not disproved, that no matter what Parisian society thought, there was nothing to justify what she proposed. She asked if I did not feel that I owed her something more for providing me with a home all this while. I told her I would always be indebted to her, but that I had no intention of settling the account in that kind of coin.

"She became very tender, dried her tears, embraced me, then finally she left the room and told me to think about it overnight. She said she would be back in the morning, early. I lay down and tried to sleep, but I could think of nothing else. Finally I just gave up, packed everything, and slipped out at about four o'clock in the morning. At first I thought I would stay with a friend, but the more I thought about it, the more I knew that if I stayed in Paris at all, I would go back to Emilie before the week was out. I was not afraid of Emilie. I wanted her more than I can say. My fear was of breaking the command of God.

"So that's why I came home."

Michel was shaken. He had envisioned it all, felt his own passion rise, and felt more than a twinge of envy. "Thank *God* I wasn't in your place," he said, breathing heavily. He swallowed hard. "Well, Gabriel"—he shook his head in near disbelief—"I admire you more than ever. The important thing is that you escaped."

"But I don't know," Gabriel answered, "that I did escape. The whole thing sticks in my mind like a hook in the throat of a fish. I see her in my dreams—day and night. Sometimes I want to plunge out of my room, saddle this horse, and go running back to her. She would welcome me with open arms. I know she would. And she was so lovely!" He set his jaw firmly. "But I'm here, and she is there, and I'm not going back. It's finished."

They rode on a little farther, and eventually their youthful ebullience rose again. At every step the deep dust fell in small, thick clouds from the horses' hooves. The sun moved gradually in its grand arc to the west, and from somewhere in the forest a killdeer called out with its plaintive, penetrating cry. A squirrel with a thickening red coat skimmed up and around a tree trunk. They were ready to turn and retrace their steps when, rounding a bend in the road, they saw a strange thing before them.

A bird sat at the road's edge—a large, majestic bird. Its dark head turned toward them, its big, piercing eyes sent a questioning gaze in their direction, and then with magnificent aloofness it looked away.

Neither Michel nor Gabriel had ever been close to such a bird before, but decided correctly that it was an eagle. But why did it let them come so close? Normally, while still far away, it would have flown. It guarded no prey. There was no nest in the nearby trees. Yet it sat without motion.

They edged closer. Only then, alarmed by their nearness, the great bird did a queer little shuffle, moving away from them, and as it did so, both wings dropped away from its body and dragged pitifully, full-length in the dry grass. Then it stopped, and with its beak reached down to each wounded wing and pulled it back into place. But the agonizing effort was for nothing, for whenever it moved again, both wings once more fell into the helpless tangle.

"It must've dived at something on the ground and hit that dead, forked limb there," Michel observed. "Look. Feathers and skin caught in the bark."

"They're broken," Gabriel said, "both of them. He'll never fly again."

"You're right. When night comes, perhaps even before, something will kill him: a fox or a wolf."

"Can we save him?"

"I doubt it, but we can try."

But when they came close, the wounded thing screamed in anger, sat back on its tail, and raised its spiky talons so menacingly that they could do nothing.

"We can't leave it here to be torn up in the night," Gabriel said.

"But it's that or kill it ourselves," Michel said.

Neither wanted the task, so Michel plucked a dry length of straw from the grass and broke it into two unequal pieces. Gabriel drew the shorter length and the lot fell to him. He had brought a fowler with him, thinking to kill small game for supper. He took it from the saddle and looked to the priming. It was good. He closed the battery and drew back the cock, sighting down the long, slender barrel.

This beautiful, majestic bird must feel nothing at all, he thought as he steadied the gun, it mustn't even be aware that it's about to die, or feel the slightest pain or shock.

In one shattering instant the cock fell, sparks flew to the pan, and the charge erupted in flame and gray smoke.

The great bird's head folded in on itself and the tangled wings came together in the wake of its backward-cascading body. The roar of the gun rebounded from a multitude of distant forest coves and came crashing back in one and then another hollow report, all in quick succession, and everything was quiet.

Gabriel spoke to the shattered thing—perhaps he thought its spirit would hear. "I'm sorry, friend. It was the best we could do."

Michel repeated, "The best, but a sorry best."

They plucked a few of the finest feathers, mounted again, and left the broken body of the dead monarch to the sun and wind and rain.

The following spring, Marie Lebrun sold the farm. She did not ask her son for his approval. Michel told Gabriel confidentially that since his father died, his mother had not thought clearly, and that her decision to sell had been a mistake. He bore her no grudge—that was not his nature—but whatever her reason for selling, to Michel the loss of the farm was a great blow.

The agreement was that the farm proceeds for that year belonged to the Lebruns, so Michel worked the land and reaped the family's last crop. By the time the winter rains arrived, he and his mother had moved into the village where Marie found work as a seamstress in the shop of a Madame DuBois, a woman of about fifty, tall, straight, with hair silver at the temples, that swept up dramatically on the top of her head, making her appear grand and forceful. Madame DuBois had never married, but because her life was full of industry and social activity, she had known little loneliness. The shop itself was a two-story affair on the winding cobblestones that served as the town's main street.

For Marie Lebrun, the move was yet one more sad conclusion to a chapter in her life. Her father had died in the flood at the mill. Her husband had been taken from her at the apex of life. Now the loss of the farm was another ending. But she was strong, and Michel was young. This would be a new beginning, and they would do the best they could.

A farmer in wooden shoes—*sabots*, they were called—walked along the narrow dirt road patiently following two swaying, lowing cows, talking to them in soothing tones, encouraging them along a path they had followed every morning for the half decade of their short lives.

A young boy burst through the door of a roadside cottage and ran bare-legged into a lush pasture, his pail rattling sharply in the clear morning air. Gabriel watched him and remembered how wet grass feels to a boy's ankles on a morning early in June.

Michel and Gabriel gazed at the slowly passing scene from the hard seat of a jolting, squeaking wagon that wound its way behind a team of two workhorses over the ancient road from Avranches to Rouen, a journey of four days in good weather. Madame DuBois had hired Michel—as she often did—to go to Rouen for a wagonload of cloth. Gabriel had come along for safety's sake.

The hardy country women of Avranches had little need for silks and satins. They chose instead the sturdy cloth woven in the Arabian town of Calicut, India. It was durable and bright, and on a background of one color—red, yellow, blue, or even black—was printed a pattern of bright flowers, sometimes interspersed with intricate, vinelike tendrils. Because it came from Calicut, it was known to everyone as calico. This inexpensive material brought color into the daily lives of even the poorer women and cheered many a Norman home.

Gabriel enjoyed these trips with his friend. While Michel dealt with the merchants, Gabriel spent his time on the quay of the River Seine. It was his favorite haunt. He walked along the banks, closely examining every ship, listening to the strange chatter of foreign tongues, trying to distinguish Chinese from Arabic, English from German. He watched merchants bid on wares brought from all over the known world—cloth from India, tea from China, wool from Scotland, and furs from New France.

He was forever awestruck at the gaping hatches, thirty feet wide and forty long, that opened the bowels of the mighty ships to the booms and tackle that loaded and unloaded their tons of cargo. Gabriel felt a magnetic attraction to these ships. They made him think of faraway places that whispered and beckoned to him until his soul ached.

When he had studied under the Jesuit fathers, Gabriel had often felt the same pull. They had talked a great deal about the missionary enterprise of the Church, especially among the native peoples of New France. He read of these mysterious, red-hued races and thought often that someday he might be sent out to work among them. But when he abandoned Louis-le-Grand, those ambitions were laid to rest.

Nonetheless, Gabriel loved the docks and the quay. As the tall ships sailed upriver, his eyes followed their fluid elegance. He feasted on the motion of every artful curve and line. His soul bathed in the glory of white sails swelled out, elegantly full in the morning breeze, tugging the vessels steadily on. Their design, their perfect grace, excited him in a way few other things did. To him these ships seemed like birds on the wing, and to look upon them filled his mind and soul with peace.

So today Gabriel sat on the dock's edge, high on a pile of great timbers brought up from the Gold Coast in the hull of a mighty four-masted French merchantman, and drank in the poetry that sailed up and down the river. Moored there before him, scarcely twenty paces away, was a man-of-war, a twenty-six-gun frigate, straining at its hawsers, its effort to rest frustrated by the river's swift current. Three-masted, a French flag floating from the tip of her spanker boom, she pointed her bow quartering away from him, so that his eye took in her magnificent grace in a single sweeping gaze.

Surely, he thought, no woman was ever more beautiful!

The masts with all their spars and rigging stood at a rakish tilt toward the stern. The jibboom ran forward and up, pointing to some invisible star in the sun-washed heavens. He imagined that she said, almost aloud, "I exist for motion. I exist to move up and beyond, to roll with the wind and crash through foaming mountains of sea. My form is my pride. I shall never place this bow under a single wave."

Just then someone hit the ship's bell, and the clear ring interrupted Gabriel's thought. A single gun-port cover rattled up on its chain and the long, black, heavy tube of a nine-foot sixteen-pounder rolled forward to give its rope slack while a workman hidden on the lower gun deck made repairs to the thick iron rings that anchored it firmly in place.

The rat lines ran from the gunnel to the fighting platform midway up the masts. The running rigging and tackle ran to every spar and boom. At first Gabriel saw the mass of rope and line as a jumble of confusion, but bit by bit he searched out the meaning of each line, standing and running, and at last a picture of perfect order came into focus. He wondered at the genius and skill of the men whose task it was to take her to sea.

At that moment his gaze fell from the frigate's rigging and went beyond her bow to midriver, where a longboat manned by a dozen hard-rowing sailors hove into sight. He was puzzled. The men bent their backs and pulled hard, but the boat moved forward in a slow and labored way. Then he saw another, with like crew, fifty feet beyond the first. The two seemed to be racing, but as in a dream, when one tries with all one's might to move quickly, yet is hampered by some unseen, powerful hand. Every motion was agonized and oh, so slow.

Then he saw the reason. A larger vessel bore into view, creeping upstream after the longboats. A taunt line ran from the stern of each of the small vessels to the bow of the ship, for they were towing it against the current.

The vessel under tow was a man-of-war, a French ship of the line, and she was wounded. Rigging hung limply from her shattered bowsprit. Her masts were broken into splintered stumps.

Fragments of sail hung loosely over the gunnel, and two gaping holes yawned at midship just above the waterline.

Gabriel had never seen anything like it. Only gradually did the meaning of this devastation steal over him. On some distant coast she had fought with something too much for her. She had tasted men's blood, smelled the acrid smoke of powder, reeled under the recoil of her own cannon, and felt the crushing bite of ball and chain shot as they tore into her sides and raked across her deck.

A hundred yards upriver from where he sat, the longboats drew the man-of-war to the quay and the crews made her fast. Gabriel approached her, walked up her boarding plank—no one questioned him—and lost himself among the men who were coming and going amid the wreckage.

The sharp, pleasant smell of the ship's oakum-tarred ropes and caulked seams cut into his nostrils. Mixed with it was the pungent odor of fresh-made charcoal, for in passing broadside to her enemy she had come so close to the enemy's guns that their muzzle blasts had set her hull's outer planking afire. The deck rolled slightly under his feet. He was careful to avoid the tangled line. The mainmast—a shaft of oak so thick he could not pass his arms around it—was broken off cleanly about six feet above the deck, sheared away by some flaming ball hot from the belly of the enemy's carronade.

Gabriel stared at the mast's great stump as though trying to extract some secret from the war-torn wood. He absently laid his hand on it. It was so massive he could not conceive of the force that had made it yield. Abruptly he jerked his hand back; a small sharp sliver had torn his palm and a small trickle of blood now ran down to his wrist. He leaned forward and looked more closely at the mast to find the offending splinter, but what he saw was a spattering of small white slivers embedded in the wood. He pinched one out and rolled it about between his fingers, wondering; and then, with a sick thrill in the pit of his stomach, he saw it was not wood at all, but a fragment of bone—human bone. The mast was embedded with bone and spattered with blood.

He stood pondering the men who, like the mast, had been broken on this deck. He imagined their screams, their unendurable pain, the deafening cannon roar drowning out the swift whisper of the surgeon's saw and the sizzle of hot iron searing butchered living flesh.

He went below. Gun carriages lay about in wrecked heaps. A burst barrel lay against the mooring bits. Fully a quarter of the deck was blackened by fire. A workman with an air of authority scurried by. Gabriel turned and called after him. The man stopped and looked back over his shoulder.

"Tell me," Gabriel asked, "what will you do with this ship?"

"Do with her? Why we'll repair her, sir. In a year's time she'll have a few new ribs, spanking oak masts, and a new suit of sails. This wounded bird will fly again."

"I never would have thought it," Gabriel said, letting his eyes wander over the debris. "Such a tremendous lot of damage."

"But none we can't care for, sir. As long as she's afloat and her frame's sound, we can fix her up like new."

The man went about his work, and Gabriel stood alone. The ship could be kept sailing for a hundred years or more, but the men who were broken on her decks could never be repaired. "Civilization," he muttered.

"Gabriel!" Michel's voice came down the forward ladderway.

"I'm down here, Michel, on the forward gun deck." He noticed that under the deck's low ceiling his own voice had a hollow ring.

Michel stooped low and came down, "It's a mess, isn't it?"

"A bloody mess! How did you find me?"

"We looked over by the frigate, and when we saw you weren't there we called up to a deckhand and asked—"

" 'We'? Who's 'we'?"

"Ah, that's just the thing," Michel answered brightly. "There's someone on deck I want you to meet. Come on up."

"Mademoiselle Lefleur, meet my friend, Gabriel Dublanche. Gabriel, this is Celeste Lefleur."

Before Gabriel stood a young woman with fair, smooth skin, golden hair made more golden by the sun, and features that were as lovely as any he had imagined in his most perfect dreams. She was obviously gentry, or at least well situated, for she wore a dress of pale blue brocade that made her dark blue eyes seem wonderfully deep.

She was the sort of person who touches another with easy familiarity, and though she did not know it, when she took his hand in hers, the effect on Gabriel was electric and so intimate that his head swam. Almost immediately he was shocked still more to hear her say with surprise, "Monsieur Dublanche, we've met before."

"Surely not," he answered. "I would've remembered."

"Perhaps not," she said. "It was in a public square—in front of Notre Dame in Paris. You were much too busy to notice me. Remember? The poor old Huguenot? You were in a rage to save him. I was with my father. He caught you when the soldiers hurled you down from the platform steps. I was crying and told you what a brave, foolish thing you had done."

Gabriel's eyes went wide with recognition. He had been touched by her words, and most especially by her tears, and had never quite forgotten. "Yes. Of course. Now I remember you," he said.

Celeste was the daughter of Pierre Lefleur, owner of a fur company that imported great quantities of fine pelts from New France. She had come to the docks that morning to see her father, who was there to meet one of his ships, and she and Michel had met by chance and fallen into a conversation.

Celeste paused and looked about at their surroundings for the first time. "This is a horrible thing," she said. "Look at the blood on the deck, and soaked into the torn sails!"

"And bone," Gabriel said.

"Bone? Where? No. Don't show me."

Gabriel pointed to the mast. "There," he said, "probably from some poor sailor's shattered head."

She looked away and her eyes filled with tears. This is a tender woman, Gabriel thought. "Let's get away from here," she said. Celeste was hardly able to contain herself until they left these immediate reminders of death and darkness.

As they walked down the boarding plank, Michel pointed out, "These ships of the line are the most formidable machines of death man has ever made."

"I believe it." Gabriel nodded.

Strolling along the quay, they spoke of other things, and soon Celeste was laughing again. The happier she became, the more her beauty shone through.

It became obvious to Gabriel Dublanche that Celeste Lefleur was a young woman of character. Her sensitive spirit and winning way impressed him forcefully. Back at home in Avranches, the memory of Celeste Lefleur lingered in Gabriel's mind.

CHAPTER 4

The Uninvited Guest

WITHIN the borders of France—that vast uneven hexagon lying westward between the Alps and the sea—stood the highest mountain in all of Europe, Mont Blanc, and the deepest forests, Fontainbleau, Compiègne, Chantilles, and Rambovillet. But the greatest and truest character of France was in her people; in the sunny, vine-covered hills, in the meadows where cattle grazed in deep, sweet-smelling clover, where young girls, milking stools in hand and wooden buckets on their arms, walked through tall grasses to relieve the fat, lowing cows of their burden. It was in the fields where men followed the plow, where reddish-gold buckwheat ripened.

It had taken generations to pull the land up from its dark wildness, to dike the rivers, to cut the squares and rectangles of green from the forests, and establish the orchards, whose pink blossoms lifted the hearts of the farmers in May. Vines whose forebears had climbed high on woody stalks to weave arbors in the treetops now twined their tendrils about long rows of treillage to produce fat sweet grapes within the shelter of solid stone walls. Apple trees, their fruit large and crisp, yielded the drink for which the Norman hills were justly famous.

The land's wildness had gone the way of the land's gods; order and civilization had come forth.

In the Dublanche home breakfast was at seven. Abel, Catherine, and Gabriel gathered about a trestle table of smooth oak polished by two centuries of Dublanches and stained by countless spills of gravy and cider. They ate steaming omelets from stoneware plates, or crêpes, small and delicately browned, or sausages, or pâtés of duck or rabbit, always with lots of butter and bread, and always with a brimming pitcher of cider.

In their civilized routine the morning broke again at nine for

37

bread and jam . . . and a mug of cider. Each day at noon, Catherine spread the table as elaborately as at the day's first meal, and at four they broke from their work for more bread, jam, and cider.

In the evening, when the church bells sounded the Angelus, Joseph François joined them at the table for tripe from Caen, slabs of red beef, or codfish from Binic. They dipped into the black iron kettle squatting on its three short legs at the table's fireside end and ladled rich brown soup onto slices of coarse brown bread as big as their plates, cut from loaves a foot thick and as long as a man's arm. Cheeses were served at every meal.

And always there was the cider, made in the press Abel's grandfather had built seventy years ago. The press was a circular trough in which a wheel of stone fixed on a shaft was drawn round and round by one of the draft horses. The heavy wheel crushed the apples, the juice was drained off for cider, and Catherine mashed the pulp into sauce. The aged cider was strong, and the color of sunlit amber, deep, clear, shining in the cup. It had the scent of autumn, sweet and faintly musky, and spoke with the tang that makes Norman cider the best in the world: cold to the lips, light on the tongue, warm to the back of the throat as it goes down.

Talk around the table was almost always lively, but when the evening meal was done, quietness fell over them. They turned and knelt at their chairs and, with rosaries in hand, began evening prayers with an Our Father, intoning with utter sincerity, "Hail Mary, full of grace, the Lord is with you. . . ."

If the weather was warm and clear, as it was on these early summer evenings in 1734, they would go to the yard together after prayers, spread quilts, and sit or lie quietly talking while fireflies winked their way up across the pasture from the river bottom and floated with gentle luminescence into the stone-fenced yard. On occasion neighbors gathered with the Dublanches and the talk ran long and pleasantly into the night. This was the fruit of honest labor: quiet minds, good friends, a life free from great surprise—a world of order and calm.

It was the hottest time of summer, late July. Work in the smithy slackened, so Gabriel and Michel had hired themselves out as a team to work in the hay fields of Dalverny, whose land lay a little west and north of Avranches. They had scythed a third cutting of clover—the year had been uncommonly wet—from a field west of the river, and today were forking the dry, wind-rowed hay into stacks where it would wait for winter feeding. The field was on a high, gently rounded hilltop; below them, all around, lay a patchwork of farms and pasture land.

The sun bore down; the air was thickly humid. As he scooped with steady swing and lofted the tan hay to the stack's top, sweat poured from Gabriel's face and into his eyes, stinging, leaving him nearly blind. He paused long enough to tie a handkerchief about his head.

"This is insane!" Gabriel exclaimed. "It's too hot to stack hay."

"It's hot enough, all right," Michel said. "But as long as you're sweating, you're all right. If you stop, that's when you'd better look out. Besides, unless I miss my guess, that cloud to the west is coming our way. If it is, things will cool off soon enough."

Michel was right. The distant cloud came nearer, rising from the west, building until it was a towering white anvil against the afternoon sky. Huge billows glistened radiantly, rising majestically to the upper reaches of the atmosphere on sweeps of rushing mist like the wings of an archangel.

Where the sunlight could not reach its inner folds and tunnels, the cloud was dark and evil looking. One after the other, sheets of hot light broke from the black recesses like flashes from a lime burner's oven when the door is quickly opened and shut. Yellow-white spears shot between earth and sky. Deep-throated thunder sounded in the distance.

The storm came on and a cool breeze sprang up, drying the sweat from their skin, leaving them suddenly cool and refreshed. For a time they worked with renewed vigor, until the outer flanges of the storm were overhead and big, warm drops of rain began to fall from the electric air.

Leaving the exposed height, Gabriel and Michel drove their team and hay-filled wagon down and east across the river toward the distant village.

The storm was like an alarm. In all the surrounding country men left their work—farmers from the fields, woodcutters from the forests, and sheep tenders from the sheltered flocks—and as if by prearrangement, they all converged in the village, swarming into the inn and alehouse that sat shoulder to shoulder with the shop of Madame DuBois.

By the time Gabriel and Michel reached the inn, dark heavy clouds vibrating with thunder extended from horizon to horizon, and the raindrops, undisturbed by any wind, fell as though their course were measured by a plumb line, making the leaves of the trees chatter and shattering the mirror faces of the newly formed pools.

The world was changed. Tension of workaday existence disappeared. The storm cloud, harsh and heavy as it seemed, gave the men a blessed reprieve from the smothering heat and the strain of their backbreaking toil.

They came pouring through the inn door, wet hats in hand, water dripping from brim and collar, laughing, greeting one another loudly, stomping and scraping their wet, mud-caked boots on the worn pine floor of the entranceway.

Each and all, a world of energy in their banter, dropped happily into chairs about the alehouse tables. Gabriel and Michel sat at the room's east end, farthest from the door, under one of the lanterns that cast a warm yellow patina on the square, thick, rough oak table.

Sharp but good-natured barbs flew back and forth. Gabriel heard someone across the room say in mock wonder, "Why, it wasn't true what I hear about young Dublanche. He *does* have sense enough to come out of the rain."

"And quicker than some I know," Gabriel returned in good humor.

The rain was a boon for Antoine and Rose Benet, the fortyish couple who owned the inn, who with their daughter Marie now rushed about among the laughter, handing around stoneware mugs of cider to every man and boy. When everyone had a fresh mug in hand, Antoine hurried to the hearth, where he built a vigorous fire to take off the chill and thick damp.

Out of the clamor, a thin little man stood to his feet. He wore wooden shoes and his baggy black trousers, dangerously loose, were held up by wide red suspenders that stood out brightly against the front of his soiled white shirt. His billowing sleeves were rolled to the elbow, exposing old, sinewy forearms. His face and throat were thin and darkened by the sun. His narrow collar lay open, revealing where the dark brown triangle of his lower throat ended and the white of his thin chest began. The collar's tying strings dangled loosely downward. His watery eyes sparkled with a happy, inner light when he lifted his mug and said in a clear voice, "A song."

"Hear! Hear! A song." A murmur of good will rose and fell

quiet again as the little man began to sing. His physical appearance had given no hint to the quality of his voice. In clear, rich baritone he sang:

> *A la claire fontaine*
> *M'en allant promener,*
> *J'ai trouvé l'eau si belle*
> *Que je m'y suis baigné.*
> *Lui y a longtemps que je t'aime,*
> *Jamais je ne t'oublierai.*

> At the clear running fountain
> Sauntering by one day,
> I found it so compelling
> I bathed without delay.
> Your love long since overcame me,
> Ever in my heart you'll stay.

Four more verses and he was done. The hush held for a moment more, then cheers and applause filled the room.

Another stood to sing, and another, until all who were so moved had done. Then someone shouted the inevitable question, "Who sang best?" Each man stood and bowed while new rounds of applause settled the contest. And as always, the first man—Henri, father of nine girls and husband of a short, rotund, happy woman— won the event. It was Henri's one claim to the special respect of his fellows, and he drank it in as dry sand drinks the fall rains.

For Michel Lebrun, this hour in the inn meant something quite different than it meant to the other men, even to his friend Gabriel Dublanche. His reason was Marie Benet. Michel first had seen Marie the day he and his mother had moved to town, and on those occasions when he worked about Madame DuBois' sewing shop, he inevitably drifted toward the inn in hopes of seeing her.

Marie was a wonderfully pleasant girl, no more than seventeen, only five feet tall, standing halfway between Michel's elbow and shoulder. She wore her long blond hair tucked under a crisp white cap, with one golden wave peeking teasingly out over her forehead. Her face, round, smooth, and fair, was Michel's idea of pretty. He had no taste for sharp angles in a girl's face or figure, and Marie had none of them. Her waist was small in a tightly laced bodice, but her face, bare arms, and breast were pleasantly rounded and full. Her striking pale green eyes danced when she talked to him. She was undeniably a coquette, yet somehow innocent and perfectly pure in appearance and manner.

Michel was in love with her, and she knew it. Even now as she swept about from one table to the next, carrying a pitcher of cider in one hand and a plate of fresh, hot bread in the other, she glanced often in his direction and smiled in a way that was reserved solely for Michel Lebrun.

The talk and laughter went on. Mugs were refilled. A smooth, white cloud—smoke from a dozen newly lighted pipes—sought its height up among the dark, wide spaces between the ceiling beams. Rose Benet stood at the door of the inn and watched the rain slide from the eaves and fall to the wet earth. "No," she reported to the men at the table nearest her, "it hasn't slacked—not a bit. If anything, it's coming down harder." At that moment a brilliant, stunning light flashed from the cloud and turned every object and the air itself to a sheet of whiteness. The light was followed instantly by a clap of thunder so loud it seemed a cannon had exploded just outside the door. Rose recoiled, snapping backward so suddenly that she nearly fell.

An appreciative murmur of awe swept through the room. "Are we hit?" asked one.

"No. I don't think so," Antoine answered, steadying Rose. "I think it missed us that time. But I've never heard it closer!"

"Heard it? *Felt* it, you mean," came a reply.

"Closer and we'd be dead men," put in another. "Somebody should check the horses."

Michel and Gabriel volunteered and slipped out into the rain to the open shelter behind the inn where the animals were stabled.

While Gabriel and Michel were out, a faint new sound, as of the slosh of hooves in mud, cut through the rush of rain. Antoine Benet lifted his eyebrows and turned toward his wife, surprised to think anyone might be traveling in the downpour.

"A carriage," Rose said, and dared to step into the doorway again. A small, elegant carriage drawn by two horses came through the driving rain and down the muddy street. The vehicle was enclosed, but forward, up on the driver's seat, a man in a three-cornered hat, his head and arms extending through slits in a heavy, brown oilskin, maneuvered the nervous span rapidly toward the inn. The carriage's tall, thin rear wheels cut narrow ruts in the soft clay, swished through the wetness, throwing twin arches of reddish-brown spray.

At the inn, the carriage door swung open. A man sprang out, bolted through the rain, and entered the inn, nearly knocking Rose Benet from her feet in the process. She bristled at the affront.

"Excuse me, madame," he said, instantly taking Rose by the shoulder to keep her from falling. "I was in too much of a rush. Just trying to stay dry—and as you can see, I was not very successful. Please forgive me."

At the sound of the man's elegant politeness and fine deep voice, Rose's hackles lay down and she began to survey the newcomer. He seemed about forty-five years old. His features were both handsome and rugged. He was tall, and a russet cape flowed from his shoulders nearly to the floor. He looked directly into Rose's eyes in a way that once more took her steadiness away. "That's quite all right," she said, a bit breathlessly. "Is there something we can do to help you?"

"Yes," he said, "there is. Do you have lodging?" He looked about the crowded room and felt a slight anger rise inside when he saw the eyes of fifty or more men and boys all trained on him.

"Yes, of course we do, sir." Antoine Benet took the initiative from his wife and thrust a large, leatherbound book brusquely across the desk toward the stranger. He dipped a white, sharpened goose quill into an inkwell and, placing the quill in the stranger's fingers, said, "Sign here, if you please."

The man wrote with a smooth, fluid hand in large letters, "Jonathan Lecharbonnier."

"Lecharbonnier," Antoine said aloud. The roomful of men still listened. "Do I sound your name correctly, sir?"

"Yes. That is correct," said Lecharbonnier.

"And you want the room for a night?" Antoine Benet asked.

"No, I expect to stay for several days. I have business here in Avranches, and I may need lodging for as long as a week."

Antoine looked him steadily in the eye. The newcomer's own gaze did not waver. "Of course, I will pay in advance." And he lay several silver coins on the desk. Antoine counted them quickly with his eye, nodded his head, and scooped them off the counter into his apron.

Lecharbonnier turned toward his alehouse audience and addressed them. "Gentlemen, I am Jonathan Lecharbonnier, on assignment in the duchy of Normandy for his majesty, Louis

Quinze. My duties are not pleasant. On the other hand, they are not repugnant as they might be. I am here to take a census of your town and the country around it for the purposes of revising the rolls used for taxation and conscription.''

Sighs of exasperation and murmurs of anger ran through the room like an undertow.

"Quite naturally you may think of me as your enemy. I sympathize with that feeling, and I assure you I shall treat you with the utmost respect. It serves no good purpose for me to antagonize you. God knows we are already under a load of taxation that is heavy enough.

"Please bear with me. Give me your cooperation and we will finish this distasteful task as soon as possible. It would be a great help to me if you would spread the word. Tell your neighbors that I am here, and let them know what I am doing. Please tell them they should call on me here at the inn within the week. Tell them also that I have the old tax rolls with me to compare with the new ones. Any indication that some resident has failed to comply will result in a thorough investigation, and possibly a heavy penalty.

"I do not wish to be impolite, but as you can see, I am soaked through and wish to get into something dry. So please excuse me. Again, gentlemen, in his majesty's name, I thank you.''

The man was a little stuffy, but all in all, considering the nature of his mission, he made a favorable impression. By this time his wet bags had been carried in, and Lecharbonnier now disappeared up the stairs.

Revision of the tax rolls went forward without incident. The citizens came and went. Most knew the man was simply doing a job that someone had to do, and treated Lecharbonnier with respect and kindness. Inevitably, a few were bitter, some glared and answered his questions with a minimum of words, and some insulted him openly. But he was always in control of himself, and if he lost patience, no one knew it.

During this same week Gabriel and Michel hired themselves out to break a pasture into farmland with two yokes of oxen. They stayed in the country for the entire week, and by late Saturday had finished. They loaded the plows onto two sledges and drove the oxen at a fast pace into Avranches, coming to the inn just as the sun was going down.

Gabriel stabled the oxen and Michel went into the inn. At the moment, the large hall was empty of customers. Rose Benet came through the back door with a stout wooden yoke across her neck with a pail of milk swinging easily at each end. Antoine was taking fresh bread from the black, oval mouth of the stone oven in the wall above the fireplace. A faint column of dark smoke poured out of the oven and fluttered up along the wall, adding a new coat of soot to the already darkened plaster.

Michel's mouth watered at the thought of the fresh milk and hot bread, but his first interest was their daughter Marie.

"Rose," he asked, "is Marie here?"

"She was here when I went to milk," the woman answered. "You didn't see her out front when you came in? Perhaps she's upstairs cleaning."

At that moment all three became aware of a quiet sound, like a quick, muffled sobbing. It seemed to be coming from the stairway. Rose looked at her husband. "Antoine, is that Marie crying?" Her voice was on the edge of alarm. They stood still, held their breath, and listened intently. Suddenly the girl's voice tore the still air with a bitter scream.

Michel was up the stairs before Rose could move. Antoine was close behind.

At the far end of the hall a door opened with such force that it struck the wall behind it, and Jonathan Lecharbonnier lunged from his room. The only exit lay behind Michel, whose large body filled the passageway. The man shouted at Michel in his powerful voice, "Get out of my way! Damn you, get back!"

Michel stood fast. At the other end of the hall, beyond Lecharbonnier, a large glass window admitted the day's last, failing light.

Lecharbonnier pivoted toward it, leaped against the glass, shattering it in every direction, and fell out of sight. Michel flew after him through the jagged opening.

CHAPTER 5

Farewell to a Friend

IT was the middle of October, and for two months now there had been no rain. The dry grasses rattled and the deep green leaves were full with settled dust.

Gabriel Dublanche sat alone on a high hill this late afternoon and looked northward. To his left, at high tide, lay the darkening sea, to his right, the undulating prairies. The grasslands, driven before a hard east wind, ran to the high coastal cliffs, then cast themselves over to be swallowed up by the restless ocean.

The wind was hot on his face. Out on the prairie, a mile or more distant, a whirlwind twisted its way from south to north, carrying a cloud of dust and broken blades of withered grass skyward in its spinning arms. The face of the sun, though its disk was distinct, shone weakly through the pallid haze.

The dry air was alive with electricity. Dust lightning played along the ground. Here and there sparks had caught in the grasses and kindled broad sheets of slanting, running flame. Long towers of white, wind-whipped smoke leaned far out over the gray sea.

For the last five days dark clouds had lain across the horizon, teasing the coastal hills with the hope of rain. Today they were nearer. Distant blue squalls played between cloud and sea. Suddenly the hot east wind died and everything sank into stillness.

Without his being aware of it, the sudden stillness made Gabriel uneasy. In his agitation he stood and walked across the brow of the hill, and began to pace among the spreading oaks that grew in a random grove on its crest. A dull agony filled his soul. A full hour passed and the light waned, but he did not notice.

A splat of cold water hit the back of his neck. He stopped pacing and jerked his head up. Looking through the limb of the old oaks, he saw that the day was gone and the sky was dark. He heard the first drops of rain striking dry leaves, slowly and unevenly, then more, and now rapidly.

Sudden fire fell from the troubled sky and rifted an ancient oak that grew at the edge of his grove. In an instant the great tree lay with its limbs on the ground and its trunk in two twisted, burning pieces. Gabriel stood transfixed in the dark. The blue flames licked in and out of the splintered wood.

The rain began to fall in earnest, and Gabriel, jolted from his lethargy, realized that he must leave the exposed hilltop. He turned and walked rapidly to the black iron gate, then along the road that wound down the hill and away from the cemetery.

The next morning at breakfast Catherine Dublanche looked across the table at her son. There were dark pouches under his eyes. He looked old and seemed distant. Catherine had been worried when Gabriel had not come home by nightfall, but she had known where he was, and why he was there. For over a month her concern for him had grown steadily. Now she reached across the table and took his hand in hers.

"Really, Gabriel," she said, "don't you think it's time you stopped mourning? He's gone, there's nothing you can do. Your sorrow won't bring him back. Pray for his soul, but you mustn't try to die in his place."

Gabriel laid down his fork, and pushed his heavy oak chair back from the table. Its legs scraped the smooth flagstone floor like fingernails on slate. Abel winced at the sound but said nothing. Gabriel went to the big bay window and stood looking out.

The rain had stopped in the night, the clouds had blown inland, and the sky was a remarkable blue. A musty smell hung in the room, a reminder of the mid-October wetness outside. Cold air had followed the storm, and the season's first frost had darkened the edges of the leaves on the spreading oak in the yard. The long dry spell had hastened the autumn; this year there would be no grand colors. The grass in front of the house, as pale as the long grasses in the prairies and meadows, now glistened with raindrops.

Catherine knew her son was suffering from more than grief. Something had snapped inside him. He was wounded, and she was afraid there was nothing she could do to bind up his wounds. He was as afraid as she. If he had known what to do to heal himself, he would have done it. But he did not know.

Gabriel grieved desperately for Michel. Added to his sorrow

was a sharp sword of guilt that cut through his heart, and made
his sense of loss deeper still.

Gabriel had been throwing hay to the oxen when he had heard
Marie's scream and Lecharbonnier's shouting. He had rushed inside and run up the stairs just in time to see Michel plunge through
the shattered window. Antoine and Rose Benet, just ahead of him,
ran into the room with the open door, and Gabriel had followed
them. Somehow it had seemed the right thing to do. He had knelt
with them on the floor over young Marie's still body. He would
never forget how she had looked. Her face was white as death.
Paths of wet tears glistened down her cheeks. Blood gurgled from
her mouth, and a terrible abrasion colored the left side of her face
red. Her clothes were badly torn and her arms deeply scratched.
   Then her eyes fluttered. As soon as Gabriel had seen she was
alive, it came hot into his mind that he should not be here but
with his friend. He had run down the stairs and out into the gathering darkness. Everything had been quiet. He had no way of
knowing where the attacker and his pursuer had gone.
   "Michel," he had shouted over and over again until his throat
was hoarse. He had run south down the street, on an impulse
turned west, and then doubled back to the inn. He was running
in circles. Then he had heard a thin, distant shout. It had seemed
to come from the edge of town, from somewhere near the brow
of the ridge that breaks off in a cliff and descends toward the
widening of the river where it joins the bay of Mont-Saint-Michel.
   Terror propelled Gabriel like a flying arrow in the direction of
the shout. In moments he was standing on the cliff's edge, searching the black emptiness for a sign. He listened intently for some
betraying sound. Except for the harsh rasp of his own hard breathing, the call of a few night birds, and the liquid slap of waves
against the base of the cliff, all was still. Somewhere down the
cliff's face a rock broke away and went rolling downward. He
heard it bounce again and again, knocking loose smaller rocks
and showers of pebbles and dirt. Then he heard it strike the water
almost four hundred feet below. The tide was in, higher than it
had been all that spring and summer.
   He wheeled in the darkness and ran back toward town. Antoine
had already spread the alarm and a string of flashing, bobbing
lanterns poured through every street and converged. They had

asked Gabriel, "Where?" And he had confessed that he did not know.

The townsmen had formed a line. Each held a lamp and stood no more than two arms lengths from his neighbor. In this manner they combed the hilltop while the women searched the town. The pale yellow lights moved slowly up and down, back and forth in the darkness. When the field produced nothing, they progressed to the face of the cliff.

Finally, at about three in the morning, a sharp call rose from a rocky point that stood out thirty feet above the water. Gabriel scrambled toward the dark knot of men and lights on the point and elbowed his way through the growing cluster. In the opening, lying in a circle of yellow lamplight, was the battered body of his closest friend.

Michel lay on his back, one arm pointing limply toward the sea, the other folded, fingers splayed across his breast. His head was thrown back, the dull eyes glazed.

The men drew Gabriel away, laid the body in a sheet, and bore Michel up the cliff and into the village.

Requiem Mass was said for Michel Lebrun two days later in the Cathedral of Avranches. Outside the sun bore down, but within the ancient stone church the coolness of night lingered. High up under the nave's lead roof, amid the Gothic arches, pigeons stirred from their roosts and fluttered about, perching first on one gray, water-streaked stone and then on another.

After the Mass, the procession to the place of burial was led by a priest dressed in a white lace robe, carrying a shepherd's staff. Behind him, the casket rode on the shoulders of six young men. They buried Michel in the cemetery on the hill, beside his father.

Young Marie Benet was not present at the burial, but was confined to her bed, where she wept much of the time. The left side of her face was swollen and a deep purple bruise the shape of a man's hand marked her cheek. Her tongue had been gashed by her own teeth.

What had happened seemed clear. Marie had been cleaning Lecharbonnier's room. He had been drunk and had assaulted her. When she had resisted, he had become enraged, tried to force her, and struck her to the floor.

What happened afterward had been for a time uncertain. Some

believed that when Michel ran after Lecharbonnier, fury made him forget the cliffs. Hot on the man's heels, he had run into the open air and fallen to his death. The theory was reasonable, but Gabriel believed Michel incapable of being blinded by rage.

The cause of death was clear, even if the circumstances were not. His body had enough broken bones to kill a man—one arm, both of his legs, as well as his back—but the back of his head was caved in, and that injury was what killed him.

The uncertainty about whether Lecharbonnier had indeed murdered Michel had ended on Sunday, the day after Michel's death. In the afternoon, Gabriel returned to the cliffs and found something that in the darkness had been overlooked. It was a large stone, a piece of round granite. He found it several feet back from the cliff's edge, directly above the place where Michel had gone over.

One side of the stone was smooth and covered with irregular patches of dark green and bright orange lichen. The other side was rough and uneven, encrusted with blood and bits of flesh and hair. The hair was the color of Michel's, and the hollow in the back of his head matched the shape of the rock.

The boy had been murdered. Lecharbonnier had lain in wait, risen up behind him, and crushed his skull.

But where was Lecharbonnier? Noticeable tracks in the soft mud had gone outward, and none had come back. This led to more conjecture among the villagers.

The bay was famed for its quicksand. Once several years ago, as an experiment, a rope forty feet long was fastened to a pyramidal block of stone that weighed three hundred pounds. The stone was set on the quicksand, and overnight sank and drew the full length of rope down and out of sight with it. Another time a ship was left stranded by the tide, and in twenty-four hours even the tops of the masts had disappeared.

Lecharbonnier was, the villagers knew, at least slightly drunk, and his judgment impaired. He tried to swim out, they reasoned, and was either drowned or caught in the sands. Either way he was dead and that was the end of it.

Gabriel had lost his truest friend. He was also tortured by a succession of "if's." If only Gabriel had reacted differently, Michel might still be alive. And deeper than his loneliness, deeper than his guilt, lay one thing more. He gazed out of the bay window at the grasses still wet with the night's rains, and he said to his mother, "I can't explain how I feel, Mama. But I know it's more than grief, because I've lost something more than a friend."

"What else, Gabriel?" she asked. "What else have you lost?"

"Mama," he answered, "I keep thinking, where was God when Michel needed him? Where was God when his father died? Where was God when Lecharbonnier killed him? I've asked the question before. When I saw the old man die in front of the Cathedral of Notre Dame, I asked it then. Where was God when the old man needed him? And I keep asking, why Michel? Why not me?"

"The grace of God, Gabriel," Catherine answered.

"The grace of God extended to me but not to him? That can't be, Mama. Not if—"

"Gabriel," she interrupted. "You're asking questions *no* one can answer!"

"That may be," he said, "but the questions won't go away. Life used to be so simple for me. You taught me so well. This house was always such a haven. And the church, I loved it so."

" 'Loved'? Don't you love it still?"

"I'm not sure. That's what I've lost: the certainty. I went away and the fathers taught me to think. They taught me to ask questions I had never asked, to be dissatisfied unless I could think it all through. And then they told me that I must have faith. How can I do both? How can I still believe in God when I see such injustice?"

Catherine came to him. He bit his lip and suppressed an uneven breath. A tear brimmed up in each eye and ran down his face.

Some movement in the sky drew his eyes upward. A wedge of geese heading south flew low overhead, so low that every gray marking was clear. They honked incessantly, gained altitude, circled, diminished to mere dots on the horizon, and disappeared altogether.

"The geese will come back," he said. "What I've lost never will."

Catherine reached up and took her son's face in her hands. The silver cross on her bosom reflected the sunlight.

"It may come back," she said with confidence. "What you believed might return."

He put his strong arms around her and drew her tightly to himself.

Cool weather passed and the heat temporarily returned. Noonday sunlight poured through the big, open south door of the smithy and the forge blazed furiously.

Abel Dublanche and his son worked that day on new iron tires for the dray that had moved freight in and out of Avranches for the last fifty years. The old tires were worn nearly through in places, and finally one had given way. The elder Poulard, who owned the dray, decided to replace them all.

Abel was as much wheelwright as he was blacksmith. The rear wheels of the dray were five feet across. Using a small wheel called a traveler, he measured the circumference of one, and then measured and cut a strip of iron from which he would fashion the new tire. Heating the iron a portion at a time, Abel bent it by hammer blows until it formed a circle. He welded the butt joints, checked the circumference, and brought the new tire to red heat. Then he punched the holes for nails, and heated it again until it expanded enough to be a driving fit on the aging wooden wheel.

With iron tongs Abel and Gabriel lay wheel and tire on the floor, and with sledges began to beat the red-hot iron into place. The wood smoked and flamed. When the fit was secure, Gabriel drenched the flames with water that hissed and steamed when it struck the hot iron, and an odor of burning charcoal rose with the dense, white cloud. The old wood cracked and groaned as the shrinking iron forced the old spokes deeper into the felloes and hub.

Abel completed four new iron bands for the hub, shrank them into place, and drove nails through the tires into each felloe. It was hot work that tired every muscle, but it was bread and butter for the table.

They had finished two wheels and were beginning on the third when they heard the mixed sounds of stamping hooves, creaking wheels, and squeaking harness in the drive. They looked up just as a well-appointed team and carriage pulled in front of the large door and stopped.

A pleasant looking, middle-aged man swung down to the ground on the far side of the carriage and knelt to examine the outer rear foot of the horse on that side. He got up and walked around the front of the team toward Abel and Gabriel. The stiffness of the ride had not yet left his joints, and he walked with the quick, wide-legged, side-to-side movement peculiar to old men when they are in a hurry. He stated his business as rapidly as he walked.

"Sir, one of my horses has thrown a shoe, and I'm wondering if you could—great day, man, it's hotter than blazes in here! How do you stand it?"

He took his hat off and fanned himself with quick, hard strokes. Then he plunged in again, not waiting for an answer. "I'm wondering if you can shoe the animal for me. We're on a holiday. Going up the coast to Mont-Saint-Michel—sort of a pilgrimage. Could you help me?"

Abel's slow, easy speech contrasted sharply when he answered, "If you'll let me unhitch her from the carriage, sir, we'll have you on your way in just a little while. The others are welcome to get out and relax under the oak up there in the yard. The boy here will get a bucket of cold water and cups."

Gabriel trotted to the house as the travelers emerged—the gentleman's wife and their daughter. All three were hot and welcomed the rest. The ladies walked up the slope to the great old tree while the men unhitched the horses.

Gabriel returned quickly, with Catherine following to welcome the strangers.

"Here you are, ladies," she said. "This is good water, and it's cool. How far have you come today?"

Just then the younger woman removed her broad-brimmed, satin hat and looked up to take the cup from Gabriel. Their eyes locked at the same instant. In chorus each blurted the other's name and broke out laughing.

Gabriel felt awkward and foolish. "Celeste, I—I'm sorry. I'm very sorry!"

"For what, Gabriel? Sorry that I'm here?"

"No, no. Of course not! I'm sorry I didn't see you when you drove in. Sorry I wasn't here to help you down from the carriage. Sorry to be so slow."

She laughed pleasantly at his awkward embarrassment and said, "Well, don't be sorry. I'm just as surprised to see you as you are to see me, and I'm certainly as pleased as you appear to be."

"You know these people, Gabriel?" Catherine asked.

"Yes—at least I know Celeste."

Celeste came to his rescue. "Gabriel, Madame Dublanche, this is my mother, Emilie Lefleur." Celeste turned to her mother. "Mother, this is Gabriel Dublanche. I met him on the quay last year. He's the young man Papa and I saw at the execution, remember?"

Soon the horse was shod, but Catherine extended an invitation for the evening meal and a night's lodging. Emilie and Celeste pressed Pierre Lefleur until he consented to stay.

When the evening work was done and prayers were said, Gabriel and Celeste left the company of the others and drifted slowly down through the pasture to the river. They talked of many things, but most of all about Michel and about the pain that Gabriel felt in his soul.

That night Gabriel felt comfort in Celeste's presence. She was very like Catherine, and he found himself telling her all his heart.

CHAPTER 6

The Girl from Rouen

GABRIEL made two long trips by wagon to Rouen before winter— to buy cloth he said, but his friends smiled and whispered among themselves that he had reasons of a different kind.

Every week letters between Gabriel and Celeste crossed in the post, and each week his admiration for her deepened. Little wonder. Celeste Lefleur was an exciting girl with a zest for life and a character that complemented his own. She was gentle as he was kind. She loved learning, so did he. She had just turned eighteen, he would soon be twenty. She spoke other languages, English and Italian. At Louis-le-Grand he had studied Hebrew and ancient Greek. She loved history and the old philosophers; so did he.

Celeste was the daughter of a burly, energetic tradesman who had begun with nothing and worked his way up. Pierre Lefleur was brusque, practical, and determined. As a young man he had obtained a royal commission to trade for pelts in New France. Now he owned a small fleet of ships, and warehouses at Rouen and Montreal.

Celeste, the youngest of three girls, had an older sister, Genevieve, who had married a merchant in Le Havre. The middle girl, Alice, served God and the Church in a convent at Fontainebleau.

Her mother, Emilie, was a happy woman, the balance wheel

of the Lefleur family. Emilie remained in the background, let Pierre take center stage, and ignored his bluster and shouting. Without his knowing, Emilie kept Pierre pointed in the right direction. She smoothed his path at home, gave him the least possible resistance, but said an occasional, firm "no." Emilie was a strong woman of consummate good sense with confidence in herself and in the man she had married.

The Lefleur home was an impressive country manor between Rouen and Duclairs, a house that sat majestically at the end of a long, tree-lined lane, in a beautiful pastoral setting, with ancient cottonwoods scattered across a wide field that every spring wore a bright blanket of waving red poppies.

Wealth had not spoiled Celeste Lefleur. She had strong opinions about the life and times of French nobility. She saw the fine veneer of delicate manners, extravagant dress, and affected speech, and recognized the corruption that lay beneath. Celeste exuded a healthy, bright sexuality without any hint of the devices of a society made silly by its own artificiality. She was both feminine and aggressive, poised but lively, happy seated at her loom or with the rich smell of fresh bread dough on her hands.

Celeste loved the outdoors. The horses that grazed in the pasture northwest of the manor belonged to her. Every day, in all kinds of weather, she rode them. They were her freedom, her euphoria, her intoxication. When astride her favorite chestnut stallion, she felt the smooth, strong rhythm of muscle and leg beating the prairie into the past. She felt the wind in her face, the exhilaration of harmony between her body and his, and the peril—the risk of commanding that which at any instant might refuse to be commanded. Such risk was life, or perhaps death, or some strange existence between the two. Let the delicate city women confine themselves to their salons, wear silk brocades, and live sedately, she thought. Life must have peril if it is to be life at all.

The dark water whirled and eddied about the blades as Gabriel pulled smoothly on the oars to guide the small boat in the slow current. He had put in two and a half miles upstream from where his father's pasture ran down to the river's east side. Now he was alone at a place so narrow that a man might easily throw a stone from one bank to the other. The water was deep.

Towering trees overhung the stream on either side, their fresh May leaves hiding the gray limbs in spring green, their branches blown by a soft downstream breeze, sweeping clean the warm afternoon air.

Soon Celeste would come to Avranches to stay, and Gabriel's life would change forever. Now, before her arrival, was the time to settle unfinished business, lest he enter his new life with a smoldering fire that might destroy it.

The water swirled steadily under the little hull. In the past nine months, Gabriel had come here again and again, rowing up and down these banks, always looking for something that might have been missed—a tree root broken by a man on the run; a footprint that escaped the washing of fall rains and winter snow, a footprint that would lead . . . where? He did not know. If he could find a piece of clothing newly risen from the river's muddy bottom, aged and rotted by the water, find it before it floated out into the bay, and follow it to a decomposed body, a collection of bones—the right bones—then the fire that burned blue inside Gabriel Dublanche could be extinguished.

Otherwise, he would be forced to go on looking until he found Lecharbonnier and did what had to be done. This one thing Gabriel had not confided to Celeste.

Never in his life had Gabriel Dublanche hated or sought revenge. When this heat flamed up inside, guilt wrenched at his heart. He tried to feel differently. He prayed. But nothing changed, except that the secret fires burned hotter.

Now, though filled with shame—ashamed that he could not free himself, ashamed that he was driven desperately to do what should not be done—he was nonetheless utterly unrepentant.

During the winter when the trees were bare and one could see clearly through the woods, he had walked both banks of the river from his home to the coast. He dared even to search the sands of the bay, though he knew that to tarry a moment too long would mean death. And he dared to search the sea caves at the base of the cliffs, caves he had feared to enter as a boy.

But in all his searching, he had found nothing.

Nor today had he found anything. The afternoon light began to fade. He pulled hard on the right oar and swung the bow upriver. On another day he would search again.

Gabriel and Celeste were married on the sixth of June, at ten in the morning, in the chapel of the Cathedral of Avranches.

Pierre and Emilie had arranged a wedding trip and the newlyweds traveled east by coach—in a style to which Gabriel was totally unaccustomed—beyond Paris, to Châtillon, in the high country where the River Seine first rises as a bubbling spring in the forest of Burgundy. Legend held that long ago a nymph was chased by a satyr, and becoming exhausted, she fell. Having fallen, she wept, and where her tears touched the ground a spring leaped up, and the Seine was born.

For centuries an old temple to the ancient river god had stood here. Then the Romans came and built a pavilion and baths, and the baths were good for love.

After the honeymoon Gabriel and Celeste talked for a while of living in Rouen, and of Gabriel's working for Pierre. Gabriel feared that in Avranches Celeste would miss the fine home and style of life she had always known. But Celeste said that her father was a hard man to work for, and that although he would pay Gabriel well, his impatience would be a needless burden. Besides, Abel needed his son's help in the smithy, and Celeste longed to taste the life of a small seacoast town. So they settled in Avranches.

It was a Sunday afternoon, the first Sunday of autumn. The sky was the kind of pale blue that only September can bring forth, and the air was crisp and clean.

After dinner, Gabriel and Celeste took two horses from Abel's meadow and rode together along the road that led from Avranches northwest to Granville.

As the horses clattered across the long, high bridge that spanned the river north of town, they skittered at the sharp, hollow sound of their own hooves; Celeste's spirited chestnut reared and backed toward the bridge's edge. Celeste dismounted just in time. Sweat stood out on Gabriel's brow, his body went cold, and Celeste's knees quivered till she could scarcely stand. They steadied themselves, took each other by the hand, and peered over the side to the river sixty feet below; broad, lazy, deadly.

"Too close," Gabriel breathed.

"Yes," she said. "My heart's in my throat. This bridge is terribly high, Gabriel. Let's get across before the horses act up again."

But Gabriel stood there, seemingly transfixed by the slow eddies beneath him. "I wonder," he said.

"Wonder what?" she asked.

"If he came over this bridge."

"Who?"

"Jonathan Lecharbonnier," he answered.

Celeste was quiet for a moment, then said, "You've not forgotten him, have you?"

"No," he answered quietly.

"Gabriel, I wish you could forget. It's a dangerous thing to go on remembering."

"I can't forget," he said. "If he's alive, he's got to pay. Michel deserves vengeance." He paused, looked around at her, and said, "Celeste, I must settle the score."

She looked up, surprised. "Settle the score? How do you mean, 'settle the score'?"

"See him in prison. See him hanged. See him shot. Kill him myself, if it's necessary." Gabriel said all of this in a matter-of-fact, steady voice, not once taking his eyes from the river. "Whatever it takes."

Celeste looked down at the gray water, up again to Gabriel. Across her face came a mixed expression of amazement, confusion, and mild anger, but she said nothing more. In another moment Gabriel drew a deep breath, and they walked on.

Once across, the road twisted to the left and switchbacked its way up the steep side of a sudden hill. Gabriel and Celeste remounted and rode slowly to the top. In all the long climb Celeste was silent, only making the necessary responses to Gabriel's questions. He wondered, for he had never seen her so quiet.

Having reached the full crown of the hill, Gabriel pulled the reins to the left, kicked his mount to a gallop, and raced off over the grassland that lay between the road and the sea. Celeste, not to be outdone, plunged after him, the spirit of the chase overcoming her distant manner, and she laughed and shouted as she and the stallion pushed past and far beyond Gabriel.

First to reach the cliffs that overlooked the sea, Celeste brought the stallion to a quick halt and jumped to the ground. When at last Gabriel reached her, she was sitting under a large maple that had grown before the prevailing winds with a distinct eastward lean. She looked up at him with a mischievous smile.

They sat for a long while under the tree and talked of many things while the horses grazed behind them. The air was wonderfully clear. High, wispy clouds feathered randomly across the sky.

The bay was quiet; no fishing boats dotted its surface, for Sunday was the day of worship and rest.

Far to the southwest, the rock of Mont-Saint-Michel rose boldly from the coast of Brittany.

All the while, Celeste's thoughts kept returning to the high bridge over the river, and to Gabriel's desire for revenge. She was troubled. The first quality that had drawn her to him was his gentleness, his revulsion at cruelty. Not once had it entered her mind that he might be capable of revenge, no matter how severe the offense might be. Justice was one thing, but revenge another, and the look in his eyes had clearly been one of revenge.

"Celeste, are you listening?"

"What? Oh." She laughed nervously and shook her head. "I'm sorry, darling. My mind was somewhere else."

"I could see that," he said. He paused and added, "There was some sort of shadow across your face. You weren't hearing me at all."

"It's all right now," she said. "Go ahead, tell me. What were you saying?"

He chuckled and continued pleasantly, "I was saying that there's a legend about Saint Michel, a silly legend in a way, but interesting. Have you heard it?"

"No," she said, "tell me."

He picked a long stem of grass and, playing idly with it, gazed across the gray sea toward the rock. "Well, it seems that long ago the great Saint Michel—the Warrior Angel, second only to the Archangel Gabriel himself—was in danger. Satan threatened to defeat him, so Michel looked about for a fortress, a place of safety from the Fiend. At last he found this great rock standing out of the sea, a habitation truly worthy of an archangel of God. So from his place high in the heavens, Michel descended to the rock, and on its peak built a fortress."

The further he went the more Gabriel warmed to his story.

"But Michel was still afraid," he continued. "Afraid the great walls were not thick enough to protect him, and the waters not wide enough to discourage Satan. So Michel spread roundabout his refuge miles and miles of shining, moving sands into which one would certainly sink if one set out to cross them. This was enough, and the angel settled down in safety."

He paused for effect, and Celeste broke in, "But that doesn't seem silly at all—not real, perhaps, but not silly either. Sometimes I'm tempted and need a place safe from the Devil.''

He laughed. ''You? Tempted? I don't believe it.''

''Oh, but it's true.''

''But that wasn't the silly part,'' he continued. ''The Devil took up residence in a humble cottage on the shore and farmed marvelously fertile lands, and the archangel grew jealous.''

''Of what?''

''He was jealous of the Devil's fertile lands, for—''

''That *is* silly,'' she interrupted again. ''An angel of God wouldn't be jealous of such a trivial thing.''

''Yes, of course. I know that. But it's just a story. Anyway, he was jealous of the Devil's fertile lands, for he himself was very poor. So he devised a plan. One day he called on his neighbor the Devil and said, 'I've come to make you a proposition.' ''

She interrupted again. ''Do angels deal with devils?'' She was serious, and he took the question seriously.

For a moment he thought, then answered solemnly, ''Once I would've said no. But one day I began to read Job. Remember, God and the Devil spoke, and God said, 'Go ahead and test my servant Job. Take everything away from him but life itself.' Perhaps angels do make propositions with the Devil after all.

''But back to the story. This was his proposition. The archangel said to the Devil, 'You love to rest, and I love hard work. Cede me all your lands. I will do the work, and you will receive half of the harvest.'

''Well, you can imagine that Satan agreed instantly. Then the saint said, 'You can even choose which share of the crops you take.' 'What do you mean?' asked the Devil. 'I mean that if you choose that which grows above the ground, I will take what grows below. If you choose that which grows below the ground, I will gladly take what grows above it.'

''The Devil agreed and made his choice. 'For the first year's crop,' he said, 'I want what grows above the soil.' 'Very good,' said the Saint. And he went away to plant his crops.

''When harvest came, the Devil found the archangel had planted carrots and radishes and beets, and for a year he had to content himself with eating greens. But he was clever, and he reversed his choice, saying that the next year he would take what grew below. So that year Michel planted barley and buckwheat and beans, and left the Father of Lies with nothing but the withered roots.

"Now the moral of that story is that there are great advantages in being a saint."

They laughed together. Then, as if to shake the stiffness from his muscles, Gabriel stood and threw a stone high into the air over the cliff's edge, out toward the water. Their laughter faded as they squinted into the dying sun to see where the stone would fall.

CHAPTER 7

On Horseback to the River

CELESTE'S happy presence lifted Gabriel out of his melancholy and diverted him from his quest for vengeance so that he happily farmed the family ground his father had left fallow all the years since his grandfather's death. The ground, rich and good, brought forth plentifully. Their house stood on the other side of a narrow bit of pasture from Abel and Catherine's, eastward, and within shouting distance.

Celeste was not content to let Gabriel bear the burden alone. How she changed that year! She replaced her fine slippers with rough boots, and followed the great draft horses through the plowed fields. She pushed her sleeves to her elbows, milked the cow and churned the butter, gathered eggs, and carried water—all over Gabriel's useless insistence that she content herself with the lighter household chores.

To Celeste the work was a release from artificiality, a proof she could earn her way, justify her existence, feel near the soil that gave them life, and be both companion and lover to the man she married.

It was not all work; there was time for laughter, free and glorious moments on warm summer days when they carried their lunch to the riverbank and sat beneath the cottonwoods, lost in each other while the deep water rolled past beneath them.

Gabriel's own *joie de vivre* returned. Past tragedies faded into the back hallways of memory. Troubling questions lost their importance. Gabriel basked in the sunlight of the present day, and its brilliant light washed out many of the past's unpleasant images.

One slight shadow did, however, come and go on the landscape of his mind. On most days he did not think of it, but his desire for vengeance never lessened. He thought of it as an unpaid debt, something he ought to do, something he *would* do—but not immediately. Lecharbonnier, if he was yet alive—and now Gabriel doubted that he was—could wait. But, Gabriel thought, I won't let myself forget. I'll wait, and always be alert. I must learn the truth, and nothing is more important than the truth. A man could not be a good man unless he was willing to sacrifice everything—even his family—for the truth.

Gabriel contemplated these long thoughts as he followed the plow and worked in his father's smithy. But mostly he thought of Celeste and the joy she brought him. He was even glad that she had delivered him from the driving immediacy of his obsession.

"I'm going to the garden for lettuce. Will you come with me?"

He was lost in concentration and did not answer.

She was standing in the door of the smithy; he was bent over a table sketching with a bit of charcoal on a sheet of new, white paper. Celeste came up behind him and looked over his shoulder. The clear black, flowing marks outlined a sleek horse rearing high, its mane and tail flying in the wind, its forelegs cutting the air.

"Darling, that's beautiful. But what is it for?" she asked. He waited a long moment, aware that she was there but still absorbed in his task, and finally answered, "It's a weather vane. Scarron the miller was in this morning. He said he would trade a year's grinding for a good, new wrought-iron vane. He wants a horse, standing high—like on a heraldic shield."

"Wonderful," she said, and then paused. "But you haven't answered me."

He looked up and smiled at her, his eyes searching her face, and said, "What did you ask?"

"Will you come *with* me?"

"Where?"

She laughed and held out a large woven basket, made of white oak splits, and said again, "I'm going to the garden for lettuce. Will you come with me? I wish you would."

"Yes." He was pleased at her invitation and embarrassed by his absentmindedness. He laughed. "Yes, of course I will."

He looked again at the sketch, wiped his hands on a clean cotton cloth, reached for her basket, and slipped his arm around her waist. Together they walked along the grassy path leading from the shop down a lane lined with mulberry trees, to the garden plot behind their thatch-roofed home.

Hordes of blackbirds sat in the mulberry trees filling themselves with the sweet, dark purple fruit. They raised a terrible din, a constant loud chatter that drowned out all other sound. When Gabriel and Celeste came near, the chatter suddenly stopped—as though a conductor had waved a baton—and the air came alive with a new sound, the muffled rush of feathered wings as the birds rose in a black fluid cloud and raced for the river.

Gabriel filled Celeste's basket with tender heads of endive. The day was getting hot. On their way back up the path, they stopped at the well. Celeste spread her skirt on the grass in the shade of the oldest, largest mulberry tree while Gabriel dropped the oak bucket from the well curb. The chain rattled musically over the pulley, and went loose when the bucket splashed into the water below. The bucket floated a moment on the surface, upset, filled, and tugged gently at the chain. The chain went tight again with the bucket's new weight, and Gabriel drew it upward with long, even, downward pulls, looping it around a short wooden arm extending from the well's frame.

He lifted the full bucket and carried it to where Celeste sat beneath the tree, then held it out. She accepted and he tipped it slightly toward her. The smooth, wet oak rim touched her lips and she drank. Trickles of water escaped around her lips and rolled down her chin and neck and wet the front of her dress. She jumped to her feet laughing and sputtering, frantically brushing the water away.

Celeste grabbed playfully at the bucket, pulling and tugging until Gabriel's shirt was soaked through, and her own full skirt was splotched from waist to hem. Cool and refreshed, they fell laughing to the grass in the tree's shade, where they lay for a time.

At last Gabriel got up, walked among the trees, and picked handfuls of mulberries. Then he knelt beside Celeste and fed them to her one by one. The deep purple stained his fingers.

Finally, after carrying Celeste's basket of lettuce to the house and leaving her there, Gabriel returned to the smithy, where he picked up the bit of charcoal and looked at his sketch. But now he hardly saw it. He was thinking of Celeste, and he asked in a whisper, "What could a man want more?"

That winter Uncle Joseph fell ill with pneumonia. The autumn's changeable weather had put him to bed with terrible chest pains and a cough so severe that each seizure left him too weak to stand. As a rule Joseph refused to be ill, but this time he was overruled.

Celeste took charge of his care. She brought him meals, and as long as his fever lasted, she remained day and night to bathe his face and arms in cool water. He made a great show of how unnecessary her presence was, but upon his recovery, secretly relished her special care as the event of his lifetime.

Winter seemed long to everyone that year. It was bitterly cold. Snow blanketed the coast for an unending succession of days. The Atlantic finger that extended to Avranches rolled gray and uneasy, never resting. When spring finally came, a great sense of liberation came with it; liberation from houses and greatcoats, freedom to breathe again the rich, sweet air of growth and life.

Celeste moved her spinning wheel out of doors to the shade of the oak in Catherine's front yard, and together the women spun away whole days. Their work went quickly, their deft fingers flying without thought as they talked of the neighborhood children, of the flowers and vegetables they had planted in their gardens, and of the new parish priest who was such a good man, earnest and hardworking. But they did wonder if he was a little young to understand the problems of the people. And they wondered, too, if God really meant that such a fine-looking man should devote his life to a celibate calling.

So the days passed and work progressed and life went on as life was intended to go. In June came the Feast of Saint Peter and Saint Paul, a holiday in all of France.

Gabriel woke while it was yet dark. He lay for a while in bed, his body relaxed and his mind at ease. Celeste lay breathing quietly beside him, and he thought, Life is good. In spite of everything, the joy is worth the sorrow. In a few hours, shortly after a special morning Mass in the village, his family would gather at his parents' home. It would be one of those days when body, mind, and soul blend together in perfect harmony—one of those rare days of exquisite and total happiness.

He rose and dressed quietly, careful not to disturb Celeste. He went out, watered and fed the horses that huffed and snorted as he walked toward them in the morning darkness. He shelled corn directly from the cobs with his thumbs and scattered it across the ground for the chickens. He collected the eggs and milked the cow. Celeste usually shared in these tasks, but today he wanted her to rest.

The sun was half an hour high when Gabriel walked through the dew-covered grass of his empty hilltop field and looked toward the bay. A spring mist was rolling down from the forest, hiding the sea beneath it like a silvery satin comforter, quieting the sleeping inlet. The sun's orange wheel had just lifted from the mist and was gradually mounting the edge of the clear blue sky.

This hilltop was Gabriel's favorite place. He came here often, especially on holy days, to settle his mind, to think, to pray. This was a glad morning, a morning for thanks. He had been married a year and nine months, and had no want. And today he and Celeste had good news to tell the family.

The whole Dublanche family began to gather at Abel and Catherine's about nine. Uncle Joseph arrived first and was sitting with Abel beneath a spreading chinaberry tree when Gabriel and Celeste came walking through the field swinging a basket of food between them.

Catherine's mother arrived a little past ten. She was eighty-three, the acknowledged matriarch of her clan. Even at so advanced an age, she kept her own small house in Avranches, where she happily received the frequent visits of her adoring children. Her hair was swept up in waves and gathered grandly to form a silver crown at the top of her head. Abel and Joseph helped her from her carriage to a chair prepared and waiting in the shade.

By half past ten everyone was there—aunts and great-aunts, uncles and several cousins and their children—thirty-three in all. The house could not contain them, so Abel and Gabriel set four weathered sawhorses under the oak and laid across them the sideboards of a wagon for a rustic table large enough to accommodate the grown-ups. The children would sit on the grass.

The women and girls, like bees in flight, hovered over the sideboards. They spread crisply starched, ironed tablecloths, white as snow, and covered them with dozens of dishes of the finest, home-cooked Norman food. An aroma rose that set every mouth watering.

A half-dozen small children ran about with the uncontrolled ecstasy that all children generate on a holiday, and once nearly upset Aunt Rénée Marie on the way from the hearth with a steaming dish of mussels, shrimp, and scallops in a sauce of vegetables and cream.

Five-year-old Martin and seven-year-old Samuel climbed the oak, ventured out onto the limb overhanging the table, and sloughed off bits of gray bark into the apricot glaze on the baked apple slices. They sent leaves floating in soft spirals to settle and sail like little boats in seas of giblet gravy and pitchers of applejack.

The first leaf boats were launched by accident, but when twelve-year-old Jacques saw the wonderful effect, he and Cousin Euclide climbed the limb to find who could put more boats to sea. These antics ended when Noel chased ten-year-old Cécile and sent her screaming into Aunt Marie's farthingale, knocking her from her feet and sending two plump baked hens rolling across the grass.

When the scurry was done, the family gathered about the table and Abel offered thanks. They ate amid good conversation and laughter, a people who knew the meaning of both bounty and emptiness.

The children sat in little clusters on the lawn, having grouped themselves by age. For the first time that day they were quiet and mannerly.

When the meal was nearly finished, Monique, the young wife of Aunt Marie's oldest son, leaned toward Celeste and, smiling, asked in a whisper, "Celeste, when are you and Gabriel going to add to this collection of fine, well-behaved Dublanche children?"

Celeste's complexion deepened to a comely red hue. She looked down at her lap and murmured something unintelligible. But then she regained her composure, stood, and cleared her throat.

"Gabriel and I have something to tell you," she said in her lovely, clear voice. Most guessed the message before it was delivered, and encouraged her with, "Now what could it be?" and "Tell us, Celeste!"

She tugged at Gabriel's arm and said in mock whisper, "Get up, dear. You promised we would do this together." They stood, each with an arm around the other's waist, and again Celeste began to blush. Several "shhhs" sounded.

"You've all guessed by now," Gabriel said, and kissed his embarrassed wife on the forehead. Joseph asked, "When, Celeste?'' And she answered, ''In December, we think.'' Applause broke out, and a chorus of congratulations and giggles of delight.

When everyone had eaten his fill, Aunt Marie said, ''We still have enough food to feed an army. But then, that's the way it always is at family dinners.''

The excess food was packed away in the baskets of those who brought it, the tablecloths readied for washing, the sideboard tables dismantled. The small children took afternoon naps, and even the older ones played at quiet games. The grown-ups sat in bunches to rest and while away what was left of the holiday in subdued talk and family reflection.

The Feast of Saint Peter and Saint Paul always fell about a week after the year's longest day, so that now when the guests began to leave, four hours of good daylight remained. Teams were brought in from the pasture and hitched, hugs and kisses were passed out freely, and everyone promised return visits.

Gabriel and Celeste were the last to go. They walked home along the roadway rather than through the field. The day had become the hottest so far that year, so when a late-afternoon breeze came to life and made the cottonwood leaves dance on their stems, Celeste sighed at the pleasant coolness, reached down for her husband's arm, and laid it around her shoulder.

But their reverie was cut short. Scarron the miller came riding up from behind and hailed them. ''Is my weather vane done yet, Gabriel?''

''Not quite, sir. It'll be a week or two yet. I've been busy in the hay fields.''

''Quite all right, Gabriel. That's not really what I came to say.'' Scarron sat his horse during the whole conversation, giving the impression he would not be long.

Scarron was stocky and had a wide, flat face. He was a pleasant man, easy to get along with, and a good neighbor. ''I learned something today that I think you'll want to know.''

''What's that?'' Gabriel asked.

''A brother of mine who lives just across the river came to our place for the holiday. After our meal we fell to talking about your friend, young Lebrun who was murdered almost two years ago— God rest his soul.'' He paused a slight moment to search Gabriel's face for a sign of interest. Gabriel looked at him intently, his eyes piercing.

"We began to talk about how strange it was that this government man should just disappear with never a trace; and my brother said he wasn't too sure that he had. So right away I asked him what he meant. He said the day after the murder he saw a stranger go by his place."

"A stranger? What did he look like?" Gabriel asked.

"Well, it was just about daylight, and this man came trudging through the pasture, moving like he was stiff and sore. The fellow didn't see my brother till he was nearly on him. Then he turned and ran like the devil himself was after him."

Celeste looked anxiously at Gabriel. His eyes were fixed intently on Scarron and a tension she had not seen in more than a year was in his face.

"Do you think your brother could describe him to me?" Gabriel asked. "I never met Lecharbonnier myself, but others have told me how he looked. I'd be anxious to hear what your brother has to say."

"Oh, I believe he could describe him, all right. He's gone home already, but it's not far to his place. You could get over there and back well before the sun sets if you liked."

"That's just what I'll do, sir. And I thank you for your information."

Without hesitation Gabriel wheeled and headed for the pasture where the horses were grazing.

"Gabriel, I wish you wouldn't." Celeste was running to keep up with his long, determined strides. "You've suffered enough over this man, a man you . . . Gabriel, stand still and listen to me," she pleaded as she ran after him. He paid her no mind, but she continued. "A man you don't even know, a man who can't hurt you anymore if you leave him alone. Please give this up!"

Gabriel still said nothing and kept walking as though he didn't hear.

She saw the uselessness of more pleas, and said with finality, "Then I'm going with you."

"Whatever you like," he said. His answer was flat and distant. A compelling anger from some almost forgotten place in the back of his mind had suddenly risen to new life.

Gabriel and Celeste saddled the horses and rode to the river and beyond in silence.

Gabriel found Scarron's brother at his home and questioned

him closely about the stranger in his pasture. When they left, Gabriel was convinced Lecharbonnier was still alive.

Celeste could not bear the look on her husband's face. Until now she had believed all this burning for vengeance was in the past. Obviously she had been wrong.

Hang Scarron! she thought. Why couldn't he have minded his own business? Nearly two years had gone by peacefully, and he had to stir all this up again.

But Celeste did not let Gabriel see her anger. She was her mother's own daughter and knew the direct approach to a determined man never works. On the homeward side of the river, just after crossing the low bridge that spanned it, she unexpectedly reined in her great chestnut and dismounted. Gabriel, not noticing at first, rode on ahead, then turned and looked back.

"Why are you stopping?" he asked.

"My horse," she answered. "He's favoring his right foreleg. I think he may have a rock under his shoe."

Gabriel turned back, dismounted, and lifted the stallion's foot. "I don't see anything," he said.

"Maybe it dropped out," she said.

"Could be," he answered absently.

Suddenly her face and voice brightened. "Gabriel, look. We're right here at the river path. Let's ride down to the place where our pasture meets the river and swim."

Even the heat of renewed passion for vengeance could not shut out the passion Gabriel felt for his wife. The prospect of swimming with her in the river brought his attention back to more pleasant sensations.

He looked out westward through a break in the tops of the mammoth trees. The sun was swimming on the silver ridge of a black storm cloud coming in from the sea. He said, "There's a storm coming. We really shouldn't risk it."

"It's all right," she pleaded. She saw plainly that she had teased him out of his dark mood, at least for the moment. "We can swim till the storm is closer. Your father's barn isn't far away, and when we hear the thunder, we can get to shelter before the rain begins. Please," she said, "let's do it."

And she remounted before he could say no.

"Where's your spirit of adventure, Gabriel?" She urged her horse forward onto the river path.

In an instant he was astride his own beast, kicking it into action.

"All right," he shouted after her. "But this is going to be very short or very wet."

Gabriel was fifty yards behind when Celeste came up to the sandy beach and swung down from her horse. By the time he reached the beach her dress lay in a heap and she was running naked across the sandbar toward the deep pool. Once in the thigh-deep water, she turned and faced him, arms akimbo, taunting him. "Come on in!" she called. "Don't be a bore!" But he sat his horse a moment longer, catching his breath in sheer admiration. How beautiful, he thought. How wonderful. She's mine, and a new life that we've created lives inside her lovely body. It's a glory!

For an hour they swam and frolicked and made love in the warm water. Then they lay on the sand, tired, laughing, pleasantly drained, the lush green leaves of great cottonwoods hushed and still above them.

"I was wrong about the storm," he said. "It must've gone around us altogether."

But at that moment a strong peal of thunder rolled down the hills and reverberated in the river bottom. Lightning cut the air. Overhead the leaves stirred to life. The horses that had waited patiently, cropping grass nearby at the pasture's edge, fidgeted and whinnied. It was time to run for shelter.

They scrambled to their feet, playfully brushed the sand each from the other, dressed in haste, and mounted their nervous horses.

The wind rose sharply and whipped the treetops. The horses, going now across the sloping pasture to the barn, broke into a gallop.

Gabriel and Celeste were less than fifty yards from shelter when a huge flash of white fire struck the ground close in front of Celeste's chestnut stallion. The concussion hit like a sledge; the blinded horse stumbled and pitched, rolling feet over body forward.

In the second Celeste's body came to rest, Gabriel flung himself off his horse and instantly was kneeling beside her. She had been thrown clear of the tumbling horse, and now lay limp and pale, a pitiful heap in the tall grass.

Rain fell in large, quick drops, washing the dirt and blood from her eyes and face. Cradling her in his left arm, Gabriel parted her wet, tangled hair with the fingers of his right hand. On the left side of her head, just above her ear, across the top of an already large swelling, he found a deep diagonal gash. She was unconscious.

He picked her up and stumbled through the grass, up the slippery slope toward the barn. The rain rushed down in sheets, and as he struggled to open the big door with Celeste in his arms, the wind tried to wrench it violently from his hand.

Once inside, he tenderly lay her down on fresh straw, wiped the droplets from her closed eyes and from the softness of her face, and fastened the gray, weathered door of the barn against the beating storm.

CHAPTER 8

The Change

THE cavernous old wooden barn was filled with the smell of horses. At the foot of the ladder that led up to the hay mow, Celeste lay on the straw, breathing even, quiet breaths. A steadily burning lantern spread a jaundiced yellow light over her pale skin.

A gentle Madonna, Gabriel thought, no sign of worry anywhere in her lovely face, so still, not a sign of pain, as though she might open her eyes any moment and say good morning. But Celeste did not open her eyes, not that evening or in the long night that followed.

Except when he ran to bring Abel and Catherine, Gabriel did not leave her side. Together the three of them watched through the night. Rain whispered on the barn's dark roof, while thunder rolled away among the hills and down the cliffs onto the bosom of the sea.

Catherine had brought fresh water from the well, gently washed Celeste's wound, wet the girl's pale, dry lips, and felt the slow rhythm of her heart. Now she sat over Celeste and fingered the beads of her rosary, or held tightly to the crucifix of silver, her lips all the while moving silently.

The horses came to the barn and scraped the door with their

hooves until Abel let them in. He gave them fodder and put them in their stalls.

Like slow, weary oxen the hours plodded on and drew the night after them. When the malingering dawn came, it did not break cleanly over the soggy land. Rather, its gray light filtered through thick clouds so heavy they seemed about to fall from the sky. The rain continued until the fields and roads ran with muddy rivulets and the barn lot was a dark brown sea.

The same wagon that had provided a table for a happy family now stood inside the barn's south door. In the morning Abel hitched the Percherons to the wagon's double tree and made a soft pallet in its oak bed. They lifted Celeste into the wagon. Gabriel sat beside her, while Abel stretched a canvas tarpaulin from sideboard to sideboard to shelter her from the rain. Without apparent effort the huge draft horses drew the wagon and family up the hill to the house.

They lay Celeste in the same bed where Catherine had given birth to Gabriel, moving it so that it sat in front of the same window. Avranches was without a doctor now, so they did what they knew to do and gave the rest over into the hands of God.

At night Gabriel lay on the floor beside Celeste's bed and listened for changes in her breathing. But day followed day, and there was no change.

"Young man up in Granville lay like that six years before he died," one insensitive old woman declared. The new young priest came every other day and offered prayers. The neighbors brought in food to lighten Catherine's load.

On the third day Gabriel went to the smithy. He wanted to be near Celeste when she awakened, but he knew now that it might be months, or never. He tried to fashion Scarron's weather vane, but again and again, at some crucial point near completion, he ruined it. He tried to weld the head of a broken mattock—a simple task—but he pumped the bellows too fiercely and when he brought the hammer down he used too much force, and where the hammer fell the iron disappeared in a shower of white sparks.

Abel laid his hard hand on his son's shoulder. "Settle down, boy," he said quietly. His voice was full of understanding. "You're not to blame. It just happened."

"Oh, I *did* it all right, Papa," Gabriel said with finality.

"If you did it, son, tell me how." Abel wanted Gabriel to hear his own voice explaining so that he could see he was not to blame.

"Papa, one evil thing leads to another," Gabriel said. "I had nearly forgotten Lecharbonnier. But Scarron came to tell me the man is still alive. Revenge flamed up inside me. I had to go. She begged me not to, but I didn't hear. She said she was going, too. I didn't even try to stand in her way. With child, riding horseback! She knew what she was doing, knew the risk, and if I hadn't been blinded by hatred I would've known it, too. But I didn't think about anything else—not the child, not Celeste, only Lecharbonnier.

"On the way back, at the river, she was trying to tempt me back into sanity. I saw it right away, and I loved her for it. Papa, but for my rage, we wouldn't have *been* in that storm!"

He sat down on a keg of new nails and put his head in his hands. Abel said nothing but, with his work-hardened left hand, squeezed his son's heaving shoulder.

In the middle of the second week, early in the morning when the sun was just breaking through the irregular glass of the great bay window and casting broken bits of rainbow on the coverlet of Celeste's bed, Gabriel wakened from his sleep, stirred by a quiet, uncertain feminine voice calling his name.

He threw back the covers of the pallet and jumped to his feet. Celeste was trying to sit up.

"Ohh," she said in confusion, "what's the matter with me? I'm stiff, and so sore."

"Don't, Celeste." He spoke softly, but with a tone she knew she must obey. He took her firmly by the shoulders and lay her back against the pillow. The wonder of the moment broke over him and his eyes filled with tears.

"Gabriel, what's wrong? Why are you crying? And why are we *here*?"

"Can you remember?" he asked.

"Yes. I remember. We were swimming, you and I . . . But that's all. I don't seem to remember coming home or undressing for bed, or anything else. What happened?"

He told her, and she hardly believed him. When at last she saw it was true, tears rose in her own eyes, and she asked, "Gabriel, the baby. Did we lose it?"

He drew her up into his arms and hugged her tight. "No, dearest. I don't think so. Everything's going to be all right."

The same evening Celeste began to take food. Within a week

she was leaving her bed every day to sit in the yard. Her head wound healed, and at the end of three months, when the first cool breezes of autumn had begun to blow, she was strong enough to do as she chose.

October. Celeste was in her seventh month, large with the child that kicked and squirmed in her belly, yet she refused to diminish her daily tasks. They were good for her, she said. "I mustn't spoil myself now, must I?"

Celeste felt about carrying her child as she felt about all of her life; it was an adventure, a wonderful adventure full of purpose and hope. She marveled at her own body and at the child within it. In spite of her plodding hardships, the heavy ambling gait, and untold other discomforts, to Celeste the weeks went by like a melody. Her face became softer, rounder, as filled with light as their home was with joy.

Gabriel breathed deeply, thanked God for his mercy, and pledged never again to cherish wrath against any man. The unpleasant episode of the summer was over.

On the twenty-third of December, Celeste gave birth to a perfectly formed son, and they named him Michel.

Little Michel grew quickly. He had his father's disposition and was the very image of his mother, except that he had Gabriel's dark eyes. He was the sensitive sort of child who could be disciplined without switch or strop. Indeed, his parents found they had to be careful how they spoke to him for he responded to gentle rebukes, but at the sound of harsh, loud tones he would sob as though the world was caving in about him.

Celeste was a perfect mother. She loved her child enough to die for him in a moment, and was as sensitive to his needs as a mother can be without becoming overprotective and coddling. It was, in fact, her maternal excellence that made the events of Sunday, January 30, 1744, so alarming.

The little family had gone into Avranches in the morning for Mass, and afterward went to Joseph's for the noon meal. Celeste had prepared some of Uncle Joseph's favorite dishes and brought them along in a basket.

Joseph lived at the Hotel de Ville in a suite of three rooms on the second story at the west end of the main wing. He kept his apartment as neat and orderly as he did his own person; every item was in its place, every dish clean, the floor scrubbed and spotless.

The parlor was furnished with several chairs that reflected Joseph's lean good taste, and with a desk that obviously had not been made in Avranches; the design was distinctly Parisian. It was strong, but not massive, with clean lines, moderately carved, and inlaid with contrasting woods. The desk sat with its back to a wide south window so the light would fall over the writer's shoulder.

Now, after dinner, the four were sitting about the table. The remains of a wild duck lay on the oval serving platter, looking like a boat overturned on a beach, with its planking torn away and its ribs left naked.

Joseph laid down his fork, leaned back in his chair, and said, "Gabriel, congratulations."

"Thank you, Uncle," he answered, "but for what?"

"For having married this beautiful, intelligent woman who is also a wonderful cook. You've done very well for yourself . . . and for the Dublanche family." He turned to Celeste. "Celeste, if I were Gabriel's age again, I would have *fought* him for your hand. You are a delight to my life."

"Thank you, Joseph," she said, blushing.

"No, it's I who must thank you." Then he paused, looked at her more closely, and into his eyes came a look of concern. "Celeste, dear," he said, "you don't look well. Have you overdone?" She was bending over her little son, wiping gravy from his face with a napkin. "Mama," the little one asked, "can I go out and play?"

She attended to Michel's question first. "Don't you think it's warm enough out, Gabriel? It seemed to me when we came in that it was." The little boy took this cue for complete approval and, before his father could answer, scurried out the door and down the stairs. Celeste turned her attention to Joseph.

"Can you see it in my face?" she asked. "You're right, Uncle. I don't feel well. My stomach is awfully uneasy. Halfway through the meal my head went into a terrible spin and then began to hurt. It's so unusual. I'm never sick."

Gabriel took her tenderly by the arm. "Celeste, come lie down in Uncle's bedroom," he said. "You're pale, and I can feel you shaking."

Celeste was unsteady on her feet, but she tried to walk without

Gabriel's help. Halfway across the room she wavered and nearly fell. Both men sprang to her side. Joseph directed her steps toward the parlor.

"You can lie on the couch in here, dear," he said. "The room is more cheerful and the air is better. Gabriel, get a comforter and pillow from my bed and bring them here."

The men sat nearby and watched her for a little while, until she fell asleep. Joseph rose soundlessly from his chair and motioned for Gabriel to follow. When they reached the kitchen, he said quietly, "Let her sleep while you and I clean the table and wash these dishes." He continued, "Has she been ill, my boy?"

"No, I don't think so, Uncle. But I have been worried about her. She's usually so active, but in spite of the warm weather she's stayed indoors for the past week and a half. And . . . there has been something else that has bothered me even more." He paused and searched his mind for the right words. "There's a sadness in her face. She seems far away from me, as though an invisible wall is between us."

"Have you had a fight?" his uncle asked.

"No. We've never fought. Not once. I've asked her what was wrong, but all she says is that she doesn't know. She may go a whole day without touching me. Always before she's taken my hand when we walk, or touched my shoulder as she walked by. But she does it less and less."

The two men were so intent on their conversation they did not hear the door open and close as little Michel reentered Joseph's apartment. In a few moments they were electrified to hear a woman's voice shout, "Get out of there, Michel! Haven't I taught you better than that?"

The shout made no sense to either of them. It was Celeste's voice, but distorted with fury. Never before had she even lifted her voice in anger. Michel came running into the room screaming in terror.

"Papa! Papa! What's wrong with Mama?"

Gabriel picked him up and both men stepped into the parlor. "Celeste, what's wrong?" Joseph asked.

"Can't you see?" she shouted. "Look at your desk. While I was asleep, Michel opened every drawer. Look at your papers. Everything is in a terrible confusion." Celeste had risen up onto her elbow and was looking wildly about.

"But it's quite all right, Celeste," Joseph said quietly. "He meant no harm, and nothing is hurt in any way."

Celeste burst into deep, convulsive weeping. Her shoulders trembled. She covered her face with her hands and shook her head from side to side in complete confusion. Gabriel handed Michel to Uncle Joseph and knelt beside her, but when he touched her arm it was as though he was not there. Celeste did not acknowledge his presence. He felt shut out, suddenly alone in a way he had not felt since their marriage, and he felt confused. Gabriel did not know what to say, what to ask. And it was as well that he did not ask questions, for Celeste would not have known what sort of answer to give.

The shadow that fell so suddenly over their lives did not lift. There were days when Gabriel felt sunshine on the verge of breaking through again, days when he saw a small upturn in the corners of Celeste's mouth, days when he felt a slight warmth radiating from her presence. But when he invited her to walk with him through the pasture, to talk in the old way after supper, or to ride through the fields, she always declined. When the warm breezes came and the voice of the turtle dove cooed in the morning light, and leaves broke out on the trees with the promise of spring, she did not seem to notice. The chestnut stallion went unridden. She did not go near the barn, and paid no attention to the care of her favorite horse.

Gabriel found himself doing many chores Celeste had once enjoyed. He often came in at midday and found her sitting alone before gray ashes that lay cold in the fireplace, the quilts hung across the windows and the room dark in spite of the noonday sun. When he entered she would appear never to notice.

For a while calm would prevail, then Celeste would burst out again with violent shouting at some small thing Gabriel or the boy had done. This was an enormous change. During such times Gabriel found he could not please her, no matter how hard or carefully he tried.

Gabriel had always been idealistic about life, especially about his family. Now his idealism tortured him. Another man might simply resign himself to a bad situation, but not he, for Gabriel could not let go of the peace and happiness they had known. He could not believe that it was gone forever. If he tried hard enough, understood well enough, perhaps he could help Celeste recover herself. So he pressed her for answers, not realizing she had no answers to give.

Strangely, in Celeste's own eyes, she had not changed. It was Gabriel and the boy who had suddenly become unreasonable and violent. She could not understand it. How could they have become so different so quickly? Why would the two she loved most in this life turn on her, choose in an instant to make her life unbearable? But for herself, though she searched, she could find no difference between what she was now and what she had always been.

Gabriel watched their little son. Michel knew something was wrong. He felt tension in the air, saw the look of defeat in his father's eyes, and saw the hard, cold arrogance that enveloped his mother, an arrogance that until recently had been so utterly foreign to her character. He felt bewilderment and pain. Some evenings, amid his loss and confusion, Michel sobbed himself to sleep.

On a pleasant, unusually cool day in July, Gabriel's heart leaped with joy. Last night Celeste had met him on the path between their house and the smithy, something she had not done in months. She had turned when they met, and fallen in step beside him, taking him by the arm, smiling. Then she had reached up and kissed him. At the house, he found the evening meal ready and everything in order. After supper the three walked through the hilltop field. Gabriel was ecstatic to see the wind playing through Celeste's hair and the blue of her eyes sparkling when she looked toward him.

When they went to bed, she lay her right arm on his chest and slept with her head nestled in the hollow of his shoulder. Soon she was asleep, but he lay awake remembering how it once had been, and thinking that it would be so again.

The next morning he went to the smithy before she awoke. Just before nine he heard her familiar step on the path and the rustle of her skirt. His heart was full from the evening before, and he felt happiness swelling at the thought that she was coming to be near him. He was standing at the vise filing the final touches on a decorative cabinet hinge, and he smiled and looked up as she stepped through the door.

One look at her face erased the smile from his lips. A sick feeling of helplessness invaded his body from head to foot. He held his breath and asked, "What's wrong?" For a long moment she did not answer. Her lips trembled. The muscles of her jaw flexed and relaxed, flexed and relaxed. Her eyes, now flaming blue, made tiny jerks from side to side. Her lips twisted and the lines of her face became distorted as she clenched and unclenched her teeth. Gabriel became aware of the great brick forge beside her, and the glowing red coals that burned in its bed.

At last she said with quiet, even tension, "Why did you leave me?"

"Leave you?" he asked. "I don't understand, Celeste."

"How long, Gabriel," she asked with a sharp edge to her voice, "how long has it been since we made love?" The question astounded him. She had rejected every overture for months on end. She continued, "Do you have any idea, or do you even care?" She spat out the question. It was a challenge and he rose to meet it.

"Yes, I do know." His vehemence equaled hers. "We last made love three nights in the third week of January, two weeks before everything"—he groped for a word that would not offend her further—"changed. That makes it almost six months—and a most miserable six months I might add." He felt uncertain, defensive, not knowing what was coming next. Her anger rose higher.

"Last night I wanted desperately for you to make love to me. Hoping beyond hope that you would pay attention, hold me in your arms for a while, and then love me." Great tears welled up in her eyes and spilled over onto her cheeks.

"Celeste!" He wanted to go on, but was so dumbfounded by the accusation that he couldn't think of what he should say. She stood glaring across the room at him. "Celeste, if I had known . . ."

"Must I spell it out for you?" she shouted. "Do you want an engraved invitation?"

He could not let her go on like that. She had to understand. He would force her to understand.

"Celeste," he said in a quieter voice, "be still. Listen to me."

She folded her arms across her breast and said defiantly, "All right. Go on." Then almost without a pause, she said again, "Well, go on! I'm listening."

"For six months," he said, "you've held me at arm's length."

"*I've* held *you* . . . !" she shouted.

Gabriel raised his voice to equal hers, "Yes! Yes, Celeste. You have. Oh dear God, I don't know what happened to you six months ago, but I—"

"What happened to me! Go right ahead and blame me. You're God. Nobody's right but you. I'd like to hear you say just once that you were wrong. But I could wait forever, because you never will!"

"Celeste, listen to me. Let's stop trying to decide who's to blame. Let's talk about it without the anger." He hesitated over the last words and lowered his voice to a reasonable, earnest tone. "We can change. We can do whatever it is we need to do to have what we once had."

She breathed hard. The skin over her cheekbones was flaming red. "I've heard that before. 'If we sit down and talk about it reasonably . . .' You love to be so reasonable, don't you! That way you come out as the shining knight, and I wind up the witch!"

"Celeste, this arguing is going to kill us! Before you say anything else, let me ask you one question. *What do you want me to do?*"

She answered quickly, "I want you to take me out of here."

"Out of where?"

"Out of Avranches!"

"Out of Avranches? But you love Avranches. You love this place. You love these people. You've always said so, that you want to live and die right here."

Her eyes narrowed to slits of rage, and she shot her words through clenched teeth, "I said that only because I knew it was what you wanted to hear."

He simply did not believe that. She had said those things a hundred times, and every time she had meant them. She went on. "You have less ambition than any man I ever saw! You would be happy to sit here in this smelly, soot-covered hole for the rest of your life. You are such a rotten poor excuse for a man!"

Suddenly her rage erupted. She reached behind her and grabbed a hoe, ran toward him, flailing at him with all her might while she shouted, "I hate you! I hate you! Oh, how I hate you!" He stepped back, frightened not by the blows but by the wild anger in her eyes. Her aim was good and she hit him on his left side and his thighs and legs with a half-dozen blows. He took them without resistance for as long as he dared, then reached out, caught the

handle, and wrenched the hoe from her and threw it across the
shop where it fell behind a pile of twisted scrap iron.

She was breathing like a caged animal. "You do think you're
God. Well I'm *tired* of living with God. I don't like him!" She
backed toward the door. Her eye fell on a book lying open on the
table. It was a leatherbound, gold-embossed copy of Locke's *The
Reasonableness of the Christian Religion.* She seized the volume
and waved it in the air, shouting. "Here's the reason we're poor!
You come down here and read while you're supposed to be working!"

And she threw it with all her might onto the burning coals of
the forge. Gabriel lunged toward the forge and reached in with a
pair of tongs just as the book burst into flames. He smothered
them in his leather apron. The book was Uncle Joseph's and it
would cost more than they could afford to replace it.

Celeste was not done. As a parting shot she shouted at him,
"Go on. Cheat and destroy everybody around you!"

Gabriel looked up from the partially charred volume and said
in an even voice, just loud enough for her to hear, "No. I won't
do that, Celeste. I would not take that privilege from you." She
bolted out of the shop and, sobbing loudly, ran across the meadow
toward the darkened house.

CHAPTER 9

Looking for a Way Out

IN the distance the door slammed behind Celeste. Gabriel, weak
and shaking, took a deep breath and steadied himself against his
workbench. Had he been in the hottest part of a front-line battle
he would have felt less threatened, for in his troubles with Celeste
more than his life was at stake.

His hands were trembling. He looked about for a task that
would take a great deal of energy and no concentration. He picked
up a long, slender rod of iron, placed a hardy in the square hole

of his anvil, and brought the rod to red heat in the coals, then began to forge nails as rapidly as he could.

He felt absolutely helpless. He could think of no way to solve the terrible conflict in which he and Celeste were locked, for it was an utterly irrational conflict. Yet he could not go on living unless there was peace between them. "Why such a needless mess?" he asked aloud through clenched teeth. "There cannot be a good reason for a thing like this. It's useless, absolutely useless."

Suddenly he felt himself thrown back into unbelief—or at the very least, onto the cold conviction that God had deserted him.

He swung the hammer with a quick, true swing. When a quarter of an hour later his father and uncle rode up to the smithy on horseback, the plank floor was spread with newly made nails.

The two men walked into the shop and instantly felt an electric tension in the air. Joseph looked at his nephew and asked earnestly, "Gabriel, what's wrong? You look as though you've been put through the Inquisition."

Abel gazed searchingly at his son's face and saw deep marks of trouble. "What is it, Gabriel? I've never seen you looking so."

Gabriel kept swinging the hammer. Tears of frustration and rage ran down his cheeks, and he bit his lower lip so tightly it bled. Joseph put his hand on the boy's shoulder and bent to look him directly in the eyes. Gabriel's swing did not break cadence.

Finally he choked out, "Celeste." In a gesture uncharacteristically bold, Abel reached out and took the hammer from his son's hand. He slipped the hammer into its place, handle-down in the rack on the anvil's wooden base. Gabriel buried his face on his father's shoulder and wept.

"Gabriel," his father said, "she's changed."

Gabriel still sobbed.

"Here. Sit down and listen to Joseph and me. All day we've been talking about you and Celeste."

Without a word Gabriel pulled himself together and sat back on the workbench. Then he looked at the two men and said quietly, "Then you've seen it?"

"Don't be absurd, boy," Joseph answered. "We aren't blind. Of *course* we've seen it." He paused for a moment as he searched Gabriel's eyes. "Everything has changed. Celeste is not the girl you married."

"Oh, God in heaven, I know it." Tears welled in Gabriel's eyes once more.

"Your father and I sympathize with you, if that counts for anything. But, above all, we want you to keep your head. Don't do something you'll regret. Frustration is a terrible thing, and anger is worse. If I can read the signs, you have much about which to be frustrated and angry."

"But what do I *do*, Joseph?" Urgency filled Gabriel's voice and he flung his arms wide. "I love Celeste. I love her as I love my own body—more than I love my own body. But I don't *understand* her. She's driving me mad. I didn't know anyone could change so much so quickly. It was like the sun going down, or a lamp blown out in the wind, as though Celeste went away and some demonic spirit came in and took over her body."

"I'll tell you what you do, Gabriel," Joseph responded quickly. "Remember." He paused for emphasis and repeated the word. "Remember. Keep it in your mind that no matter how she infuriates you, no matter how unreasonable she is, no matter how she blames you for things you have not done, for thoughts you have never had . . ."

"Have you been outside our door listening, Joseph?" Gabriel asked with a slight smile.

Joseph went on. "No matter what she says or does, you've got to keep reminding yourself that *it isn't Celeste's fault.*"

Gabriel looked up sharply and asked, "What do you mean by that?"

Joseph reached into his waistcoat pocket for the black leather pouch that contained his pipe. He filled the pipe and reached into the kindling box for a long splinter. He laid the end of the splinter among the coals in the forge bed until it flamed, touched it to the tobacco, and drew on the stem. When the pipe was lit to his satisfaction, he resumed.

"A year ago I was in Paris for a month—you remember, don't you? Well, while I was there, I spent an afternoon with Georges Marichal. Marichal was one of the founders of the Royal Academy of Surgery back about, oh, twelve or more years ago.

"Surgery is coming into its own in France. Some of the doctors still look down on it, thinking surgeons are barbers yet." Smoke ceased to rise from the bowl of his pipe. He reinserted the flaming splinter and puffed until the smoke rose in small, thick clouds again. "This last year a new law went into effect. It frees surgeons from the barbers' guild. Now no one can practice surgery in France without a university degree—a great step forward.''

Gabriel, in considerable mental pain, was becoming impatient. Wanting Joseph to come directly to the point, he said, ''Uncle, I've no idea what you're talking about.''

''You're right. I'm sorry. I was talking with Georges Marichal, and he told me about a surgical case he himself handled just last year. It seems he had a patient who had worked in the government gunpowder factory at Essonne, just about twelve miles south of Paris. Have you ever seen a powder mill? Well, the buildings are constructed of loose boards, barely nailed on, so when there's an accident, it all blows apart easily, and it's *rebuilt* easily. Absolutely no question whether or not there will be accidents in a powder mill; there will be. They blow up, all of them. The infernal black stuff goes at the spark of a cat's whisker.

''Well, about seven years ago in the plant of Essone, fifteen thousand pounds let go all at once. It took three minutes for the explosions to rip through the factory. The whole place and everybody in it would've been destroyed if the main cache hadn't been in a building surrounded by redoubts.''

Joseph again saw impatience building in Gabriel's eyes and hurried on. ''I say all that to tell you about Marichal's case, a man who worked in the powder factory at the time of the explosion. He was a long way from the cache, so he wasn't burned. But some of those loose boards were blown almost out of sight into the air. One of them came down and struck the ground near this man, rebounded, and hit him in the head. He was out for days, but finally came around.''

Gabriel's interest suddenly came to life.

''*Before* the accident,'' Joseph went on, ''the gentleman was as congenial as a saint. But a few months after the board laid him out, his whole personality changed. No one could help him, including Marichal. He got to be a regular rowdy, knocked his wife and children about, and when he came back to work, nobody— absolutely nobody—could get on with him. And it got no better, but worse and worse right up until last spring when he died.

''Marichal performed a surgical autopsy. He opened the man's head and found a growth, a cyst he called it, twice the size of a walnut, nestled right into the surface of the man's brain where he had been struck by the board. Marichal probed the cyst with his lancet, and a white, milky fluid gushed out.

"Marichal is convinced this fluid was accumulating and making the cyst bigger and bigger. The bigger it got, the more it pressed into the man's brain. He said there had been bleeding into the brain's tissue as well. Marichal is certain there's a connection between the bleeding around the cyst and the way the man changed.

"I'm not a surgeon, but I expect Marichal's right. It's not a new thing for a man to get hit and sooner or later go out of his head."

For several minutes no one said anything. Gabriel had never heard of such, and he sat with a solemn look on his face, his eyes fixed unseeing on the iron weights that lay atop the great bellows. He felt a mixture of powerful new emotions. He felt relief, for if this were true, Celeste was not to blame for her harsh words and behavior. Neither was *he* to blame, at least not in the way she had said he was. He had not mistreated her after all. He also felt a sense of great dread, for this could also mean that Celeste was doomed—and all their happiness as well.

Gabriel stood and asked quietly, "Joseph, if you're right, is there a cure? Can she be helped?"

Joseph drew a deep breath and answered slowly, "I asked Marichal if he could have helped the man with some surgical procedure. He did not know. He believes that if he had drained the cyst surgically, it would only have filled up again, perhaps even more rapidly, and shortened the man's life all the more.

"Gabriel, the important thing is that you remember that Celeste cannot help what she is. Somewhere inside her troubled brain the old Celeste still lives but simply cannot get out. Be kind to her, as I know you have been—for your boy's sake and for the sake of the girl you used to know."

"But she might die," Gabriel said vacantly.

"Yes. In another year. In five. Maybe in old age. No one knows. We never do."

Celeste's anger subsided within the hour. Afterward she realized how violent her outburst had been, and all that day she thought of nothing else. When Gabriel came home in the evening, she was subdued but distant. As they prepared for bed that night and she saw the bruises she herself had inflicted on him, she became silently contrite, and in the dim lamplight Gabriel thought he saw traces of tears on her cheeks. The tension between them dissipated, and a kind of helpless melancholy hung in the air.

In the very early morning hours, unable to sleep, Celeste quietly left their bed, opened the heavy timber door—by sheer strength of will forcing it not to squeal on its dry hinges—and softly walked in her nightdress and bare feet out onto the fresh-cut lawn.

There was no moon, and the night sky was deep, set with brilliant, silver-white sparks in an unending ocean of black.

She breathed deeply and let the fresh, cool air into her lungs slowly as she gazed through the heavens at the myriad stars. Slowly she ambled to the strong rock wall that divided their lawn and the upper orchard. A light dew lay on the grass. It was wet and cool on her bare feet. The nighttime fragrance of apple blossoms lay on the air and, like eiderdown on a soft breeze, floated into her consciousness. "How sweet the trees smell," she said quietly to herself.

The top of the wall—high as her waist, and an arm's length across—had been built of the larger stones gathered from the orchard and fields when the fields were first claimed from the wild, centuries ago. In the eight years of Celeste's marriage, the wall had stood there, reminding her of the past, giving her a feeling that the present was secure. But now everything was uncertain and she felt a sickness rising within.

Celeste leaned on the massive stone wall, felt the texture of rocks worn smooth by half a millennium of winds and rains and hands. The stones were warm to her touch—warm yet with yesterday's sunlight, comforting in the cool night.

Carefully she placed her bare foot in a lower crevice and climbed up, then stretched full-length along the wall's top and gazed upward. For a while she tried to sound the depth of the black, star-pointed night, but soon her mind began to spin slowly with the impossible task and she felt so helplessly, infinitely small that she turned her thoughts to other things.

The rocks beneath her smelled of a curious, contradictory mixture of odors—musty-old but washed to freshness by rains and bleached clean by the sun. The smell of the dew-covered grass rose heavily and lulled her into a sweet calm. The only sounds came from a cricket still awake somewhere among the stones, and the rustle of a bird disturbed from sleep in its nest. The liquid call of a nightingale floated up from some tree down along the dark river.

As a young girl, Celeste had often felt the tenderness of the night, but now that seemed so long ago. "What's happening to me?" she whispered.

Celeste's violence of yesterday had broken open a door in her mind, and a discomforting, pale light now poured through to show her, however briefly, that these miserable times were not Gabriel's doing, and that in some strange way she could not understand, neither were they her own. The pale light grew until she thought, Am I losing my mind?

A terror rose within her. Tears welled slowly in her eyes, broke over, fell from her cheeks, and wet the stones beneath her head and in the darkness were absorbed into the time-smoothed surface. She turned over and pressed her soft cheek against the stones, feeling the warmth through the thinness of her gown, spreading her arms wide to embrace the wall's sturdy width. How disappointed in life she had become! How disillusioned, how in need of strength.

"Dear Mother of God," she prayed. "My protector and guide through all my childhood, am I going mad?" She began to sob. "Save my husband, and save my child. Save my soul to everlasting life. And, oh please, save us all from myself." After a long while, her deep emotions exhausted both her mind and her body, and a numbness crept into her brain. The reprieve of sleep enfolded her in its arms.

"Celeste." Gabriel spoke softly and laid his hand on her arm. The sun was just up. Doves were cooing in the orchard. Her eyes opened slowly. When she realized where she was, Celeste reached out and put her arms around his neck.

"Oh, Gabriel," she said. "I came out here to think, and I fell asleep. I didn't mean to." She hurried into the next sentence. "Gabriel, I'm so sorry about yesterday. Please forgive me."

"Forgive you? No, dearest. I'm the one who needs to be forgiven. In some way that neither you nor I can see, this all goes back to the sin of *my* heart, not yours. You're the purest, finest woman in the world. The fault is mine."

Though Celeste did not know what he meant, she felt deeply relieved. Still sitting on the edge of the wall, she buried her face in his shoulder and cried.

* * *

In that summer of 1744 Normans looked with fear toward their southern border and the duchy of Brittany. In late May smallpox and typhus had broken out in Brittany and now extended through all her length and breadth. The warmer the weather had become, the higher the death toll had risen. Death now lay only twenty miles from Avranches.

Whenever Gabriel heard of a case of typhus or smallpox within fifteen miles, the news affected him for days. He would begin to think what it would be like to lose Celeste or Michel, and the mere idea was more than he could bear.

On a warm day in August, Gabriel and Abel were laboring hard over a heavy shaft from Scarron's mill. The shaft had been bent by the high waters that followed last week's flash flood, and now the bend lay on their biggest anvil, glowing red, throwing off waves of heat in the already stifling smithy. Abel steadied the shaft while Gabriel swung their heaviest hammer with all his might. He stopped for a moment to rest and was panting heavily when he said, "The thing haunts me. If Celeste or Michel died from typhus or the pox, I don't know how I'd go on. Yet it rages closer and closer, and there's nothing we can do about it."

"No. Nothing at all," his father answered. "Some folks believe God sends these things to keep our numbers down. They say that without them, the world would become so crowded there wouldn't be enough food to go around, and the whole race would die out."

"I doubt that," Gabriel said as he swung the hammer again. "It's hard for me to believe that God sends terror on innocent people just to keep them thinned out."

"Does what we think make a difference?" Abel responded. "These things seem to happen to everybody alike, no matter what they think."

"It makes a difference in how a man feels about God, that's certain," Gabriel said. "I have a hard time with a God who causes such things."

"Any less of a problem than with a God who *permits* such things?" Abel asked. Gabriel was surprised to hear that from his father, and he did not answer. Abel continued, obviously quoting something he had heard from his brother. "Voltaire says that for every one hundred people born in France, sixty will have smallpox sometime in their lives. And that out of that sixty, twenty will die. It's a terrible figure. Joseph says that out of all the women in all the nunneries of France, two hundred thousand are there to hide their pox-marked faces from the world.''

''A high price to pay for piety,'' Gabriel grunted as he swung the hammer down fiercely.

''Well, if it's real piety, no price is too high. Don't you agree?''

Gabriel broke cadence and stood shaking his head. ''I suppose so. I don't know though, Papa. I'm confused about what I think.'' His eyes searched nervously through the far corners of the room. ''After all that's happened to us, I don't know anymore what I believe. I've just about given up on 'truth,' whatever that is. I'm just going on, trying to live as happily as I can before the next blow falls. That must be why I'm so uneasy over the pox and fever.''

Abruptly Abel asked, ''Do you ever think of leaving here, Gabriel?''

''No. Not really.''

''But you said Celeste wants to go. She wants to be back in the city, wants you to make a better living. Don't you think you should at least consider it?''

''If I thought it would help, I suppose I would. But I don't have confidence in the future. Things get better for a little while, and then they just turn on us and get worse than ever.''

''Gabriel,'' Abel broke in sternly, ''I don't often try to tell you what to do. But I think you should move to Rouen.''

Gabriel was shocked. He looked at his father as though the entire idea was new to him. Abel went on, ''She wants you to go. And you can't tell, it might make a difference. If Celeste were close to her own mother, she might get better. And you're worried about smallpox and typhus. I hear there hasn't been a single case of either in Rouen so far this summer. If you could live there at the manor away from the city—it might be the safest place you could find. If I were you, I'd do it.''

''Pierre, I cannot go.'' It was one of Emilie Lefleur's firm ''no's.''

Pierre was determined to cross the Atlantic and look into his business affairs in New France. For reasons he could not determine, last year's profits had fallen off drastically. He strongly suspected that somewhere in his ranks he had a Judas—someone diverting furs for his own profit, or embezzling money and skillfully changing the company books. At any rate the problem had to be dealt with, and Pierre felt he was the one to do it. It would cost him at least a half year. Good passage one way could be made in less than sixty days. Allowing four months for travel and two months to ferret out the thief . . . perhaps he could do it in less time, but not likely.

He wanted to go early next spring, and he wanted his wife to go with him.

"The devil, Emilie! Why do you have to be so obstinate?" Pierre paced back and forth in their parlor. "Something has to be done, and soon. What in the world is holding you?"

"Pierre," she answered, "you know very well what's holding me." She paused for a long moment and struggled with the words as redness and tears rimmed her eyes. "I'm terrified for Gabriel and Celeste. Something is horribly wrong, and I've no idea what. I've written Gabriel in care of Abel and Catherine, begging him to tell me. He writes back that everything is well, but I know he's not telling me the truth."

"Oh Emilie," Pierre bellowed, "*how* do you know it? It's your imagination!"

"No," she answered, "Celeste's letters are not the same. They're distant, there's nothing warm in them. Something is wrong. So, Pierre, I am not about to cross an ocean with you or anybody else while Celeste may need me." She looked up at him from her place on the plush, gold sofa. The edge went out of her voice as she said, almost pleading, "Pierre, you could send someone else. Talk with your captains. Write letters. You have friends in Montreal who can look into it for you. These children may need your help, too."

At that moment, far to the south in Avranches, Gabriel Dublanche was tying a bedroll to the back of his bay mare. He strapped it tight, put his booted foot into the stirrup, and swung up into the saddle. He pulled the brown tricorn tightly on his head, and spurred the animal out onto the road that would take him to Rouen.

When Gabriel finished speaking, Emilie was stunned. The problem was deeper than she had suspected. It was to her credit that she did not try to fix blame on either Celeste or Gabriel, and she made no effort to excuse either of them. Nonetheless Emilie had never seen Celeste in a rage. No matter what her son-in-law said, she could not envision it.

When Gabriel suggested that his little family come and live nearby in hopes that this might make a difference, Pierre responded with characteristic enthusiasm.

"Yes," he said. "Yes, that's a grand idea." And he immediately offered Gabriel a place in the business as his adjunct. "After all," he said, "I need someone to help me, especially now. You can move up right away, in a company coach. I'll send it down for you. Bring only what you need to move in with us until we can make other arrangements."

Before the day was over, Pierre realized that he could go ahead with his trip the coming spring. Not only could he show Emilie the world, but his youngest daughter and grandchild as well. This time Emilie's "no" was not so strong, and this time Pierre prevailed.

Gabriel returned to Avranches and, not knowing how she might react, broke the news to Celeste cautiously. She screamed with delight and threw her arms around him. Even in his enormous relief, Gabriel's confusion at her response was heightened. Celeste's emotional state was utterly unpredictable. She might ride for days on a mood of joy, only to plunge again into deeper despair and vindictiveness. And her judgment on the smallest matters rode the tides of her emotions. In the next few days, her lethargy disappeared altogether, and as she busied herself packing, her excitement became boundless.

Abel and Catherine took the news well, for though it tugged hard at their hearts to see their children go, they understood that this was the best possible opportunity for a new beginning.

Joseph François was certain that the move would be beneficial, but he felt far less optimistic about the venture to New France. He had doubts about French involvement on the North American continent. It was a distant, dark land of unimaginably vast forests, peopled by wild, primitive breeds that ate their defeated enemies alive. Besides, France was now entangled in the War of the Austrian Succession. Joseph had heard that only last May, to regain fishing rights on the Grand Banks, France had attacked an English island off the North American coast. The attack had been launched from Louisbourg, a French fortress on Acadia. If Gabriel and Celeste did go to New France in the spring, they would pass through those contested waters.

"But it's a chance to begin again, Uncle," Gabriel said simply.

"Fine," Joseph replied. "I only wish for you a safer place to do it. I don't think you understand that New France extends all the way from the Alleghenies to the Rocky Mountains, from Mexico to the North Pole. Though we have forts from New Orleans to Hudson Bay and control all the major rivers of the continent, remember that the English there outnumber us twenty-one to one. So few Frenchmen cannot defend that territory against them.

"I marvel at the Italians," he went on. "They know when to leave well enough alone. Their Columbus the Genoese discovered that land, and John Cabot the Venetian, and Verrazano the Florentine, and Americus Vesputius, another Florentine. But they leave the Spaniards, the French, and the English to fight over it and to conquer it. When it's all done, the Italians will go and live there. Just wait and see."

Uncle Joseph thought this a clever point, but it was wasted on Gabriel, who was too absorbed by the prospect of the venture to give it thought.

By the first of September, Gabriel, Celeste, and Michel were settled in the Lefleur manor northwest of Rouen, preparing for the coming spring.

CHAPTER 10

The Passage

THE unsettled weather of March had run the usual arpeggios of unpredictable wind and calm, warm and cold, wet and dry, and the month was nearly gone. The twenty-fourth day came and gave France its first full taste of spring. The wind alternated between the mildest of breezes and perfect calm, the sky was clear, without a cloud, and the scent of fresh buds and new grass filled the air.

Two longboats, each manned by ten oarsmen, towed the Dutch flute *Petulant* away from the quay at Rouen and pulled her out into the strongest current of the River Seine.

The *Petulant* was an armed merchantman of three hundred tons, eighty feet at the waterline, round in the stern and broad of beam, able to carry twice as much cargo as other vessels her size.

True, she was slower than ships of sleeker line, making her more vulnerable to pirates that lurked in the shipping lanes, but she carried sixteen twelve-pound cannons that her well-drilled crew could fire at two rounds each, every three minutes.

Unfortunately, pirates were not likely to be the problem this voyage. With the outbreak of hostilities, the greatest danger lay in meeting a British man-of-war. The *Petulant* would sail through waters that lay between Isle Royale and Isle de Terre-Neuve, very near Acadia, the center of recent conflict. Her sixteen guns would be no match for a British man-of-war twice her size, mounting seventy twenty-four-pounders.

Nonetheless, Pierre Lefleur had refused to delay his voyage any longer. Evidence continued to mount; someone was robbing him blind. Pierre judged the risk of British attack on a merchantman to be small, so small that he had no misgivings about taking his wife, daughter, son-in-law, and grandchild with him.

So, on March 24, the *Petulant* sailed with a full cargo of goods for trade with the American peoples; heavy wool blankets that would bring four beaver pelts each, countless yards of broadcloth, tons of iron pots and copper kettles, hundreds of mirrors, hand axes, smooth-bore guns, ingots of lead with powder to match, and keg after keg of glass beads of all sizes and description.

With good luck and heaven's blessing the *Petulant* would complete the passage in sixty days, Pierre and Gabriel would accomplish their mission, and she would return in the fall laden with bales of marten, lynx, otter, bear, and beaver pelts that would bring extravagant prices at European auction, especially in fashion-conscious France.

The fur trade had become the economic base for the North American colonies, both French and English. In 1715, three hundred ships had carried furs for France. This year the number would be above eighteen hundred, an increase of six hundred percent in less than three decades.

Pierre was expanding his fleet accordingly. The *Petulant* was one of four ships he had purchased new from Dutch builders just last year. Even with the mysterious losses of the last twelve months, his fortune was growing rapidly.

Pierre and his family took two cabins in the quarter gallery of the stern near the captain's cabin.

Captain Joachim Lamotte, in Lefleur service for eight years and one of Pierre's best men, had taken command of the *Petulant* when she came off the ways, and in her first year of service he found her to be an excellent vessel. She had an amazing ability to right herself after being thrown nearly on her beam in heavy seas. This was a comfort, since early spring passage of the North Atlantic was often violent.

Captain Lamotte had purposely waited for the equinox to pass before setting out, knowing that on the twenty-fourth of March they could ride an outgoing tide. At each equinox, spring and autumn, remarkable tides called "Mascaret" climbed the river to points beyond Caudebec-en-Caux. These were great tidal bores, spectacular displays of water fighting water as gigantic incoming tides challenged the outflowing river. The inbound water bore hard against the banks and sent geysers shooting high into the air to curl back and crash thunderously into the stream again. And then, having spent its fury, the Mascaret would flow quickly back into the sea from which it had come.

Now, on the twenty-fourth, on this outgoing flow, the *Petulant* rapidly wound her serpentine course toward Le Havre.

Neither the Lefleurs nor the Dublanches had been to sea before, so as the *Petulant* left the river and ran before the wind into open sea, they stood at her rail and watched the waters roll beneath them. The Seine's current extended into the channel and marked the ocean with boiling, grayish-brown silt—the soil of France washing away.

Honfleur to the right passed behind them, and then Le Havre to their left. The protecting lands fell away and an unobstructed north wind heeled the *Petulant* to port and drove her proudly through ten-foot seas. The silt of land disappeared and the channel's waters became clear, a marvelous, deep translucent green.

By midday of the twenty-sixth, they rounded the great Norman cape and bore due west; by nightfall Europe had disappeared behind them.

Now Gabriel stood on the forward deck, alone in the darkness. The sea below was faintly luminescent with plankton, and yet seemed somehow unspeakably dark. It had been hard to leave Abel and Catherine behind, harder than he had supposed. Somehow it had been different from their partings when he was a child. Catherine had tried to hold back her tears, but she could not. As the time came for her and Abel and Joseph to leave the ship, she wept and tried to smile. She had reached behind her neck, unfastened the silver rosary her father had given her thirty-five years ago, then tenderly placed it about the neck of her son and tucked the cross in place beneath his shirt. They had embraced tightly for long minutes, each sobbing quietly. Then she had kissed Gabriel and said good-bye. She still had been standing at the water's edge on the river's north side when the ship had rounded the first curve and she had slipped from his sight.

Now Gabriel gripped the crucifix in his right hand as he gazed out across the dark waves that lay ahead, and he thought of how he loved them all, especially Catherine.

At that moment the full moon broke from behind a bank of clouds that lay over his homeland, and he turned to look. The mainmast and top spar formed a cross over the moon's silver face. Gabriel prayed to the God of whom he was no longer certain that He would bring them all safely together again.

"May I get you some water, maybe a little food?" Gabriel stood by the bunk where Celeste lay, her face like dry ashes, lifeless and gray, a wet cloth covering her forehead.

The ship rolled and fell rhythmically into the wide, deep troughs of the endless sea. Celeste felt that nothing solid or firm remained anywhere in all the world. She was in a universe of undulation; falling, then rising and falling again. Her stomach tried to stay in one place while her body rose and fell with the ship beneath it.

"Oh Gabriel, let me die." And she doubled up and lay like an unborn child.

Celeste was not alone. By this time, five days out, each of the new seafarers had tasted his own bile. Surely before long they would learn to live with the incessant rolling.

Pierre had already made the adjustment and, characteristically, was with the crew trying to learn everything there was to know about handling the vessel and trying to show them that he could do it all better than a seasoned sailor. Such demonstration seemed to be what he lived for. Already he had mastered the sextant and compass, or at least thought he had, had been aloft helping take in sail, and had taken one full watch at the helm. Pierre was the kind of man who had to be occupied. This natural inability to rest, combined with a reasonably good mind, was responsible for his success, but his unrelenting drive galled the men who worked for him, and it galled his family.

"Oh, well," Emilie would say. "He's a good man. But for his impatience and shouting spells, I have no complaints."

But when the shouting spells came, she complained in plenty. His temper had made it hard to keep good help at the manor, and his outbursts embarrassed her. After more than one childish display she had said to him, "Now, don't you feel like a man? You certainly set everyone straight tonight at the Fouquets'. Soon no one will be left who will dare invite us to dinner." She would sigh with exasperation and say, "I think you'll never grow up."

And Pierre would sit and listen without a word. Emilie was just an oversensitive, excitable woman, he thought. But all his friends knew that Emilie was right.

Michel, who was now seven, proved to be the best sailor of all. The third day out, Emilie left her cabin for fresh air and found him climbing in the rat lines just above her reach. At that moment she had a shouting spell of her own, and made it abundantly clear to everyone that the child was not to be left alone again.

For Gabriel and Michel, this voyage was the best of all times. The two had always been close, but during the passage Gabriel had almost nothing to do but enjoy his son.

They stood for hours together, leaning against the polished wooden rail of the high stern deck, gazing down into the churning wake's hypnotic foam. The seabirds hovered above them on starched, white wings, wheeling in the air, diving into the roiling green waters, rising again with some unlucky fingerling fighting against the grip of a tenacious beak.

But Michel liked best to go to the bow and, with his father, climb out over the open sea to lie in the hammocklike net stretched under the bowsprit. He laughed and squealed with delight as the bow dipped low and the upward-rushing water threatened to sweep over them. Once a great roller struck the bow and drenched them with a rebounding geyser that took the little boy's breath and left him wide-eyed, soaked to the skin, clinging desperately to Gabriel's neck, gasping between laughter and tears, their cheeks pressed tightly together.

On the thirty-first day, with a mild sea running, the ship in trim and reaching smartly, Captain Lamotte called for a gun drill. Michel was ecstatic. Gabriel took him to the gun deck, where chains rattled as the crew raised the gun-port covers, swabbed the bores, loaded, and rolled the cannon into position to fire.

Gabriel pressed his hands over Michel's ears just as the forward gun let go. Shattering thunder and fire erupted in rapid succession from all sixteen iron throats, stem to stern. Eyes watered and noses rebelled at the sting of the acrid smoke that filled the low-ceilinged deck. The crew reloaded and fired again and again until Lamotte was satisfied.

The next morning, Gabriel and Michel walked in the semi-darkness of the closed gun deck. The little boy climbed up on the carriage of the great forward gun, ran his hands over the smooth, cool iron, looked into his father's eyes, and announced that some-day he was going to be a soldier.

All their lives both boy and man would remember this voyage. They would remember being together amid the enchantment of the rushing, translucent green water, the smell of oak timbers wet with salty sea, the prickly feel of new hemp line, the groaning and creaking of timbers, and the whispering of the wind as it sang in the taut rigging. The boy would remember his father's nearness and his strong arms about him, his laughter, and his calm, mas-culine voice in his ear.

He would always remember that his father loved him and was near him when he was a boy of only seven.

It was their fifty-seventh day at sea. Impatient sailors looked for excuses to be in the rigging, anxious to be first to sight land.

Celeste had long since become accustomed to the ship's roll, and the voyage had become as pleasant for her as for Gabriel. This morning she awakened on fresh white sheets feeling strong and well. As she opened her blue eyes, the sun's first light poured through the ship's hinder windows and threw its bright gold on the west wall of her cabin, sweeping from floor to ceiling and back again with the rise and fall of the stern. She thought how like being in a swing it was, or in a child's cradle as it rocked to and fro.

Celeste was eager to see this strange new continent. The voyage had touched her old sense of adventure and teased her out of herself. She felt good from head to toe, except for a mild, per-vasive weariness that on some mornings made her want to stay abed. More than once she had even ventured into the rigging with Gabriel, and sat on the lookout platform high above the deck. The ship's roll was more pronounced on the platform than down be-low, but Celeste had held on tightly and, true to her old nature, learned to relish the wide, oval pitch and yaw.

From their high perch, Gabriel and Celeste had watched the horizon for land, cheered on a school of dolphins racing the ship off its starboard side, and talked of what they would find in New France. Pierre might ask Gabriel to become his overseer in Montreal, and this new land might someday become their home. To Celeste, it all seemed good, and new hope rose in her heart.

There had not been a single event to mark the passage as unusual. They had seen only one ship the entire time, an English sail on the horizon five days ago. It had run a parallel course for a full watch past noon, then heeled off to port and gradually dropped from sight.

As the Atlantic's silver foam passed beneath the *Petulant*'s barnacled oaken hull, the days of spring passed with it, swirling into a pleasant symmetrical wake of memories that each voyager would one day hold sweetly in mind as one holds the dried bloom of a faded rose.

That evening, still sailing with the wind from the starboard stern quarter, a blue-green line rose and lay on the west edge of the sea. By sunup next morning, they were sailing into the vast mouth of the Saint Lawrence River.

How different was the scene before them from the one they had left behind! The banks of the River Seine had been bustling with activity, but here there was no sound from the waiting land. The trees advanced from the hilltops to the water's edge and stood like tall, dark sentinels come forward to protect their continent from invasion. All signs of life were hidden in the forest, furtive, unseen by the adventurers—life that was wild, elusive, utterly untouched by man.

As he looked at the dark forests, Gabriel feared the uncivilized man-life veiled somewhere among the trees, man-life that knew no Christian principle, that fought in savage ways, then ate its human prey; man-life thought to be unrestrained by heavenly revelation, scripture, or church; man-life gradually giving way before a superior civilization.

Gabriel remembered how Jacques Cartier had named this river. Cartier had sailed into its mouth two hundred years before, on August 10, the Feast of Saint Lawrence. Saint Lawrence had lived in the third century, a deacon in the church of Rome in the time of Sextus II. When the emperor had demanded the treasures of the Church, Lawrence had gathered together a group of the Roman poor and presented them to Sextus saying, "These are the treasures of the Church."

For this bold, witty impertinence, Sextus roasted Lawrence alive over open coals on a grid of red-hot iron. Gabriel hoped the river's name was not a portent for their party as it had been for some Jesuit missionaries before them.

As they sailed on, the river narrowed. At d'Anticosti it was ninety miles from bank to bank. Upstream where it was joined by the Saquenay, it was a mere fifteen miles across, and finally, at the Ile d'Orleans, more than three hundred miles from the sea, just below the city of Quebec—an Algonquin word that meant "a narrowing"—it was merely a mighty river of nearly a mile's breadth. It was here, after rounding Ile d'Orleans and passing the mammoth falls of the Montmorenci, that they looked westward and had their first glimpse of the city. Here a great promontory rose up from the water, an immense rock of great breadth and height, like the throne of some river god who sat to judge all who passed beneath his feet. The city of Quebec, a fortress of stone, sat on the rock's crest, with its houses and rambling rock palisades, its large old buildings with roofs punctuated by half a dozen spires of cathedral, seminary, and Jesuit dwellings. Gabriel marveled at the buildings spilling over and running down to the water's edge: civilization, the first they had seen in seventy days, hunched on that mighty bend of the Saint Lawrence.

But Quebec was not their destination. The *Petulant* pushed beyond, and the river narrowed still more. Tree-crowned islands rose around every bend. Finally, on the thirteenth day beyond Quebec, a thousand miles inland, the crew anchored the *Petulant* at the island city of Montreal.

CHAPTER 11

The Island City

AT the river's edge, Pierre and Gabriel sought out a red-brick building on the stone-paved waterfront. Above a thick oak door hung a large oblong sign; letters in dark blue script against an ivory white background proclaimed simply LEFLEUR PELTRIES.

Inside the spacious main office, smooth, freshly swept wooden floors glistened and smelled sweetly of oil. Sunlight flooded through a large window with many small glass panes of irregular thickness, giving the room a light, airy feeling conducive to efficient work.

Four accountants sat on tall stools at high desks, each in the center of one quarter of the room. Each desk was equipped with an inkwell, two or three long white goose quills in their holders and a penknife lying near at hand. Large red leather account books stood upright in their cases along the west wall.

A short man of slight build led Pierre and Gabriel through a door to an inner office where they found the overseer of Lefleur operations in North America.

"Gabriel Dublanche," said Pierre, "allow me to present to you Monsieur Edmond Charcot. Charcot, this is Gabriel Dublanche, my son-in-law and my adjunct."

"I'm happy to meet you, Monsieur Charcot." Gabriel bowed slightly from the waist toward the tall man who stood ramrod straight.

"And I, you, Monsieur Dublanche. I hope your journey was a pleasant one."

Edmond Charcot had thick, wavy hair, white but for a few strands of strongly contrasting black mingled in the wave just above his forehead. His shoulders were wide, he was meticulously dressed, his voice was deep and masculine, and he had a face that Gabriel imagined most women would call handsome. He had been in Pierre's employ for six years, having come highly recommended by business contacts in Paris, and during that time had lived up to his reputation for efficiency, and for having the ability to make almost any enterprise turn a more-than-acceptable profit.

Charcot turned to Pierre and said gravely, "Monsieur Lefleur, I am extremely happy to have you here in your American office." He paused for a moment and continued, "But I am equally sorry that you have made this long voyage for such unpleasant reasons. And I am embarrassed to find that by this time I have not earned your trust for handling such matters myself."

"My coming is no reflection on you, Charcot. None at all. But this . . . difficulty has been afoot for so long, I felt it was time to give it my personal attention. And frankly, I like to deal with these things myself."

"Thank you for your confidence, sir," Charcot answered. "Since you have come all this distance, I do hope you have brought some fresh ideas for getting to the heart of our problem."

"Fresh ideas or not," Pierre responded characteristically, "I have come armed with a suspicious nature and considerable energy for the task."

"Suspicious, sir?" Fire leaped into Charcot's eyes.

"I mean that I come with a mind open to any possibility. As my starting point I shall be suspicious of everyone in my company and out of it."

"Including me, Monsieur Lefleur?"

"Yes, Charcot, including you. I have no reason to think you're involved, but the kind of money in question is enough to tempt the king himself—just a matter of human nature. I hope you take no offense."

Charcot turned casually toward the window and stood looking out over the quay. "No offense taken, Monsieur Lefleur," he said quietly, but Gabriel noticed that he took out a clean handkerchief and wiped perspiration from the palms of his hands. He kept his gaze on the river as he asked, "Do you feel, Monsieur Lefleur, that you can confide in me your method of investigation?"

"Certainly, sir. My son-in-law and I will be here early tomorrow morning to begin examining the company books. We will go to the warehouse and inspect the premises inch by inch. We will talk to every man in my employ, beginning with you and going right down to the warehousemen and canoemen. We will talk to men on the streets, to local officials, to the police and soldiers.

In other words, we will search for information until we find something that rings a bell. What we do after that depends on what we find.''

"I see," said Charcot. "Well, your method sounds very like the one I have pursued for months. I wish you better luck than mine.'' He paused, clasped his hands loosely behind him, breathed deeply, then said, ''I assure you that I have reported every finding to you. Twice I have come very near dismissing everyone in the entire company and hiring a new staff. But I have not done it, since in this vast wilderness empire it is extremely difficult to find men who are capable of performing the operations required in this office.

''We have sustained at least some of our losses through theft from the warehouse. This is an especially difficult problem, since the warehouse faces directly on the waterfront and the ships are so close. It is quite easy for—''

"Easy!'' Pierre's voice was almost a shout. ''Man, theft must not be *easy*. It is your job to make it next to *impossible*.''

Charcot spun quickly and easily from the window, never releasing his hands from their casual clasp behind his back. Gazing directly into Pierre's eyes with a glint of fire, he said in a voice of urgency and strength, "Monsieur Lefleur, I am in total sympathy with your dilemma. It is my dilemma as well, for I am your servant. This is your establishment, and if you wish to burn these buildings over your head, it matters not one whit to me. However, I insist that you never speak to me in that tone again. Do we understand each other, Monsieur Lefleur?''

Gabriel caught his breath. Pierre's eyes were wide and his mouth was open. Never before had anyone but Emilie spoken to him in that way. He paused for several moments, meeting Charcot's burning gaze without wavering, then said in an even, quiet voice, "Yes, Monsieur Charcot. We understand each other perfectly.''

Montreal was the last city west. Beyond it for thousands of miles was nothing but wilderness.

The city itself sat on a large island that lay diagonally to the points of the compass, an island that measured ten by thirty miles, formed by the converging of two rivers; the Saint Lawrence, which came from the southwest, fell over a series of rapids and then widened to flow smoothly along the island's southeast side, and the Ottawa, which descended from the northwest and split its flow to join the Saint Lawrence at the island's southwestern end and again at its northeastern tip.

The dominant feature of the island was an ancient volcano with a crater in its peak, the rim of which reached eight hundred feet above the river. The volcano sat majestically halfway up the island's length and near its southern shore. The city itself was cradled on a narrow ledge between the mountain's foot and the river.

One hundred and thirty-five years ago, Samuel de Champlain had founded Montreal as a base for missionary operations, but now missionary and merchant divided the city between them. The long trade routes from the Great Lakes and from the western and northern forests converged at Montreal, so that every year French canoemen paddled tons of furs out of the wilderness and here transferred them in bales to warehouses or to the holds of ships bound for European ports.

The stone fortress Ville Marie was the city's central building. Chapelle Notre Dame sat nearby. Scattered about these were merchant shops and dwellings that rivaled any in the motherland. The city was the habitation not only of wilderness adventurers, but also of government officials, men of business, tradesmen of all kinds, and, of course, their families. Montreal was a long-established, thriving city.

It was now late spring, and the weather was open and warm. Emilie Lefleur and Celeste were making a grand tour of Montreal's shops. As they walked briskly together through the narrow streets, their spirits ran high. They had just emerged from a millinery, and the sharp, clipped ring of horses' shod hooves striking hard cobblestones provided a background to their animated conversation. A cobbler dressed in a long, dark, shining leather apron, his sleeves rolled to his elbows, swept the sidewalk in front of his business. His broom made a clean, whisking sound that somehow lifted their spirits even higher. He paused in his sweeping to let them walk by, smiled, and nodded a pleasant good morning, then watched as the two women rounded the corner. A scream split the air, followed instantly by strong masculine voices pouring out a jumble of surprised, unintelligible exclamations. The cobbler gripped his broom tightly and followed the alarm.

Emilie Lefleur lay full-length on the walkway, perfectly conscious, her face an embarrassed red. She was half crying, half laughing. Celeste knelt over her, frantically rubbing the back of her hand. Two men stood nearby talking uncertainly between themselves. One of the men was tall, the other shorter; both had skin of deep, carmine-tinged brown. The most striking thing about the taller one was that, but for a narrow cloth passing between his legs and looped over a leather waist thong front and back, he was absolutely naked. Further, except for a narrow strip of bristling hair that began at his forehead and ended above the back of his neck, his head was cleanly shaved. His shorter companion was more decorously dressed, with a bright blue blanket draped grandly about his right shoulder. Both wore soft, pliable leather shoes.

Fainting—so fashionable a practice among the women of France—was an art unknown to these Huron men. They looked with wide eyes for a moment and, when sure this foreign woman was in no real distress, backed away and continued along the street, occasionally glancing back, chattering rapidly between themselves.

"Madame, are you all right?" The cobbler leaned his broom against the nearest wall and knelt over her.

"Yes. Oh, yes." Emilie laughed. "I'm perfectly all right. Those men took me so by surprise. Except in paintings, I have never seen anything like them in all my life!"

The cobbler smiled kindly. "We have Hurons and Ottawas in our streets every day, madame. It won't take you long to become accustomed to them."

The grand house of the Marquis Delachaux blazed with the light of cut-glass chandeliers, hummed with conversation, and sparkled with candle flames reflected in the wineglasses of his guests, dozens of the most important people in Montreal. The marquis, mayor of the city, fond of masquerade, dancing, gambling, and dining, entertained lavishly every month.

Tonight Pierre, Emilie, Gabriel, and Celeste were among his guests. The marquis welcomed them warmly to the city and made every effort to court their good favor.

The evening was well under way when, beginning at the entranceway and advancing to the farthest corners of the large room, the loud hum of conversation fell suddenly to a whisper, punctuated by baritone "ahhs" and feminine gasps.

Edmond Charcot had entered and his presence had been formally announced. The whispered exclamations, however, were not for Charcot, but for the young woman on his arm. She was Angelique Fontaine, newly arrived on the ship *Dorrill*. This was the first time Montreal had laid eyes on her.

Angelique Fontaine was more than beautiful—she was exotic and stunning. Her skin was dark, and she radiated a voluptuous magnetism from which no one in the room could turn away. On every mind there were two immediate questions: "Who is this striking woman?" and "What mixture of bloods could possibly produce such an effect?"

Today was Angelique's twenty-sixth birthday. She was at the peak of young womanhood. A black velvet choker circled her graceful neck. Her gown—rich, soft silk, flaming red—flowed from below the crest of her dark, smooth shoulders, opened deeply to display her full bosom, formed a tight bodice, and rushed on in cascades and rivulets to the floor. She was the very epitome of the highest in Parisian fashion.

Her black upswept hair she wore bound above the back of her neck. She held her head high. She was regal. She was perfectly possessed. She was in control.

Charcot was proud of his acquisition, and the pride shone from his eyes. Yet the women of the party, surveying the flash in the girl's eyes and the haughty set of her chin, whispered to one another that even the dashing, suave Charcot might well have met his match in this young woman.

The days passed quickly. Pierre and Gabriel examined the books exhaustively and found no irregularity. They made daily inspections of the warehouse, talked with the guards, mingled with men along the wharf, and still found nothing. But they did notice one singular thing: since their arrival, nothing had been stolen.

One citizen of Montreal, Antoine Lemonnier, Pierre had taken into his special confidence. Lemonnier, like Pierre, owned a fur trading company. The two had met at the Marquis Delachaux's party.

Lemonnier was a strange-looking man. His hair was black and long, trimmed in ragged bangs just above dark, full eyebrows that inscribed perfect arches over his big, black eyes. His overlarge nose was square at the end, and his eyes, always half-closed, made him appear perpetually drowsy, when in fact he was simply relaxed in perpetual self-confidence. His lower lip jutted past his upper in an everlasting pout, and his mustache was sparse, more like pig whiskers than human hair.

This entire set of features sagged with a just-past-middle-age look, especially in the semicircles below his dark eyes, in the lines that ran from the sides of his nose downward, and in the fiftyish bulge of his jowls.

All in all, Antoine Lemonnier was not easy to look at, but when he spoke, an inner light came on. In the man's eyes Pierre thought he saw something that made him worthy of trust. He was a witty man, clever, and above all discerning, for he observed his fellow beings with an uncanny shrewdness that made them feel they could hide nothing from him.

Pierre gleaned one vital thing from his frequent conversations with Lemonnier. More than once he said to Pierre, "Watch Charcot. You cannot trust him." Pierre took the advice, and yet he discovered nothing.

Summer neared its end. Within two months the upper river would freeze and all opportunity to return to France would be lost. Pierre could not stay longer, but he had a proposition for Gabriel.

"Remain here," he suggested. "Watch Charcot. If you find nothing by this time next year, bring your family and come home. If you do find what we're looking for, I'll reward you well. If Charcot is our thief, and if you want his job, you can have it."

Gabriel and Celeste chose to stay.

That year Montreal enjoyed a lingering autumn. Celeste found it pleasant, and when winter came and the snows began to fall— measured in feet rather than in inches—she squealed with childish delight. She spent hours outdoors with little Michel, taught him the thrill of snowflakes on eyelashes, made statues from the ice, and held tightly to his hand as together they learned to skate on the deeply frozen river. Normandy's occasional snows were nothing like the winters of Montreal.

For Gabriel it was a time of rebirth. He watched Celeste revel in her new surroundings, again becoming the girl he had married. Coming to New France had been an enormous risk, but by the end of December, from all appearances, it was paying off.

Then January came. The snow-laden winds blew in sudden, unexpected bursts of fury that lasted for days. There was no reprieve, and the drifts mounted higher until the streets were impassable to a mother and her child. The cold was abysmal. One had to wear a scarf over one's mouth outside or suffer frostbitten lungs and die.

The house in which Gabriel, Celeste, and Michel lived was near the upper edge of the city, on the north side of a narrow street. The house was built in the old style, of wood, with double walls three feet apart, the space between filled with ashes and sawdust as insulation against the bitter cold. Their home was moderate in size, with living and dining rooms on the ground floor, a low-ceilinged kitchen with a stone oven behind the dining room, and two sleeping chambers up the narrow stairs.

Now, in the midst of winter, their breath froze in long, decorative feathery scrolls on the thick, deep-set windowpanes. On bright, sunny days the scrolls were gold or silver. When the sun was red in the east, they blazed a deep orange. When the sky was clouded, as it was much of the time, the scrolls were the color of lead.

When the wind did not blow for several days on end, the breath of the town's livestock and its human population froze and hung in the streets as a perpetual gray mist. Even the river was hushed into silence under a thick, impenetrable sheet of ice.

In spite of her every inner effort, the terrible winter began to pull Celeste down. She had not dreamed that such cold existed anywhere on earth, nor had she dreamed that a winter could be so long.

A sense of imprisonment descended upon her. The unspeakable cold drained her strength away until she was unable to fight her own inner torment. Still the snow continued to fall, and the cold held on. Celeste began to break.

Days of pleasantness alternated with days of depression, tears, and irritability. To both Gabriel and Celeste, the bad periods seemed a hundred times longer than the good. Celeste's old, bitter facial expressions returned. She became less and less reasonable, more and more cutting with her words, and by the first of February threatened every day to leave on the first merchantman downriver in the spring.

Michel cried in his bed at night. Gabriel could not think clearly. Celeste turned her back on them both.

Their new life turned into a winter of despair.

CHAPTER 12

The Girl from Trinidad

EDMOND CHARCOT shunned intimacy, or perhaps it would be more accurate to say that intimacy shunned Charcot. It was easy enough for one to like him at the outset, but the better one knew him, the less there seemed to be to like. He won confidences easily, then used them for his own gain, for he was a perfectly self-centered man.

It is not altogether true to say that he had *no* intimacies. Of the kind that meant warmth, loyalty, or rich human love, he had none, but of the carnal kind he had plenty. They were his "bread of life."

Such was his interest in Angelique Fontaine.

Angelique's mysterious origins tantalized the people of Montreal. It was whispered among them that in her speech was more than a touch of the Caribbean, and in Angelique's face they thought they saw combined the races of Africa and Spain and France. They were nearer the truth than they would ever know, for indeed Angelique Fontaine *was* an octoroon, a product of the slave trade and of French and black ancestors who made love on the white sands of Trinidad's Sena Bay. Her childhood was shrouded in mystery. There was a rumor—no one knew from where it had come—that her French father and Spanish mother had been lost in a wreck at sea. It was certain, however, that she was the adopted daughter of a wealthy Boston merchant.

From the very look in her eyes and the haughtiness in the shape of her mouth, they knew she was a woman of utter independence. There was something untamed about her, an inextinguishable light in her eyes taken by some as thirst for excitement, but which was in fact a kind of beneficent defiance of custom.

But when she spoke, and as she moved about the city, when she reached out and touched man or woman or child, they also felt a kindness, an unexpected tenderness that spoke of love and true consideration for humankind.

And of why Angelique was in Montreal, they knew only what she had told them. She had become bored with Boston and its proper social life. Rumors of this bustling French city had caused her to want to see for herself, and so she had come.

It was February, and for almost a year there had been no attempt at theft. Then, one bitterly cold night toward the end of the month, a rear door of the Lefleur warehouse was splintered and fifteen bales of furs and twenty trade guns were stolen.

From signs in the snow, it was clear that the thieves had used two large horse-drawn sleighs to carry their plunder away. But once in the street their tracks mixed hopelessly with hundreds of others and could not be followed.

Gabriel took charge of the investigation, but quickly reached a dead end. He questioned both guards only to find that they had been roaring drunk. Gabriel found this odd. He had gone many nights to the warehouse, and had always found the same men sober and alert. That they should be drunk on that particular night was clearly more than coincidence.

The guards shamefacedly confessed that three bottles of French wine had been arranged neatly in the snow outside the rear door of the warehouse. They were slow-witted men and had suspected nothing. Since no attempt had been made in months, they reasoned, it would be harmless for them to drink a little. But for these men, of course, there was no such thing as "a little."

The planted wine pointed the finger at no one. Charcot explained that he had hired these proven sots as a gesture of goodwill toward their suffering families. That was at worst suspicious, at best even admirable.

The loss was considerable, and after a month's investigation Gabriel seemed no closer to the answer than when he had first set foot in Montreal.

Another month passed. In late March the weather grew unexpectedly warm and the snow began to melt on the rooftops and in the streets. The ice spanning the river was covered with slush and began to break. With new warmth, spirits revived and the work pace of the entire city quickened.

But the thaw brought no relief to Celeste. The constant dripping

of water from the eaves maddened her. The unbearably damp
south winds rattled the shutters and whispered around the cor-
nices until she huddled herself in the innermost room of the house
where she could not hear. Sometimes she shook uncontrollably,
and often wept away half her day.

Even on her best days Celeste averted her eyes from Gabriel's
when he entered the room and remained coolly indifferent, never
touching him, moving quickly to one side if they met in a doorway. And when he reached out to her, as he often did, she would
slip deftly away.

Twice during the long winter she had begun to babble, speaking, but making no sense, and soon every day she was stammer-
ing, searching for words she could not find. Her face would fill
with tortured confusion, and Gabriel saw it. He strained to listen,
to catch her meaning, struggling on her behalf, nodding vigorously when he understood, feeling desperately for her when he
could not.

"I can't . . . can't say it," she wept aloud. "Why? It isn't . . .
it isn't a hard word. Why can't I say it?" If she wanted to say
"door," "opening" was the word that came out, or "dwelling,"
instead of "house," "brightness" for "light."

Only then, in helpless frustration, would she lay her head on
his shoulder and ask, "Oh Gabriel! What is wrong with me?"

And Gabriel would explain again.

But sometimes when Celeste's anger flared, it was hard for
Gabriel to heed Uncle Joseph's advice. Sometimes his own temper was close to the edge, and an invisible wall began to grow
between them.

Gabriel believed that if Celeste would come out of the house,
time would not weigh so heavily on her shoulders, that if she
would mingle among the friends she made when they first came,
her confusion would lessen. The mayor was entertaining again on
the thirty-first. "Please, Celeste. It's important that I be there,
and I want you with me. It would be good for you, and good for
me. Come along. Let's go and have a good time."

But she would not go.

The mayor's chateau sat on a lower slope of the mountain, elevated grandly above the city. The night was black and the windows of the house blazed with light. As Gabriel approached on

foot from below, the house reminded him of a beacon raised on a point of land to mark a dangerous coast.

Gabriel's feet were cold and wet as he stepped from the ice water of the street and walked up a dry flagstone path to the house. He reached for the big brass fleur de lis on the front door and swung it against its anvil three times. A servant opened the door and announced Gabriel's arrival.

Madame Delachaux—well past her prime, corpulent, and chatty—came quickly to greet him. She reminded Gabriel of a hen running to peck kernels of corn thrown on the ground.

In a short while Gabriel was absorbed in the evening's warmth. Being away from the house that had become such a sad, dark prison, he felt a degree of relief. But he also felt bad about going out when Celeste could not come with him. She *could* have come, he reasoned, if only she would have. He himself needed to be out from under the load for a little while, even if she refused. He thought how stubborn she had been, how unreasonable, and within him, anger began to rise.

"Don't you think so, Monsieur Dublanche?"

"What? Oh, excuse me," Gabriel answered, startled and embarrassed. The stocky man next to him politely waited for his response. "I'm afraid my mind drifted. What did you ask?"

"We were just discussing the war. Aren't you afraid it may obstruct shipping in the spring?"

"Yes," Gabriel answered. "Yes. I'm afraid it might. . . . But I hear Russia may enter the war on Austria's side. Perhaps that will end it all."

He felt foolish for having let his mind wander, and soon he excused himself from the little knot of people and began to walk among the other guests. He noticed that Charcot was not there and wondered why. And he was even more surprised to find that Angelique Fontaine was there without Charcot, for Charcot had a reputation for being jealously possessive of his female consorts.

Gabriel chuckled to himself. He suspected heavy-handedness did not work especially well with this young woman, and that with her, Charcot had his hands more than full.

Angelique's strange beauty and her air of mystery fascinated Gabriel, as she bewitched all men. Throughout the evening, whenever he saw her, he caught his breath. It was a shock to his system to be in the same room with such loveliness. He was trying hard to keep his mind on a conversation with a black-robed seminary student from the Place des Jesuites, but his thoughts and his gaze kept drifting back to her.

He had talked with Angelique only once before, and on that occasion he sensed Charcot's uneasiness with the familiarity. He knew Charcot would become especially chary if Gabriel should try to know her better.

So he was surprised when he found her once more in the crowd and discovered that she was much nearer, and looking directly at him. Their eyes met, and as if meeting an old friend, she smiled warmly. Immediately she excused herself from the conversation and made her way toward him.

As she came his way, he thought how strange it was that he had never seen her dressed in anything but red. Tonight it was red of a milder hue, an elaborate brocade, cut lower than normal modesty—even for that time—allowed. She was altogether a daring young woman.

"Monsieur Dublanche." She spoke his name in a contralto voice that was warm with enthusiasm. "It's been so long since last we talked," she said, "and I've thought about you often." She extended her hand for the customary kiss.

"Mademoiselle Fontaine," he said, and bowed. "I'm surprised to hear you've thought of me at all, but I'm pleased that you have."

"I see you are alone tonight, Monsieur Dublanche," she said, looking about as if making one more effort to find Celeste in the crowd. "Is your wife ill?"

"Yes, I'm afraid she is," Gabriel answered. "But she insisted that I come without her."

"I'm sorry she is indisposed," she said, "but I'm glad you've come. I, too, am alone, and I hope you will not think me too bold if I suggest we dine together."

Of *course* he thought she was bold. What else could he think? But stunned with surprise and hardly able to conceal his considerable pleasure, he answered simply, "I would be honored."

At that moment dinner was announced.

During the dinner Gabriel found Angelique Fontaine as much a delight to be with as she was a delight to see. Her accent and intonations captivated him. When he asked, she told him she spoke three languages quite well; French was her father's tongue, Spanish her mother's, and she spoke two kinds of English—the kind

spoken by proper Bostonians and the kind spoken on the bucca-
neer island of New Providence.

"New Providence?" Gabriel expressed surprise.

"Yes," she answered, and told him her story.

Others at the table interrupted their own conversations to listen,
and soon all the room was silent but for Angelique's warm, feminine voice. She was not at all bothered by being the center of
attention.

She spoke for a long while, and then stopped and looked about.
"Well, I'm afraid I've taken over this conversation. Now, please,
someone else must do the talking for a while."

Ignoring her suggestion, Gabriel asked, "And after Boston,
Angelique?" He was surprised to hear himself use her first
name, but he relished it as it passed pleasurably over his tongue.

"After Boston?" She laughed, reached out, and squeezed his
hand. "I will tell you about 'after Boston' another time." Gabriel
felt a warm excitement at the thought that there would be another
time.

Dinner ended. A carriage waited to take Angelique home. To
Gabriel's disappointment, she made no offer to take him to his
door. But when she turned to go, and he assisted her with her
cape, she gripped his hand. His eyes followed as she walked
smoothly out the door, the cape fanning grandly behind her. Only
when she was gone did he become aware of a piece of paper
folded and pressed into the palm of his hand. He slipped the
clandestine note into his waistcoat pocket and left the party as
soon as he could.

Gabriel Dublanche blushed as he walked homeward. The night
had grown colder, and what had been slush underfoot was now a
hard layer of ice over the cobblestones. He would not get wet on
his way home, but there was considerable danger of falling.

The strangest mixture of guilt and ecstasy milled about inside
his breast. Gabriel was no philanderer, or at least he did not think
he was. He thought of Emilie, the woman in whose home he had
lived in Paris. Could he be sure that he would escape again—
especially now that he had known a woman's love, and been es-
tranged from Celeste? He could not be sure. But somehow, rather
than being filled with revulsion at the thought of betraying his
wife, he was absolutely taken with the wonder of this girl who
tonight had come so close to him.

What experiences she had known! How intelligent she was, even brilliant. So self-possessed, so physically perfect. Then a new thought struck him. Why was she attached to Charcot? And how was it she had dared to spend the evening with Gabriel? Well, what did it matter? At that moment he was willing to take almost any risk to have the thrill of her company, even if for only a little while.

Something within spat out a warning: "Stop right where you are, and take a good look at all of this." Gabriel spoke sternly to his galloping emotions and tried to cleanse himself of the obsession that rose within. But no sooner had he flushed them out of his system than they began to rise again.

The folded piece of paper! He had not even read it yet. He reached beneath his cape and felt in his waistcoat pocket with his forefinger. Yes. It was still there, still warm from her own hand, or at least, so he imagined. He hurried along the deserted street.

When Gabriel entered his house, Celeste was asleep. The burning wick of an oil lamp beside her cast long shadows from the bed-posts against the wall and illuminated her face with a soft amber light.

She was relaxed. The tension was gone from about her mouth and eyes, and he thought she looked for all the world like the girl just out of school that he had met on the quay at Rouen more than ten years ago.

As a midmorning breeze dispels the fog, so Celeste's loveliness expelled the note from his mind. He sat on the edge of the bed, looking at her silently. He bowed his head in his hands and tears rose in his eyes. What is going to become of us? he thought. Then sorrowfully he asked under his breath, "How could God ever have let it happen, that such beauty and love should be dashed against a rock in a storm?"

He rose from the edge of the bed without disturbing her, walked softly to Michel's room, looked in on him, adjusted the covers about the little boy's shoulders, and descended the creaking stairs to the kitchen.

He lighted a candle and set it in a holder on the split pine table, then reached into his pocket, withdrew the note, and held it to-ward the flame. Better never to read it, he thought.

As the edge of the paper began to scorch and turn brown, a new and disconcerting thought flamed into his mind. What if the note is *not* a flirtation? What if Angelique's warmth were only a masquerade to allow her to tell him something? Suddenly it struck him hard that she had to have written the note *before* she came, that rather than a casual flirtation, this was something she had carefully planned.

He snatched the paper from the flame and pinched out the fire that had kindled on its edge. He unfolded it and lay it flat on the table where the candlelight reflected warmly from the expensive white vellum. It read,

> Monsieur Dublanche,
>
> Please forgive me for my forward behavior. If things have gone as I planned, by the time you read this we will have created quite a stir at the Delachaux's party. I hope this causes you no great embarrassment. It was the only way to satisfy myself about you before sharing with you an important secret.
>
> That you now possess this note means I have concluded that you are reliable.
>
> I must meet with you again very soon—but this time it must be privately. I have a story that you must hear, for it is essential to the success of your mission here in Montreal.
>
> Tomorrow I will come to the Lefleur offices. At some unobserved moment, signal with either a nod or a shake of your head whether you will meet me at the Chapel Notre Dame two hours after sundown tomorrow evening.
>
> I think it best that you burn this note after reading it.
>
> > Faithfully,
> > Angelique Fontaine

Even in the candle glow Gabriel's face burned red with humiliation. How foolish I've been, he thought, like a stupid schoolboy. How can I face this woman again?

But he took a grip on himself and shunted the embarrassment aside for the more serious consideration. Of course he would meet her. He must.

He read the note twice more to be certain of every detail and, with a reluctant hand, held it out to the flame of the guttering candle.

CHAPTER 13

The Night of Discovery

NEXT MORNING, April 1, found Gabriel at the Lefleur office, trying to better acquaint himself with the business as well as distract his mind from the coming tryst with Angelique. He studied the lists of canoemen, their terms of service, their wages, and where they had come from.

All day long Gabriel watched Charcot's face for signs of uneasiness or for an indication that something out of the ordinary was afoot. But the man's face was as inscrutable as ever. He was perfectly calm and self-possessed.

About noon a warm southwest wind began to blow, raising the temperature dramatically, and by three, dark clouds were rolling down the river valley, spreading low overhead. By four, large, warm drops of rain were pelting against the windowpanes. Now it was evening. A hard rain roared on the rooftops, and the cobblestones disappeared as the streets ran full. Melting snowbanks and fields of ice were releasing the imprisoned water of winter, setting it free to flow down the rocky slopes. Bright flashes of light cut sharply through the deepening gray as the season's first thunder rolled and boomed among the houses and along the banks of the rising river.

Gabriel left the Lefleur office and hurried through the downpour to his home. There he refreshed himself, played with his son, and ate. Celeste was in a pleasant mood. Her speech was clearer tonight than it had been in many days, and she and Gabriel sat for a long while before the open fire, talking like the lovers they had always been. Occasional drops of rain found their way down the chimney and small clouds of steam rose from the burning logs.

Gabriel confided in Celeste about the mission that lay before him and told her he must be gone for a while. "Expect me no sooner than midnight," he said, and kissed her lingeringly. He took Michel by the hand, led him up the stairs, and put him to

116

bed. "In the morning we'll go down to the docks together to watch the river rise," he promised. In the candlelight, the little boy's eyes glowed with anticipation. Obediently he rolled onto his side and snuggled his head deep into the soft pillow. As his father drew the covers about his shoulders, Michel felt loved and secure.

Downstairs again, Gabriel cast a broad, black cape about his shoulders, pressed a three-cornered hat on his head to gutter the rain away from his face, and drew on a pair of boots that reached to his knees. Just as he stepped out the door, he was struck by a new thought. He turned back to a weathered chest that sat against the east wall, its six shallow drawers running its full width, containing papers related to the Lefleur business. On top of the chest sat a wooden box of fine walnut. Gabriel lifted the lid of the smaller box and from its red velvet-lined interior took a dueling pistol.

He was not suspicious of Angelique Fontaine, but it was possible she was not what she seemed, and it was also possible that some other interested party might have gotten wind of tonight's arrangement. A secret meeting on a dark night . . . it would present a good opportunity to get rid of him.

With a puff of linen on a cleaning tip, Gabriel swabbed the pistol's bore free of oil, then loaded and primed it. He dipped his finger in hot candle wax, then rubbed it around the edges of the pan. He closed the frizzen, rubbed on more wax, and when satisfied it was watertight, slipped the pistol's hook over his belt, pulled his cape about him, and ventured out into the pouring rain.

Once away from the house, Gabriel could see nothing. The lightning had long since passed, and the night was utterly black. Rain was still falling in sheets. Though he knew the route and distance to the cathedral by heart, Gabriel had to feel his way along the stone buildings or become hopelessly lost.

At last he slipped into the narthex of the great stone church and stood dripping, still enshrouded in blackness, for inside no candles burned. A soft breath of damp air, smelling of old stone and lichen, chilled the wet skin of his right cheek. He felt his way toward the source of the draft, and soon entered the nave by its great central door. There at last, he saw light. On each of the long nave's supporting columns, a candle flickered in its sconce, and at the far end, before the locked tabernacle in which lay the Holy Eucharist, burned a flickering perpetual flame.

He stood for a moment looking down the long, dimly lit aisle toward the altar, then perfunctorily knelt, crossed himself, and stood to listen.

"Gabriel," called a warm, familiar feminine voice from somewhere near the front, almost lost in its own echo. "Gabriel. I'm here, near the altar."

He walked forward, every step ringing on the polished stone floor like a hammer on an anvil, and at last found her in the shadow of the foremost column.

She reached out and took his hand. Her touch, as warm and electrifying as before, distracted him for a moment. She pushed back the hood of her cape, and when he could see her eyes, he said to her in a whisper, "Angelique, forgive me last night's foolishness. I was presumptuous. Tonight I was nearly too ashamed to face you."

She cut off his apology. "Gabriel," she said—he was pleased to hear his first name on her lips—"I should beg *your* pardon for leading you on. You could think nothing other than what you thought. But let's lay that aside until later. Just now I've something more important to tell you. I never know when I'm being watched, and there may be little time."

He nodded.

"Gabriel, you must do something quickly, or Charcot is going to escape."

"Charcot!" he hissed. "Then he *is* the one. Somehow I knew it from the first. There was something about that man that simply would not let me trust him." The high roof gave their urgent whispers a hollow, distant ring.

"Yes," she said, "of course he's the one. I thought you had guessed it, and only needed more information for his arrest."

"And can you give me that?"

"Yes, I can."

For a moment she was silent, and in the vaulted nave the rain beating heavily on the lead roof rattled softly. The candlelight from the sconce behind Gabriel reflected in Angelique's liquid eyes, and in them he saw his own dark image silhouetted. He saw also that once again she was dressed in red. Angelique picked up her story where she had stopped the evening before.

"My new father is one of the principal men of Boston," she

said. "We live on an estate of thousands of acres with a mill and barns and a magnificent home on the Neponset River south of the city.

"Everyone believes my father made his fortune in shipping. And partly it's true. His ships make regular voyages to the Indian Ocean and trade between there and the coast of New England.

"But my father also takes supplies secretly to the pirates of Madagascar—everything they need; food, clothes, medicines, tar—and of course he is paid well with their plunder, sometimes in gold and silver, often in goods that he sells wherever he can in the ports of India and Egypt. He—"

Gabriel could see no connection between her story and the business at hand and broke in. "But I came to find out about Charcot, not about your father," he said.

Angelique looked at him with a cold, steady gaze and said nothing. He wavered under her gaze, realizing that this woman would tolerate no lack of confidence.

"I'm sorry," he said. "Please go on."

She paused a moment longer, then continued. "About four years ago," she said, "out of nowhere, Charcot came to my father and made him a proposition. He said that he was the North American agent of a French fur company, that my father could do very well buying furs directly from him—furs he and his men would steal from the company warehouse. There was little risk, and my father agreed. Charcot was right. It has been profitable for both my father and him. In short, Charcot is selling Monsieur Lefleur's furs right out of his own warehouse."

"We should have known." Gabriel sighed and shook his head. "But how does he do it?"

"Easily," she answered. "He hires weak men—men like the drunken guards. If he steals in the winter, he takes the furs over the ice to an island downstream. In summer they go by dory to the same island. When there are enough in storage, my father sends a schooner upriver and takes them off in the night."

"Why are you telling me this?" Gabriel asked. "Aren't you afraid for your father?"

"No," she answered. "I've sent word to warn him."

"Then your interest here isn't Charcot after all. You're here to look out for your father's interests, to warn him if something goes wrong."

"That's right," she said. "And I knew sooner or later you

would find the answers. It's getting too warm for Charcot. Another week and he will be gone. You can be certain of it." Then almost as an afterthought, but with a hidden flame of emotion, she added, "I don't want him to get away."

"Somehow I thought you cared for him more than that," Gabriel returned, hoping for a denial. He was not disappointed.

"Care for him!" she exploded. "Not at all! We have suited each other's purposes. As a lover, he's swine." She smiled and said, "I was stupid enough to tell him that. My back and thighs are purple with bruises. In all honesty, Gabriel, I want him put away, and I think you are the man to do it."

Gabriel saw the picture clearly now. He was her instrument against Charcot. Yet he did not feel in the slightest demeaned and was drawn all the more powerfully to her. Within Angelique's gloriously exotic exterior, Gabriel saw an extraordinary person with strength and character. And there was something exciting about being a part of this bold, fascinating woman's thoughts.

"So you're looking for revenge, and I'm your weapon," he said rather flatly.

"Well," she answered, "I would rather say that I am performing a surgery. Let's say I am removing a boil from the buttocks of society—and you are my scalpel." She smiled a clever smile as she said it, and Gabriel broke into a laugh that echoed in and out among the arches and columns of the nave. In the faint candlelight, smiling so, her face was even more beautiful than before. He said, "All right. I'm your instrument. Take me to the island tomorrow and show me the cache of furs as proof of what you say. All Lefleur furs are marked with a brand. Then we will go to the authorities, ask for Charcot's arrest, and take them to the evidence."

"That's perfect," she answered. "I'm certain the men in his employ will testify against him. Every one of them hates him with a passion."

"You've thought this out to the last detail, haven't you, Angelique?" he added reflectively. "You're as intelligent as you are beautiful.

"By the way," Gabriel continued, "where was he last night? I'm surprised he let you out alone. For that matter, I'm surprised you could get away to meet me here. Charcot strikes me as a jealous man."

"He has learned he cannot control me," she answered. "When

he finds I've been out with someone else, he rages for a while, but then he calms down. Besides, he has other women. His magnetism is strong. There are, in fact, half a dozen well-married women in this city who are more than pleased to share his bed. He has a hideaway on the waterfront for that purpose, since the women dare not be seen coming and going from his house. This is not Paris, you know.'' She paused for a moment as though weighing some additional thought, then said, ''Gabriel, there's one other thing. It might help you to know that his name is not Edmond Charcot.''

''He uses a false name? Why?''

''Because of some crime he committed in France before coming to this country. He killed a man, I think, and he's running from the hangman. You can see why I have no remorse about—''

Gabriel's interest suddenly rose. ''Do you know his real name?''

''Yes. He confided it to my father. His real name is Lecharbonnier. Jonathan Lecharbonnier.''

''No, Gabriel! No!''

Angelique rushed desperately through the blinding, driving rain close on the heels of Gabriel Dublanche. Guided by some sixth sense, like a bat that flies unerringly in blackness, he plunged through the deluge, his wrath fired by years of bitterness that lay like burning coals in his soul. It seemed that every great sorrow of his life could in some way be traced to this evil man. Tonight his wrath had discovered its rightful target.

The moment Angelique had uttered the name Lecharbonnier, Gabriel had stopped breathing, and his gaze had frozen. Angelique Fontaine was not given to fear, but his cold stare had knifed a chill into her heart. Hatred had risen up within Gabriel like rising water, and any dam of restraint had crumbled before its boiling fury.

Angelique had seen instantly that some terrible thing had happened in his mind. She had grabbed his shoulders, trying to shake him back to sanity, but he had neither seen her before him, felt her hands on his shoulders, nor heard her words in his ears. Without explanation he had turned and run past the tall columns to the narthex and out into the rain with Angelique close behind.

''Gabriel, you can't!'' she called out. ''You'll ruin everything.''

He turned to face her in the blackness.

"If you do this thing," she said, "you risk yourself and everything you have—your wife, your child. And you risk me and my father. Gabriel, you must not!"

He did not answer, but turned again and walked with visible resolve toward Lecharbonnier's secret retreat.

Within minutes they were on the waterfront. The continued roar of the rain mingled with the sound of the river as it washed against the bulkheads and tugged hard at the dark line of moored ships and boats.

From a low, compact stone building a yellow light gleamed through a narrow curtained window. Gabriel stopped by the heavy front door.

Angelique came up behind him. He looked down at her. Her earnest dark face, wet with rain, showed no fright as she sternly said, "Gabriel, don't do it."

He answered in a tone equally determined, "You won't stop me, Angelique." Gabriel held his breath. With his right hand he reached under his cape and felt the firm, checkered butt of the pistol. With his left he grasped the door handle and, with a sudden quick movement, pushed hard.

The door burst open and slammed against the wall behind it. At the same instant Gabriel stood at the center of the room with the cocked pistol pointed directly at Lecharbonnier's bare chest.

The yellow light Gabriel had seen in the window poured from the flame of an oil lamp on a bedside table. The room was small and tidy, but smelled of dampness and mold. Its central furnishing was a double bed that sat with its head against the east wall.

In this bed Lecharbonnier sat bolt upright, staring in fury at his sudden intruder. Beside him, clutching desperately for sheet and blanket, not knowing whether to flush with humiliation or go white with terror, lay Monet Duchamp, daughter of the Marquis Albert Colbert Duchamp, the king's prosecutor in Montreal.

At that moment Angelique stepped out of the darkness and stood beside Gabriel. She looked directly at Lecharbonnier, smiled a slight smile of disgust and disdain, and then spoke. "For such a humble room you certainly have noble furnishings, Edmond. Don't you think, though, that your newest piece looks a bit out of place? From the expression on her face, I think your . . . companion would rather be at home with her father."

Lecharbonnier found his voice. Ignoring Angelique, he demanded loudly, "Dublanche, what in God's name is going on? I have not the slightest notion what you are about; but whatever it is, put down that pistol and tell me what you think you're doing."

For the first time Gabriel spoke. "Tonight you are not the inquisitor. Tonight you will answer questions that burn in *my* mind." Neither Lecharbonnier's upright position nor his steady, hard gaze changed. Gabriel went on. "First, I want the truth about the robberies, and bribes, and the cache of furs on the island downriver, and a schooner that takes them off in the night, and a merchant from Boston."

Lecharbonnier's face did not change, but his eyes shifted in an uncertain way. Gabriel continued. "Next, and far more importantly, I want to know if you are indeed Edmond Charcot."

At this, Lecharbonnier's countenance changed. His fierce anger faded and sudden fear took its place. Boldly, but with a faint tremor in his voice, the man asked, "What possible difference could that make to you, Monsieur Dublanche?"

Gabriel's response was slow, deliberately measured, and drawn out with exquisite tension. "It makes quite a lot of difference, Monsieur. The king's prosecutor will want to know by what name he emasculates you for the rape of his daughter—"

"Damn it, Dublanche. This is not rape! This girl was as willing as—"

"And he will want to know by what name he should prosecute you for theft of Lefleur furs." At this, Lecharbonnier fell silent and turned his cold stare to Angelique; she glared back with a steady coldness of her own. Gabriel took a new grip on the butt of the pistol and continued.

"But, most importantly, the executioner will want to know by what name to call you when he takes off your head."

Lecharbonnier's arrogance now deserted him altogether. His breath came faster, and his gaze began to dart about the room. He said unevenly, "Talk sense, man. I don't understand."

"Perhaps if I addressed you as Jonathan Lecharbonnier you would better understand," Gabriel said evenly.

"A man can have whatever name he likes," Lecharbonnier answered nervously. "It is no crime."

"Certainly not your worst crime." Gabriel remembered the limp and bloody form of his friend; rage and nausea swept through him. "Michel Lebrun," he said, and waited to see a sign of recognition on Lecharbonnier's face.

Lecharbonnier, impatient and irritated, answered, "The name means nothing to me. Nothing at all."

"To the contrary. At this moment that name means *everything* to you. Think harder: 1734, Avranches." At the name of the village Lecharbonnier stiffened in ill-disguised shock. Gabriel went on. "An inn. A young girl named Marie Benet. A cliff. A rock. You did not know Michel Lebrun, and he did not know you, but that made no difference twelve years ago. And I assure you, monsieur, it makes no difference at all tonight."

Lecharbonnier's face was white. The girl lay in a confused huddle on the side of the bed, tears running down her face, wetting the pillow she clutched tightly to cover her breast. But for the steady beat of the rain on the window and Lecharbonnier's labored breathing, the room was utterly quiet. The man was like a dog run into a corner, looking for a way to bolt but finding none.

Lecharbonnier himself broke the silence. His mouth was dry as he ventured weakly, "We could make some arrangement. I'm in a position to pay you. I'll make it worth your while if you lay down that pistol. Tonight you can leave here a wealthy man."

Gabriel answered, "Michel Lebrun was my truest friend. I was there when they found him. I held his dead hand. I saw his mother die of grief. Your offer is obscene."

Gabriel's eyes became intense, and he leveled the pistol at Lecharbonnier's chest. The girl whimpered, and Lecharbonnier's face grew ashen.

Angelique put her hand on Gabriel's arm and whispered, "No, Gabriel. No."

Lecharbonnier echoed quietly, "No. Monsieur Dublanche. Please. I beg you. No." Minutes ago all had been exquisite pleasure, and now, in a sweat of agony, he looked death squarely in the face. He could not bear to think of his own death, of sheets soaked in his own blood, of wealth left unspent, of stepping into unconsciousness never to awaken, or worse, into flaming hell. Lecharbonnier's hands began to shake, and he crossed himself repeatedly as he whispered to Angelique, "Angelique, in God's name, stop him."

"Monsieur Lecharbonnier," Gabriel said, "at this moment I can think of no reason for you to live, and I can think of several very good reasons for you to die." Then with resolution he added, "If there is a God in heaven, tonight I do Him service."

Savoring his long-awaited moment of revenge, Gabriel squeezed the trigger.

Lecharbonnier was not a slow man. When to his stunned delight the pistol's priming failed, all the tension in his body flung him forward toward Gabriel. Lecharbonnier was in the air for only an instant, but in that instant Gabriel drew the cock, closed the frizzen, and pulled the trigger again. The man's face was but a hand's breadth away when the closed room rang with a deafening explosion and fire erupted from the bore.

Lecharbonnier fell hard against Gabriel's legs, knocking him forcefully against the wall. Gabriel regained his feet, stood above the man where he fell, then turned him over. The ball had entered the middle of Lecharbonnier's left eyebrow; the skin of his face was charred black by flame and powder. A flap of skull lay open on the back of his head; thick, dark blood spurted spasmodically and ran down to the floor. His chest rose convulsively as he gasped. Then the body twitched and was still.

CHAPTER 14

The Escape

GABRIEL'S hands shook violently. The girl in the bed fainted. Angelique leaned against the closed door and looked up at the ceiling with half-closed eyes, shaking her head slowly. "Oh, Gabriel, what you've done. What you have done."

She was not sorry for Lecharbonnier. As far as justice was concerned, the scales were better balanced now than they had been five minutes before. But this was murder.

"Now what are you going to do?" she asked him. "Where will you go? What is going to become of your wife and child?"

Sudden sickness gripped Gabriel, and he jumped to his feet. "I've got to go to them!"

"No." Angelique stood her ground, barring the door. "No,

you cannot. This girl is going to wake up, and when she does she will be out of her mind and run screaming to her father. She will forget every shred of shame and tell him everything. You and I don't know what he will do then. He may be so glad to be rid of Lecharbonnier that he will give you a parade and celebrate with fireworks. On the other hand, he's a public official. It would be hard for him to explain why he does not hang a murderer, for he'll certainly not reveal that the victim was killed in bed with his daughter.

"No," Angelique continued, thinking fast. "Here is what you must do. You must go downstream to the island where the furs are cached. There is a small cabin there and food. No one will go there with the river high, and you can hide for a few days until I find out what they decide to do with you. I will go to your wife and child and try to reassure them; then I will come out to you."

The girl began to stir. She rose up in bed, looked about, saw the dead man lying on the floor, and fell back, wailing hysterically.

The rain beat against the window. A clock on the wall read a quarter past midnight. Gabriel lighted a lantern and went out into the rain to find a boat.

Angelique picked the girl's dress from the floor where it had been shed in the haste of ecstasy, pulled the sobbing girl upright, and slipped the garment over her head. "Don't wail for him," Angelique said firmly, giving a disgusted jerk of her head toward the body lying on the floor. "You haven't lost a thing. He would've sucked you dry and pitched you aside like a squeezed-out lime. You were just one more in his very long line. I'll go with you to your father, and together we'll tell him what happened." The girl wailed louder.

Gabriel returned, dripping, and started to ransack the room for supplies. He found two heavy blankets, a fowling piece, dry powder and shot, some food, flint, and steel. A dozen times in his comings and goings he stepped around the obscene mass that seeped blood onto the floor.

They determined to leave the body exactly as it lay, for Angelique would hide nothing from Duchamp. Truth would be the best course.

Gabriel faced yet another problem. Could he reach the island in this rain and darkness, on a rising river filled with ice floes? A pity he could not wait for the light of day.

When the boat was loaded and the girl dressed—she had calmed, though her hands shook a little and she wiped an occasional tear from her face—Gabriel climbed down the sheer rock wall of the quay, jumped into the dory, slipped the line, and pushed out onto the rushing, black water.

Immediately, strong currents caught the boat and the river bore him along with a will of its own. He bent to the oars with all his strength and made directly for the opposite shore. Even so, the torrent swept him dangerously near the northwest cape of Isle Saint Pierre.

He could see nothing at all, not his own hands, the oars, or the boat that carried him. He could not see the island on which he nearly ran ashore, but he thought he felt branches and floating things reaching out to snare him in the blackness.

Unseeing, he passed between Saint Pierre and Isle Sainte Helene, moving always closer to the river's southeastern edge. Lonqueil and Tremblay fell behind to his right. He had fought the darkness and currents for an hour, his shoulders and arms aching to rest, when suddenly the boat slid to a stop. Gabriel took an oar and reached about in the blackness, and found that he had run aground on a submerged bank of mud. But as he tried to push off, the blade of his oar only knifed deep into the slime.

Was the mud bar narrow, or was it so wide that he could not hope to dislodge the boat? If he went over the side to push, would the footing be firm or would he sink? What a predicament *that* would be, he thought, to be stuck waist-deep in mud with the river rising.

Morning light was yet hours away, and there was nothing to do but wait. He feared the pouring rain would fill his dory before morning, and he had brought nothing with which to bail. Occasionally cakes of ice hit the boat, rocked it, and scraped on by. With nothing else to do but wait, Gabriel sat in the stern, drew his heavy wool cape about his legs, and pulled his hat down over his face to fend off the downpour and conserve whatever heat his body could generate. Even so, after an endless hour the cold overcame him, and he began to shake uncontrollably.

Worse, Gabriel was as miserable mentally as he was physically, stunned to think that though he hated death and violence, in a terrible rage he had killed a man, and that now he would be hunted for his crime and well might die. He plunged into deeper agony when he thought of his family and especially when he thought of little Michel. He imagined the disappointment the little boy would feel, and it pained him more deeply than all else.

The hours oozed by. After Gabriel had sat a long while, with the rain running down his collar, assaulted every minute by involuntary fits of shivering, it came into his mind that it was not Lecharbonnier's body he had seen lying on the floor, but his own. Perhaps *he* had been killed, and had seen his own cast-off form bleeding there, and that now his spirit was crossing the River Styx, that he was in hell, and that the black and wet would never end.

But, just as this thought occurred to him, the faintest glow touched the horizon toward the north. The north? he wondered. Why there? In another hour the glow had grown into the first light of dawn, and he realized he did not know north from south, east from west. The light revealed rain continuing to fall in gray sheets. The boat was half full of water now, so he took off his hat and used it to bail. When the light grew strong enough, he looked about and saw a large, tree-covered island no more than two hundred yards below him, a black silhouette standing against the faintly visible clouds.

Suddenly he felt a slipping, a movement. The river, rising gradually, floated him free of the mud, and he moved rapidly toward the island's high banks. A thick old tree, its roots undermined by the flood, had fallen into the water on the island's right side. Gabriel pulled hard on the oars, made for the tree, caught its wet limbs, and drew the boat into the eddy-filled cove formed by the tree's upriver side.

Gabriel drew the boat up onto the bank, turned it over, lay his provisions underneath, and covered it with brush. Immediately, hoping desperately that this was the right island, he began to search for the fur cache.

The island was at least three miles long, a half mile wide, and covered with thick timber. Gabriel made his way along the shore to the downriver end, then climbed a high point of rugged gray rock and looked about. From there, to the northeast, he sighted a spire on the river's nearest shore. This he took to be Boucherville. He looked back to the southwest toward Montreal and saw the top of Ville Marie's stone fortress.

He looked toward the island's interior. If this was the right island, at its center there would be a house built of hewn timber and stone, with two rooms and a concealed cellar filled with bales of furs marked with the Lefleur brand.

An hour or so past noon he found it. It was well hidden and appeared to be nothing but a trapper's cabin. Gabriel brought his provisions from the boat, found dry clothing, and struck a fire on the hearth. The sky was yet gray and the rain still falling, but dry and warm, he lay across the bed of willow poles and fell into an exhausted, fitful sleep.

It was morning of the third day, and still the rains fell unabated. The Saint Lawrence had crept above her banks and now threatened to submerge Gabriel's island, or to eat it away piece by piece. Already the lower expanses were under water.

On the nameless island's upper end, Gabriel sat in a clump of trees and, through the gray morning light, watched the river rush toward him. He had found oilskins in the cache and now sat wrapped in them, the rain running in shining gray streams down the folds of the cloth and onto the wet, glistening rock on which he sat. The air was cool. Clouds of mist steamed from the river's confused surface and obscured the distant shores in every direction.

About the granite rocks below him the water swirled and eddied. Great cakes of ice swept by. Some wedged themselves against the rocks or careened off grotesque old logs that protruded from the face of the muddy flood.

Underneath, from the riverbed, the warming waters coaxed bubbling vapors from fermenting vegetation long buried in the slimy mud. Frogs and turtles broke free from their winter prisons. The aroma of fresh spruce buds on the trees blended with the crisp, cool scent of clear rain.

Gabriel watched longingly for a boat to come out of the mist. Angelique had not yet come, and his panic mounted higher and higher until he felt he would burst. Every moment of these three days and nights he had spent contriving little plots to explain to himself why she had not come. She had gone to Duchamp, Gabriel thought, and he had arrested her on the spot. Now the authorities were trying to force her to reveal his hiding place. Angelique, his only lifeline, was sitting in prison wondering how to get word to him. How strange, he thought. His only lifeline, and yet he hardly knew her.

It was a God's wonder that he had found the right island and that he had made it through the ice floes without being crushed or sunk. Thinking of the ice made him aware of another possibility. Perhaps, because of the high water and ice, Angelique had decided she could not come, or perhaps she had tried and her boat had been crushed or capsized, and she had drowned.

But, he thought, she wouldn't have tried to come alone. She's no fool. No, he thought again, Angelique was certainly no fool. If only he had listened to her. "The wrath of man . . ." He remembered the biblical warning and shook his head at his own capacity for evil, a capacity that had taken him totally by surprise.

As he sat in the rain with nothing but bleak despair about and within, it was hard to remember that he had once been happy, that he had once known peace of mind. Life is a muddle now, he thought, like the roiling river, full of mire and silt. He remembered, "The wicked are like the troubled sea, when it cannot rest, whose water cast up mire and dirt."

Am I wicked? he wondered. When I was a child, I loved God. Or I thought I did. Did I really love Him? If I did, why has everything gone wrong? Why has everything I've prayed for been lost?

He remembered Lecharbonnier crossing himself again and again. Am I better than that godforsaken man? Gabriel asked himself. Why should I think that I am? No matter how we began, he and I, in the end, were both alike.

He wondered how Celeste had taken the news. Had it unhinged her completely? Had she strode about, raging and throwing everything she could put her hands on? Or had she lapsed deeper into that blank stare, into her mental cocoon? Even more painful were his thoughts about his son. What did the boy think of his father now? Did he cry himself to sleep last night? Oh Lord, Gabriel thought in anguish, how I prayed for a child! How I loved him when he was born. How I prayed that I would be a good father. God, how could you refuse to hear the prayer of a father—especially a prayer asking for strength?

Gabriel could not imagine a satisfactory answer. Unless it was, as he had come to suspect, that there was no God. It was an honest doubt, but other than its honesty, the thought seemed to him to have no merit at all. He reached for the crucifix Catherine had given him, but his fingers caught only the loose rosary. How had he lost it? Did it matter?

He pictured his son weeping. Had he not told Michel that he

would be there when the boy woke next morning? Bitter tears rose in Gabriel's eyes, ran down his face, and mingled with the warm rain.

And what would Michel think when he heard his father had killed a man? Would they be sure to tell him that Lecharbonnier was a very bad man? Had they told him yet? Of course they had; there was no way to keep him from finding out.

Gabriel peered through the mist. At any moment, he thought, the bow of Angelique's boat would emerge and she would tell him that all was well. He would climb into the boat with her, and tonight he would be at home with his wife and child.

Whether Angelique came or not, he had made up his mind about one thing. He would not stay on this island another day. The agitation of uncertainty filled every part of his body until it was impossible for him to sleep or to think clearly about anything.

If she doesn't come today, he vowed, I'll set out before dawn tomorrow—for good or ill.

Gabriel got to his feet and turned toward the island's interior. But as he turned, a darkness moved behind the face of the mist, and a green glow caught his eye. He stopped where he stood and waited. The darkness moved nearer the island. A boat, but not the boat he wanted to see. This boat was larger, a cutter on her way downstream. She moved abreast of the island, and he saw her name clearly, the *Candide*, no doubt on her way to Quebec and on to the ocean, the first vessel to leave Montreal after breakup.

Gabriel remembered seeing this cutter perched on its ways a short distance from the warehouse, waiting out the winter on-shore. She was small, about forty feet long with a sixteen-foot beam, easy to save from the crush of winter's freeze.

She had a grandly sleek profile, a rakish set to her single mast, a long bowsprit, three graceful jibs forward, and a schooner's mainsail so large that in cross winds she drove forward with a perilous yaw. But she was fast, and when winter ended, she was always the first to take news to the outside world.

Likely on board the *Candide* were passengers bound for France. How he wished he and Celeste and Michel were among them. He felt a sinking in his chest as she passed by, so close he could see deckhands moving about.

She faded quickly back into the mist. The last he saw of her was the glow of her green starboard running light and the white lamp that gleamed from her stern.

Angelique had watched Gabriel's boat until it disappeared from the small circle of light thrown by her lantern. She had returned to the room, placed a cape about the shoulders of the quivering girl, snuffed out the lights, and led her home.

"I am not sorry the man is dead," said Monsieur Duchamp. Duchamp was a good man, disappointed in his daughter, but kind and tender. "I'm afraid Monsieur Dublanche is an unfortunate victim. He may even be the instrument of justice, but I'm afraid he must be charged with murder and stand trial. I will be forced to dissociate myself because of my daughter's involvement. Of course I would like to see Dublanche go free, but I am not in a position to make that decision." He turned to the girl. "Monet," he asked her again, "have you told me everything?"

"Yes, Papa," she said, "I have."

"And all of what you have said is true?"

She nodded, and Duchamp turned back to Angelique.

"Then, Mademoiselle Fontaine, would you be so compassionate as to say nothing of her presence? After all, she contributed nothing to the crime."

"Yes," Angelique said. "You have my word."

Duchamp smiled with warm appreciation.

"Thank you most sincerely. My family will always be in your debt." He drew in his breath and continued, "I will tell the governor that I am dissociating myself because of my intense dislike for the victim, and that is no falsehood. But now I must send men to the scene, and I'm afraid I must accompany them."

On the same morning of Lecharbonnier's death, shortly after dawn, Angelique Fontaine knocked at Celeste Dublanche's door, startling her from sleep. Celeste welcomed her warmly, but when she learned why she had come, her face turned to a lifeless mask. For a long while she looked into her caller's eyes and then stared past her. She did not speak.

Angelique told her every detail, from the passing of the note to the murder itself. Celeste's expression did not change. She asked no questions, made no exclamations, wept no tears.

"Can I help you, Madame Dublanche?" Angelique's heart was

filled with pity for Celeste. "May I bring you a glass of water, help you with the child, anything at all?"

Angelique moved to the couch where Celeste was sitting and put her arm about her shoulder. Celeste was cold and tense, and her face gave no indication that anyone else was present in the room.

Someone knocked at the door, but Celeste seemed not to hear. For a moment Angelique waited, then rose from the couch and answered the knock. Before her stood a contingent of men from the fortress Ville Marie. They asked if Gabriel Dublanche was there, and when she told them he was not, they asked to see Madame Dublanche. Angelique ushered them in. The captain stood with his feet apart, his hands clasped behind his back, looked closely at Celeste, who in no way acknowledged his greeting, and said, "Madame Dublanche, does this belong to your husband?" He held out his left hand, palm-up, and revealed a silver crucifix. In script on its back was engraved the name Catherine Dublanche. The sturdy ring that had held it to its chain had been twisted open. The captain continued, "We found it this morning in the hand of a dead man—a man who only last night was shot to death with a bullet through the head." He paused, waiting for Celeste's answer.

But Celeste sat as she had for the last quarter hour, looking straight ahead and saying not a word. "Madame Dublanche, answer me, please."

Angelique answered for her. "Captain, I told Madame Dublanche the terrible news only a few moments ago. I'm afraid she's in no condition to answer questions, and as for myself, I do not know whether the crucifix belonged to Monsieur Dublanche or not."

The captain wrapped up the crucifix, and placed it in his pocket. He looked intently at Celeste for one more moment, and then the men left. Angelique stayed. Then, when the two women were alone, Celeste broke her silence. In a flat, unemotional tone she said, "Mademoiselle Fontaine, please leave my house at once."

"Leave?" Angelique leaned forward, puzzled.

"Please."

"But Madame Dublanche—Celeste—I've come to help you."

"I do not want your help. I'm certain there is more to the story of Mademoiselle Angelique Fontaine and Monsieur Gabriel Dublanche than you have told me. Now please go."

Angelique bit her lower lip and stood to her feet. "I will go, Madame Dublanche," she said calmly, without a trace of anger, "but you wrong me, and you wrong your husband. I have told you everything."

And she left, wondering. Celeste had shown no concern for Gabriel. She did not ask where he might have gone, nor did she express any interest in Angelique's welfare or thank her for bringing word. Perhaps it is only the shock, Angelique thought. But the more she dwelt on the question, the more she came to believe that Celeste was in the grip of a silent, cold rage.

Angelique did not return to the Dublanche house. That evening she learned that Celeste had booked passage for two on the first sailing of the cutter *Candide*.

Nightfall found Gabriel sitting in front of his fire listening to the rain drip, drip, drip from the eaves.

Suddenly he sat upright, shutting out every thought in order to listen. From somewhere out in the soggy undergrowth came a muffled sound. An electric current shot through his body when a voice called out, "Gabriel."

Angelique had finally come, but not alone. A large man followed her in. Like a barrier to freedom, he filled the doorway.

"Gabriel," Angelique said, "this is Paul Robertson. Paul is a clerk for the Lefleur company."

Gabriel breathed a great sigh of relief and said, "Yes. I've met Monsieur Robertson before."

Angelique continued, "He helped me get here. . . ." She paused and watched Gabriel's eyes. "And you're going to need his help to get away."

Gabriel's eyes widened. He whispered, "To get away?"

"Yes." Her voice was softer than before. "I'm sorry, Gabriel, but the prosecutor says he cannot let the murder pass. He agreed that it was well for everyone that the man is gone, but feels if he did not prosecute, it would be a glaring omission of his duty."

"And everyone understands that I'm the killer?"

"Yes," she answered. "I hid nothing." She paused for a moment and asked, "Have you missed your crucifix?"

Gabriel raised his right hand and felt again the loose chain about his neck. "Yes. But I don't know where I lost it. How did you know?"

Angelique smiled sadly. "You lost it in the hand of a dead man.

When Lecharbonnier grabbed for your throat he caught the crucifix. They pried it out of his dead fingers. It has a woman's name on the back—Catherine Dublanche.''

"My mother.'' Gabriel's gaze fell to the floor and he put his head in his hands. "What will this do to her?'' Then he brightened and said, "But she won't hear the news for a long while. Perhaps this can all be cleared up in time to save her the shock.''

"No, Gabriel. Right now the marines stationed at Ville Marie are searching everywhere for you, house to house, island to island. You're going to have to stay here a little while longer. We'll put out the fire, and make it appear that you've been here and left. Then you must hide in the cellar. Paul and I will conceal the cellar door under a pile of firewood, and you'll stay there until the search is over.''

"And after the search?'' Gabriel asked.

"After the search, Paul and I will help you. In a few weeks the Lefleur canoes will be setting out for the interior. Paul will enter you into the register of canoemen—not under your real name, of course—and you'll go into the interior with them.''

Suddenly Gabriel felt caged. In a tone near anger he protested, "Now wait. You've laid your plans, but you haven't asked me. There are other choices. I can go to the prosecutor and surrender. I'll do what has to be done to put the whole thing behind me, and—''

"I'm afraid not, Monsieur Dublanche.'' The large man spoke for the first time. In perfect French, accented with a pronounced Scottish brogue, he continued, "You did kill the man. You did it in a mad fit, and God knows he deserved it, but the law makes no such fine distinctions. As surely as you go back, you will die.''

Gabriel sat staring with empty eyes into the fire, properly subdued, trying to take it all in. After a few moments he asked, "How far into the interior?''

Robertson answered, "Over a thousand miles.''

Gabriel shook his head slowly.

"I won't do it. I won't leave Celeste and Michel.''

Angelique's large black eyes were sad in the firelight.

"Celeste is already gone, Gabriel. She and Michel sailed this morning on the *Candide*.''

PART TWO

1746–1747

CHAPTER 15

Toward the Unknown

THE sky was perfectly clear. A pleasant springtime chill hung in the damp early-morning air. A cast of deep green had settled on the trees that grew thickly along the riverbanks, filling their arms with new life. The bright rays of the early-morning sun warmed Gabriel Dublanche's back as he stood outside Fort de la Chine on the southwest end of Montreal Island, waiting for Paul Robertson and the Lefleur canoemen to gather.

It was Monday morning, the fourteenth of May, six weeks after the death of Jonathan Lecharbonnier. It had been a long and bitter wait.

Gabriel's mind was like a boil, infected with hatred for the dead man whose curse insisted on hanging over his life. He was angry at being forced to hide, wounded by Celeste's desertion, and struck with sharp, deep pain at the separation from his son. If only Pierre had been here; he would have helped, he would have understood. But Pierre was four thousand miles away and did not yet know. It would be at least another seventeen days before Celeste and Michel would arrive at Rouen and break the news. Ocean passage being what it was, they might never reach home at all. They could at this very moment be dead for all Gabriel knew.

For the first time in his life, Gabriel felt alone, truly alone. Every tie to those he loved had been cut; he'd been separated irrevocably from every old friend, every familiar face. His world was new, but it was a grimy world, cursed with utter loss.

Last night, with a full moon to show him the way, Gabriel had come from his island by canoe as far as the foot of the de la Chine rapids; he had then cut across land and reached Fort de la Chine an hour before sunrise. He now was about to step even deeper into this dark continent.

This morning the canoemen would come from outlying farms up and down the river valley and converge at this place to begin the incredibly long voyage into the interior. The thought of the gathering men made him uneasy. What if someone recognized him? On the other hand, he reassured himself, while some might have heard his name, none would know his face. Gabriel did know the clerks, and they knew him, but Robertson had assured him they could be trusted, for they, too, had disliked the man known as Charcot, and had pledged themselves to silence.

The sun was two hours from the horizon when the first men stepped from the bordering forest and signaled for a light canoe to ferry them across. They came alone and in little groups, Frenchmen and mixed bloods all—French-Ottawa, French-Huron, French-Iroquois—recruited from Boucherville, Pointe Claire, Isle de Jesus, Saint Pierre, and from as far away as Three Rivers.

Gabriel had never seen such men. They appeared to have been bred for the task at hand. Most were five and a half feet tall or less, their legs short, their hips narrow so that in the canoes they took little space. But their upper bodies were a contradiction, with broad shoulders and strong backs that could carry hundreds of pounds on the treacherous carries.

Obviously they were men with a sense of romance and style. Each was a splash of color; tassel-tipped knitted wool hats were everywhere, some blue, most red, and many sprouted feathers or plumes. The men wore them pulled down nearly to their eyebrows, set at a jaunty angle with the top half neatly folded over to form a ridge on top and pinned to one side with a silver cross or brooch. To offer some protection against the black clouds of mosquitoes that hovered over the wilderness lakes, every canoeman wore his dark hair shoulder length.

Their broadcloth and calico shirts, in every color of the rainbow, were long-sleeved, and hung to midthigh, partially concealing the fact that they wore no pants. Rather, an azion, or breechcloth, of wool ran over a belt in front and behind, passing between their brown, sinewy legs. As protection against brush and rocks, each wore a pair of deerskin leggings suspended by a cord that ran from the belt down each leg. On their feet they wore only soft deerskin moccasins.

As they materialized out of the forests, the men came shouting and laughing and clapping one another on the back. These were friends, old traveling companions who had been apart since the previous autumn, and now in the excitement of reunion they gestured wildly and made animated inquiry about health, family, and fortune. Gabriel looked on and thought how like children they seemed, uncomplicated, straightforward, obviously lovers of life.

But in the pit of his stomach, Gabriel felt an emptiness, an uneasiness at being part of these men whose lives were so different from his own. Would they tolerate him? Could he keep up with the pace? With the exception of three of the younger ones, all of them had voyaged before, every one of them had grown to manhood knowing that someday he would be a canoeman.

Robertson had warned him that the work was hard, and that each night he would lie down with every ounce of his strength drained away. Gabriel was strong, but never before had he labored as hard as this task would demand. Gabriel thought, That will be good. I won't be able to think of anything but staying alive.

The rest of the morning they spent preparing the canoes— sewing, caulking, patching, making watertightness certain. Though he had seen these canoes from a distance, this was the first time Gabriel had examined one closely. Built by the Chippewas—a skill passed from generation to generation over centuries of time— each canoe was a work of art, a poem composed of ribs of white cedar, a skin fashioned from the bark of the yellow birch sewn with thread from fine root of red spruce, and caulked with melted resin of the white pine. More graceful than any boat or ship Gabriel had ever seen, they reminded him of the dragon ships his mother told him about in his childhood. Did the old Norsemen reach these shores and inspire the Chippewa design, he wondered?

But between these canoes and the ones the Chippewas made for their own use, there was one great difference: size. These were made especially for the fur companies, and were enormous. Six feet across at the center, thirty-six feet or more long, they were called "six-fathom canoes." Each carried seven thousand pounds of freight, and a crew of fourteen men with their gear.

Now the great canoes sat empty, floating lightly in the water, fourteen of them, quietly waiting, every line flowing with consummate grace between high-pointed prow and stern, painted with bright greens, reds, and whites; the most striking man-made objects of the great north.

Paul Robertson did not ask Gabriel by what name he wished to be called, but entered him in the roster as Gabriel Leclair. As the two men stood together on the riverbank above the canoes, Robertson wrote it down, saying, "I always liked the name Leclair. You'd better get used to answering to it, at least till we get past the Height of Land. After that, it won't matter what they call you."

Just then Gabriel felt a firm hand on his shoulder and heard a resonant masculine voice say, "Monsieur Paul, I have not had the honor of meeting this young gentleman. Please introduce us."

Gabriel could not at first believe the mismatch of the man and his manner. A pleasing voice, perfect diction, manners refined as any that one might encounter in Paris; Gabriel's ears registered style, taste, and a ring of kindness. But the man was a simple canoemen, dressed like all the others, his red cap set back on his head and shocks of perfectly white hair streaming down and gathered behind his ears.

The old man's face was like the north country, riven by crevices, obviously the product of a lifetime of smiles and laughter. One eye closed over an empty socket, while the other jigged and danced about.

His nose looked as though it had been pinched in a blacksmith's vise, much too large for his face, narrow, and all edge. And yet, for all his facial imperfections, the man's teeth shone white in the morning sun; even, unstained, not one missing.

His shirt was new, but his leather leggings and moccasins were stained dark with the grease of spilled food and the dust of thousands of portages. His sinewy old thighs and hips were exposed from knee to belt, and his loincloth sagged beyond the limits of decency, a condition of which he was no doubt aware, but with which he was not at all concerned.

Robertson introduced the old man to Gabriel as August Bonaventure. Flashing a broad smile, his one eye twinkling with inquisitiveness, Bonaventure began to ask questions. "I have not seen you before, Leclair. Your speech tells me you are from our mother country. Am I not correct?"

Question followed question. "How long have you been here? Why on earth did you come? Do you understand how rigorous a canoeman's life can be?" He looked Gabriel up and down and asked, "Do you really think you are up to it?"

Bonaventure may have been an intrusive old man, but Gabriel liked him for his good humor, and he sensed that his presence would make the entire venture more tolerable. When at last the old man turned to go, his one eye reflected a flash of morning light as he said to Gabriel, "Leclair, there is not a man here who would not gladly give his life for any other man in the brigade. Count on us. We are your friends."

Suddenly there was a bustle of new activity as the men laid new-cut saplings in the bottoms of the canoes to help evenly distribute the weight of the men and packs. The freight—blankets and strouding, coarse woolen cloth, calico, pins and beads, scarlet yard goods, gartering, flour and pork, silver animals, crosses, and brooches—all packed in big canvas sacks, each weighing ninety pounds, was spread on the shore. There were forged hand axes and copper kettles, shot, powder, and guns. But no Lefleur canoe carried rum or brandy wine for Indian trade, for Pierre had a conscience, and he followed the instruction of the Jesuit fathers who had seen firsthand what rum and brandy had done to American family life throughout the interior.

In a flurry of activity the men carried the sacks down to the water. Soon the canoes, floating more deeply now, were loaded and waiting, while nearly two hundred Lefleur voyagers stood by, ready to embark.

Whole families—parents, children, wives, old and dear friends—had come to see off many of the men. True to their childlike character, unembarrassed by shows of affection, the men broke in sobs, and from one end of the gathering to the other rose anguished, tearful wails.

Bonaventure's wife and married daughter embraced him as though their hearts would break. "Be careful, little one," he said to his daughter as she squeezed him tightly. "You'll break my ribs and I'll not be able to go."

"Oh, Papa," she said, "I wish I could, then you would stay with us always." And she squeezed all the more tightly.

All this weeping, all these tears, all the tenderness conspired to make Gabriel feel more alone than ever. He stood at the crowd's edge, nauseated with loneliness, terrified of the unknown interior, drawn toward France, his homeland, as strongly as if he were tied to it by a cable, wishing desperately that he had not consented to this scheme, and feeling very sorry that he had no one to tell *him* good-bye, when on his bare forearm he felt the touch of a soft young hand and looked about to see Angelique Fontaine standing beside him, tears coursing down her lovely dark face.

In a rush of emotion he threw his arms around her and held her tightly, nearly lifting her from the ground. Gabriel was not in love with Angelique, and she was not in love with him, but they were now bound together for life. Her tears were for them both.

Finally they simply stood and looked into each other's eyes, his hands on her waist, her arms resting on his. It would be easy to fall in love with this compassionate, lovely woman, he thought. But he remembered Celeste.

"My heart is breaking for you, Gabriel," Angelique said. "I don't want you to go away."

"Angelique," he answered in a quiet voice filled with urgency, "come with me."

"No. It's not possible," she answered.

"Yes," he urged. "There's nothing to keep you, and Robertson would be glad to have you come."

"I cannot, Gabriel. In another week I will go downriver to Quebec and stay there for a little while. Then I'll go on to Boston before the summer's end. I want to come with you, Gabriel, but I can't." She continued, "If it had not been for me, this would not have happened to you." The lower lids of her dark eyes swam with tears.

He shook his head vigorously. "No! Not true, Angelique. Lecharbonnier is responsible for all this."

She looked into his eyes and wondered that he had not yet seen it—that a man does what he does not because he is forced to do it, but because that is what he wants to do, that Lecharbonnier could not be blamed for the actions of Gabriel Dublanche. But her heart went out to him in spite of that blindness, and she felt that if only they had come together in another time and place, she could have loved this man.

"I almost didn't come," she said. "I was afraid someone would be watching me, and that I would only lead them to you. But I couldn't bear to think of you here, alone, with no one to tell you good-bye. I wish there were some other way. I think we could become very good friends."

"And I think we already have." Gabriel smiled tenderly. "Thank you, Angelique, for coming. Thank you for being my friend." He paused, smiled slightly, and wiped a tear from her left cheek. "And thank you for your tears. I won't forget them . . . and I won't forget you. Until I come back to Montreal, I'll see your face in my memory. And when I return, I will find you, no matter where you are."

"Do, Gabriel," Angelique pleaded softly. "Please do."

Suddenly, from the water's edge, Robertson's voice rang out. "Time enough. Let's be on our way!"

The chorus of weeping rose again, but Angelique looked up at Gabriel and smiled. She put her arms around his neck, stretched on tiptoe, and kissed him. He was surprised, for she kissed him lingeringly, as one would kiss a lover. His head swam with the tenderness of her soft, full lips—exquisitely sweet—beyond description, outstripping imagination.

Robertson interrupted them without apology. "Gabriel, this is your canoe. I'll be in right behind you."

In the space of three minutes he was paddling in rhythm with the others, and fourteen clear ringing voices rose around him, singing the song old Henri of the red suspenders had sung a dozen years ago.

> At the clear running fountain
> Sauntering by one day,
> I found it so compelling
> I bathed without delay.
> Your love long since overcame me,
> Ever in my heart you'll stay.

Gabriel paddled awkwardly, with his face turned toward Angelique, who yet stood waving on the shore. He watched her recede into the distance, turned, and set his eyes toward the wilderness.

CHAPTER 16

Over the Edge

ONLY once that afternoon did the men stop singing. The brigade had paddled for an hour and a half, traveling west from Fort de la Chine, past the northeast side of Isle Perot, and was rounding the western tip of Isle de Montreal when the song grew soft, then stopped altogether. Without signal each man quietly lifted his paddle from the water; the canoes lost momentum and glided soundlessly to land.

The voyagers waded ashore, fell in line, and climbed silently up a staircase that had many years before been cut in the hard red rock, each step now worn smooth. Something restrained Gabriel from asking why they should be stopping here or why the mood of the men had changed. But soon he saw.

At the top of the rugged promontory, exposed to the fury of western winds and to the storms of winter and summer, fastened firmly to the unyielding rock where it stood looking out over the Lake of Two Mountains, sat the church of Saint Anne. Saint Anne's would be the last place of worship they would see for many months to come. It flashed through Gabriel's mind that it might be his last for many years.

The men entered reverently, crossed themselves, and knelt to pray, asking Saint Anne, mother of the Blessed Virgin, to give them strength and protect them on the long voyage ahead. Then, one by one, they dropped coins in a box for a Mass to be said on their behalf.

Robertson did not kneel, but stood at the back of the little sanctuary with his head bowed while the men completed their devotions. Robertson was a devout man, a member of the Church of Scotland, neither welcome nor inclined to take part in these Catholic proceedings, but he respected his men and their beliefs. This he was able to do only because he had strayed sufficiently from his stern Calvinist raising to doubt that God would damn a man for a mistake in judgment. If in order to reach heaven, he reasoned, it was necessary to understand Christ perfectly, there was no hope for anyone. Rather than doctrinal perfection, Robertson relied on the words "the merciful shall obtain mercy."

But Gabriel Dublanche held back for a different cause. Now, even more than when Michel was killed over a decade ago, he was bitter and unbelieving. Not only had he lost his homeland, his family, and his friends, he had lost his God as well. He did not kneel because he had no one to whom he might pray.

Even so, long habit and the desperate love he felt for his little son, for his mother and father, and even for Celeste, made him want to pray. Yet he fought the impulse, for it seemed to him that those for whom he had prayed with the greatest fervor had all come to the greatest harm. Now he risked prayer for no one but himself, for, he thought, he had nothing more that could be taken from him, nothing but life itself, and at this moment that would be no loss.

No one asked why he did not kneel, and no one inquired about the silver chain that dangled loosely from his neck, though each saw plainly that he wore a rosary without a Christ.

Dropped from the edge of the earth—that was the feeling in Gabriel's breast.

Though the Genoese had proved that the world was round, if Gabriel Dublanche paddled westward for thrice five thousand miles, he would not again find civilization as he had known it.

On the Lake of Two Mountains, the flotilla of canoes crossed twenty-five miles of quiet water, and then, where the lake narrows at Pointe Fortune and Saint André, they entered the mouth of the treacherous Ottawa River. For the next three hundred miles this stubborn stream would force them to fight for every inch of ground gained. Between here and Grand Portage on Lake Superior they would empty the canoes eighteen times, carrying both craft and cargo around rapids, obstructions, and falls. Another eighteen times they would carry the freight and float the lightened canoes over shallows and rapids.

A spirit of fierce competition drove Gabriel to keep up with his companions. "Who can carry the most packs at one time on this portage?" they would call. And rather than walk along, they ran, no matter how crushing the load.

All the while Gabriel, resentful at his forced retreat, grew moody and held the men at arm's length. For a while the voyagers tried to tease him out of his withdrawal. But after a while, discouraged by his unresponsiveness, in spite of their innate friendliness, they let him alone. Gabriel's sense of isolation deepened.

Days began before sunup and ended only when the long, northern light faded and the river disappeared into darkness. Except for breakfast, noon, and the exhausting carries, the paddles dipped endlessly, plunging, pulling hard against the relentless current, lifting and dipping and pulling again, forty times every minute, sixteen hours every day, six days every week, in sunshine or in storm.

It is the nature of a river to wind and snake its crooked way among the lowest crevices of the earth. The hills and even the meadows rose to shield it from all breezes that would otherwise cool the laboring voyagers.

Gabriel often bowed over the gunnel to empty his stomach, or knelt beside a portage trail and retched until every internal organ seemed ready to pour from his throat and mouth.

As he dogtrotted along the trail, the great packs jiggled and rubbed and chafed the skin of his back. Where the loads met projections of bone and muscle, blisters rose and festered. Every night the sores forced him to lie facedown on his blanket, too exhausted to sleep, while his arms and legs quivered violently and he waited for merciful oblivion to swallow him.

Every morning, after what seemed only moments, Robertson's voice would call out, "Up men! On our way!" Choruses would rise from the awakened men, "No. Not already!" or "Drown the clerk," and Gabriel would force himself from the blankets and begin his trial by water all over again.

Every morning his muscles screamed to be still. When he lifted the sacks to his back again, the coarse cloth tore at the blisters and made them raw and red again.

On the eleventh day they turned from the Ottawa into the Mattawa, a swift, narrow stream that, while only thirty miles long, would oppose them with even greater vigor and threaten them with greater dangers. Before entering its boulder-guarded mouth, the voyagers took off their caps and bowed their heads while a man in every canoe stood and begged God for protection against the hazards of this turbulent stream.

The voyagers were ending their second day on the Mattawa, their thirteenth from Montreal. They had finished the carry around Paresseux Talon, the Lazy Heel, the hardest portage between Montreal and Athabasca, and had fought on another three miles beyond when the light began to fail. Here, on the Mattawa's north side, a beach of sand sloped gradually up from the water's edge. Dark majestic spruce grew above the banks, making the cut of the river seem like a deep, green canyon.

Toward this beach of sand the steersman in the lead canoe now turned his bow. Within minutes the freight was unloaded and stowed under oilcloth sheets beneath the overturned canoes.

The cook from Gabriel's canoe was a thin little man, past forty, with a wrinkled forehead and a black, bushy mustache that drooped on the sides. His name was Pierre Hippolyte, but the men called him "Le Renard," the Fox. Nicknaming was a game to the voyagers, every man being called by some name exactly opposite to his most outstanding characteristic. True to the custom, Pierre was less than bright, but he was good at heart and pleasant as any man among them, though he irritated them with his incessant chatter. He had no teeth, and as he talked, his quick lips bubbled the words like air percolating upward in a kettle of water, breaking the surface musically with little pops and gurgles.

In the evening's faint remaining light, Le Renard flitted about to prepare supper. His legs were bowed from many years in the canoe and from carrying loads beyond his strength, and now, with quick, rocking steps, he darted here and there through the soft sand. Having filled his biggest kettle with river water and having set it over blazing logs, he now poured in flour, then cut in big pieces of a mixture of dried meat, berries, and melted fat. The resulting soup they called "rubbaboo."

Gabriel was amazed at how the men ate this concoction. If in a hurry, they poured it into some small hollow in a nearby rock, let it cool for a moment, and like dogs, lapped it with their tongues. They had become creatures of convenience and necessity.

When the meal was over and his utensils put away, Le Renard shuffled toward the overturned canoe beneath which Gabriel lay exhausted and stood for a moment, waiting for Gabriel's recognition.

"Monsieur Gabriel," he finally said. His high voice was quiet and apologetic. "Monsieur Gabriel, if you do not mind, I would like to talk with you."

Gabriel rolled onto his side, lay his head on his bent arm, and looked up. Firelight flickered orange on Le Renard's weathered face, and reflected from his small, close-set eyes.

"What is it, Pierre?" Gabriel winced as he spoke, for moving had irritated the painful blisters on his back.

"The sand feels better to sleep on than last night's rocks, doesn't it, Monsieur Gabriel?"

"It does, Pierre," Gabriel answered wearily. "It surely does."

The older man paused for a long moment and then began, "Monsieur Gabriel, I hope you will pardon me for intruding, but I can see that every day you grow sicker and weaker than the day before. You are falling farther and farther behind. You break the paddle's rhythm and stumble badly along the track."

Gabriel drew a deep breath. "You're right. I tell you the truth, Pierre, I don't know if I'm going to make it. I may die before Grand Portage."

"Would it offend you if I offered advice, monsieur?" the man asked as delicately as he knew how.

"No, Pierre," Gabriel said, "I wouldn't be offended. If you have advice for me, please give it."

"Thank you, monsieur. Thank you. I will tell you what I think. I think you have three problems. First, you are not accustomed to this hard way. Eventually you will grow stronger."

"Well, not so far, Pierre," Gabriel responded. "You said yourself I'm getting weaker every day."

"But, that is because of your second problem. This work is hard, and you do not eat enough. You lose flesh from your body and strength from your arms and legs. You must eat more, much more."

"But I lose everything I eat, Pierre. Even now my throat's raw from vomit and bile."

"Yes, I know," Pierre argued. "You eat in the morning and lose it in the morning. You eat at noon, and lose all of that in the hot afternoons. But tonight, you ate nothing. You came straight to bed, hoping to sleep.

"You must eat at night, let it strengthen you as you sleep. Then eat in the day as well; perhaps small bits that will lie light in your belly." He handed Gabriel a small sack closed tight with a drawstring. "Here. I've cut pemmican for you. Tomorrow, eat from it as you paddle. And tonight, before you sleep, come to the fire and eat a bowl of rubbaboo."

Gabriel smiled up at him. "I expect you're right, Pierre. I'll do it." He paused, then asked, "But what's my third problem?"

"Third problem?" Pierre asked uneasily.

"Yes. You said I had three problems. What's the third?"

The little man stumbled for words, then said, "I do not know, monsieur, but I can see that it is a problem of the mind—something that makes you suffer in your heart. Perhaps more than any other thing, it is taking away your strength. A man such as I should not give advice on matters like these to a man such as you, but—"

Gabriel broke in impatiently, "What do you mean, Pierre, 'like you,' 'like me'? What am I like? What are you like? How are we different?"

Pierre smiled apologetically. "I am . . . Le Renard. That is what they call me because I am slow." He tapped his forehead and grinned. His empty gums glistened in the firelight. Then he went on. "But you, Monsieur Gabriel, you are a smart man. So"—he chuckled nervously—"I should not presume to tell you what is good."

In the quiet moment that followed, Gabriel thought sadly of the pride men take in the differences between them, and the all-too-neat categories into which even simple men place themselves and their fellows. At length he answered, "Pierre, I once thought that I was—as you say—a smart man, but now I do not know. Even if I am, I doubt my life has been better than yours. In fact, I expect you have made fewer mistakes, and hurt fewer people, than I." He paused again, and then said, "So go ahead with your advice. I want to hear it."

Pierre nodded his head and smiled gratefully. "Thank you, monsieur. You give a foolish man courage. I was going to say, I think you should tell someone your secret. If the blisters on your back could be opened, and then you let them rest, they would heal. If the blister that festers in your mind could be opened, and then you had rest, perhaps it, too, would heal."

Gabriel lay still thinking, while Pierre sat with his arms around his knees, looking down at his own feet, embarrassed that he had said too much. Finally Gabriel answered, "Le Renard is a truer name than I knew, Pierre. Thank you. I'll do as you say." Then he struggled to his feet, sat down by the fire, and ate his fill of Pierre's rubbaboo.

The next day the Mattawa ended, and the flotilla ran smoothly out onto Lake Nipissing. After crossing to Nipissing's southern shore where it flows into the French River, the brigade exploded with laughter and shouting, for since leaving Montreal, the French was the first river to flow in the direction of their travel.

Three easy days brought them to the great lake of the Hurons, where they bore west along its northern shore. After emerging from Georgian Bay and passing Birch Island, the brigade divided. Seven canoes would follow a southern route to Mackinec and there disperse to trading posts on Lake Michigan.

Gabriel's canoe was among the other seven that continued along the northern shore of Huron until coming to the short River of Mary and to the foot of the mile-long rapid known as Sault Sainte Marie. There they portaged upward to the head of the sault and at last stood gazing northwest across the greatest freshwater sea in all the world, the one Father Marquette one hundred and thirty

years before had called "Superior," but called by the peoples
who lived on its shores "Chi-o-ni-ga-mig," the Great Water.

Gabriel's condition had improved so much that he now relished
the hard labors of this voyage. New tone filled the muscles of his
arms, and he had not vomited in days. The last two hundred miles
had been by lake, a straight course without carries, and the blisters on his back had rested and healed.

But more important, Gabriel had found a friend and opened
his mind to him.

At first he had thought it would be Robertson to whom he would
tell his troubles. Robertson knew Gabriel's past and knew his
mental agony. Besides, Robertson was a good man. He was scru-
pulously honest, gave fair measure, made true entries in the company books, and every Sunday insisted that his men gather around
him for scripture and prayers.

Yet in spite of what Robertson knew, in spite of his intelligence,
his integrity, and his fairness, Gabriel felt in him a certain absence
of sympathy. Gabriel did not want someone to pity him, but he
did need someone who could tell him he was not an utterly evil
man, that there was still hope for his life's redemption, and that
God, if indeed there was a God, might in mercy answer even the
prayers of Gabriel Dublanche.

But Robertson, Gabriel now saw, was too stern a man to feel
empathy with a murderer, too much in control of himself to understand that other men are truly weak, and too reserved to give
the emotional assurances Gabriel craved. Calvinist that he was,
he might even tell Gabriel that he had been damned from the
beginning, and that his sins were only confirmation of his lostness. Gabriel could not risk hearing a verdict like that. Even
though he doubted the existence of God, he still could not live
without words like "purpose," "value," "evil," and "good."

Deep within, Gabriel knew he would welcome the appearance
of someone who could restore the confidences on which his life
had been built. Although faith in life and purpose seemed utterly
irrational at this moment, still he longed for the simple beliefs he
had once held. Right now, more than anything, he needed the
confidence necessary simply to go on living. And he was sure
Robertson could not give him that.

So Gabriel had turned to the human flame that presently warmed
him most, the simple, unassuming Pierre Hippolyte. Gabriel had

opened his heart to this man, and Pierre had responded with the kindness he sought.

Le Renard had no theology—at least he would have said that he did not. But he did have two qualities Gabriel needed. He was a kind man who felt deeply, and he had never doubted as Gabriel now doubted.

Pierre had wept silently as Gabriel told him his story, and then one night, camped on the north shore of Georgian Bay, Pierre had told Gabriel a story of his own.

"I live alone," he said, "on the edge of Trois-Rivières, a small village a day and a half downriver from Montreal. But Trois-Rivières has not always been my home. When I was a young man, full of life and happiness, I had a wife and a little girl, and we lived together in the valley of the Montmorency, north of the Saint Lawrence, not far from Quebec. We had a little farm, and in the winters I trapped for beaver and sold them to a fur buyer who came our way every spring.

"We were very happy, we three, my wife Eva, my child Anne, and I. Anne was the light of my life. But in the autumn of twenty-five, I went deep in the woods to hunt for winter meat, and was gone for several days. I came home with a fine doe across my shoulders. When I entered the clearing, I called out, 'Eva! Anne! I'm home.' But no one answered. Then, on my way to the house, I saw it—a new grave marked with a cross of rough sticks broken from a tree.

"Eva was alone in the house. I found her by the small south window, the sun lighting her worn face. She did not lift her eyes when I came in. She just sat, holding in her hands a little doll I had made for my child. Two days after I had gone into the woods, Eva had been cooking their supper, and little Anne had been helping her about the hearth when Anne's dress caught fire.

"Before my wife could reach her, the fire was all about the child. Anne was terribly burned, but did not die until two days later, and all that time the burns hurt her and made her scream with pain. She called out for her papa, saying that if only I would come I could make the hurt go away.

"You will know, my friend, that my heart was broken. My dear Eva was never again the same, and before Christmas she died also." As Pierre spoke big tears rolled down his simple face, glistening orange in the firelight, dripping from his chin.

"For eighteen years now I have been alone. I tried to forget by becoming a canoeman, but one doesn't forget such things, monsieur. It is always with me, like a pain in my side that will not go away. But these are my friends, and they make life good for me.

"Besides, if my wife and little girl had lived, perhaps some more terrible thing would have overtaken them. They might have been stolen away by the Iroquois, or my little one might have turned from the faith, so, please God, it is better this way. My suffering is a small thing. And"—here his voice became brighter—"it is not all over. I will see them both again. Our love will begin just where the fire took it from us."

He lifted his wet face and his small, close-set eyes glowed in the firelight. "And so it will be for you, Monsieur Gabriel. If Le Renard can go on, so can you. As he has for me, God will send others to help you."

It was now past the middle of June. The brigade had stopped north of Sault Sainte Marie to rest and make repairs before pushing north. Three days had passed. The other voyagers now slept, but Gabriel Dublanche sat alone on a gentle knoll and studied the night.

It was cool and fresh, the sky deep and black, unmarked by cloud or mist, filled with stars, some large and alone like fire ships set adrift on a dark, shoreless ocean; others so small they were visible only as part of a vast cloud of stars, none of which shone brightly, but together glowed, like colonies of microscopic life floating beneath the surface of a warm, still sea.

Hushed by distance, a waterfall whispered on the Sainte Marie. A young land breeze filled with night games teased the trees' fresh new leaves, and begged them to play.

Behind Gabriel heavy rotting smells crept out from hidden depressions in the forest floor to blend with the fresh clean scent floating upward from the water's edge. The sweet aroma of late spring poured softly from leaves, blades, and tendrils of luxuriant, verdant life growing everywhere along the great lake's forested shore. Before him, invisible in the utter darkness, its presence revealed only by the sound of its calm washing on the sand and the smell of its waters, lay Superior, stretching its vast arms league after league into the distance, like some giant in its bed, unable to rest.

Gabriel turned and peered southward through the darkness. Between the boughs of the trees winked burning pinpoints, lights from many distant fires. In his body Gabriel felt a cadence, a rhythmic concussion that he could not hear except now and then when the ever-changing breeze blew his way from the fires. When he heard it with his ears, there was also the melody of many voices singing in time with the deeper beat.

At the back of his neck a feeling entered Gabriel's body, flowed into his trunk and limbs, and coursed to the ends of his fingers and toes; it swelled and grew within him, a good feeling, a need to know, and something deeper yet that whispered of a supernatural kinship between himself and a people he had not seen.

This was their land, their lake, the place of the Ojibway. Because Etienne Brule had first met them here, living about Sault Sainte Marie in 1618, the French called them the Saulteurs, people of the falls. Some called them the Chippewa. They spoke of themselves as the A-wish-in-aub-ay, the Spontaneous People.

As he gazed at the minuscule lights of their fires, a curious thought struck Gabriel. It was to these very people he had wanted to come when he was a boy at Louis-le-Grand. He had heard stories about how Father Jean Brébeuf had come among them as a missionary, and how the Iroquois from the south had risen up and killed him. No wonder God did not let me come, he thought. I wasn't worthy. And now, rather than a missionary, I'm a fugitive.

Gabriel turned and gazed northward. The pole star was high in the heavens, and except for the bear that wheeled in its never-ending circle, Polaris was alone. Nothing now stood between Gabriel and the great emptiness that was the northern forest—terrible in winter cold, formidable in isolation. Tomorrow, if the weather held, they would be off again. They would cross Superior, and in a few days more Gabriel would see this land of lakes and forests in which he was to hide, a land that—at least for a time—would be his home.

CHAPTER 17

Beyond the Height of Land

WITH a start Gabriel's eyes opened wide. The first thought that came to his mind was that this was the twenty-third of June, and that he was now thirty-one years old.

He counted on his fingers the days out of Montreal. Celeste and Michel were still somewhere on the Atlantic, and his father and mother yet blissfully ignorant of what he had done. Somehow that cheered him; present enough for the day, he thought.

He rose to find a wind blowing softly from the southeast. That was good. Warm sunlight poured across the great inland sea as white-tipped waves rose up line upon line, marching away in unending procession to the farther shore.

Breakfast was over, and the voyagers, refreshed, anxious to be on their way, scurried about until the canoes bobbed waiting in the water, loaded and ready for travel. Once out on the lake's breast, makeshift sails caught the wind and bore them in a daring course north-northwest, over against the eastern end of Michipicoten Island and on under the towering cliffs of the northeastern shore.

It was an easy day, the steersman standing in the stern ruddering while the wind carried them on. The others lay propped against the great canvas bags of freight, smoking small clay pipes with short reed stems, or they sang, played cards, talked, or simply slept the passage away.

Though the voyagers had been raised and nourished in the bosom of the Church, they were a superstitious lot. Perhaps the Ojibway were right, they reasoned. Perhaps there were indeed spirits in the water, the sea, and the air. So, in order not to offend, and perhaps to win an extension of the winds that today lightened their load, a man in each canoe threw precious tobacco to the waves as an offering to La Vieille, "old woman of the wind."

And they chanted, *"Souffle, la vieille, souffle."* "Blow, old woman, blow."

The day passed pleasantly. The thin birchbark hulls rolled easily over the broad breast of the fluid deep, thrumming with life, keeping pace with the waves that sped along beside them. While the sun was yet high, with many miles behind, the brigade put in and encamped at the mouth of the White River.

When they rose next morning, the wind was gone. The air possessed an exaggerated clarity, without the slightest hint of mist, and distant islands seemed near. Up the shoreline from the south, directly over their heads, flew a great blue heron, its slow, heavy wing beats becoming slower as its long legs extended and it settled on the river's north side in the shadows of a deep marsh. Though it landed far away, its guttural squawk rang hollow along the riverbank and somehow seemed not at all far.

The stillness, the clear air, things far seeming near, sounds ringing clearly from a distance—to the weather-wise voyagers these were portents all. Within three days, they said, there would be wind or rain or sudden storm.

So they set their course to follow the shoreline, never to venture from sight of land.

There was no storm that day. The wind did not oppose them, but neither did it help them. It was a day of constant paddling under a clear sky with no relief from the rays of the terrible, burning sun.

Sweat soaked Gabriel's headband, stood glistening on the browned skin of his arms, beaded on his neck and shoulders, and gathered on his spine, trickling in rivulets down the small of his back, tickling maddeningly. When the sun began to fall before them, the sea became a golden mirror, blinding them, making the course hard to hold. Gabriel was grateful to be on the canoe's right, shielded from the worst of the glare.

But again the rigors of the toil were lessened by constant singing. The voices of the voyagers were as important as their skill or their strong backs, for the songs buoyed their spirits, metered the paddle stroke, and gave them constant pleasure.

Their melodies were not the bawdy *chansons* of sailors, but songs from home, songs they could sing to their mothers and sweethearts with never a blush, the most favored being, *"A la Claire Fontaine"*—"At the Clear, Running Fountain." But there were many songs new to Gabriel—some love songs, some about the homeland these men had never seen, some bright and fast, others slow and dreamy—and he learned to sing them all. Of fifty songs, Gabriel had two favorites, *"En Roulant Ma Boule,"* and *"C'est le Vent Frivolant"*—"Arolling My Ball," and "It's the Frivolous Wind."

What the songs did for the others, they did for him: renewed his strength, took his mind from that which was behind, and made him eager for things that lay ahead.

The third night the voyagers spent on Isle Saint Ignace, just south of Superior's northernmost point. Next morning they rose in darkness to a warm, damp wind blowing from across the lake and a feeling of change in the air. Robertson was worried. Their route from Isle Saint Ignace to Grand Portage would thread among several islands and then across the open, unsheltered mouth of Thunder Bay, ninety miles in all. The more prudent course would be to hug the shore of Thunder Bay, but it would also add days of travel. Robertson made his choice. They would try and outrun the coming weather.

Just before sunrise, they launched their canoes onto the lake's uneasy breast. Because the shore was rocky and the water chopped furiously, they worked hard to keep the frail hulls from being washed back onto the angular boulders where they would be torn to pieces. Four men stood about each canoe in heaving waist-deep water, fighting to keep their own footing and at the same time to hold the craft while it was being loaded.

With everything aboard, men in the stern and bow held off the rocks with poles while the others climbed in. Then, with a concerted sweep of the paddles, they spun each bow into the wind, and with vigorous, deep strokes, propelled their flotilla toward open water.

The sun was barely above the horizon when it disappeared again behind a thick layer of slate-gray clouds marked with rolling black patches that dropped down gusts of chilling wind. The sea rose higher and turned to dark marble.

Their task was a hard one. They must travel due southwest, parallel to the northern shore but well away from its rocks—almost impossible in the climbing wind. Numerous islands lay in their path, all too small to provide relief by leeward passage.

The wind was in their faces, slightly from the left and growing stronger, sweeping up from Superior's most distant point, having blown across two hundred and fifty miles of unobstructed sea. They met the great rollers head-on, aiming the bow directly into each wave, knowing that if one caught them from the side they would be swamped or overturned. As each roller came on the men poised their paddles in midair, then in unison dipped and pulled with all their might, and the high, sharp bows answered the surge of power by riding up and over. The water ran hard at the gunnel's edge, but not a drop came aboard.

Whatever Viking blood ran in Gabriel's veins rose up to answer the call. Like the foam on the face of the waves, exhilaration flowed in his heart. Here I am, he thought, in a craft made from the mere skin of a tree, held together with tree-root string, crossing a deep sea in a growing storm.

When the rollers bore them up on the crests, they could see land far to the north, but when in the troughs, mountains of surrounding water obscured their sight.

They toiled on, yet in the space of an hour progressed no more than two miles. Then, above the whistling of the wind and singing of the water past their hulls, even above the chorus of unending song, came the dim, angry rumble of thunder. The rumble grew louder, the clouds darkened and lowered. Bright jagged lines of forked lightning cut across the deep, blue-green background of sea and cloud.

Far ahead sheets of rain began to fall, coming in such torrents the clouds themselves seemed to descend and the sea rise up to meet them. When he saw the advancing rain, Robertson, in the lead canoe, ordered the steersman to make for the shelter of the nearest island. The steersman swung his sweep to the right and angled the bow away from the oncoming waves as much as he dared. In desperation the men pulled with all their strength for the small, nameless speck in the distant mouth of Black Bay.

Every man bent his back, forcing every ounce of muscle into the paddle's sweep. The steel-gray water swept around the thin hulls with such speed the skin thrummed a single, long, unchanging note. In a voice that rang above the roaring wind the steersman sang out a new song, "It's the Oars." Ninety voices picked up the melody and the canoes leaped forward.

When at last the bow of the first canoe scraped into the sand, the rain was right behind. Some of the men snatched the great packs from the canoes, threw them on the beach, and covered them against the storm, while others pulled the canoes from the water, turned them over on the sand, and tied them down, then spread tarpaulins above and blankets below.

Then, faces flushed, breathing hard, exhilarated at the victorious effort, the canoemen crawled beneath their hasty shelters and broke out their pipes, still singing as the rain beat down harmlessly over their heads.

In the gray, cold wash of the wet and windy day, every heart was light, as stories, songs, and laughter passed among them. But Gabriel pulled a thick, woolen blanket about his shoulders and thought of home.

At the same moment, five thousand miles away, the frigate *Amiable*, having received French passengers from the *Candide* at Acadia, docked at Rouen, France. Celeste Dublanche and her son Michel stepped onto the quay, hired a carriage, and drove to the home of Pierre and Emilie Lefleur. There, with sullen arrogance written boldly across her once lovely face, Celeste broke the news of Gabriel's infidelity, his crime, and his desertion.

Pierre found the pill hard to swallow. He loved Celeste more than he loved his own life, but she could be mistaken, especially in her present state of mind. Gabriel was not above wrongdoing— no one was—but Pierre knew that if Gabriel had done this thing, he had done it under duress, and that even now he must be struggling in an agony of guilt and separation.

Many bales of Lefleur furs had been recovered from the river island, and for that Pierre was grateful. His old friend from Montreal, the unconventional, sagacious Antoine Lemonnier, had sent a letter that followed Celeste, saying he would care for the Lefleur enterprise until Pierre could dispatch a new overseer. But all this was overshadowed by the dark fate of his son-in-law.

Pierre and Emilie were not content to break the news to Abel and Catherine by letter, so on the very next day, they took Michel and left for Avranches. Celeste did not go, saying that she could not bear to see the place where they had once lived "so happily."

If Gabriel had been lost at sea or killed outright, the effect on Abel and Catherine could not have been greater. They mourned for him, both because he was gone and because of their unspeakable disappointment in what he had done. Amid many tears, their prayers rose day and night on his behalf.

Pierre made Abel and Catherine a promise. He himself would

return to Montreal to search for Gabriel. But, he warned, if Gabriel was found, the consequences might be more severe than if he were lost to them forever.

For three days wind and rain locked Robertson and his men in the mouth of Black Bay. For the most part they had no concerns but to rest, eat, and stay dry and comfortable.

On the fourth day the weather abated and they completed the last leg of their voyage to Grand Portage.

Grand Portage stood on the shores of a small bay on Superior's northwest side, halfway between its northern tip and Fond du Lac, the western "end of the lake." Here the shores were gentle and easily accessible, marked only by an occasional bluff. Tree-covered hills rimmed the bay and then, marching to the north, inscribed an undulating line across the sky.

The houses at Grand Portage were sturdy, built of hewn posts that stood upright at the corners, with logs mortised horizontally between. They appeared to grow from the earth itself, to have been here forever. And in fact, the post was not new. When the Europeans and Ojibway had met near Sault Sainte Marie a hundred and twenty-nine years before, the Ojibway had quickly discovered that the Europeans wanted furs, and that they were willing to pay well for them. The Ojibway began to hunt and trap for trade, and once each year they left their home and journeyed to Montreal or Quebec with their pelts. Then at last, much to Ojibway delight, the traders had come to them and had established trading points here and there in the forests and on the lakeshores.

On their own ground the Ojibway were a smiling, easygoing, peaceful people. Many French traders found them so compatible that they came to live among them, took their lovely, dark-eyed girls as wives, respected their beliefs, and settled down to raise families and live as they lived. Unlike the English to the south, the French were not there to claim land or tear the Ojibway from their ancient ways. Consequently, the Ojibway welcomed the French as brothers.

So, about forty-seven years ago, at the turn of the century, French traders had built this fort. Its chief attraction was access to the Pigeon River, doorway to the deep north. But to reach the point at which the Pigeon became navigable, one had to make a nine-mile carry—and thus the name "Grand Portage."

At Grand Portage, the men from Montreal met other voyagers

who had just arrived from the interior forts in the northern lake regions—Fort Dauphin across Lake Winnipeg, Fort Bourbon at Winnipeg's northern end, Fort Rainy on Rainy Lake, and far away Fort Athabasca.

Through the long winters, clerks at these forts had traded with the Ojibway, the Cree, the Assiniboine, the Muscotay, and the Gros Ventre. They baled and branded the furs and then, with breakup in the spring, brought them to Grand Portage, took on new supplies and trade goods, and turned back to the north again.

The trade was a great relay, two teams running to a central place of meeting, exchanging cargo, and racing against the coming cold to reach their starting points again.

Once at Grand Portage the Montreal men were free to do as they pleased. What some pleased was to eat an abundance of good food, sleep as long as they liked, drink brandy wine until they were senseless, and consort with the Ojibway girls to their heart's delight.

Revelries like these were new to Gabriel Dublanche. The closest behavior he had seen had been during his student days in Paris, and now as then, he stood apart from it. Again he thought, These men are like children. Despite their faith in God, their consciences are as unfettered as the wind itself.

Robertson spent his days negotiating with traders for furs and replenishing the food supply for those returning to Montreal. He himself would not return, for he had business at the fort on Rainy Lake and would go there to spend the winter. Gabriel would go with him.

For a few days Gabriel also was at leisure. The more time he had on his hands, the more he thought of Celeste and Michel. It was then that the idea came to him: he would begin a journal. And in happier days yet to come, as Michel grew, Gabriel would read to him of his adventures in the great American wilderness. At the post he bought paper, and then whiled away his free hours in recording his memories of the passage from Montreal to Grand Portage.

On the second of July all of the Montreal men but Gabriel started for home. Two and a half weeks later, his business done, Robertson took Gabriel and a band of winterers and set out through the ascending hills that stretched to the northwest.

That night they camped on the banks of the Pigeon River where the winterers had left their north canoes overturned and tied down among the trees. In the north, streams were shallower, and portages more frequent, so the north canoes were smaller, twenty-five feet long, six feet at the beam, and carried about half the load of the Montreal canoe—three thousand pounds and a crew of ten.

Gabriel soon discovered that these men were far more daring than the Montreal voyagers. In fact, the winterers looked down on the Montreal men, called them "pork eaters," and disdained their hardiness and endurance.

The streams here were often narrow, rushing through rocky gorges and over deep, sudden falls. The voyagers of the north delighted to test their skill against these hazards, and often Gabriel's heart was in his throat as his canoe became airborne over the lip of a chasm, or the bowman executed a ninety-degree turn to keep from dashing into a dark rock wall. The craft suffered frequent damage, so that every night, and sometimes in the day, the men pulled them to shore, melted gum, and cut new bark for repairs.

So it was that Gabriel's hard work began all over again. On the entire journey from Montreal to Grand Portage they had carried on thirty-six portages. Between Grand Portage and Rainy Lake they would carry on thirty-six more, thirteen of these before reaching a stream that would run with them. The carries all had names: Partridge, Big Rock, Caribou, Fowl, Moose, Big Cherry, Slimey, Little Cherry, Watap, Long, Marten, Perch, and Height of Land.

At the first portage the river plunged over a hundred-foot precipice. But their path was up, over shallow soil and great slabs of brown rock, wet and slick from the spray of the falls. Twice a canoe and the men under it came close to slipping over the edge. Gabriel noticed that places like these were marked with crosses, some old and weathered, some new.

By now Gabriel's body was in fighting trim and his endurance matched that of the most seasoned voyagers. He pressed forward with the best of them, and often led the brigade over the rough portage trails.

Gabriel was in the lead when they topped the Height of Land, the edge of a great plateau that stretched hundreds of miles north and west, where the water flow of the continent divided. Now once again the rivers and lakes would run in the direction of their travel. Gabriel dropped his heavy sacks and stood gazing out over the vast new terrain.

As far as his eye could see was forest: tall pine, resplendent maple, white-barked birch with pale green leaves that shimmered in the light breeze, great balsam, majestic fir and spruce pointing tall fingers into the heavens. Rolling hills far in the distance marked a blue line where land met sky.

But the most breathtaking feature of all was the lakes. In the unobserved past some primordial event of unlimited power had forced from the rocks hollows and dells that now were filled with the rains and melts of a thousand springs and winters. Gabriel was standing lost in the beauty of the sight when Robertson, coming up from behind, said sharply, "No time to linger, Gabriel. Let's move!"

Gabriel picked up the great sacks, slipped the tump line over his forehead, and dogtrotted behind the last man down to the river's edge. Soon the canoes, too, had been borne across and they were on their way again.

There had been an edge to Robertson's voice, and Gabriel took notice of it, wondering if the presence of a murderer—and a man Robertson surely took to be an adulterer as well—had begun to wear thin on the good man's conscience.

Gabriel was surprised to find that his desire to live had returned. He was well; he believed they had outdistanced all possible pursuers; and now the land's exquisite beauty lifted his spirits. He had begun to hope again, to think, to lay plans. He now dared to dream that after a year, perhaps two, in this beautiful wilderness, he might return to Montreal and find passage back to France. There he would go to Celeste and Michel, pick up the threads of his life, and start over again. And, he reasoned, while I'm waiting I must not let remorse kill me.

With this dream had come gladness. He began to enjoy the men, joined them in their campfire talks, joked with them, laughed, and played their little word games. On the trails and in the canoe, he sang with a voice as loud and joyful as the rest. Le Renard would have been delighted. But Robertson was not.

Now five days past the Height of Land, having come through Gunflint Lake, the great Saganaga, down the Ottertrack, and up the Basswood River, they stopped at sundown to camp at the southern tip of Crooked Lake, just above Lower Basswood Falls.

Supper was done, the canoes were freshly caulked, and the men sat on the broad rock where their fire was built and began to sing.

A short man with a face broader than it was long drew from his wooden chest a violin and began to play the lively "On Our Way to Paris," a drinking song extolling the joys of wine and the beautiful flowers of a lover's heart.

To everyone's surprise, Gabriel jumped to his feet and began to dance. He jigged and reeled through two songs and had begun a third when Robertson's strong, deep voice cut through the music. "That's enough! No more."

Jacques Vallee dropped the bow to his side, the clapping stopped, and the men all turned in stunned silence to Robertson.

"Dublanche." Robertson motioned toward the river. "I want to see you, over there."

A murmur ran through the cluster of men. "Dublanche?" they said. "Who is Dublanche?"

Gabriel said nothing but, his arms limp at his sides, walked out of the circle and followed Robertson to the river's edge, where the big man turned on his heel and faced him with fury in his eyes. Gabriel stood with arms crossed on his chest and looked up into the big man's face, prepared to defend whatever ground Robertson was about to invade.

"Dublanche—"

"We agreed not to use that name," Gabriel interrupted in a calm, firm voice.

"It doesn't matter what I call you out here." Robertson's Scottish brogue was thicker than ever, and his *r*'s rolled with anger.

"That may be," Gabriel answered. "But nonetheless, I'd like them to know me as they found me." He looked hard into Robertson's eyes.

Robertson was too enraged to be deterred. "When I met you, you were a poor, repentant man on the run. But now it looks to me like you're over all that, maybe even glad you left a dead man in Montreal. And you know what I think?" Robertson's intensity grew. "I think your heart's too light. I think you're glad to be done with responsibility, glad you haven't a wife and child to care for anymore!"

Gabriel's eyes widened with anger. The accusation was not only unjust, it was outrageous. He stared at the big man, then, breathing hard, pushed his face up close to Robertson's. With barely controlled fury he said, "Don't . . . don't ever say that again."

"And if I do," Robertson snarled, "will you kill me, too?"

Gabriel turned white and his arms shook at his sides. "Robertson, you have no idea what I think or how I feel. You don't know why I killed that man or what determination it takes to keep me here. I think you want me to grovel for the rest of my life. I think it galls you for a man to pick up the pieces and go on living. I think you're mad at God for not striking me down on the banks of the Saint Lawrence when that girl kissed me. You can't stand the thought that God in his heaven might forgive a man like me." Gabriel's words were coming faster. Suddenly he paused. Robertson glowered but said nothing.

"Well," Gabriel asked, "am I right or not?"

"Dublanche," Robertson answered in a voice just above an intense whisper, "stay as far from me as you can. I can't stand the sight of you." And with that, he turned and stalked away. Gabriel, avoiding the firelight and the men, bit his lip, walked up the riverbank, and disappeared into the trees.

CHAPTER 18

Huntermark's Lodge

WILHELM HUNTERMARK was seventy-four years old, born of pure German stock in the Mohawk-Schenectady valley west of the Hudson River in 1672. He was a tall man with full white hair, dark blue understanding eyes, a wide protuberant brow, a strong nose above a thick mustache, and a bush of white beard growing around his square jaw.

When a boy, Huntermark had lived and trapped among the Mohawks. In 1694, against her Quaker parents' wishes, he had married sixteen-year-old Melody Fry, and together, lured by the promise of the peaceful Ojibway and the fur-rich Canadian wilderness, they had come to New France.

Now, just a day's walk west of Crooked Lake, Huntermark lived alone. As he did every year about this time, he had camped at the base of Lower Basswood Falls, waiting for a brigade of canoemen to whom he could trade his winter's catch for a year's provisions.

He had spent the past five days out on the lake, fishing. Now, having taken a large catch of pike and walleye, he sat cutting the fish into strips and hanging the strips one by one on a long, green-sapling rack over a low fire to dry and smoke until cured.

Today was July 14. The sun had set, and Huntermark crouched on his haunches beside a fire of hot coals, enjoying the final bite of walleye. A big silver-gray dog sat across the fire from him. She had just finished a large slab of fish, and now her tongue made repeated passes backward along her upper lips as she cast her eyes anxiously toward Huntermark, hoping he would throw an extra piece her way.

As he threw the stripped skeleton into the fire, Huntermark said aloud, "Fish, you were a fine meal. I thank you for coming to my evening table." He got up and washed his hands in the cold, clear river, talking to himself in low tones. Suddenly he became aware of loud, angry voices from somewhere upstream. He stepped into the trees beside the trail and moved cautiously in the direction of the voices. The dog followed close behind.

Huntermark arrived on the edge of the clearing just in time to see Robertson enter his white canvas wall-tent and let the flap fall behind him. He knew Robertson, having met him for the first time on this very spot twelve years ago, but he had never seen the young voyager who shot up the riverbank and into the woods.

Gabriel walked aimlessly, remaining in the woods until all light was gone. When at last he had burned off his anger, he found his way out of the forest and back to the fire.

Robertson sat in the firelight with the men, and Gabriel was surprised to see a stranger sitting beside him. Everyone in the circle sat quietly, listening to what the two men were saying.

"How long has it been, Huntermark?" Robertson asked. For the sake of the other men, the two were speaking in French. The man calculated a moment before answering. "Fifty years," he said in a voice pleasantly coarse with age. "Forty alone."

"That's a long time for a man to be alone in this country," Robertson said. "Ever think of packing up and coming out?"

The man sat with his forearms over his knees, his big left hand gripping his sturdy right wrist. "I think about it, Scotty. I know I'm pushing my luck. The odds are against me if I stay out here alone much longer.'' Suddenly he laughed. ''But then, Scotty, think of it. The odds are against a man my age no matter where he lives.'' As his laughter subsided, he paused, grew serious, then picked up a stick and poked it into the fire. ''No, I couldn't stand to go back east. This is my home. Everything I've got in the world is here. There's no one back there waiting for me, and I'm content just as I am. Does get lonely, though.''

Robertson drew on his pipe and sent up a swirl of smoke. He fanned the smoke away with his hand and said, ''If you want to leave here in the spring, we'd be glad to have you come along. Passage won't cost you a thing.''

Huntermark rolled back and laughed again as he said, ''Won't cost me a thing! I've watched you fellows work this river. I know what it would cost me.''

As Gabriel listened, a plan began to form in his mind. Suddenly he spoke from his place outside the circle. ''Monsieur Hunter-mark, being lonely, perhaps you would be willing to take a partner for a while.''

A general rustle went through the group of men as all eyes turned toward Gabriel. The firmness of Gabriel's tone told Wilhelm Huntermark that the young man's question was a serious one. In the flickering firelight, he took Gabriel's measure.

''Voyaging too hard for you, son?'' he asked.

''Not too hard, monsieur, but I have reason to leave it.''

''I'm afraid,'' broke in Robertson, ''that I've done the boy wrong. Tonight I told him to get out of my sight.'' Then he turned to Gabriel and said, ''Gabriel, I'll say it right here in front of everybody. I was wrong. You have my word on it. You're as welcome in this brigade as any man here.''

Gabriel was moved by Robertson's apology. The man was as big in heart as he was in body. He stumbled for words, nodding his head awkwardly, and finally said, ''Yes. Thank you, Paul.'' He paused, looked around into the tops of the dark trees, and with a lower voice, almost as if talking now only to himself, he added, ''But still, it might be best if I stayed here. I'd have time to think . . . in a different way.''

Robertson turned again to Huntermark and said, ''He's a good man, Wilhelm. Works hard. Has a lot on his mind right now, but if he wants to stay with you, and if you want him, he'd make a good partner. Maybe you should take him on.''

The old German sat in contemplative silence. He looked first at Gabriel, then studied the back of his hand for a moment. Slowly he began to nod.

"All right. I'll take him on."

A band of Chippewa that always spent summers on the west end of Saganaga had built a canoe for Wilhelm Huntermark, one much shorter than those to which Gabriel had become accustomed, and in it the two men spent the following week fishing the deep waters of Crooked Lake.

When the brigade of voyagers had disappeared from sight on the lake's long face, Gabriel had felt empty, but he was glad now to be in one place, to be done with the incessant hurry, and to have the company of one good man.

The fishing was fine, and before it was over they had taken a large number of lake bass and a hundred pounds or more of walleye and pike. Fishing was best in the mornings and toward the close of day. During the hours between, they cut hickory for fire to smoke the catch or simply rested and, in the hours after sunset, cleaned and sliced the fish for drying.

Always one of the two stayed awake in the night to feed the fire and to drive off any marauding raccoon or bear that might try to make a midnight raid on their winter's store. For Huntermark this new arrangement was a welcome improvement, since it enabled him to sleep the whole night through.

When finally satisfied that they had caught and dried enough fish to last the entire winter, they left Lower Basswood Falls with their catch strapped to wooden frames on their backs. The provisions they had bought from Robertson—a hundredweight of flour, half as much of pemmican, a hundredweight each of lyed corn and dried peas—they cached at the falls to be retrieved later. On the ninth day after they met, the two walked into Huntermark's clearing.

His wilderness home sat on the south slope of a long ridge of hills. Below the clearing, three hundred yards through heavy growths of aspen, white spruce, and oak, was a small lake that Huntermark had dubbed the Little Vermillion. The name had come to him the evening he first saw it fifty years ago when the lowering sun had thrown a deep red across its liquid surface.

His clearing was halfway up the side of the ridge, high enough to be safe from floods and to catch the summer's cool south breeze, low enough to be sheltered against winter's screaming north winds. Here a large shelf jutted out from the hill, then dropped steeply down to the lake. The top of the ridge was another two or three hundred yards above the clearing through a forest as thick and heavy as that below.

In the clearing itself a few large trees grew, great old birches mostly, several so large that two men could not clasp hands about their trunks. The biggest of these stood midway between the cabin and the clearing's west edge. On the great tree's south side, the side bathed every day in sunlight, some words had been skillfully carved. The carving was old, and now the white bark around it had curled and framed each letter:

Wilhelm & Melody Huntermark
June 26, 1696

At the foot of the same tree, directly beneath the carving, was a greenstone marker, engraved in a similar, carefully executed script:

Melody Huntermark
Beloved Wife of Wilhelm
Born 1678–Died 1706

Across the top and down the upper third of the stone's face grew a covering of blue and orange lichen. Wild ivy, a few of its leaves blushing a mild red, twined over the dark earth of the grave. Together the colors lent a bittersweet beauty to that pain-drenched rectangle of soil.

When Gabriel saw the stone, he looked quizzically at Huntermark, but the old man kept walking and said nothing. As if to draw attention away from the grave, he nodded toward the house.

"That's it," he said, "your home for the next year, God willing. If we like each other, could be for longer."

An irregular circle of tall birches stood respectfully at a short distance around the house, as if to give it room and yet shelter it overhead with their spreading, white arms.

The house was not at all what Gabriel had expected. He had heard that trappers' cabins were nothing but dirty, roofed holes in the ground, but Huntermark had done better. This house was built of logs hewn square, and so could be called a cabin, but it was more than that. It reminded Gabriel of the country cottages in his motherland, descended from the strong homes of the ancient Celts and Scandinavians. The logs were pine, a foot through, interlocked at the corners, and the spaces between them were filled with a hard, gray clay.

A high-pitched roof—very like roofs on the houses in Normandy—topped the walls and was thatched with thick bundles of beige meadow grasses. Gabriel was surprised to see that this cabin had real windows, not just openings covered with thin-scraped deerskin parchment that let in just enough light for one to know whether it was day or night. It had glass windows—one in the front wall east of the door and one in the west—large, wide, and high enough to let in an abundance of light.

He wondered why the eaves were so low, but when the door swung open—a heavy door on two wooden hinges cleverly joined with pegs of ash—he found that he must step down to enter. Inside, the room was surprisingly spacious. The floor was three feet below ground surface, and the back wall was carved directly into the hillside. Huntermark had built his lodge for comfort against the north's terrible cold. Gabriel knew at once that even in the worst weather this house would be warm and secure.

The big fireplace in the hillside wall had a wide opening that reflected the heat back into the room, and it was faced with flat, native stone of the same variety that covered the floor. The stone was like slate, smooth and easy to clean, and Huntermark, as he was in all matters, had been meticulous in its care.

Gabriel let his eyes wander up the rafters to the high ridge of the thatched roof. Everything combined to give an air of space and even luxury. But the thing that amazed him most was a shelf along the west wall, just south of the window, a shelf lined with half a hundred books, among them a German Bible, an English copy of the King James, Cervantes' *Don Quixote de la Mancha*, Pascal's *Pensées*, the plays of Cyrano de Bergerac, Augustine's *Confessions*, Plato's *Dialogues*, and Shakespeare's *Hamlet*, *A Midsummer Night's Dream*, *Romeo and Juliet*, and a volume of his sonnets.

In sheer wonder Gabriel lovingly fingered their leather bindings, then looked up at Huntermark.

"Not what you'd expect of a trapper's cabin, is it?" Huntermark examined Gabriel's face for the answer.

Gabriel, still trying to take it all in, said, "No. No, it's not."

He paused and added, "But then, so far, you're not what I'd expect of a trapper."

Gabriel's new home could not have pleased him more. Huntermark's cabin sat back far from the chain of lakes and streams the voyagers and tribes used as a waterway. This was a vast wilderness, and the number of native inhabitants was far from being great enough to fill it. In this place Gabriel would rarely see any human being other than his new friend. It was the perfect place to hide.

Wilhelm Huntermark's dog was a big female of no particular breed, with heavy fur well suited for the northern winter. She stood over two feet tall at the shoulder, was short of muzzle, and had enormous feet and a long tail that inscribed a spiral over her back. Her short, alert ears pointed forward and, like her deep eyes, were expressive and quick. She was silver-gray, near black around her eyes, down her front legs, and along her hackles.

She was a mature dog, five years old if Wilhelm calculated correctly, but he could not be precise about her age, for she had not always been his. He had gotten her when she was about a year old from a trader going south on Crooked Lake.

Huntermark had not given her a name, but simply called her "Dog." She was a good companion, never complained about the food, and never argued over the work that had to be done. But the thing Huntermark liked most about this animal was that she reminded him of a dog he had known years before. In truth, the earlier one hadn't been his. It had belonged to Melody.

In the year 1705, Huntermark told Gabriel, he and Melody, both young and in the very prime of life, had canoed together to Du Lhut's Fort, in those days the only post beyond the fledgling Grand Portage other than York Factory, and that was clear up on Hudson Bay. It was, he said with sadness, in the last year of her life, though at the time of the trip they had no inkling that she was ill.

At Du Lhut's Fort, Melody had seen the puppy and immediately fallen in love with her. She had begged Wilhelm to let her take her home. The factor had thought the dog was half wolf, but Huntermark had disagreed. "She likely has some wolf blood in her veins," he had said, "maybe more than just a little. But the dog is certainly not a wolf. Too broad through the chest, legs shorter than a wolf's, and a wolf that tall would be more than half a foot longer in body. And look at that tail," he continued, "how it curves up. No wolf ever had a tail like that. She's got big feet, all right. But a wolf's would be twice the size."

Wilhelm was soft as damp clay in Melody's hands, especially when she laughed and begged in her little-girl way, so he had grinned and said yes. And he had always been glad, for it was during the following winter that he realized that she was ill.

She began to lose the roundness from her face and became listless. Toward the end of spring, when the drifts had melted and the days were alternately cold and warm, she began to labor at breathing. One morning at dawn her breathing stopped. "Simply stopped," he said. She was only twenty-eight.

"Lord," he said to Gabriel one evening at the fireside, "how I loved that girl. She was light as the fresh, clear air of spring. Never complained. Always ready to go or stay . . . or to do whatever she had to do.

"When we made the trip up here from the Mohawk country, I feared she might not make it, slip of a girl that she was. But she just kept on keeping on, and always had a smile at the end of a day, no matter how steep the hills we'd climbed or how fast the rivers we'd crossed. The day she saw this place, she said, 'Oh, Bill! This is the place! *Our* place! Let's stay here. Please! It's a wonderful spot to have our children.' " A single tear broke over and ran down Huntermark's right cheek, and he shook his head. "Children we never had. I built this house the first year. Wouldn't have been so particular if it had just been me . . . but I built it for her. Wanted her to have the best I could give her.

"Most women would've gone out of their minds at the loneliness, but not Melody. She thrived on the isolation, and on the sheer beauty of the place." He drew a deep breath and looked up into the darkness among the rafters. "The days we spent together . . . the things we did. And right now I can see her face just as she was.

"Sometimes I'm glad she didn't get old. Too full of spit and vinegar to get old. Too beautiful. The blush of youth was still in her face. The rot of age hadn't time to set in."

Gabriel's thoughts turned inward, and he thought of Celeste. If only he could remember Celeste as she had been rather than as she had become. If only those who loved him could be spared the thoughts they must now have. Some things were indeed worse than death. Then Huntermark interrupted his thoughts with words Gabriel had heard Pierre Hippolyte say.

"Besides," he said, "I'll see her again . . . someday."

Huntermark leaned forward over the dog that lay on the floor between him and the hearth and kneaded the full, deep fur about her throat. "But until then, this dog makes me feel a little closer to her."

"What became of Melody's dog?" Gabriel asked.

"I don't know," the old man answered. "After Melody died, she would wander off once in a while, and then one day she just went away and never came back."

The dog on the hearth stretched languorously and yawned a high whine that finally ended in a lazy, full-throated groan. She found as much pleasure in the man's company as the man did in hers, taking assurance from the strength of his large hand on her shoulder and from the firm, confident look in his old, blue eyes.

At first Gabriel wondered if the animal would be jealous of his coming, but she was not. She accepted him as a friend, welcomed him joyfully to the warm dwelling, nuzzled his hand, and wagged her furry, spiral tail. Even so, her affections and deepest devotion still belonged to Huntermark.

CHAPTER 19

The Boulder

SUMMER in the north woods does not linger. The first hint of autumn came with a faint yellow glow in the highest leaves of a tall, big-toothed aspen on the edge of Huntermark's clearing.

By mid-September every voice of nature testified in unison that the warm months had indeed fled. Every ridge and hilltop, every valley and shore, every rivulet and meadow proclaimed that autumn had stolen in to fill its all-too-brief space in the cycle of seasons.

In another two months the cold would be upon them. Heavy

snow would fill the trails, the lakes and streams would become ice-bound, and winter would lock them in its unrelenting grasp.

At this moment food and warmth were still abundant, free for the taking, but if the two did not give diligence to gathering and storing, then terrible misery, perhaps starvation and death, would come before winter's end.

It was evening, the fourteenth of September, 1747. Gabriel drew out the writing paper he had bought at Grand Portage, and once again wrote in the journal begun there.

Michel . . .

This morning, Huntermark and I went down to the lake, not for fish this time, but for something else he says we must have to make it through the winter.

I was surprised to see that the tall, feathery grass growing in the shallow mud-bottomed inlets of Little Vermillion is really wild rice, something like wheat, but with grains half an inch long and quite black. Huntermark says that it's the staff of life for the Ojibway, Assiniboine, and Cree, and that five hundred pounds of it, along with rabbit, bear, elk and woodland caribou meat, will keep a family of five fat and healthy for a year.

Today was a good day to begin the harvest. The weather was calm and very still. We poled the canoe out into the rice just before the sun came up. The sky was a light blue and feathered with long wisps of flowing cloud that made me think of the heads growing at the tip of each of the tall grasslike stalks. The air was crisp and cool, so cool that there was a slight glaze of ice on the water, and as the bow of the canoe pressed through, the ice made a high, thin cracking sound, like delicate crystals breaking.

With a hickory pole cut for the purpose, I steadied the canoe, while Huntermark drew handfuls of grass, bent them over the canoe, and shook out the grain. It was perfectly ripe, and the grain showered into the canoe's bottom like sleet against a windowpane. When we had all we could safely carry, we made for shore and spread it out on sheets of birchbark to dry in the sun. Tomorrow we'll put the rice in an iron kettle and parch it over a fire.

I'm feeling well, Michel, enjoying the fall—enjoying it much more than I thought I could under the circumstances.

I think of your mother every day, and I'm glad to know that Pierre will be watching over you. Pierre is good at heart; he loves you and will take good care of you until I am home again.

It was the last day of September. The season changed more quickly now. Every morning brought some new taste of autumn splendor, every bend in the stream and trail unveiled some hue of gold or magenta that Gabriel had never seen on the grandest of Normandy's fall days.

It was the profusion, he thought, the variety of the north woods and its waterways that outstripped France, profusion nearly untouched by the hand of man. The lands of Normandy had been cultivated and laid out in orderly blocks, the rivers diked and dredged for centuries. French forests were carefully managed and the underbrush cleared away. The deer were neither wild nor tame, but lived in great parks of land, owned and hunted by nobility.

But here the rivers were pristine; nature determined their flow. Here the crops grew wild and the animal life roamed freely.

One thing made all this possible. The Europeans looked upon the land as a thing that men could divide among them and own. The American peoples revered the earth, felt it was their mother, lived in harmony with it, believed that all land was for all men, and touched it only with reverence. They called the caribou, wolf, and deer their "forest brothers," and took only what they needed to live.

Huntermark explained the native American ways to Gabriel, and told him that it was a matter of spirit. Gabriel again felt within him the pull of life he had felt that first night on Superior, when through the trees he had seen the glint of native campfires.

On the third of October, he wrote:

I have yet to talk at length with any of the people who inhabit this northern wilderness. At Grand Portage I met a few, but we were there so short a while there was no time to win their confidence.

Yet I feel a kinship with them. It's strange. Even when I was a child, I felt this closeness—perhaps a prophetic closeness—to a people about whom I had only heard a few stories. And now, here I am in their land. And such a land it is.

This morning, very early, I was out in the meadow that extends from the east end of Little Vermillion. I love that meadow, and whenever I can, I go there to think.

Months ago, in a late spring storm, lightning had burned the meadow's south side. Now, against the gray residue, asters bloom in a variegated sea of bronze. Bunches of berries the color of a rooster's comb hang from the mountain ash. Underfoot the bracken has changed to russet, even though the moss beside it is still a constant green.

There are bogs in the meadow, low-lying places where for centuries the ground has been filling with rotting pollens and leaves. The black new-made earth now quivers when you walk on it, and is covered with coarse plants, brown and copper, that spread out like a carpet beneath a grove of pines growing there. Huntermark calls these pines by the name larch. Larch needles turn pure gold in autumn, and a sudden breeze will make them shed every needle in a single instant.

I was in the meadow just as the sun rose. In the night a fragile coat of frost had silvered the matted beige grass. I looked behind me toward the sunrise just as the sun rimmed the ridge and glinted through the tops of the balsam firs, and I could see exactly where I had walked, because everywhere I had gone, from the edge of the meadow to where I stood, my feet had rubbed the frost from the grass, and left a dark path through a field of silver.

Sometimes I am lost to all the world by simply reaching up, plucking a bright red leaf from a maple, and slowly turning it between my fingers, gazing into its universe of beauty.

Someday you will read this, Michel. If you do, you will know that today I've wished you could be here with me. The wooded hills are bright yellow and flaming red, toned here and there by dark evergreens. Where the leaves are already gone, the trunks and limbs seem gray and somber. I feel at rest inside, even though you are so far away, because when I see it all I begin to think again that there is a God who made this world, and that somehow that same God watches over you.

It's a glory.

* * *

Huntermark had a taste for rich red meat. Its robustness contrasted wonderfully with the flat monotony of fish, and if the two men could procure some, they could endure the hard winter ahead more joyfully. In addition, both men were in need of thick, strong hides from which to make new shoes. Gabriel needed the hides to make cold-weather clothing without which he could not survive.

So on the tenth of October, while sitting in the light of their hearth fire, the dog stretched out to receive full benefit of the reflected heat, Huntermark told Gabriel it was time for them to hunt.

Next morning they rose early, left the lodge, and climbed northwest to the top of the ridge. They scrambled across the great outcropping of granite monoliths that stood above the lodge like a fortress wall, and continued through the forest to Huntermark's favorite hunting grounds.

After a night of deep rest, they rose an hour before the sun and prepared for the stalk. Then they sat, dressed for warmth against the chill of the October morning, Gabriel with a skin of silver wolf about his shoulders, Huntermark in a bright red coat made from a Hudson Bay blanket. The coat's hood gathered about his neck in a way that made him look regal, and Gabriel marveled in admiration. Huntermark was a man of keen intelligence. He'd a fine broad forehead and a calm self-assured mouth. His deep blue eyes looked piercingly from under relaxed lids. Gabriel felt fortunate indeed at the match they made.

By evening the hunt was ended, and the meat of a large elk was ready to be carried home. All in all, they had garnered a fresh hide, two hundred pounds of meat, and antlers for knife handles, buttons, and scraping tools. Their winter larder was full.

It was the end of October. A sea of bright yellow aspen leaves quaked on petioles grown loose, and in every burst of wind countless waves let go and showered the earth, blowing end over end, rushing along the ground with a sound like millions of scurrying field mice, on and on until some bush, tree, or patch of grass stopped their onward rush.

Even on windless days, maple leaves fell away from their twigs and floated downward on their backs in lazy whirlpools, spinning slowly to the ground. Fallen leaves buried the animal trails and made little dams in the streams, where pooled water wore coats of white froth mottled with patches of gold, sunset orange, and fading yellow.

As the vegetation died and the world became cold, a burst of activity among small animals broke the silence, an irresistible, universal drive to burrow secure shelters and store pine cones, seeds, and fungi from rotting logs. Beaver swam across still ponds carrying limbs of aspen and birch, storing them against the time when the water would freeze thick and deep, imprisoning the aquatic creatures between a low ceiling of ice and a floor of mud. Birds gathered to fly southward, the harsh call of the jay rasped through still air, and the beating of wings whispered across the water and through the dusky evenings.

Then came the rains. On those wet days when the clouds dropped down upon them, the two men sat indoors by the fire, replacing snow shoes, cutting and sewing furs into caps, thick mittens, warm leggings, and deep-piled coats, making their own preparations against the coming cold.

It was on such a day that Gabriel gradually opened up to Huntermark, and one by one led his secrets into the open. He knew that every secret shared was a risk taken, for any one of his failings might offend the older man and raise a wall between them. "I was stupid and naïve," he said. "I thought that if a man loved God, he led a charmed life." Now, his naïve trust gone, all he had left was bitterness and regret. He confessed his guilt and wept at how terribly his crime had cost him.

Huntermark was a stern man of enormous integrity and straightforwardness. But he was as warm as he was stern, and did not shut Gabriel out. As he listened, the old man leaned forward in his chair, looking at Gabriel. When he had heard it all, including Gabriel's confession to murder, he sighed a deep sigh and leaned far back with his elbows propped beside him, touching his fingers together in a contemplative gesture. He gazed for a long moment into the hearth's blazing coals. Then, in a voice that was filled with sad resignation, he slowly shook his head and murmured, "The fruit of your body for the sin of your soul."

Gabriel did not understand. Looking up, his eyes red and watering, he asked, "What did you say?"

"The fruit of your body for the sin of your soul," Huntermark repeated. "You were wroth." He emphasized "wroth," for he liked the word, and wanted to speak its full weight. "You were wroth, and you killed a man. But for that you have given your son. My heart weeps for you, but you will never be free from the sentence, except by some extraordinary grace of Almighty God." Then Huntermark looked away from the fire. "I pray for you some happy ending, but I confess to doubt that it can ever be."

"But Wilhelm," Gabriel answered, "in a year, maybe two years, I will go home, and somehow I'll pick up where we left off. I have a wife and child and parents. There's a life to be lived, and I intend to live it."

"I wish you well, son, but whatever comes, good or ill, remember, the wrath of man does not work the righteousness of God—and more, it does not even work the happiness of man."

The lodge stood on the edge of winter well prepared. The ground about it was raked and clean. A large pile of firewood was carefully stacked under an arborlike shelter against the cabin's east wall. Inside, baskets full of wild rice rested on the rafters, slabs of meat and fish hung below, bundles of herbs lay above the door, and sheaves of grass for weaving mats and baskets lay in one corner. Freshly made candles and cattails soaked in bear fat were ready to provide light on long winter evenings.

On the mantel sat a small basket filled with spruce shoots collected fresh last spring for the making of winter tea, something prescribed by the Chippewa as protection against scurvy. A cluster of beaver traps on chains hung from a nail driven into the cabin's south wall. Scraping tools, knives, and awls lay oiled in a chest, waiting to be used in preparing the furs for next summer's trade.

Already the snow was falling, but each time it fell, warm winds followed, bringing rains that washed the snow away. Brown leaves lay soaking in creek beds and depressions where the rain and wind had swept them. Large stones covered with thick, green moss shone wetly under the weeping clouds. On these wet autumn days, the giant firs on the ridge stood silhouetted against the gray-roofed heavens, dim in the falling rain and blowing mists, their tall heads concealed in the lowering clouds.

On the third of November a cold wave swept down from the northwest, and on the fourth a light, feathery snow began to fall.

The first flakes found Huntermark and Dublanche down the

slope east of the cabin. Last night a bear had left his tracks, and Huntermark wanted its fat for grease and its heavy fur for a new robe. They were building a pen of thick logs that would trap the bear when he came in for the bait.

As they worked, the cold deepened, and Huntermark told Gabriel that winter was here to stay. Soon the ground would freeze and they could begin to trap for beaver. The thought invigorated them, and the air rang with their pleasant laughter, with the sound of stamping feet, the beating together of hands for warmth, and the barks and whines of Huntermark's excited dog.

When the pen was finished, baited, and set, they turned up the slope toward home. Darkness came. They had finished a large meal of wild rice and smoked walleye, had given the dog a slab of fish, and were putting away the cooking utensils. The fire had burned down to coals and Huntermark was about to throw on a new log.

As Gabriel hung the large skillet on its peg in the rock wall left of the fireplace, a sudden, unfamiliar sound caught his ear. Ever so slightly, the skillet began to rattle against the stone wall, and in a matter of seconds began to jump on its peg as though it had life. The men looked at each other and the dog whined as underneath them the earth quivered and bounced. The noise rose from rattle to roar to crash; the ground pounded and all the pans flew from their pegs.

Suddenly a mighty rending of the cabin's roof threw the heavy rafters helter-skelter. Great bundles of thatch fell to the floor as a sudden rush of air blew out the lanterns. The pounding faded into the distance and suddenly all was quiet but for the whisper of rice pouring from ruptured baskets in steady streams to the floor.

In the northeast corner the dog whined. The two men lay on the floor where they had thrown themselves. Slowly they lifted their heads and stared in the firelight, their white faces red from the light of the glowing coals. Tense and still, they braced for the next blow, the next falling timber, while about them dust, thatch, and bark drifted tardily downward.

Rice baskets continued to rain down on them from the remaining rafters. Dried fish and hams and ribs swung lazily to and fro. Cold night air blew about them, and flakes of snow large as breast feathers of white geese drifted to the floor through the torn roof.

When he was sure the cataclysm was over and the last beam had fallen, Huntermark dared to look up. An ancient maple, a tree of mammoth size that had grown for decades on the upslope just above the cabin, now lay across the walls from north to south. Under its great weight the walls creaked and groaned, but stood firmly.

"Dear God in heaven." It was a prayer, not an oath, the first words Huntermark spoke after starting to breathe again.

"A boulder from the ridge," Gabriel said under his breath.

"An *enormous* one," Huntermark agreed. "Big enough to cut through all the forest and lay that tree in our lap. It's a God's miracle we're alive."

Gabriel reached a taper into the hearth fire, relit the lanterns, and with his friend went out to assess the damage. But with the meager light they could see nothing other than the nearest tangled debris. There was little they could do until daylight.

They reentered the cabin, and for a shelter stretched a sheet of canvas from the mantel to the floor. Satisfied with their ingenuity and warmed by the coals of the hearth reflecting from the canvas, they spread their robes and went to bed.

In the fire glow they talked for a while of the job ahead and agreed it must be done quickly because of the cold. Before drifting off, Huntermark said something about the mercy of God. Gabriel thought for a moment, said nothing, and soon both were sound asleep.

They woke at first light. The air outside their lean-to was very cold. Large, dry flakes were falling thick through their sundered roof and covered the smooth stone floor. On the canvas lay a thick, soft mantle of white that slid soundlessly down when Gabriel turned on his side and brushed the fabric.

The men dressed, ate a quick breakfast, and went out to survey the destruction. Up the slope, where yesterday there had been solid forest, a wide path now opened before them, as though a team of woodsmen had come through with axes. Tangled masses of trunks and limbs lay along the path's edges; whole trees had been torn up by the roots, some upended, their naked roots caught among the limbs of trees still standing. Below the cabin, the path continued down to the lake. Down the great cut the two men went, clambering over debris and working their way through twisted trunks and limbs until they stood overlooking the water.

Before them lay a vast granite boulder twice the size of the cabin itself, its great mass resting half-submerged in mud and water, surrounded by new ice, sunk deep, never to move again.

"It jumped our clearing," Gabriel said in awe, "from the ledge above the cabin's north wall, out over the shelf where the cabin sits, and then on down."

"And that eighty-foot maple helped it pass over," Huntermark added. "Heaven and earth," he exclaimed, "look at that thing! You know, that may be the very rock you and I stood on when we climbed the ridge the last warm day in October. Thank God it didn't go then."

Up on the ridge they found a vast space between the remaining boulders, like a gap in the teeth of some terrible giant. There was no wind, only snow falling thickly over the valley that spread white before them. They sat down beneath one of the balsam firs and laid their plans.

The first order of business, they decided, was to clear away the great maple.

"We'll take axes," said Huntermark, "and trim away its limbs, then top it and cut its base away. Then, with poles, we can pry from underneath until we roll the main log right off the edge of the cabin. After that we'll rebuild the rafters and rethatch the roof. It'll take a day or two to get the tree off, much longer to rebuild."

The work progressed well. On the afternoon of the second day they were ready to roll the great trunk from the walls. Huntermark stood on the north wall where the ground was level with the cabin roof, and Gabriel on the south wall. The silver-gray dog watched from the ground. Each man held a stout pole half again as long as he was tall. Each laid a hewn block between himself and the tree, inserted the end of his pole between the block and the log, and laid his weight on the pole's upper end. True to their expectations, the tree rolled slowly toward the cabin's west edge.

The walls groaned and creaked beneath the weight, but held steady. Little by little they moved the blocks forward and pried again. When the maple was less than two feet from the edge, Huntermark's hewn block slid sideways and fell inside the cabin. Rather than taking time to climb down and retrieve it, he slipped the pole beneath the log and pulled up hard. This new maneuver required more effort than he had supposed, but he followed through with all his might until the heavy mass yielded, rolled over the edge, and fell to the ground so heavily the walls jumped beneath them with the impact.

"We won! We did it!" Gabriel shouted with jubilation. Huntermark said nothing. Gabriel looked toward the older man. Huntermark was standing, bent from the waist with his hands on his knees, staring at the ground.

"Something wrong, Wilhelm?" Gabriel asked.

"Maybe," Huntermark answered. "Shouldn't've lifted so hard on the pry." He pressed against his lower right side. "I pulled something in my side," he said. "Burns like the devil."

He tried to straighten, but the burning doubled him over again and the intense pain made him vomit. Gabriel ran around the wall to Huntermark's side.

Once down, the old man stretched out on the ground. Gabriel opened his coat, unlaced his friend's waistband, and pulled it down to his groin. The old man's body was lean and white, the skin loose with age. Halfway between his navel and the joint of his thigh a soft mass the size of a large egg rose beneath the skin.

"You've ruptured yourself, Wilhelm," Gabriel said to him.

Wilhelm lay still, breathing shallow breaths to ease the pain. "A boy's stunt," he said with disgust.

"This ever happen to you before?" Gabriel asked.

"Twice," Huntermark answered with difficulty, "once down on the Mohawk, once since. It's all right. A doctor helped me with it the first time, showed me what to do. Just let me rest awhile first."

He lay quiet for a time, and then, with his eyes closed and his face drawn up in pain, he said, "When I pulled up on that pry, the muscles in my stomach wall split. A loop of gut pushed through. Now the muscles have clamped down on it and won't let it go back." He paused for breath and continued, "We've got to make those muscles turn loose and let the gut slip back in."

Gabriel felt uneasy at the prospect. "How on God's earth are we going to do that?" he asked.

The dog laid down beside Huntermark and licked gently at his face. Huntermark seemed not to mind. "Go get a rope from the cabin." A sudden spasm of pain made him bite his lower lip. When it passed, he continued, "Go get a rope and throw it up over that limb." He pointed to a large birch limb directly above him. Following his orders, Gabriel threw the rope over the limb and tied a loop at one end.

"Now, slip the loop over both my feet. . . . Good. Now anchor yourself somewhere and draw me into the air, head down."

Gabriel remonstrated, "You're in no shape to—"

"Do it," Huntermark said evenly.

Without further objection, Gabriel obeyed, and drew the old man into the air as one would draw a bucket of water from a well.

Huntermark swung by his ankles, head down, and arched his back. Twice before he had resorted to this, and twice the muscles had parted and the intestine had slipped back into its place. But now, nothing happened.

Even in the cold, sweat rolled from his face into the long, white hair that hung down toward the ground. He closed his eyes and arched further back but the muscle did not separate, and the intestine still did not return.

Huntermark relaxed his arms and let them hang limply to the ground, and rested. He said breathlessly, "It's always worked." Gabriel could see he was in agony. Then, throwing himself suddenly and relentlessly into the effort, he arched his back again. Nothing happened. Again he went limp.

"It's got to work," he said. "The blood in that loop is cut off. If it won't go back in, it'll rot."

Gabriel's uneasiness grew to near panic. He backed up, wound the rope around the trunk of a nearby tree, tied it, and hurried back to his friend's dangling form. "Here," he said. "Let me help you." Gabriel put the palm of his left hand squarely in the small of Huntermark's back, grabbed his shirt collar with the other, and together they bent his body back as far as they dared.

Again, nothing.

Huntermark's face was red and his head pounded from the downward flow of blood.

"Get me down," he said to Gabriel.

"But what will we do?" Gabriel asked.

"I don't know. We'll try this again after a while, maybe. Just get me down for now."

The seriousness of their predicament fell over Gabriel like cold water. If the loop refused to go back, this man would die. Huntermark rested on the ground for another half hour, then Gabriel drew him aloft again. Nothing.

Gabriel went in, rebuilt the fire, and carried his friend to their makeshift shelter.

Behind thick gray skies the sun slipped over the edge of the world. Night came on, and the snow continued to fall.

* * *

That night Wilhelm Huntermark slept hardly at all. But as daylight approached, the pain subsided, and he eased off into sleep. Gabriel stayed nearby.

When Huntermark woke about midday, Gabriel was busy at the fire.

"Did you rest, Wilhelm?" he asked quietly.

"No," he answered, "but it was better than nothing." He paused, realizing that Gabriel had a solemn, determined look in his eyes, and that he was working at the hearth with some special purpose. "What are you about, Gabriel?" he asked.

Gabriel held a knife in the fire until its blade glowed red. Huntermark asked, "Don't you know you'll take the temper out of that blade and ruin it?"

Gabriel looked over to his friend. "We've got to get that intestine back in. I'm ready to try anything."

Huntermark's mind was clear and he instantly saw Gabriel's meaning. "So you think you're going to cut me open and put it back, do you?" the old man asked somewhat defiantly.

"You know of another way?" Gabriel returned, a tinge of impatience in his voice.

Huntermark's reaction was quick. In spite of the pain, he shook his head. "No. I don't know of another way, but I won't let you do it. I've always said that nobody's going to cut me open."

Gabriel turned and stared for a moment at his friend, then said resolutely, "But I've thought about it. It's not far under the skin, and I'm certain I can do it. We'll tie you down so you can't move. I'll take a clean knife and cut a half circle around the bulge, lift up the flap, pull the muscle apart with my fingers and tuck the gut back in. Then I'll sew the flap down. If the bleeding's bad, I'll cauterize the wound with a hot knife." He turned back toward the fire. "I only wish I had thought of this last night."

Huntermark lay still for a few moments. "I don't doubt you could do it, son," he said. "But there's something in me that says no. I'm not afraid to die, and one way or the other, it's time."

"Stop it, Wilhelm!" Gabriel flared. "You've got more life in you then most men half your age." He looked up at the snow still falling through the open roof, then said, "Besides, I can't stand to lose you. You're the best friend I've had since Michel died—or since Celeste . . . changed." He paused. "You've got to let me try."

Huntermark was moved by Gabriel's affection. For a long minute he struggled with his emotions and then said, ''All right. If it means that much to you, do it.''

Gabriel lifted Huntermark from the floor to the table where he gently laid him down. He worked at a frantic pace, and soon everything was in place. Huntermark bore the pain well, and in half an hour the work was done. The knife's cut hurt no more than the rupture itself, and before long the old man was peacefully asleep.

Gabriel went out into the forest and wept with relief. He was relieved to know that he had done the best any man in his place might do. He had seen what needed to be done and he had found the courage to do it. Now Huntermark was in the hands of . . . of whatever power there might be.

Yet Gabriel was afraid. When he had uncovered the intestine, it was already black, and he had no reason to believe he had done the work in time to save his friend.

It is one of the most maddening ironies of life that its greatest events sometimes hinge on its smallest happenings. A single cone falling from the highest limbs of the tallest balsam fir, one seed washed into a tiny crevice, sprouts in spring sunlight and warmth; a handsome sapling emerges, its roots growing down deep into the fissure, enlarging it ever so gradually, rain seeps into the cleft, then the cold, and soon an icy wedge prying against a boulder that has stood for millennia.

On the morning of the sixth day after his accident Wilhelm Huntermark died. He was seventy-five years old. Gabriel wrapped his friend in their finest fur robe and buried him beside Melody.

Gabriel had never thought before about how a lone man might bury another with any sort of dignity, but he thought about it now. He dug through the few inches of frozen earth, then down to where it was yet warm. He carried the body to the grave's side, climbed into the grave, took the old man tenderly in his arms, and reverently laid him down.

For a long while Gabriel himself sat in the grave at Huntermark's feet, struck dumb at the loss of this man who had become both his father and his friend. At last, he laid a large piece of birchbark over Huntermark's remains, clambered awkwardly out, and shoveled in the freezing earth. The dirt hitting the stiff bark rang hollow, and each ring struck Gabriel hard in the pit of his stomach.

When done, he stood silently over the grave for a long while. The big silver-gray dog nosed at the mound, whined pitifully, and began to dig. Gabriel pulled her away, knelt beside her, and circled her neck with his arm. The wind rose about them, filled with thick swirls of new snow, and moaned in the limbs overhead. Soon the big flakes covered the patch of dark earth and gathered in small drifts about the feet of the man and his dog.

CHAPTER 20

The Outcast

By mid-December the cold lay like brittle iron on the face of the Little Vermillion. In the murky dusk, thick ice cracked and boomed like thunder. A heavy blanket of soft deep snow muffled the land from horizon to horizon, and silence filled the still, blue-white world.

Bears lay in their dens; squirrels huddled in their nests; beaver hid in their dark caves, eating saplings from winter store. The merganser, mallard, blue goose, and myriad hosts of chattering summer birds had long since deserted this home for the warmth of the south. Even the loon had taken its strange laughter and fled this boreal land.

Yet life was present. Hundreds of miniature footprints marked the snow; mice scurried out of their darkness to find food; lynx, rabbit, marten, otter, and fox were abroad and as busy as ever.

Huntermark's death profoundly changed Gabriel's existence. For the first time in his life he was isolated from every human being. From their meeting the two men had been busy from first light with the work of living: cutting wood, carrying water, preparing food for winter, mending clothes, washing, making plans for the trapping season.

Gabriel's routine did not change with his friend's death. He did the same things alone that they had done together. For two weeks after Wilhelm's death he had worked at the cabin, picking up the winter stores, cleaning out the scattered debris, and repairing the rafters and roof. Soon the work was done and the lodge was as sound as before. Yet everything was different, and the difference lay heavily on Gabriel's shoulders. His steps were slower. He wanted to sleep more—and yet he woke up earlier. Winter deepened, and color fled.

The winter's vast silence was a burden to him. Soundlessness covered the meadows. The stream's gurgling songs were sealed off by thick sheets of ice and the ice in turn was covered by feet of snow. No grass rustled. No bird song brightened the air, no rain beat staccato rhythms on the roof or windows. The only sounds he heard were the crunch of his feet in the snow, his own breathing, the clank and clatter of his work, or his own voice as he talked to himself or to the dog—the one living being that stood between him and insanity.

One afternoon while he was baiting an empty trap, Gabriel was startled by a sudden movement. Instantly he was frozen by surprise. A rising chill tingled between his tightening shoulders and plummeted down his stiffened spine. A large beast sat on his haunches not ten feet away, looking at him quizzically.

Never before had Gabriel seen a wolf of any kind, let alone a great gray timber wolf of the Canadian north. The animal was so near he could see every marking; the points of reflected light in each yellow eye, the deep fur about its throat splaying fitfully in the soft wind that breathed among the trees.

Gabriel's hands became clammy, and sweat broke out on his face.

The two gazed fixedly into each other's eyes. The beast cocked his head to one side, looking for all the world as if he were about to say, "And what are you?"

Then the wolf grew unaccountably nervous. He turned his head this way and that as if wondering which trail to take, then moved away. Suddenly, as though pursued, he broke into a run, up and over a hillock, going so rapidly that bits of dry snow flew like bursts of white powder to either side.

The wolf was an outcast from his pack and had spent three full winters alone before encountering Gabriel. It was shortly after this first meeting that the young wolf took to lying in the evenings on the high ridge directly above the cabin, resting there among the firs.

On one such night, his belly full, he lay on a rock that crested the ridge and watched the valley below. The wind was blowing softly from the south, sweeping up the slope to where the wolf lay.

On the rising breeze a river of odors floated. The young gray cocked his head first at one angle, than at another, sniffing continually, separating one scent from the other, until suddenly he came to a new one, one he had never known before.

The new scent excited him. He rose to his feet and began to pace, stopping now and again to lift his nose into the air and sample it once more. A restless impulse to find the source rose within him. Before descending, he lifted his face high and bathed the starry night with his lonely music.

Gabriel sat by the fire lost in contemplation of the large hide spread out before him on the floor. Two days after he had buried Huntermark, he had remembered the log pen they had built together and immediately had gone to check it. He had found a bear that for several days had had nothing to do with its time but try to chew its way out. By aiming through the gap chewed in the logs, Gabriel had shot it squarely between the eyes.

He had spent the entire next day skinning it, cutting the meat into usable pieces, and rendering the fat. Eventually he would convert the skin into a fine robe, eat the meat, and use the fat to oil his guns and waterproof his footgear. He had fleshed the hide that day, then rolled it into a bundle and stored it in the cabin's coolest corner to await the time when he could work on it in earnest.

Tonight he had chosen to unwrap the hide and finish the work. It lay spread out on the floor before him. He sat in his chair, puffing quietly at his pipe, gazing at the pelt, wondering how to make the best use of it. His mind wandered back to Huntermark. How helpless I would be, he thought, but for those brief months with Wilhelm. Gabriel would not have imagined that he could learn so much about how to survive in such a short while. Huntermark had been a good teacher. Gabriel owed his life to him.

Then he heard it in the distance, low at first, full of throat, a long, rising, plaintive note that ascended until it seemed the voice would break. Even so the wail rose higher still.

- Huntermark's dog lay before the fire. Her ears rose and pricked forward. She growled a low growl and came to her feet as her hackles stood from shoulder to tail. A queer sensation ran up

Gabriel's spine, as though he had hackles of his own. The dog went to the door and scratched impatiently for Gabriel to let her out.

The following day there was no sign of the dog. The howling had stopped within minutes of her leaving, and Gabriel had begun to fear for the safety of his only friend. But on the third night there was a scratching and whining at the door. He opened it and the dog bounded in. She lifted her front paws to his shoulders and joyfully licked Gabriel full in the face.

Such goings and comings were common in the month that followed. Sometimes the dog was gone for a night, but at other times for several days and nights together. It became obvious to Gabriel that the dog was now attached to the wolf. This did not strike him as unusual, but it did unsettle him, for he did not know how he could continue without her company. She was almost always with him on the trap line or hunt. Each evening after supper the dog had come and stretched out beside the fire. Gabriel would draw a few spruce buds from the basket and brew a small kettle of tea, then sit down by the dog, mug of tea in hand, lay his arm over her deeply furred shoulder, rub her chest, pick flecks of bark and twig from her coat, and inspect her pads for cuts and bits of rock. All the while he would talk to her and she would seem to understand, and even sometimes answer with a whine, an uplifted brow, or by cocking her head.

It was no wonder he was uneasy at her absences. She was just a dog, he reasoned, but life would be intolerable without someone, even a beast, to keep him company.

So, after she'd been a long time away, his heart lifted when he heard her feet come padding through the snow, and he would reach gladly for the latch and receive her rambunctious greeting with a strong embrace of her furry shoulders. He knew that in another month she would give birth to a litter of . . . of what, wild dogs? Tame wolves? He didn't know, but he was sure that when it happened, it would happen somewhere other than the lodge.

Now it was January the fifteenth. The cold was deep. That night as they sat by the fire, Gabriel with his usual mug of spruce tea in hand, the dog's head came up from the floor and she cocked her ears to listen. Then he heard it, too, the far distant bark, and then the lonely, hollow wail that still chilled his bones.

She got up from the hearth and trotted quickly to the door. He followed her, lifted the latch, and opened the door wide. Soon a new voice joined that of the wolf, and a clear harmony filled the cold night.

She did not return again.

PART THREE

1747–1748

CHAPTER 21

Along the Ottertrack

IT was now early March. For six weeks Gabriel had been utterly alone. With every day that came he descended deeper into himself. Confusion swirled about in his inmost mind. He dreaded each day before it began. Each morning, with what little will was left to him, he forced himself from his bed and to his work.

Every night he took to the bed again without fire or light and huddled for warmth under robes that exhausted him with their weight. His depression deepened until on some days he did not rise at all. Often he forgot to eat, or remembering, hadn't the will to prepare his food.

The lodge was unswept and littered. He fleshed his catch indoors and did not bother to sweep up the fallen shreds of fat. His soiled clothes lay about everywhere. When he carried in firewood, tree bark and dirt fell to the floor, and there they remained. Eating utensils were scattered about, encrusted with layers of rancid food. A heap of traps lay in the southwest corner where he had thrown them.

The hearth was filled with ashes he had not the will to carry out, mixed with the partially burned bowels and bones of lynx, beaver, and marten. Their raw hides were tossed about on the floor and across his bed. Even the cold could not suppress the reek of rotten food and uncarried night soil.

When Gabriel tore his clothes he did not mend them. After he killed and gutted the daily catch he did not wash, and now his hands and face were smudged with patches of dried red blood and brown excrement. He did not shave, nor did he wash or trim his dirty black beard or tangled hair.

Gabriel was half aware of his condition, and in that half awareness he was miserable, but his mind was too dark to think that in some way he might help himself, and there was no one there to tell him what he must do, or to draw him out of his darkness.

* * *

It was the seventeenth of March, nearly spring, but winter retained its hard grip. The cold was bitter, and the snow grew ever deeper. Gabriel came into the cold cabin with nine fresh pelts over his shoulder, which he let fall to the floor in the middle of the room. Then he gathered up an armload of wood, scooped a hollow in the deep ashes of the hearth, and struck a fire.

He knew he must eat something, so he put water on to boil, dropped in three or four spruce buds to ward off scurvy, and cut a thick slab of meat from a hock that hung beneath the rafters, a hock from the elk he and Huntermark had killed in the fall. The water boiled and the tea simmered and Gabriel ate his meat. But the food was tasteless and flat. He slouched in his chair and stared at the meager fire on the dirty hearth.

Then, slowly, unaccountably, there crept into his consciousness a sound. He hesitated in his chewing, and then, in order to listen, stopped altogether. He couldn't believe what he heard. Cautiously he rose from his chair and went to the south window. He could scarcely see out, for the glass was smeared with grease and soot, a filmy residue from those times when he had wiped the frosty glass with unwashed hands. Now he wiped the glass again, succeeded only in rearranging the film, bent forward, peered and squinted, but saw nothing.

But still he heard it, unmistakably: the hollow ring of an ax. Suddenly convinced that the sound was real, his movements became quick and wild. He threw open the door and stepped out into the receding light. An orange brilliance lay on the snow, the sky was clear, the air like crystal.

Like music, the ax blows rang through the frozen woods. Gabriel searched frantically for its source. Then he saw—in the aspen grove that grew not fifty yards from the cabin, up the ridge and east a ways. A man wearing a light blue blanket coat was swinging an ax, cutting firewood.

Now Gabriel heard his voice. The man was singing songs Gabriel himself had heard the voyagers sing. Was it possible, he thought, that a man or men could be wintering here? That another human being might live close by without my knowing it?

Gabriel broke into a run, hallooing as he raced toward the stranger.

The man turned to face him, dropped the head of his ax into the snow, leaned on its handle, and smiled broadly. When Gabriel reached him he threw his arms about the man, buried his face on his shoulder, and wept.

Gabriel expected the man to be as ecstatic as he, but the man seemed not at all surprised or even especially pleased. His greeting was as unemotional as if the two had talked only yesterday. Gabriel thought he detected something disconcerting in the man's eyes—a look of pity, perhaps, or condescension, the kind of look one might have when meeting another who was ill or insane.

Nonetheless, Gabriel was beside himself with joy. Along with his happiness, he poured out a great volume of questions. "Where did you come from? Do you live nearby? Are you a voyager? Are there others with you? Will you stay with me tonight?"

The smiling stranger answered with short, simple sentences in a dialect of Normandy. Yes, he said, he had left voyaging to become a free trapper. His cabin was several miles away, up to the northeast over the ridge, not far from Crooked Lake. He was running a trap line that he had laid only recently, found himself too far from home, had decided to sleep in the open, and was laying in firewood for the night. The man was friendly and quickly accepted his invitation to stay.

But Gabriel could not escape those annoying, unblinking, bright eyes that seemed so full of understanding and yet so empty. And the man's smile never faded from his face. Gabriel felt increasingly uneasy.

Together they carried in the freshly cut wood, built up the fire, heated a large kettle of water, and hurriedly began washing pans and plates. Gabriel scrubbed residue from cups that had lain in the corner for a month, scalding each with hot water from the boiling kettle.

He ran a large piece of meat onto the spit and poured rice into a smaller pot of boiling water.

While the food was cooking, Gabriel picked up the broom and began to sweep the cabin floor, all the while pouring out words as though a dam had broken inside. The stranger sat politely and listened, sometimes looking down into the fresh cup of tea, sometimes following Gabriel with his strangely bright eyes.

Gabriel told the man everything: how he had come to be there, all about Huntermark and the dog. And in turn the man told him his story: that he had been born in Le Mans on the bank of the Sarthe in northwest France, and that he had gone to school in

Rouen. He, too, poured out detail after detail, with no sign of stopping.

Five months it had been since Gabriel had last heard a human voice. Now he soaked up every word.

The two stayed up late. Gabriel asked every question he could think of: weather, voyagers, France, war, the Church, crime, punishment, guilt . . . loneliness.

It was near dawn before Gabriel told the man that he was exhausted. He cleared off the bed that had been Huntermark's, offered it to his new friend, and retired.

It was noon when Gabriel awoke. Bright sunlight poured through the south window and reflected radiantly on the smooth, freshly swept floor. As the haze cleared from Gabriel's mind, he remembered the man, and a warm feeling of happiness swept into his breast.

He rolled over in his bed and called out the man's name. There was no answer. He was surprised to see the bed empty, the robe turned back just as he had left it.

Gabriel stretched out both arms above his head, felt the ripple and tension of waking muscles course through his body. "He woke up early," he said in a sleepy voice. "Went out to run his line." He swung his feet over the side of his bed and said enthusiastically, "I'll find him and help." But first he built a fire from the banked coals, washed the grime from his face and hands, dressed, then ate a bite, and started toward the door.

As Gabriel's hand touched the latch, he noticed a puzzling thing. The door was locked—locked from the inside. The great bolt lay across it as if no one had gone out, or as if someone else had bolted it after another's exit. This put Gabriel in a quandary.

He lifted the bolt and stepped out into the fresh, cold air. The sky was clear, the sun bright, and in the night no new snow had fallen. Gabriel looked about and called out the man's name. No answer.

He walked to the edge of the clearing and looked down the slope. No one was there. He searched for fresh prints in the snow, then suddenly realized with a chill that there were no prints but his own.

Gabriel set out in the direction from which the man had come and reached the grove where yesterday he had found him cutting wood. He studied the ground carefully. Again the only prints in the snow were his own. No wood chips lay about. All the trees were standing just as they had stood in the past; there were no new stumps.

But, he thought, I stood on this very spot last night and watched him cut this tree into sections.

Gabriel's mind began to whirl. Here were two sets of facts— the set in his mind, and the set that lay before his eyes. Each seemed true, but one had to be false.

He caught himself and leaned back hard against a thick birch. Then slowly, despairingly, in utter confusion, he slipped to his knees in the snow. "Mother of God," he prayed aloud, and his own voice startled him, "I'm insane."

For two nights and two days Gabriel slept. The morning of the second day he awoke rested, surprised to find that his mind was clear and all his panic gone. Moreover, he knew that he was not insane.

Huntermark had once told him of trappers with phantom visitors. The isolation was too much for them, and after weeks without the sound of a human voice or the sight of a human face their minds had begun to produce what they had wanted: apparitions, sounds. That's all it was.

That day, with his mind at rest, Gabriel appraised his circumstances and made a firm decision. He would go home, home to France and to his family. He would finish the year's work, run the lines, dress the hides, and stretch and bale the furs, but when the ice broke he would load the canoe and leave. He would bypass Montreal, go to Quebec, and board ship to France.

Having made that decision, Gabriel began to work with peace of mind. Now he had purpose, a place to go, something to work toward, and with new purpose he found energy and drive flooding back into his body and mind.

Within days the south winds began to blow. Though deep cold still ruled the land and massive drifts lay high against the cabin walls and across every trail like slothful white giants, if one listened quietly and felt with one's soul, he might sense that the winds held in their slender soft fingers the first living breaths of spring.

April dawned. The sun mounted higher in the heavens every day. As it shed direct warmth over the land, the winter white diminished. Patches of soil appeared, and the sleeping earth awakened to the soft persuasion of warm winds and gentle golden brightness. Faint hints of green appeared as tender shoots unfolded into the light of day. Where the sun struck the lower marshes, they softened, and water began to rise underneath.

By mid-April the white-backed snow giants remained only in the shelter of the deep forest, in the shade of the balsam, and on the north sides of overhanging banks of earth. Their essence ran down in rivulets and swelled the valley streams, rushing, gurgling, leaping over rocks and crashing with a roar around sudden turns in their rocky beds.

The meadows were awash and warm. Rich blankets of marsh marigolds enfolded the low-lying meadows and creek banks. The partridge spread his fan and puffed his chest and drummed his call to any female that would listen. Red-winged blackbirds reconnoitered the meadows for food, lighted on long stalks of blue-eyed Mary, and blended their songs with the bright simmering warmth of the sun. The ice sheet on Little Vermillion was inundated by its own melt. Inflowing streams cut their way into its floes and then ran under to lift and break them into ever-smaller pieces. The streams were clearing, the water paths opening. By mid-May they would be fluid highways ready for travel.

Gabriel's catharsis did not fail him. His hope grew, and along with it his strength. He smiled often and laughed with the bird song. By the end of April he had finished his furs, so that now they stood in bales. He portaged Huntermark's birchbark canoe over the easterly trail that led to Lower Basswood Falls, then returned to the cabin three times in three days for what remained.

On the morning of April 30 he was up before dawn, said goodbye to Huntermark's lodge, crossed himself at the graves, and set out.

After three days of paddling Gabriel reasoned that he was halfway to Saganaga and a quarter of the distance to Grand Portage. The going was hard because he was moving against the current, a condition that would not change until he reached the Height of Land.

On the fifth day, paddling in a light rain, he entered the Ottertrack River. In late afternoon the sky grew darker, the clouds lower, threatening a downpour. Gabriel began to watch the passing bank for a place to make camp. Soon he turned the bow toward the gently rising south shore, leaped into the shallows, and pulled the little craft out of the water.

The bank was clear and level, mottled with fresh green grass, but too low to be safe from a rising river. Gabriel carried his cargo and provisions forty good steps to higher ground, then pitched a simple canvas lean-to, its back to the light breeze and gentle rain. In the lee of his tent he built a fire.

Gabriel was weary of body, but relaxed and at peace. His spirits were high, his appetite considerable. His homeward journey begun, he felt like celebrating, and so began to cast about for something out of the ordinary to eat, something better than wild rice and dried fish. He remembered that when the voyagers grew tired of pork or fish or rubbaboo, they searched the marshes for duck eggs. With wild onion and fresh bass they were a fine treat. He cast a baited line into the river, then left it to search for nests among the new cattails growing in a bordering marsh.

Soon he sat under his tent, a good fire before him, the rain pattering gently on the canvas above his head, and a refreshing meal in his contented belly. The world outside his lean-to was dark with wetness, but his bed was perfectly dry. The sun went down and night settled in. The rain grew heavy, thumping an unfailing rhythm on the tarpaulin, and lulled him into deep sleep.

It was just after midnight when consciousness seeped falteringly back into Gabriel's mind. As he wakened, he gradually became aware of something new, a vague uneasiness creeping through his body, a mild nausea growing oh so slowly.

The rain was pouring now, beating hard against his shelter, and the darkness was so complete that he could see nothing at all. Gabriel tried to ignore this uneasy feeling inside, believing it would quickly go away, but it did not. It only increased, centered itself in his bowels, and soon sent fingers of tenderness out to his skin so that each square inch of his body and limbs was sensitized painfully to every touch.

Sleep would not return and he began to roll from one side to the other, trying to find a position that would ease the pain.

The pounding of the rain intensified, as did his nausea. The pressure in his abdomen became greater and his bowels wrenched with violent tearing. He clenched his teeth and dug his fingers into the soft ground in an effort to bear the torment. He cried out, then doubled up beneath his blanket. He grasped his belly with both arms and rocked gently, rolling from side to side.

At last his discomfort eased. The battle seemed done, and exhaustion settled in. He drifted blissfully into sleep, only to be reawakened within the hour, and to find that whatever had torn at his inwards had doubled its assault.

The hours of agony and darkness dragged by without end, until a faint gray light seeped through the heavy clouds and spread over the sodden ground. The rain thundered against his shelter and in the background he heard the river rising.

Gabriel began to shake with chill and longed for heavier covering, for a better shelter, for the warmth of a fire, but his fire was out, its ashes soaked and dead. He trembled uncontrollably and his teeth clicked rapidly. He painfully eased the covers aside, rose, and lay dry wood for a new fire. It was an exhausting effort that required every bit of self-discipline he could muster. In agony he laid his supply of small dry twigs in place, then the kindling, then the larger wood. He struggled not to rush, knowing that if he did, his effort would fail and there would be no fire.

He reached into his pack, drew out steel, char, and tender—then struck a spark into life. He lay the black char with its widening red glow into the tender and began to blow. As it smoldered in his hand, its thick white smoke rushed up into his nostrils and set him to coughing. His abdomen gripped him with a terrible new force. But he was desperate to have this fire, and blew until it burst into flame.

He lay the blazing mass under a pyramid of twigs, watched the living orange rise and take hold, first on the kindling, then on the larger wood.

Again he slept.

When at mid-day he awoke, the fire was again out and his chill had deepened. Darkness came again. His stomach contorted savagely to empty itself. He had no strength to leave his shelter, but expelled the putrid stream from under the tent where the merciful, still-falling rain washed it away.

With the emptying of his stomach came tremendous relief. For a while his lucidity returned and he thought about his condition. I've been sick before, he thought, when I was a child. And I've been alone before. Oh, how I've been alone. But I've never been sick *and* alone at the same time.

A childhood vision rose in his mind. Catherine sat on the edge of his soft bed and lay damp cloths on his forehead. He remembered that in those days, whenever he had been sick, always she had been there, that when the violent contractions doubled him over, she had cradled his forehead in her cool palm and spoken kindly to him. She had comforted him. She had surrounded him with love.

For a moment at least, the memory was enough to calm his mind. But it brought tears to his eyes. He missed her so, her love, her gentleness. There was a place deep within where he was still only a child, and in the most adult places of his mind, Catherine still reigned supreme.

Then the nausea began to rise again. The pains returned and his fever climbed higher. He slipped into deeper, longer periods of unconsciousness, and the rain continued to fall.

CHAPTER 22

Wind Lake

GABRIEL was suspended somewhere between consciousness and oblivion. No matter how he struggled, he could not waken from this world of confusion and sickening pain, a world in which he could neither move nor speak.

He was drifting down. The earth dissolved beneath him. Round about him were faces, some he recognized, some he did not, faces that like mist changed from form to form, then to nothing, and evaporated into darkness.

Time lost its meaning. Somewhere a loon cried out. Between the first note of its call and the dying of the last echo, Gabriel passed from life to life; from the building of Egypt's pyramids to the rise of Alexander, to Charlemagne, to Ulf the Walker and Charles the Bold. Before his eyes kingdoms rose and withered into dust, but he himself was imprisoned in the bowels of the earth, set free only as the last note of the loon's eerie melody died away.

It seemed to Gabriel that darkness gave way to light. The rain stopped. The clouds disappeared. He lay pinned to ground baked dry and hard under a brilliant copper sky. As the sun blazed down, his lips burned and his tongue clung to the roof of his parched mouth.

All sound faded away, the cricket's rasping chirp, every bird song, the rising river, each as silent as though they did not exist, or as though Gabriel had been struck instantly deaf.

All trees and grasses withered. The ground, split with dryness, cracked wide and long and deep. A great fear gripped him, fear that the earth would tilt beneath him, that he would roll into one of the great crevices and fall for ever and ever. Indeed, the earth began to rock, and he dug his fingers hard into the pebbled ground until they ached and bled.

Still the sun grew hotter. Every heartbeat was like nails driven through the softness of his temples.

Suddenly there was a change. From deep within the open crevice that had yawned open nearest his side came the sound of hissing. Slowly he turned his head to the left and saw them, small, black, shining vipers, each with a single crimson stripe from nose to tail, slithering out of the earth onto the hard ground.

By the thousands they came, milling about until the ground seemed in motion—aimless in movement, tongues flicking, tasting the air, winding over and under their own sleek bodies in impossible knots, spreading wider and wider afield until they encircled him. They slipped between his fingers, sliding like slime under and over his arms, poking into his ears and nose, searching for some opening by which to enter his body.

Gabriel compressed his lips and tried to will his nostrils closed. He fought desperately against the invisible bonds that held his arms to his sides, wanting to fling the serpents through the air, back to their horrendous pit. But his arms were frozen, and he succeeded only in twisting and writhing like the snakes themselves.

Then to his left—somewhere near his head—the vipers wound themselves into a ball and melted together before his eyes, forming a mass of fluid black, elongating slowly into a single, immense snake that began to move toward him. Its nose touched his bare side, made its way between his body and the ground, sliding under the small of his back, winding itself around until it encircled Gabriel's trunk in a thick, black, muscular coil, tightening as it wound.

Gabriel found that he could not breathe, that when he expelled old air from his lungs, the coil tightened, and he could not take new air in. Now in the throes of death, he opened his mouth wide in a silent scream and fought to free himself. Blackness began to encircle his field of vision, moving rapidly inward until all that remained was a single pinpoint of light, a candle about to be snuffed out.

Then, at the moment of death, in that strangely measured moment when he hung suspended between life and total loss, as the earth receded and dark eternity opened her mouth wide to receive him, while he struggled not with reason but with the agony of existence, then it was that a single breath of cool air touched his burning cheek. He opened his eyes.

Across the dark chasm, out on the edge of the sunbaked earth, a creature sat. A fox, yet in winter's coat, thick, soft fur, white as the first fall of snow. For a long minute the fox gazed calmly, steadfastly, into his eyes. Then, with purpose in her movement, the fox rose from her haunches and advanced toward the dying man and his captor. At her approach the beast about Gabriel's body drew back its hideous head and struck at the intruder, at the same moment tightening its coils sharply. But in a single swift move, the fox parried the strike and sank her needle-sharp teeth into the soft flesh behind the serpent's head.

Instantly the constricting coils began to slip. The thick muscles went limp, and the serpent fell away. The great constrictor again became a small black viper, dangling, squirming helplessly from the mouth of the snow-white fox.

She tossed her head sharply. The wounded viper flew twisting through the air, fell into the crevice, and the ground closed over it.

The melodious call of a thrush broke the unnatural silence. The air stirred with coolness. Blue shadows of tall pine fell across Gabriel's face, and soft green grass sprang up like a lush carpet beneath him. Somewhere in the grass a cricket sang.

The fox came near, nuzzled Gabriel's face, and licked his wounds. The pain vanished. Deep, delicious rest filled his body with ease and his mind with peace. But before his eyes closed in long sleep, he looked once more on the snow-white fox. On her breast was a patch of red where her once spotless fur was now soaked with blood.

* * *

Gabriel Dublanche woke to the movement of his own body. He lay on a woven mat stretched taut on a frame of slender poles. Someone was carrying him from a shelter into the sunlight and across a clearing. There was talking, all in hushed, respectful tones. Some of the talk he understood, for it was in French; some he did not, for much of it was in a tongue he did not know.

A woman's voice, lovely and soft, said, "Here, Father. Let's put him here."

He opened his eyes. The sky was an indescribable blue, and the sun's rays filtered through the top boughs of the tall pines standing above him. Moving feet rustled around, and the soft grass compressed as he was laid down upon it. The earth felt cool to his body and the air pleasant to his face.

"Look, his eyes are open." It was a male voice this time, quiet and calm.

"Yes," the woman spoke again. "I think he sees us. He's waking up."

Gabriel's eyes closed as two hands lifted his shoulders from the mat and placed a rolled length of soft, thick blanket beneath his head. Someone gently drew another blanket over him and folded its edge beneath his chin.

"Friend," said the man's voice, "I think you're going to be all right." The man paused and said, "We took the liberty of looking through your gear. Is your name Gabriel?"

He lay there, eyes still shut, puzzling over the question. Its meaning came to him gradually, and he uttered a single raspy syllable.

"Did he say yes?" the young woman asked.

"I think he did," the man replied. In the background murmured an undertone of conversation—male and female.

"Gabriel," said the man, elevating his voice a little as though trying to speak across a room, "open your eyes again. Can you see me? No. Don't try to move. You've been a very sick man, Gabriel. Young men from our town found you six days ago down on the Ottertrack. You were lying near the bank, not far from dead. Now, Gabriel, I'm going to lift your head in my hands. This young woman will give you water. You must try to swallow."

Strong hands lifted his head and shoulders, and the smooth round rim of a pottery cup touched his lips. The young woman tipped the cup and cool water trickled into his mouth. He found it hard to swallow; in his unconsciousness he had vomited such a profusion of bitter bile that his throat was sore and raw. Even so, the water was blessedly sweet.

The effort took all his strength, and soon he drifted back into peaceful sleep.

The four men who had found Gabriel had made a pallet of two saplings and one of Gabriel's blankets. On this they had carried him to their town on the northeast shores of Wind Lake, four miles due east of the Ottertrack.

A crowd had gathered as they brought him in, and a woman ran to find There-Is-Something-That-Knows, a tall man about fifty years old, with streaks of white running from his crown down the full length of his long black hair. Something-That-Knows was a Mide, a member of the grand rite of Me-da-we-win, the sacred society of the Chippewa nation that held in its keeping the secrets by which the people approached the Master of Life, Creator of All Things. Me-da-we-win also held the secrets of medicine and healing.

Something-That-Knows had stood over Gabriel's wasted form and looked down upon him thoughtfully. Then he had gone to his lodge, and after a time returned with a cup and, little by little, had poured the contents down Gabriel's throat. Then Something-That-Knows had pointed to an open space, told the young men to build a lodge, and sent one of the children to go for a young woman to care for the stranger. He also sent for Father Dumarchais.

It was Father Dumarchais and the young woman chosen by Something-That-Knows whom Gabriel had seen when he first regained consciousness. After drinking the water, he had fallen asleep again, and the young men had returned him to his new lodge. It was there the next day that he came to fuller consciousness, opening his eyes to a spacious dome made of white canvas stretched over arched saplings. Daylight streamed through its walls with such brightness that it forced him to close his eyes again and avert his face. When he turned his head the whole world spun round and over, and he grabbed at the ground to keep from flying off into space.

When his universe stopped spinning, Gabriel opened his eyes again, little by little so they could adjust slowly to the light. He found that if he moved his head with caution, everything stayed in place and he was in no danger of falling from the earth.

The next thing Gabriel saw, hazy and indistinct, was a figure kneeling beside him. Soon his eyes adjusted fully, and details began to fill in; lines, shades, and colors became clearly delineated one from the other.

The kneeling figure was a woman. Her face came first into focus, and a hazy memory formed in his mind. She gracefully extended her left hand and felt his forehead. Her hand was as soft and gentle as the cool morning air that whispered under the white edges of his lodge. Not since he was a child, or perhaps since his happier days with Celeste, could he remember having been touched with such tenderness.

He tried to lift his head.

"No. Don't stir," she said in French, and to be sure that he did not rise she placed both hands on his shoulders. "You must conserve your strength. You're much too weak. Do you know that you almost died?"

"How long have I been here?" he asked weakly. His throat felt like gravel.

"This is the seventh day," she answered.

She was hardly more than a girl. Her skin was dark, a mild brown deepened by a constant blush of carmine. Her cheekbones were high and her lower jaw wide. Her long, black hair was parted in the middle, drawn back and tied on both sides. Below her delicate ears it was bound together in braids with lengths of white braided yarn. Two perfect feathers, also white, tipped with black, lay over her left ear, and pointing downward, rested on the cascade of hair that fell over her shoulder.

Every feature flowed together to create such beauty that even in his sickened condition, Gabriel was awed. But most beautiful of all were her eyes. Each was framed above by a fold of skin that hid its inside corner and gave them the shape of almonds and, in a way that he did not understand, wonderfully increased their loveliness. They were deep eyes, big, dark, and full of light.

From the moment he saw her, Gabriel felt the sum of this young woman's beauty and knew somehow that it harmonized with the mind and spirit that lived within her.

He let his gaze wander over her face for a few moments and then asked, "Who are you?"

"My name is Philepenca," she answered. "Something-That-Knows has chosen me to care for you until you're well."

"Until I'm well," he repeated reflectively, trying to clear his mind. The haze persisted; his speech was sluggish and faintly slurred.

She reached out and brushed his hair tenderly from his forehead as she answered, "Seven days ago four of our young men were fishing on the Ottertrack. They found you lying outside your shelter near the riverbank. You had crawled through mud and it seemed you had been trying to reach the water when your strength failed. You had collapsed in a pool of your own vomit. The young men brought you here nearly dead. I think you ate something poisonous—some plant, bad meat, eggs that were spoiled, perhaps."

She felt his forehead again and touched her lips to the back of his right hand. "But the fever's gone now. You're getting well."

Distantly Gabriel remembered his meal at the river. It seemed a lifetime ago. "Can you tell me where I am?"

"You are among the A-wish-in-aub-ay, the Spontaneous People. Sometimes we are called the Ojibway, sometimes the Chippewa. We have come from the forests that border the great sea far toward the sun's rising. Now we live here, north of the sea that your people call Superior."

Just then a shadow covered the doorway and Gabriel heard another familiar voice. "Do I hear talking in there? Is our patient awake?"

"Yes, Father."

The man stooped lower, came into the lodge, and knelt beside the girl. His face looked like the craggy rocks that overlooked the shores of Crooked Lake, rugged and chiseled by long seasons of water and rain. He was dark, but his was the complexion of a European tanned by the wind and sun. Gabriel judged him to be at least fifty-five years old and knew immediately why he was here among these people. A black broad-brimmed hat was pushed back on his head, he wore a black dust-covered cassock, and a stiff white collar ringed his throat. It was the familiar attire of a Jesuit priest.

Like the girl, his most striking feature was his eyes. In spite of the darkness of his skin and the blackness of his hair, his eyes were the color of smooth gray slate laced with blue clay, shining as though washed in the water of a cold, pure spring.

His lips were thin, and he smiled pleasantly.

"Son," he said with a chuckle, his manner of speech casual and easy, "when they dragged you in here cold as a whet rock and limp as a wet dishcloth, I thought they'd gone to a lot of work for nothing. And here you are awake with eyes bright as Spanish dollars.''

"Was it that bad, Father?" Gabriel asked with a weak smile.

"Oh, it was, it was. I don't think I've ever seen a man further gone and come back to tell us about it." He looked at the girl and said, "But then, no man's ever had a finer nurse to help him." She smiled and dropped her eyes in thanks.

"I think that must be true, Father. My thanks to you both."

"You're as welcome as you can be, Gabriel," said the priest. "But tell me, were you headed upriver or down?"

"Upriver, Father. I left Montreal a year ago with a Lefleur brigade. For ten months I've been on a small lake northwest of Lower Basswood Falls. I was on my way back east with furs to trade."

"Didn't happen to see an old man named Huntermark by any chance?" Dumarchais asked.

"Yes," Gabriel answered, "I was living with Wilhelm Huntermark."

"I know Huntermark well. He's a good man. How was he when you left him?"

"He's dead, Father. He died from infection late in the fall."

Father Dumarchais was clearly saddened by this news. Gabriel told him how it came about, that he had been alone through the winter, and that he was now on his way back to France.

"But I'm afraid I've lost track of time. What is today, Father?"

Dumarchais thought for just a moment and said, "Well, it must be about the thirteenth—no, the twelfth of May."

"The twelfth!" Gabriel exclaimed. "Then there's still an outside chance I might reach Quebec in time to find a ship to France before winter. If I can be up and away in another week, I think I can make it."

Dumarchais' smile made his eyes twinkle. He said, "Why, son, you won't be strong enough before the end of *July*. You'd best forget about reaching home this year."

Gabriel's face fell, and Dumarchais responded seriously but kindly, "Gabriel, there are some things a man just can't do. Remember what à Kempis said, 'Man proposes, but God disposes.' You'll get back to France when God sees fit, not a day before."

CHAPTER 23

The Priest and the Dreamer

A SHORT distance south of the mighty Saganaga, curled among wooded hills, lay the body of water called Wind Lake. It was a small lake, a mile and a quarter long, a half mile at its widest, but its uneven shores wound in and out, sometimes among high, rocky bluffs, sometimes met by gentle escarpments of rock or soil, but everywhere surrounded by deep forest of pine, birch, maple, and fir.

Here it was that an A-wish-in-aub-ay town sat on a broad tree-scattered slope whose east and south sides ran directly into the water and whose north and west sides broke over into gently rolling, thickly timbered hills that were full of hidden dells, sudden valleys, and small meadows. Forty families made their summer homes in this village, three hundred people, young and old, more women than men, many children. Their houses were small, oblong rooms framed by long saplings sunk into the ground, bent and tied overhead, covered with woven reed mats and topped with sheets of birchbark to turn the rain. A few lodges, like Gabriel's, were of European canvas secured from the voyagers, but mostly they were made in the old way. Sixty such dwellings spread across the slope, some close together, some in a circle about a common fire, others set apart to themselves, all underneath the protecting trees.

The Wind Lake people were fortunate. Most A-wish-in-aub-ay towns moved four times a year, once to an autumn camp to fish and harvest rice, then on to small family clearings deep in the forest where they hunted through the winter. Again in the spring they gathered among the maple trees to make sugar, then finally moved on to a summer encampment to plant gardens.

The good fortune of these people lay in the fact that the forest about Wind Lake had many sugar trees, the soil plentifully produced corn, beans, squash, and pumpkin, and in the lake's shallows, tall, feathery rice grew in profusion. So the Wind Lake people lived here from the time sap rose in the sugar trees until freeze-up in the fall; only then did they disperse into the deep forests to hunt. In the spring they gathered together again, as they had done just a month ago.

This morning Gabriel sat just outside his lodge leaning against a backrest Philepénca had made of slender willow wands. The girl had cared for him wonderfully, feeding and washing him in his illness, administering medicines prescribed by Something-That-Knows, and reviving his roughened skin, burned by winter wind, cold, and sun, with fragrant oils. More than that, she had given him friendship that made his days of convalescence pleasant and his life seem worth living.

Nearly a month had passed. In some ways the time seemed shorter, Gabriel thought, for when one is in a strange place and among new people it goes quickly. Soon he would be thirty-two years old. Why, he thought, the average life span is hardly more than that. Where have my days gone?

At first he had been bitterly disappointed at the delay in his return to Europe, but now he was glad to be here among the A-wish-in-aub-ay. He felt he had inadvertently stepped into an ancient stream of rich, orderly life that had purpose and value.

Through a wide opening in the trees he could see men fishing from canoes on the deep lake's calm blue water, and beyond, the lower hills were bathed in the morning's bright, warm light. The hills were mottled, dark green where the firs and pines grew, light charcoal gray with the faintest hint of lime haze among the aspen and birch. Overhead, birds sang pleasantly in the boughs.

In the camp a new fragrance filled the air, for the season's last sugar-tree sap was running. From big copper kettles hanging on a sturdy pole framework over a brisk hardwood fire, billowy white clouds of steam wafted their way upward and, blending with the air, thinned into disappearing wisps.

The place was a perfect anthill of activity as both grown-ups and children scurried about. Women stood above the kettles, stirring and sampling their mixtures with wooden spoons. Children came out of the surrounding woods with little buckets of sewn birchbark full of sap, went directly to the kettles, and poured in their contents. Both men and women carried wood to feed the fires.

Tomorrow, after many hours of boiling and continual stirring, the thick, heavy syrup would be poured to harden in birchbark cones and little molds carved in wood: stars, moons, beaver, turtles, and flowers. For an entire year the decorative bits of candy would season meat and fish, sweeten fruit and cereals, and on hot summer days be dissolved into cold water for a refreshing drink.

Today there was talk of the work being nearly done, for this would be the last run of sap from the leafing maples.

Gabriel was startled by a small sound. Standing near and a little behind his right shoulder was a child. She did not lift her eyes, but stood silently and gazed steadily down at her own small moccasined feet.

Gabriel smiled pleasantly at her and in a gentle voice said, "Hello, little one. Who are you?" She did not look up. He reached around and took her small brown fingers in his hand. "Look up at me, dearest," he said. But the more he pleaded, the more reluctant she became.

"She doesn't understand you." It was the rich, warm voice of Philepenca.

Gabriel looked up to see her walking toward him. "She doesn't speak French?" he said.

"No, not yet," she answered. "Soon she will become a catechumen, and then she will learn. For now she knows only the language of our people."

"She's a very shy little girl," he said.

"No," Philepenca responded. "She isn't shy. We teach our children never to look up in the presence of their elders unless they are bidden to look up, and as I said, Deer-in-Water doesn't speak your tongue." Philepenca knelt and put her arm around the child's shoulder, then with her forefinger lifted the little one's chin. Deer-in-Water smiled sweetly, and her teeth glistened in the morning sun. She threw her arms around Philepenca's neck, squeezed her tightly, and then in embarrassed pleasure turned and ran away as fast as her feet would carry her.

Gabriel looked after her as she ran and with great feeling said, "Your people have the most beautiful children I have ever seen." He paused and with the same intent gaze continued, "And they are so very wise."

"Wise?" she asked.

Gabriel turned his searching gaze toward Philepenca and said,

"They know in their hearts who loves them, and who is good, and who is worthy of their trust."

Philepenca said nothing, but she recognized the compliment. The carmine in her cheeks deepened and she looked away.

"Philepenca, they trust you because they know you." He paused and continued, "Your heart is written in your face, not only in purity, but in sheer beauty. Even the children are not so lovely as you." She did not know how to respond to such words, and to put her at ease he changed the subject by asking, "When will I meet Something-That-Knows? I want to thank him."

"Thank him?" she asked.

"Yes," he answered, "for choosing you to bring life back to me again."

He was so earnest that she broke into pleasant laughter and said to him, "When you're well and about, then you can go and meet him. He is the kind of man who is not likely to come to you."

Suddenly a new thought burst into Gabriel's mind, and with immediate enthusiasm, he said, "Philepenca, teach me to speak your tongue!"

"I would be happy," she said, smiling.

Immediately she sat down beside him and began to explain. She rubbed the broadcloth of his shirt between her thumb and forefinger and said *"manido wegin."* Touching her soft deerskin shoe she said, *"makizin."* Pointing to the lodge behind them she said, *"wigiwam."* So the lessons began and so they progressed. Within days he saw that it was an intricate tongue, rich with words softly spoken, the most musical language on the continent, as polite and classical among native North Americans as French among native Europeans.

Day by day Gabriel's vocabulary grew. He learned the names of the birds: *shawshaw* the swallow, *opechee* the robin, *wawa* the wild goose, and *shuh-shuk-gah* the heron—and of the fish: *nahma* the sturgeon, *ugudwash* the sunfish, and what to call the whispering of the wind in the tree tops, the *si-si-quad*.

Gabriel's disappointment at being detained lessened. At last he was wholly glad to be on Wind Lake. What was a month or two, he reasoned, when it came to crossing an ocean? Besides, he had discovered a people to whom he had always been drawn. He had stepped, quite by accident, into a way of life with which he fell immediately in love. Or *was* it an accident? Perhaps Le Renard had been right. Perhaps he was sent among them to learn.

* * *

It was nighttime in midsummer. Gabriel sat just outside the door of a bark-covered *wigiwam* in a circle of quietly talking friends. At the center of the circle a fire burned, its light reflected from the glistening eyes and dark faces of a dozen men.

The calm, assuring drone of conversing voices drifted in from other fires and other circles. Children played in the shadows where dark night met the farthest reach of firelight glow, the sounds of their scurrying feet mingling with the murmur of the camp.

Somewhere on the eastern edge of the town, near the water, a young man sat in the darkness outside a lodge and played a simple, haunting melody on a flute of cedar. Somewhere a girl listened. The mellow, rich tones drifted over the *wigiwams*, flavoring every conversation, making the hearts of even the very old tender with remembrance.

Gabriel listened, too, and thought of his wife so far away. He wondered that a single moment could have changed their lives as it had: a carefree frolic, a rising storm, a flash of light, shining muscles tumbling in a great brown mass—and Celeste on the ground, so still, so broken, so forever changed.

The immediate conversation faded from his mind. What life have I lived, he thought, that I deserve such sadness? Did God foresee my evil and punish me beforehand?

Sometimes Gabriel was actually happy, but if he dwelt on these things long, sadness swept over him and he began to brood. He had no right, he thought, to be happy here in this remote corner of the world where pleasantness seemed to cover the land as waters cover the sea. Certainly others—his father, his mother, Celeste, little Michel—had not escaped the terrible consequences of his stupidity.

His thoughts drifted in and out of the firelight talk. He caught fragments of the conversation—accounts of the winter hunt, tales of the Dakota who had fled west, rumors of the Iroquois menace to the east.

A tall, handsome young man who sat directly across from Gabriel—Two Babies by name—passed a new elkskin pouch around the circle. He had made the pouch during the winter, and had covered it with intricate flowers of white, blue, red, and green beads, work of which the young man was justifiably proud. As it came to his hands, Gabriel nodded enthusiastic approval, and Two Babies responded with thanks.

While first one and then another spoke, Gabriel learned four new words and put them in their proper places. He could understand far more of their language than he could speak, but he could now carry on a passable conversation.

Then, feeling a sudden urge to be alone, he rose without a word and ambled through the dark trees, down to the lake's edge. It was not far to the beach, but as the sand pressed soft and damp against his moccasined feet, the sounds of camp faded behind him.

The breeze had fallen, and the lake was perfectly still, smooth as glass, reflecting the black jagged line of firs on its far eastern edge. The late-rising moon—four days past full, shimmering pale yellow—looked twice on Gabriel, once from just above the trees, and once again from the still, deep lake. The night air smelled of fresh water and rotting mud. A great horned owl asked Gabriel who he was. A fish jumped and splashed noisily back into the water again, spreading circles of silver outward in the moonlight.

There was peace here, so far from the splendor that was France and the glory of the European nations and the conflict in which it seemed that continent was forever embroiled.

Is there no evil among these people? he wondered. If so he had not yet seen it. To him they seemed as civilized as the peoples of Europe. They were certainly as intelligent, certainly as skillful.

His thoughts were deep, blissfully at peace. Were it not for my family, he said to himself, I might stay here forever.

Somewhere to his left a twig broke sharply. Gabriel became aware of the aroma of Father Dumarchais' pipe and looked around to see the priest's tall figure coming toward him.

Nathaniel Dumarchais had lived among the A-wish-in-aub-ay north of Superior for thirty-six years. He traveled from place to place, spending the summer in one town, the autumn in another, and the winter and spring in yet others. He was an unassuming man who preferred to be called simply Father Nathaniel.

Father Nathaniel was born in Bordeaux, France, on the Garonne River in 1690, fifty-seven years ago. He had first put on Jesuit robes at the age of nineteen and stepped into the North American forests at twenty. In the intervening thirty-seven years he had endeared himself to all the Chippewa who lived on the northern shores of Superior.

Father Nathaniel was moderately tall, about six feet, lean, with black hair that had whitened at the temples. The blackness of his hair and the darkness of his wind-burned skin gave dramatic emphasis to his light gray-blue eyes.

Because Father Nathaniel had helped Philepenca care for Gabriel, the two had seen each other often, and had quickly become friends. Dumarchais was more than content among the Chippewa, but he had a certain thirst for the companionship of this fellow countryman, so that already they had passed many hours in conversation.

"Father Nathaniel." Gabriel greeted his friend with a strong note of gladness in his voice. "Come sit beside me and enjoy the night."

The older man responded with equal enthusiasm. "I thought I saw you come down to the water, Gabriel," he said, and sat down on a slab of bare rock. Its stored warmth felt good in the coolness. "It's a fine night—moon on the lake, everything still and calm."

"It is," Gabriel answered, his tone showing clearly that the tranquility satisfied him deeply.

"You look to be stronger every day, son," said Dumarchais. "How do you feel?"

"Oh I feel fine, Father. As though I was never sick."

"Good, good," the priest responded. "But what about your plans to go home? I don't think I've heard you mention that for a long while. You're not thinking of staying with us, are you?"

"No, not permanently, Father. But I admit I was just thinking that if it were not for my family I might do that very thing. I've had more peace since I came to Wind Lake than I've felt in years." He paused, then added, "It's not just the place, of course. It's the people, too. I've come to enjoy them a great deal."

"Do you enjoy any one of them more than others, Gabriel?"

"Yes," Gabriel answered, the darkness hiding a faint blush. "But I suppose that's inevitable, isn't it, Father? I have the impression that you feel much the same as I do on that score. You do have a special affection for her, don't you?"

"That's no secret," the priest said clearly. "I was here the spring she was born. Most beautiful baby you ever saw."

"How long ago was that, Father?"

"Oh," Dumarchais said, "that was . . . let me think . . . it was the year before cholera broke out in '29—nineteen years ago."

"That's how old she is—nineteen?"

"I'm sure that's right. Yes, it is. She's nineteen."

"I could've sworn she was older than that," Gabriel mused.

"Well, that's because she acts older than that. She's always been a serious girl. Her folks died in the cholera outbreak and her grandmother raised her. With those big dark eyes, she always seemed to look right into my soul. When she was old enough for catechism, she had a love for God that not many grown-ups have. Her first confession was so truthful, completely honest; big tears were rolling down her cheeks." The priest sat in contemplation for a moment, then went on, "And she's never changed. The same humility, the same love, the same devotion—and nobody enjoys life more than Philepenca."

"Philepenca. That seems a strange name for a Chippewa child, Father."

"Well . . ." The older man leaned back and looped his arms about his knees. "In a way I'm responsible for her name. Before she was born I told a story around the council fire one night, about the son of Massasoit of the Wampanog people down in New England. He was the chief man among his people and led a rebellion against the English. Before he was killed, he proved himself a great man and distinguished himself with great wisdom and heroism. Everyone called him King Philip. Philepenca's mother— she was carrying the child at the time—heard the story and greatly admired Philip, so when the little girl was born she named her after him. It is a strange name, but that's how it came to be."

Father Nathaniel's pipe went out. He knocked its bowl against the rock slab, filled it again, and drew out his flint and steel. He fumbled in the dark for a piece of char, struck a spark into it, pushed the glowing bit of cloth down against the tobacco, and drew. The smoke rose in the darkness, and with it the agreeable aroma everyone associated with Dumarchais.

Then, after a few moments' silence, he added, "She's a dreamer, you know." The old priest said it in an offhand way, but Gabriel did *not* know.

"What do you mean, Father?"

"I mean that she has dreams . . . and that her dreams have meanings. Even when she was small she had dreams that came true."

"Like Joseph in the Old Testament?"

"Very much like Joseph. One morning when Philepenca was seven, her grandmother, old Wah-Wah-Taysee, came to me and said that Philepenca had dreamed, and in her dream saw water standing around the trees here on the shore of Wind Lake. Wah-Wah-Taysee wondered if I thought it meant anything. I said that I did not know, that we would wait and see. The very next week hard rains fell and the water rose until it stood around the trees. Nothing like it in all the fifty years the A-wish-in-aub-ay had lived here. Philepenca said it was just as she saw it. There have been other times, too.

"Even the Mide respect her dreams and her wisdom, so they have entrusted her with the knowledge of the Great Megis. The Great Megis is a huge seashell that the Mide say rose many years ago from the great salt sea toward the sunrise. The sun's rays shone from its back and the people lived well. Then the Megis sank again into the sea and the people were sickly. The Iroquois rose up and oppressed them, so they came west. When they reached Superior, they say the Megis rose from its waters, and life became good again."

"What does it mean, Father?" Gabriel asked.

"The Great Megis is the symbol of the Great Spirit's revelation of truth to His red people. The Great Spirit, the Master of Life, the Gitche Manitou has entrusted it to the Mi-da-we-win, the medicine society. Only certain persons are ever received as members. But because of her dreams, her wisdom, and her compassion, they've entrusted Philepenca with the society's great secrets, even though she is only nineteen. It's because of this she was chosen to help you when you were brought to the village nearly dead."

It was growing late. Gabriel looked back toward the village. The circles were breaking up, the people scattering and walking slowly to their lodges. Mothers called their children. Fires were being banked one by one. The young man with the love flute had retreated to his lodge.

Father Nathaniel stood up. "Well Gabriel, I don't know about you, but I'm going to turn in."

"I'm not tired, Father," Gabriel answered. "I'll be up after a while."

So Gabriel sat on the shore and looked out across the moonlit water, thinking he may indeed have come to Wind Lake for a purpose, and wondering at a girl whose dreams came true.

CHAPTER 24

Among the Spontaneous People

AUGUST 1747 was hot and dry; there were no summer showers, no cooling winds, and the sun beat down relentlessly. Even at night every *wigiwam* was stifling, so to escape the swelter all the Wind Lake people slept under the stars.

The fish, also trying to escape the heat, lolled about lazily near the lake's bottom. The nets could not snare them there, and the fish refused the bait sent down on hooks. So the people abandoned fishing until the weather should break and become cooler.

Industry in the camp ground to a standstill. Only essential chores were performed. Fires were lit only when necessity demanded. Dogs lay in the shade, breathing fast, tongues hanging long and loose from the sides of open mouths, too dry to drip saliva onto the dusty earth. In the gardens, bean vines shattered and the long brittle leaves of the corn stalks turned white and rattled when brushed. Broken clods crumbled and the ground cracked. Women carried water in birchbark buckets from the lake to their squash and pumpkins, but in spite of their efforts, most of the crop withered and died. Only the corn did well, for the yellow ears were already full when the terrible heat came, and the blistering sun ripened them all the more quickly and dried the corn in the ear, making it easy to shuck and shell.

During this hot, dry month, Gabriel spent much of his time with the young Chippewa man called Two Babies. Two Babies was—he told Gabriel—twenty-seven winters old, unmarried since the girl he loved was of the same clan as he, the Loon totem. Marriage within one's clan was as forbidden among the Algonquian peoples as marriage between brother and sister was forbidden among the Europeans.

Two Babies was a tall man with fine red-brown skin, serene, deep eyes, an aquiline nose, a handsomely formed mouth, and a firm, resolute jaw. The entire forward part of his head was shaved clean and his hair at the back cut short. He wove three long eagle feathers into the hair at the very top of his head and tied it upward in a tuft. Large silver rings hung from his ears. His face, shoulders, and forearms were tattooed with carefully executed, colorful, geometric designs.

His only clothing in summer was a colorfully embroidered breechclout that fell midway between his loins and knees, and soft-soled moccasins. His shoulders were broad, his body finely muscled, and his dark skin glistened with fragrant herbs and oils. During the fall and spring months he added leggings and a blanket, which he wore with as much style as Louis XIV had worn his satins and plumes.

Gabriel had first felt drawn to Two Babies when Father Dumarchais told him the origin of Two Babies' name.

"He's a twin," Dumarchais had said, "the secondborn. When a woman gives birth, she hangs by both hands from the ridge pole of her lodge while the child slips out and the midwife catches it. Two Babies was the second, and when he was born his mother said, '*Two* babies.' Two Babies he's been ever since."

"Identical?" Gabriel had asked.

"Absolutely," the priest answered. "You couldn't tell one from the other."

" 'Couldn't'? What happened to the older one?"

"His name was Silver Otter. He was murdered," Dumarchais said, shaking his head at the memory.

"Murdered!" Gabriel had exclaimed. It was the first evidence he'd seen or heard of violence among these peace-loving people. "How did it happen?"

"Well, Silver Otter had taken a wife—a girl from the Wolf totem—and a young villager, Blackbird, was jealous. Blackbird was the son of Strong Ground and came from a good family, but he was surly, always had it in for somebody. For a year or more the elders had kept their eyes on him, afraid he was going to 'rub somebody out' as these people say.

"One day a trader came through and gave Blackbird brandy wine. Blackbird got just drunk enough he didn't care what he did, and began to swing his long-bladed knife. Silver Otter said to him, 'Let's go to your lodge together, my friend.' Just as smooth as you please, Blackbird reached out and put that blade right below Silver Otter's third rib—into his heart.

"Two Babies and his brother had been as close as two brothers can be, yet Two Babies didn't seem bitter. But he did want justice. And more than anything, he knew Blackbird, and knew if Blackbird had killed once, he'd kill again.''

"So what happened?" Gabriel had asked.

"While everybody gathered around Silver Otter, Blackbird slipped right into the woods. Two Babies took four men and went after him, brought him back two days later to stand before Silver Otter's family.''

"What do you mean, 'stand before his family'?"

"In these people's system of justice," Father Nathaniel had replied, "a victim's family has the final say about what happens to a murderer. They can kill him outright or they can adopt him to take the dead man's place. In this case Two Babies himself led Blackbird to his parents' lodge—Tapinawa was the father of Silver Otter and Two Babies. Tapinawa and his wife came out, and Two Babies sat down beside them while the elders gathered around and Blackbird stood and waited. Two Babies' father got to his feet, made an oration, walked four times around Blackbird, and announced he would adopt the man as his son.

"I was there when it happened. Well, I had my eyes on Two Babies and it was plain from his expression he thought his father was wrong. This man shouldn't live to kill again. Blackbird smiled in a nervous, relieved sort of way and stepped forward to embrace his new father. As he did, Two Babies stood and sunk a tomahawk to its haft in the side of Blackbird's head. Blackbird dropped like a sack of corn. Nobody could deny that justice had been done— and that was all of it.''

"Quick and simple," Gabriel had said.

"Quick and simple," the priest had echoed.

Soon after that Two Babies and Gabriel became firm friends. Often at sunset they would canoe out onto the lake to escape the heat and to talk.

This was just such an evening toward the end of August. South of where their canoe drifted, a long, slender peninsula reached out like a finger from the farther shore. Between them and the peninsula three large white-spotted loons swam and burst out with an eerie laughter. Children's voices and laughter drifted faintly across the water from the village. A weed thrush burst out with high trills. In the distant forest a night bird sent out his hollow call. The dark bosom of the lake rose and fell as though breathing in sleep. The two men felt at ease together.

The day's blue blended into gold and the gold into dark. Gabriel said thoughtfully, "It's hard for a man to hold something in his heart and not tell it to his friend."

There was silence, until at last Two Babies asked, "Is some such thing in your heart, my friend?" More silence. "If there is, please know you can trust me."

Then carefully, as though stepping on ice that might break, Gabriel related his story of death and evasion, how his friend had been killed and how he had met the murderer and taken his life.

When he was done, Two Babies gave no sign of shock, but sat quietly. Finally, knowing that Gabriel expected some judgment of him, he said, "You did the right thing, my friend."

"The right thing by your way of life," Gabriel answered, "but not by ours."

"That I do not understand," Two Babies said. "Among the A-wish-in-aub-ay you would be praised for the way you dealt out justice."

"But there are too many of us," Gabriel answered, "and our laws shield a man from personal revenge. Among our people, revenge belongs to the state."

Two Babies shook his head gravely. "Revenge belongs only to the Master of Life," he said.

Gabriel looked at him blankly. "Then you acted for the Master of Life when you tomahawked Blackbird?" he asked.

"I did not take revenge on Blackbird," he answered.

Gabriel wanted to blurt out, "What do you call it then?" but instead he said calmly, "Why was his death not revenge?"

"I did not kill Blackbird because I hated him," Two Babies answered. "I did not kill him to avenge my brother's death." He turned and looked directly into Gabriel's eyes as he said, "I killed Blackbird so that he would not kill someone else's brother. If one is kind to the wolf, he is cruel to the rabbit. That was my purpose, to be kind to my people."

Gabriel said nothing, but sat taking the measure of his friend's words in silence. Two Babies dipped the paddle and drew it gently. The water gurgled around its blade in invisible little whirlpools and the canoe moved forward again.

At last Gabriel said quietly, "I hated Lecharbonnier. When I took his life, it *was* revenge." Two Babies said nothing, but paddled slowly to keep the breeze moving about them.

After a thoughtful pause Gabriel asked, "Is this the way of your people? They never seek revenge? Their only object is justice and the saving of life?"

The younger man shook his head. "No," he said. "Many of the A-wish-in-aub-ay go to war gladly. Many times they have avenged the life of a single man with the lives of an entire village of the Nadowessioux, the people you call the Sioux. We can be a violent, vengeful people. Some call us the Chippewa 'roast until puckered.' That is what our people have done to some of their enemies."

"Roasted them over a fire until their skin puckered?"

"Yes."

"But not you?"

"No. Not I, and for the most part the Wind Lake people would not be guilty of such a thing."

"Why are the Wind Lake people different from other of the A-wish-in-aub-ay?" Gabriel persisted.

Two Babies shook his head as though he could not believe Gabriel's question, then answered with obvious feeling. "You are like others of your people," he said. "You make us all alike. You think if you have seen one of my people you have seen us all. But we, like you, have among us different kinds: the workers and the lazy ones, the kind and the cruel, those who make war and those who make peace, those who love and those who hate. Man is what man is. Just as you, we have evil men among us. And among us we have men and women as good as the best of yours.

"But the Wind Lake people have listened closely to the Master of Life, and He bids us not prey on each other. Father Nathaniel, in the name of your God, says the same. The Master of Life and your God are one. The Wind Lake people seek to do right, and that is why we are a peaceful people. I cannot speak for the others, but I can say for myself that there is no revenge in my heart."

Gabriel was properly subdued. "So you would kill only to prevent killing," he concluded in an even voice.

"Yes," the younger man assured him.

"Do the A-wish-in-aub-ay have enemies in these forests?"

Two Babies shifted his weight and pulled on the paddle, then laid it across one strong, bare leg. "Not now," he said. "After our people came to the northern forests, for a long while they and the Nadowessioux lived in harmony. But then bitter rivalries rose between us, and we drove them to the west. For a time they settled on the banks of M'de Wakan, Spirit Lake of the Dakota. The Nadowessioux found M'de Waken to be a fine lake, rich with fish, set in the heart of fertile grounds that they called Minnesota, 'sky-tinted land.' There they began again, and have not returned.

"Yet the war club has not been buried, so that even now, the Nadowessioux and the southern Chippewa send war parties to raid each other in revenge. But the Wind Lake people, unlike their Chippewa brothers on Superior's southern shores, have no taste for war. We want only to live life as well as it can be lived. So we dwell at peace, and only from afar do we hear of the battles between our southern brothers and the Nadowessioux.

"But our most ancient enemy from the east, the ones you call the Iroquois but we call the Adders, sometimes raid to the eastern shore of Superior. Our people fear them yet. They worship a hideous god they call Agreskove. Agreskove is a god of war, and his eyes are full of blood and pain. The Adders follow his example. The greater their cruelties, the more success Agreskove will give them against their enemy. Have they made Agreskove to suit their hatreds, or has this devil shaped them in his likeness? I do not know.

"Father Nathaniel told me they tortured another priest, Father Jean de Brébeuf, many years ago. Without mercy. God had appeared to Brébeuf in his dreams, and told Brébeuf how he would suffer. So when the Iroquois built a scaffold and led him up, Brébeuf was not afraid, and began to preach to them.

"They tried to silence him, but could not. They struck him and shouted at him. He was a big man, hardened to pain, and just kept on preaching. At last they cut off his lips and cut out his tongue and ran a red-hot iron down his throat, then stripped him naked and set him afire. While the wood burned about him they poured a caldron of boiling water over his body. They said to him, 'You told us the more we suffer on earth the happier we will be in heaven. Out of friendship to you we are working to make your sufferings greater. You will thank us later.'

"Then they speared him, drank his blood, cut out his heart, and ate it. For they believe if one eats a brave man's heart, his courage will live on in them."

Two Babies fell silent. The sky was dark now and all the stars were out. A meteor traced a streak of silver across the heavens.

Gabriel stared through the darkness. His mind went back to the open square in front of the Cathedral of Notre Dame, and he saw again, as clearly as if it had been yesterday, the old Huguenot, as the executioner, in the name of God, crushed his windpipe and broke his bones. Gabriel shook his head sadly at the atrocities committed in the name of God. And what is worse, he thought to himself, is that Two Babies—a "savage"—is a better man than I.

Out loud, Gabriel asked his final question, "How long since the Iroquois ventured into these forests?"

"Not for a long while," Two Babies answered, "Not for a long while."

It was now early autumn, when Father Nathaniel found Gabriel sitting on the ground outside his lodge, legs crossed, a blanket about his shoulders, a roll of birchbark on his knee, and a short length of charred grape-vine in his hand.

"What on earth are you doing?" the priest asked, looking down in amazement.

"Writing, Father," Gabriel answered, and glancing around the village, he explained, "a journal I've been keeping for my son Michel. These people are too rich to forget." He looked at the priest for some sign of approval, but instead the older man smiled, shook his head, and walked away. Gabriel thought it a strange reaction, but continued to work over the piece of white bark, carefully inscribing letters on its white surface. He had laid a rough stone at his right knee and often stopped to rub a new point on the end of his charcoal stick.

Several minutes passed, and once again an ambling footfall rustled in the dry grass and disturbed his thoughts. At first he chose to ignore the disruption, but when his visitor stood above him for a full minute, obviously waiting for him to look up, Gabriel felt compelled to acknowledge the new presence.

He was surprised to see the black-cassocked Dumarchais again, standing there looking down at him, a wide smile on his face, and holding out a small walnut writing desk. Gabriel reached up hesitantly, took the desk, and turned it about, examining it as though a thing of this kind didn't belong so deep in the wilderness.

"Open it," the priest said.

Gabriel found a small brass latch beneath the lid's edge on the forward side and pressed it. With a quick snap the top opened.

Inside was a bar of dry ink, an empty bottle, three well-shaped goose quills, a penknife, and perhaps fifty sheets of fine cream-colored vellum.

Gabriel looked at the charred bit of vine and birchbark on his lap and smiled at his own foolishness. The priest grinned and said, "We don't have to do it all their way, Gabriel." Then he turned and walked away, chuckling to himself.

Between his eye and the sun, blue swirls swam in involuted curves like the curls of a chambered nautilus, and the water within the bottle grew thick with cloud, until shining through the liquid, the sun's disk became only a spark of dark silver.

When the water was a deep royal blue, Gabriel sharpened the nib of a quill and took a sheet of vellum from the lap desk. He held the sheet up to the light and, running his fingertips lightly over the paper's surface, examined its texture, fine and white as new cream. A clear, bold watermark proclaimed "Duvalier & Son, Paris."

He had seen nothing so finely delicate since leaving Montreal. Idly he wondered if he could make something like it from the pulp of rice straw, and resolved to try. But later.

Gabriel dipped the quill and began.

September 20, 1747—Moon of Shining Leaves

It has been a long time since I last wrote, Michel, but just as when I began this journal on Little Vermillion, I am again thinking of you, thinking you may want to know the things I've thought, and done, and seen during my time in the American wilderness.

I was on my way to you when I fell ill and would have died had not four "savages" found me and brought me to this village. Though for some time I've been well enough to travel, something within compels me to stay until the coming spring. I've been here for nearly five months now. And I wish more than ever that you could be here with me.

The people who found me and saved my life call themselves the A-wish-in-aub-ay, the Spontaneous People, for they don't know where they came from, except to say that the Master of Life created them "when the world was new." They are a handsome people, on the average taller than Frenchmen, with darker skin, well-shaped features and bodies. They are gentle, peace-loving, and have received me with as much affection as if I had been born among them.

You would feel at home here, for rather than working for money, these people work for their existence, just as the peasant farmers in Normandy. But here, no one owns the land; they share it. They plant gardens and raise vegetables. For meat they hunt, fish, and lift great nets into the air on poles to catch whole coveys of dove and pigeon, which they boil with wild potatoes or with dried blueberries and rice.

There is a fine simplicity in all their ways. For example, they name their months according to what happens at that time of year. June is the moon of strawberries, July, the moon of blueberries. March is the moon of the broken snowshoe, and November the moon of freezing.

Though I hear their lives are very hard in winter, in spring and summer this is a land of wonderful abundance. In the months I've been here, I've often gone into the woods and fields to gather berries of all kinds: chokecherries, raspberries, cranberries, bear berries, and creeping snow berries. Because of its shape, they call the strawberry "heart fruit." From the forest we also harvest wild ginger, hazelnuts, roots of the wild bean, a plant called mountain mint, acorns from white oak, hickory, walnuts, butternut, chestnuts, and even seeds from the blossoms of sunflowers.

"I've come to relish wild rice boiled with hazelnuts, blueberries, and wild onion, or wild rice with roasted elk, seasoned with juniper berries and maple sugar.

I've found work here, so I'm not idle. I've built a forge, a very large one. It stands fifty paces from the lakeshore, beneath an ancient oak very like the one I played under when I was a child.

The forge is built of randomly shaped blocks of native greenstone, mortared together with sand and lime. The chimney of the forge is half again as tall as I, and so great in girth that two men can barely join hands about it. The hearth of the forge is also of stone, built up to a height just below my waist, wide as my two spread arms and as long. The hearth is hollowed out to receive the charcoal, and the leather pipe from the bellows enters from beneath.

The great bellows is of wood and leather and hangs from

two of the tree's largest limbs. And the anvil is so large that to lift it I must crouch at the knees, hook one arm under its horn and the other beneath its heel, brace my shoulders, and stand. It's anchored to a section of tree trunk by lengths of iron rod driven and bent over its feet.

Until now the people have known nothing but to throw away broken tools. Now I can repair their axes, grubbing hoes, knives, and scraping tools. I've also made them plowshares, spear and arrow points of iron, and I mend the cracks in their kettles and dishes.

But Michel, I am like your grandfather. The work I love the most is ornamental. A day's walk south of here, at the base of a high cliff, is a large open vein of pure copper. The Wind Lake people believe the copper is sacred, and everything made of it they hold in high regard. From it I make emblems they dangle about their necks, and useful things such as small kettles and knives.

In turn the people supply me with meat and clothes. I have a garden of my own, and I've dried enough pumpkin and squash to last me the entire winter.

Every day I begin some task at the forge, and evening usually sees it done.

What peace I find in working again with my hands! What pleasantness to be among such a gracious people, especially after that miserable winter alone! God forbid that I ever have to exist alone again! Here I have the laughter of children around me, and all day long I see men and women working and playing, loving and living.

Now, in this place, among these people, the forest that nearly drove me insane gives me peace. The Wind Lake people believe the animals of the forest have spirits, and they call them "animal brothers." They think of the trees as being alive. They say, "Our animal brothers and the trees have peace. So look at them and you will find peace, too. It is the way of the Master of Life."

So I go into the forest and I walk among the trees. I lean against the great strong trunk of a giant sycamore, and sure enough, a quiet rises within me and covers my mind like an ocean, and like the ocean's tide, it washes the decaying weeds from the beach of my mind and leaves me clean.

I suppose it's the peace that makes me want to stay here until spring.

Less than a month later, in the Moon of the Falling Leaf, there was great excitement when toward evening, just before the sun's setting, a runner burst out of the forest. Instantly a crowd gathered around him.

"Where have you come from?" they asked. "What news do you bring?"

When the runner caught his breath he answered, "I come from Bow-e-ting. I've traveled eight days by canoe along the shore of the lake, then north on foot. I've been to four villages with a message. When you have heard my message, I will carry it west to tell the people of Rainy Lake. Please take me to your principal men."

The chief men took him aside, heard his message, and called the town together.

Women left their kettles simmering over fires. Children left their play. The voice of the water drum reached out onto the lake and into the forests; within half an hour everyone gathered in front of the great lodge of the Me-da-we-win to listen.

Black Duck, the town's principal chief, stood before them and raised his hands for silence. The crowd hushed, and Black Duck spoke. "A messenger has come from the sunrise with news for us. Give him your ear and you will hear for yourselves."

The man stood and said, "People of Wind Lake, I bring you news from the People of Bow-e-ting. It is news that will stir your hearts beyond my words to tell. Twelve nights ago, near the end of the Moon of Shining Leaves, the People of Bow-e-ting learned that a war party was marching on the land of the A-wish-in-aub-ay, a war party of our enemy, the Adders."

The people gasped and some rose to their feet ready to prepare instantly for war. Black Duck raised his hand again; the murmur and stir subsided.

The runner continued, "Immediately our principal men called a council and raised a war party to go out and meet the Adders. Five hundred men answered the call, and ten nights ago the war parties came together near Bow-e-ting.

"It was evening, our warriors had just lighted their fires when from over the ridge they heard yelling and laughing. They supposed it was a camp of Frenchmen, but wisely sent young men up to the crest to look over and see. It was the war party of the Adders, they said—nearly a thousand.''

Again a strong murmur ran through the crowd, and again Black Duck motioned for quiet. The Wind Lake people prepared to hear the worst. The runner's voice fell low. His feet moved with his words as he sang, ''The scouts told their leaders that the Adders were drunk about their campfires. Then every man among them''—his voice rose and fell and his feet moved faster—''every man put out his campfire and took up his weapon and put on his paint for battle. They waited then for nightfall. While the Adders slept all drunken, they walked in among them.''

The suspense was too great for the Wind Lake people. Every man and woman stood. The water drum beat in cadence to the runner's words, and every foot shuffled in time as the runner's voice reached out through the torchlit darkness.

''Then the warriors fell upon them and with their war clubs beat them senseless, drove their blades into their dark hearts, and sent them to the land of spirits in such numbers that not one remained among them. Then they sent word back to their *wigiwams*, back to their wives and children, the Adders come no more among us . . . the Adders come no more among us . . . the Adders come no more forever!''

With his last words their joy exploded in unrestrained dancing. The people laughed and shouted; the drums grew louder, feet moved faster. Even Father Nathaniel stopped to the music and joined in the song. He clapped Gabriel on the back, took his hands, and drew him into the crowd.

Fat old women frolicked with handsome young men. Those too old to dance sat in the great circle and in the doors of their lodges, clapping in time with the drums and rattles, rocking backward and forward to the rhythm. Smiles were everywhere.

As Gabriel whirled in and out through the crowd, cold sweat soaked his shirt. The Iroquois had been too close. The Wind Lake camp had escaped terrible battle, most likely a slaughter in which the women would have been captured and the children butchered. Father Dumarchais would have gone the way of Brébeuf.

The dancing lasted past midnight, and next morning the town was up early preparing a great feast of thanksgiving to the Master of Life.

CHAPTER 25

The Girl from Wind Lake

"GABRIEL, will you come with me?"

It was the end of October. South of the village, Gabriel had squatted on a rock slab that ran gradually into the lake, and was washing his hands. Philepenca had walked out of the village toward the woods and had seen him. On sudden impulse she had turned and come up behind him.

Gabriel had just come from the forge, where he had made a belt knife. Now he was scrubbing his hands with sand and ashes, working the mixture hard into the crevices at the bends of his fingers and under his nails, frustrated in his efforts to get out the black soot and animal fat that stubbornly clung there. He kept rubbing and working, but looked up when he heard her voice, smiled, and answered, "Go with you? Where are you going?"

He wanted to say, "Of course I'll go with you." He felt a boyish thrill to think she would ask him to go—it made no difference where.

"To look after my rabbit snares," she answered. "I set them yesterday. A weasel or fox will eat my catch if I don't get there first. Will you come?"

"I'd like that very much!" One more time he swished his hands back and forth in the cold water, rubbed them vigorously together, then stood and dried them on the white cloth draped over his shoulder.

As they walked away, out of the field of rushes and cattails growing in the shallows, a flock of startled mallards leaped noisily into the air and flew low across the water. Caught by the wind, they were borne south, becoming only specks lost in the black line of trees along the lake's southern edge.

The autumn sky was dull. The dark clouds stretched from horizon to horizon like an uneven sheet of lead hammered by some unskilled hand into waves of irregular thickness and color. The dark clouds stretched from horizon to horizon. A mild, cool wind blew from the northwest and stirred the lake into rippling motion, building combers that ate at the farther banks, but left the camp shore calm and quiet.

Within the forest, there was peace; only the tops of the firs were touched by low-swooping breaths that made them sigh. Only now and then a darting, uncertain wind dived down among the maples and oaks and rattled their broad, dry leaves.

The grass underfoot was dead, and it whispered to the passing of their soft moccasined feet. Up the side of a tall, old white oak, a sumac vine twisted, reaching out with fragile tendrils, slipping tiny feet into crevices and dark cracks beneath the giant's bark. A colony of beige five-pointed earth stars spread their arms in the dark brown humus at the base of a vast old oak that must have been centuries old. Under its limbs were scattered large acorns, smooth and brown, each of which wore deeply knurled caps like a Frenchman's beret.

Where only firs grew there was no underbrush at all, and the forest was a roof supported by myriad columns, while all below was a spacious room, clear, open, stretching away into the distance like some ancient Greek pavilion. It was a good place for two to walk on an afternoon so perilously balanced between the easy warm days of autumn and the chilling cold of winter.

Beneath the hardwoods the forest floor was covered with autumn color. As Gabriel and Philepenca walked, their feet made the crisp, new-fallen leaves snap and rattle softly.

Between the man and the woman there was no hesitancy to speak their hearts, for by now each was comfortable in the other's presence. Nearly every day for half a year Gabriel had seen Philepenca at least at a distance. By now he was filled with admiration for her, and his heart swelled with desire to know her better.

Often he had gone to the lodge where she and her old grandmother Wah-Wah-Taysee lived. Philepenca had welcomed him, conversed with him, and had as many questions for him as he had for her. Questions about the world beyond her horizons, about great canoes that looked like white-winged birds, about houses that could not be moved, and about a water with waves sometimes as high as the forest's tallest trees.

His questions were about her childhood, about the wisdom of the animal brothers, and most especially about the dreams she had dreamed. For beyond her marvelous femininity, he was drawn by the mystery of her spirit, something deep, beyond words, beyond logic, something transcending their vastly different cultures, something he had doubted, but in which he hoped to believe again.

And sometimes, when in the evening they had sat before her lodge, she would say in a voice quiet and low, ''Do you hear it?''

And he would answer, ''There are so many night sounds, which should I hear?''

And Philepenca would answer, ''The trees, their murmur as they brush their branches together when the wind moves among them.''

''The trees,'' she had once said, ''are the glory of the Master of Life. They shield my people from the blistering sun in summer and in winter give them warmth and food, and they shelter us and the animal brothers from the bite of the bitter cold winds. And,'' she continued, ''sometimes the Master of Life speaks to me through them.''

She paused and lifted her alert eyes to the whispering darkness in the treetops, then nodding, said softly, ''Tonight, the trees are at peace.''

At other times she would say the trees were restless or were sad, but always when she spoke of them he saw in her eyes a longing that he, too, might hear, and come to understand.

And when, as she sometimes did, Philepenca became hurried and preoccupied, the trees did not speak to her at all. Then she would disappear from the town and be gone for a day, or perhaps three. And when she returned, Gabriel could see that her heart was at peace and that she had heard them once more.

Today as they walked together through the forest to tend her snares, their feet whispering among the grasses, he asked, ''Can you hear them now, Philepenca?''

And she answered in her soft voice, ''Yes. The Master of Life speaks to me today, and the trees are happy.''

''And what do they tell you?'' he asked.

''They tell me that now, for many days, life will be good for the A-wish-in-aub-ay.'' She paused and looked at him, then said, ''And they say that after the storm the days will be good for you . . . and for me.''

He looked at her sharply. Her face flushed slightly, and perplexed by her own words, she looked away.

The moment passed quickly. Gabriel vaguely decided it meant nothing more than a premonition of his imminent return to France.

Shortly they came to the edge of a small clearing and found Philepenca's first snare. The place was shielded on every side by trees but was open to the sunlight. Bushes grew thick there, many of them covered over with the tendrils and scarlet leaves of creeping vines.

Philepenca pointed to a narrow path running beneath low bushes, a trail worn by the soft feet of rabbits who made the low growth their refuge and home. On one of these trails she had set her snare, a small net that she herself had woven of fibers stripped from the underbark of basswood saplings.

The net had fallen. Hunched down inside was a large rabbit, almost white, his fur newly grown to protect him from the coming cold. He sat helpless, crouched within the net's strands, his large black eyes wide, searching, fearful of the human creatures bending above him. He quivered and, in a desperate effort to escape, made quick, spasmodic movements.

Even when Philepenca deftly stripped away the net with one hand and took hold of the rabbit's back feet with the other, he made no sound. But when she placed her right foot on his head, he called out wildly in short, high-pitched squeals.

With her foot on the rabbit's head and his rear feet in her hands, she jerked sharply upward, and the neck broke cleanly. Then, holding the limp creature high, she examined it closely.

"In the summer, this rabbit was brown," she said. "But see"— she pointed to a grizzling in the fur—"soon it would've been like the snow so that the fox and lynx could not see it. And look at its feet, so big, like the cedar and sinew shoes my people make to walk on top of the snow." She smiled a pleased smile, shook her head in wonder, and said, "The Master of Life has made him so—to protect the rabbit from those that would take his life."

Gabriel smiled faintly at her naïveté and said, "But he has not protected it from you. You have killed it." He felt an instant pang of guilt at having said it, for it was a callous remark, certain to devastate this simple forest child and strike a wound to her perfect faith.

He was surprised to hear her laugh and say, "Oh no, Gabriel. You do not understand. Let me tell you. Once when I was sad and could not hear the voice of the trees, I came into the forest, to a place very near here, to an opening in the woods where I could quiet my heart and listen. It was seven winters ago, and I had just passed from childhood. Snow was on the ground, but the bitter cold had not yet come. I sat at the foot of an oak on the clearing's edge, folded in the warm new fur of a bear, and spoke to the Master of Life what was on my heart.

"Suddenly a woodland caribou appeared on the other side of the opening, and very near me three great gray wolves stepped from the trees. The caribou and wolves stood looking at each other. The caribou did not run, but stepped toward the wolves, who only lifted their noses and sniffed the air—they were having a talk about death, and it was not time for the caribou to die—so the wolves turned about and trotted back into the forest and the caribou went his way.

"There is order in this world. There is a time to live and a time to die. My people do not kill for the joy of killing as the foolish Europeans do to prove that they are men. We kill for meat and clothes. This small animal brother came into my snare because it is his time, and he is to help us live well through the winter. Gitche Manito is the master of his life as well as the master of mine.

"There is nothing wrong with dying—except that it takes from us for a while those who love us. It is only ours to strive for a good death, to die well when the Master of Life says our time has come."

Gabriel's sophistication suddenly looked very foolish to him. She waited for his response, but he said nothing. She did not interrupt his silence. It was well that she did not, for he was thinking about this remarkable woman.

She's soft, he thought, as soft as a woman should be, yet she's strong enough to do whatever must be done, and clear-minded enough to see the reasons to do it, just as Celeste used to be. All the beauty and fragrance of womanhood, but not the slightest thread of foolish false femininity. If only they could have met when Celeste was well, how they would have loved one another!

Philepenca's second snare was by a small stream that trickled down a crevice in a wooded dell. The stream had been crippled by two months without rain. This snare was untouched, just as were six others. But of the ten snares she had set, three held rabbits. She would take them to her lodge, remove the hide from each in a single piece, and preserve the furs to be cut into strips from which she would make the warmest of all coverings, a rabbit-skin blanket. The meat she would preserve by drying it over slow fires, and the bones she would pound into powder and later boil with the dried meat in a rabbit-vegetable stew.

It was late afternoon by the time Gabriel and Philepenca started back. The hidden sun was descending rapidly behind the gray clouds. While yet far from the village, deep in the forest, they found themselves on the edge of a clearing Gabriel had never before seen. He was astonished, left almost without breath to see standing in the clearing's center one giant maple tree. Its great height was further accentuated by the fact that it grew upon a hill in the midst of a meadow. All of its leaves were still intact, every one at the height of its autumn color. The other trees stood about on the meadow's edge, and seemed to be respectful subjects paying homage.

Without a word between them, the Frenchman and the A-wish-in-aub-ay girl sank to the ground, gazing, inscribing deep into their memories an indelible print of the wonderful tree.

After a time Philepenca broke the silence softly, speaking as if to the tree itself. Gabriel turned toward her and watched her lovely face as the words rose from deep in her heart. He felt that even if he had not been there, she would have spoken. She said, "One morning in the early summer, when I had been in the world seven winters, Grandmother called me to come and eat. She had prepared a meal of *man-o-min* and fish. The wind was calm that day, and the sky was clear, so we ate about the fire in front of our *wigiwam*.

"I came when she called, filled a dish of bark with the rice and boiled fish, and sat down. Then I saw. On a square of birchbark, Grandmother had laid a small piece of charcoal. And I knew. It was a sign from her to me that I must make an important decision.

"The charcoal meant it was my time to go out into the forest and wait to see if perhaps the Master of Life would come to me and give me a gift that would always be mine, a gift by which I would serve him. But she did not force me to go. It was my choice. Many children choose not to go. But when I saw it, my heart filled with joy. I wanted to leave the rice and fish and go immediately. But I restrained myself and ate.

"Then, without a word between Grandmother and me, I picked up the charcoal and walked into the forest. I did not know where I would go."

Philepenca paused for a long while and a gentle smile played about her lips as she let her mind go back. Then she spoke again. "I came to this meadow, to the foot of this great tree. And this is where I discovered his gift to me, and first learned that I would be a dreamer.''

She paused in her narrative, and for the first time since entering the clearing looked at Gabriel. Then with joy in her eyes Philepenca said, ''It's good that we've come here together, for I have told my first dream only to Father Nathaniel and to Wah-Wah-Taysee. Now, if you do not mind, I will tell it to you.''

Gabriel sensed the wonder she felt in the moment, and somehow felt it, too. Softly he answered, ''I would be honored to hear your dream.''

In her gentle voice Philepenca began, ''The leaves were green and full on the tree, and its winged seeds were falling, some settling like whirling birds beneath its limbs, others carried by small puffs of breeze out into the meadow, and some even beyond into the forest. The air seemed full of them, like dragonflies spinning round and round as they went.

''I sat here . . . right here where we are sitting, and filled my eyes with the great sugar tree's beauty, and I asked the warm south wind to carry my heart's wishes to the Master of Life, for he is too sacred for us to approach. We hardly dare speak his name.

''Then I began to dream. Though I was not asleep, I dreamed, and in my dream I saw an animal sitting at the foot of the great tree. It was very beautiful, small and white—as white as the snow. Never before had I seen such a forest brother. Since, I have heard that something like it lives to the north and toward the setting sun.

''It was a fox with a coat like an ermine. She saw me here, then she rose, and came and sat proudly before me.

''Then, in my dream, she spoke and called my name. She said I would have the gift to dream, and that with this gift I would help my people.

''Soon I understood. The creature was me, and I was the creature. But in the world of spirit it was more than me. The white fox served the Master of Life and had been sent to be my guide. She is the lesser spirit between me and the Great Spirit.''

Again Philepenca paused, lost in her thoughts, just as Gabriel was now lost in his. At last she spoke again. ''Since that day I have dreamed many times, and the old fathers say that my dreams are dreams by which our people can plan. And now I believe my dreams even more . . . for before the last winter white melted, while it was still full on the ground, I dreamed again. In my dream I saw a face looking up to me out of deep waters.

"When our hunters carried you into camp that day in the moon of sugar making, I saw your face and knew that I had seen it before. For you were the face looking to me out of deep waters."

At that moment, far in the western sky, the sun broke through, and its light fell full on the grand maple. Instantly hidden life sprang into every leaf and stem. The oranges, the scarlets, the residual greens and foreshadowing browns burst into a full symphony of color.

Gabriel and Philepenca drank its magnificence deep into their souls.

In the time it takes to draw four deep breaths, the cloud closed again, shut the sun away, and the incomparable moment was gone—gone except in the memory of the man and the woman who saw it.

They sat in silence, awed as if their coming to this place, at this time, had been intended, perhaps by the Master of Life.

CHAPTER 26

The Winter Encampment

IT was the Moon of Freezing, November, the third day. Hard snowflakes, almost like sleet, began to fall in the early afternoon. As they fell, the dry foliage on the oaks rattled softly, and the brown leaf carpet that lay on the ground changed slowly to white.

Children ran with their heads tossed back, laughing mouths wide open, catching the tiny white spheres as they fell. Gabriel sat at his lodge door, a thick Hudson Bay blanket about his shoulders, tending his fire and cooking his evening meal. The snow hissed in the hot coals. As night came on, the hard flakes turned to large feathery wisps of snow, looking for all the world as though a great flock of northern geese flying above the clouds had molted.

Next morning the women going to the lake for water found they had to break a thick layer of ice before dipping their copper kettles. This was the silent signal; the time had come for the Wind

Lake people to break into families and go to separate winter camps.

Gabriel wrote in his journal:

November 4, 1747, the Moon of Freezing

Last night the weather turned suddenly cold, and the lake is frozen. Within two days the village will divide and everyone will go with his near family to a winter camp where hunting will be good.

Father Nathaniel has gone to the camps of the Pigeon River people, several days east of here. We expect him to return sometime early in the moon of making sugar or the moon of flowers.

I've been invited to go with Sitting Ahead and his wife White Marten. The group will include his children, his two brothers, his own father, his father's sister Wah-Wah-Tay-see, and her granddaughter Philepenca; in all, eight dwellings and perhaps forty people. They are good people, Michel, and I wish you could come to know them as I have.

There, just as here, I will have a dwelling of my own.

November 21, Moon of Freezing

I think we are well prepared for rough weather. My lodge is simple, but adequate, only four good paces long and nearly as wide, with a roof just high enough for me to stand with two or three inches to spare. I built it after the A-wish-in-aub-ay fashion.

I began by cutting thirty-six slender poles and planting their large ends in the ground about a cubit apart, eight poles on each of two sides and ten on each of the other two. I bent the smaller ends in an arch to meet and, where they overlapped, tied them with basswood cord.

Then, around this framework, I bent other slender poles, this time horizontally, on four levels, two spans apart, and tied them where they cross the upright saplings.

This framework forms a dome, to the sides of which I've tied two layers of thick-woven bulrush mats. For a roof I've sewn sheets of birchbark, laid them on top, passed cords over them, and staked the cords to the earth on either side. A firepit in the center, beneath a smoke hole cut in the roof, allows me to heat this crude room rather well.

Across the smoke hole I've tied a short stick. From this I hang two crotched limbs of chokecherry tied together to form a double hook. I hang one of these hooks on the horizontal stick, and on the lower hook suspend my copper kettle above the fire.

I finished the lodge just in time. The snow has been falling steadily for several days now, growing deeper and deeper. Around the outside of my lodge I've driven wooden stakes a foot and a half from the walls and packed this space firmly with cedar boughs and moss to seal out cold drafts. The snow will improve the seal.

Our eight lodges stand in a circle around a small "court," where we keep a fire burning day and night, and a rack of meat drying. My lodge is on the court's north side, fortunately for me, for my door is away from the prevailing winds.

Across the circle is the lodge of Sitting Ahead, his wife White Marten, their four children, and White Marten's old father Niskigwun, meaning Ruffled Feathers, a name that fits him well. To my left is the lodge of Gagewin and his wife, Ajawac. The meaning of his name is Everlasting Mist, and hers, Wafted Across. They have three children, two boys just becoming men and a little girl of perhaps nine winters. Gagewin's parents live with them. They appear to be very old, but if I've calculated correctly, neither is much beyond sixty, and perhaps not that. Exposure to the elements ages them prematurely. Yet I'm convinced that at least five of the Wind Lake people are somewhere near one hundred years old. One of these is Wah-Wah-Taysee, Philepenca's grandmother. The lodge on my right is hers.

One small lodge is certainly not spacious enough to house a man, his wife, her parents, and their three children in the European fashion, yet they seem to get along quite well, generating less friction than a French family might in the same circumstances.

By comparison, I have room to spare, and we all have plenty of food, for these are industrious people. I am perfectly content, and believe we are ready for anything the winter might throw against us.

* * *

December 15, Moon of the Little Spirit—or as the Nadowessioux call it, "Moon When the Wolves Run Together"

It is getting colder by the day.

I had not imagined that anywhere in the world were a
people who lived in such circumstances as my people here.
This is hardship of a most difficult kind.

And yet, they are so very close to everything that's real.
I would not have thought that living in such a dwelling
could bring me so near to the earth and sky.

Just now it is night, and the wind howls about my lodge
and whistles through the little opening above my fire. The
snow grows ever deeper in the forest. The heavy caribou
skin that covers my door flaps furiously. Snow blows in
little drifts about the door and spins through the smoke hole
to melt above my fire. It is easy to understand why the
A-wish-in-aub-ay believe that every tree, every breath of
wind, every flake of snow has a spirit. We do indeed live
in a wondrous, mystical world.

January 10, 1748, Moon of the Big Spirit

The cold is incredible!

My fire never goes out. Even so, a white sheen of frost
has edged through the smoke hole, creeps along the thatch,
down every pole, and now thickly covers all the upper parts
of my walls.

I am never perfectly warm. If I piled on wood enough to
beat back the cold, I would turn my lodge to a bonfire and
incinerate myself with it; there are tales about those who
have tried.

I have learned that one does not fight the cold; the
A-wish-in-aub-ay do not try, but accept it for what it is,
hard and heavy, a great white leech that sucks the very life
out of them.

The nearest I come to being warm is when I'm in my bed
of cedar boughs, on a hair-covered caribou hide, spread
over with two thick Hudson Bay blankets and a bearskin.

I've been away from the European settlements for nearly
two years now, and all of my woven clothing is gone—worn
out. The Wind Lake people buy cloth from the voyagers,
but at present they have no extra, so I dress in their soft-
tanned leather; shirt and pants of skins, a cape of nearly a

whole hide of elk. The cape is a simple arrangement with a hole in the middle through which I slip my head. It drapes over my shoulders, reaching almost to my knees—simple, but incredibly warm. Whatever powers shaped the world and its life planned well. Now I understand how it is possible for the beasts to survive this horrific cold.

Only one thing is harder than staying warm; that is staying clean. Where in this cold does one get water to wash? All the streams and lakes are frozen, and my people dig no wells. Many times a day I add snow to the copper kettle above my fire, but beyond what I need to drink, it yields little. Always the water has an abundance of foreign matter floating in it—soot flies up from the fire, fine ash falls from the smoke, bits of grass and bark from the roof. I've learned to ignore the scum and black specks and to drink the water with as much relish as if it had been drawn from a fine deep well.

To conserve body heat we rub our skin with a mixture of crushed puccoon root, bear grease, and ashes. The grease holds in our natural heat, and the puccoon cuts down the foul smell of the fat. It also darkens the skin so that I look very nearly like the A-wish-in-aub-ay.

The air in my lodge is almost always a haze and the inside roof is black with soot. You can imagine, I think, how the particles of smoke attach to the grease on my skin.

But it's all right, for the others do the same, and no one is thought the worse for it.

I make us sound filthy, but we are not. We do wash, and we use powders and oils from the forest's plants, so that our skin is soft to touch and sweet to smell.

In fact, A-wish-in-aub-ay knowledge of plants for medicine and cosmetics far outstrips anything I've seen before. They are a resourceful people!

And they are gentle. Their civilization is shorn of all superficiality, their beliefs are profound, and they have an absolute sense of honor. Their two chief values are their devotion to the Master of Life and devotion to each other. They are tender toward their children, husbands and wives are devoted to each other, and the free flow of feelings between them is wonderful to observe.

Surely the measure of a civilization is not in whether it

builds cities and lives in houses that cannot be moved, but in the compassion its people show to one another and the determination with which they press toward greater compassion.

I often think of Huntermark's lodge above the Little Vermillion, with its stout clay-chinked walls, huge stone fireplace, tight glass windows, and even at this moment its rafters yet filled with enough food to see a man and his family through the harshest of winters. Yet, if this very day I could somehow reach it through the deep snow, leave these eight bark-covered *wigiwams* and go there, I would not. For no matter how terrible the cold, isolation is worse.

Better miserable in the company of others than comfortable alone.

February 18, 1748, Moon of the Crusted Snow

While the men hunt, the women stay in camp and butcher what we kill. The great drying racks above the common fire are heavy with strips of moose and elk.

Three days ago, on the fifteenth, I killed a bear. I came on him by accident—or I should say we came on each other—at a place about four miles from here. He was about ten feet from me, and every bit as startled as I. When he reared high to sniff the air, I shot him near the white patch on his breast.

When the bullet hit, he cried out with an almost human cry that sounded like, "Oh Lord!" And he fell down dead.

It was a large beast, and the women are still rendering the fat for oil. I intend to tan the robe and give it to Philepenca.

February 24, 1748, Moon of the Crusted Snow

The snow is falling so heavily that everyone is inside; we keep busy weaving mats, sewing, making new fishing nets, canoe paddles, etc. Some of the women are making birchbark transparencies, a thing the A-wish-in-aub-ay do by piercing the bark with their eyeteeth to make pictures of fish, animals, or flowers.

Two Babies spent yesterday in my lodge. He is a good hunter and quite pleasant, but he is like none of the others. He does everything his own way and tends to stay to himself. Everyone thinks him a little eccentric, but he has deep thoughts, and I have learned a great deal from him.

Yesterday he made a cedar flute. I asked if he intended to do some courting in the spring, and he said he did not, but had a friend who might, and that if the time came, his friend would certainly need a love flute. So he was making it for him.

He doesn't seem to hear me when I say that with breakup in the spring, I'm leaving for France.

March 23, 1748, Moon of the Broken Snowshoe

For several days the south winds have blown steadily. There is a feeling of spring in the winds, but they come across Superior so sharp and damp, they cut through me like a knife. Even as I write, my back shivers with the chill and my bones ache. The ache reminds me that I am growing older and in three months will be thirty-three.

There is much talk of moving back to Wind Lake. Sap in the sugar trees will soon begin to run.

Three of the men have gone to join a party on an extended hunt clear into the Rainy Lake region. Game is plentiful there, they say. But then, game is plentiful here as well. They are going for the thrill of the journey and the hunt, but I have more pressing things.

Two Babies stayed behind to help move the camp. In the last two weeks he and I have done some pretty fair hunting on our own, taking a moose and a caribou, so that once again the drying racks are heavy with new meat.

April 15, Moon of Sugar Making

Winter in the deep woods is giving way to spring. We and all the other camps have come again to the shores of Wind Lake. Believe me, it is good to be among old friends! The maple sap is rising, and with it the spirits of the people, all of whom are happy and optimistic.

But rather than sugaring, I have a task of my own. Every day I gather the freshly risen gum from the evergreens, and I boil it to make pitch. Our people use the pitch to make torches, but I will use it to caulk the canoe that will take me to Montreal, and from there, Michel, I will come to France, and to you.

CHAPTER 27

A Bruised Reed

It was the first day of June, clear and warm. On the shore of Wind Lake, where the gentle escarpment of rock runs into the water, a loaded canoe floated ready and waiting for Gabriel Dublanche.

Gabriel had said his good-byes to Father Dumarchais and his other friends. At this last moment he stood facing Philepenca, the girl who had nursed him to health and who had made him believe again that life was worth living. Her eyes brimmed with tears. "It isn't for you to go, Gabriel," she said.

"But I must," he answered. "I have someone waiting for me."

She heard the determination in his voice and so made no reply, but despairingly dropped her gaze to the ground. Gabriel reached out and caressed her arm. She looked up and smiled. He smiled in return, lifted the last bundle to his shoulder, and turned toward the canoe. Two Babies, who would go with him as far as Grand Portage, had taken his place in the bow, and Gabriel was about to step into the stern when he heard a thin shout. Far out on the water a light canoe bore rapidly toward them. He stood and waited.

Within minutes the canoe beached. Three men jumped out, drew the craft ashore, and extended greetings to the curious crowd. Two of the men were French, and the third was the tall Scotsman, Paul Robertson. After a warm greeting, Gabriel, knowing that Wind Lake was not on the voyagers' regular route, apprehensively asked, "Paul, what are you doing here?"

"Wintered at Grand Portage," Robertson answered, "on my way now to Rainy Lake. We heard a rumor that a young Frenchman named Dublanche lived with the Chippewa on Wind Lake."

He paused, reached inside his vest, and drew out a leather pouch, then said, "I've a letter for you."

One thought sprang up in Gabriel's mind. It's from Celeste, he guessed, and it says "Come home." No need to hide any longer. So strong was his conviction that even before he broke the seal, he began to laugh; his heart was filled with happiness.

He opened the letter. The hand was not Celeste's, but the large flowing script was a hand he knew; it was from Pierre Lefleur, the date, July 20 of the preceding year. It read:

Gabriel:

I am writing to you from Montreal where I have been eight weeks trying to learn your whereabouts. Early tomorrow I will leave for France on the *Destiny*, captained by André Beal.

I came to Montreal expressly to find you, thinking that surely you had hidden in the southern hills or made your way to Boston with the young woman who was with you the night of Lecharbonnier's death. Only yesterday, while paying the governor my last call, I had the good fortune to meet this young woman. Mademoiselle Fontaine confided in me that you had fled to the interior and that she believed Paul Robertson would know your exact whereabouts.

According to Celeste, this young woman was your mistress. Having seen her, if it were true, I could hardly blame you.

I have wished very much to know the straight of what happened the night of Lecharbonnier's death, and Mademoiselle Fontaine has helped me on that score. Though I have not found you, I at least go home with a satisfied mind.

Frankly I doubt I will ever set eyes on you again, Gabriel, for whatever you do, you must not entertain ideas that this thing has blown over. Lecharbonnier was the intimate of several important officials in the homeland, and his death was a financial loss to at least three of them. Each of the three would be glad to see your head roll. So, please, for the sake of us all, do not try to come home.

Even so, what I am about to say will make it even more difficult for you to stay away. There is no good way to break the news to you. Celeste is dead.

After she came home—I'm sure you knew she returned,

but perhaps you did not know that she came to live with us—she grew less and less rational. Her temper was a terror to us all, for there was no one against whom she would not lash out. It was impossible to reason with her.

Before long, I was convinced that you were quite right, that she was ill, the result of the accident years ago. It was in fact a seizure—on March 10 of this year—that took her life. Her eyes rolled back in her head, her muscles grew rigid, and she could not breathe. Within minutes she was gone. It was a terrible day for us all. And yet I must say, after years of torment, she is finally at peace.

I want you to know, Gabriel, that Emilie and I do not hold you responsible for her illness, nor for the sad way in which she lived out her last years. And we understand why you did what you did to Lecharbonnier. It was foolish in the extreme. It had terrible consequences. But we understand.

I am grateful to you for uncovering Lecharbonnier's thievery. Had you only handled it differently . . . but you did not. What is done is done.

Your parents grieve for you. They have aged unbelievably in the last year. Abel has grown stiff and his hands are so gnarled that he can no longer work. He tells me that Catherine is close to tears much of the time.

Little Michel is doing well, living with us and growing to be quite a big boy. At first he asked every day when you were coming home. When Celeste died he cried for weeks, but before I left he had settled down somewhat. You know how we love him, Gabriel, and that we'll care for him with the same devotion you would yourself were you here.

Our hearts are broken, but we bear up well. We have something to hope for in Michel, so we try not to let him see our pain. Always we speak well of you, and we tell him that you cannot come back, that you did not desert him.

We want to hear from you, but it is best if you do not write. A letter falling into the wrong hands would betray you. And Michel might not understand how it is that you can write, but that you cannot come to him.

I am giving Paul a small package for you, something the governor helped me get my hands on. I know it will mean a great deal to you.

We pray for you, Gabriel, and you have our love.

> Very Affectionately Yours,
> Your Father-in-law,
> Pierre Lefleur.

With the two forefingers of his right hand, Gabriel smoothed the long-folded paper against his knee. His face betrayed no emotion at all. He sat in a state of numbness and shock, smoothing the paper with long slow strokes, staring at some meaningless pebble that lay before him on the ground.

Then he spoke quietly. "Paul, the letter says . . . you have a package for me."

Robertson had the package in his hand. It was a small wooden box wrapped in a sheet of paper. A piece of cotton string circled it once lengthwise and once around the middle and was tied in an uneven bow. Gabriel slipped the knot, unwrapped the paper, and slid the top of the box from its morticed slot.

The morning sun glinted brightly from the silver arms and the bowed head of Christ. It was the crucifix his mother had given him the day he left Rouen, the one snatched from his neck the day he had killed Lecharbonnier.

The night was dark and cool. When he had received the news, Gabriel had plunged south into the forest alone. Still he pushed ahead, unconsciously following an animal trail that wound along the water's edge.

Madness was upon him. He did not think of where he was going, but was driven and tormented by what he felt: anger, terrible desperation, a hopeless poverty of soul, frustration at having searched diligently and not having found, of having believed and of having been betrayed.

"We will never see you again . . . Your parents grieve . . . Celeste is dead . . . Michel weeps and wonders where you have gone." The words slammed an iron door in his face. "Dear God, what is left to me?" Gabriel cried.

He stumbled on till all light was gone. The winding, twisting trail looped about the lake's southern end and then led eastward through the deep pines, up a ridge, over into the next valley. In the blackness, a bush of thorns caught him suddenly in its arms, biting and ripping at his face and hands until at last he tore himself from its grasp. Exhausted, he felt about for a small open place off the path where he might lie down.

At last he slept, and in the morning woke to the warm sun pouring gladly through the tops of the fresh, green leaves. When Gabriel opened his eyes, he could not remember where he was, how he had gotten there, or why. But in a moment it all came flooding back and a wave of nausea clamped hard about his belly.

He did not think of food, but jumped to his feet and set off hurriedly down the trail again, having no idea where he was or where he was going, knowing only that the path always sloped down.

At midmorning he came to a river, shallow and broad, fast-flowing and cold, with the sparkling light of the morning sun dancing on its wide breast. He stood on its eastern bank and looked across.

Beyond, a range of towering rock palisades and high jagged hills lofted their profile against the sky. At a distance so great he could scarcely discern it, coming through a notch in the high ridge, a waterfall inscribed a vertical silver line on the face of the dark brown rock.

Though he could not tell why, the falls called to him, invited him to come, to climb, to see. Perhaps it was a hidden path home. Perhaps somehow he could find Celeste's spirit, happy free sprite it once was, waiting for him there. It was an irrational thought, but some unaccountable force pulled him toward that ridge.

Immediately he crossed the river and turned downstream. In less than an hour he came to the place where the tributary from the falls joined the larger waterway, and he turned to ascend its narrow, rocky face.

Gabriel found himself passing under tall firs with boughs so thickly entwined that the ground below them lay in perpetual shadow. Here the air was chill; small banks of last winter's snow still lay, melting ever so slowly. His course paralleled the stream, which, though at times hidden from his sight, was never far away, and always its undertone throbbed among the trees. The valley alternated between strath and chasm, but always continued upward toward the distant ridge.

The narrow river was violent and wild, leaping rocks, tumbling noisily over miniature falls. It hissed down deep granite fissures, tossed out of its channel, thunderously beat itself into misty spray against solid rock embattlements, threw itself into sudden right-angle turns, and careened in its mindless rush down and away.

Gabriel's going was hard. He slid helplessly down rock-bordered ravines, clawed his way up their granite sides until his nails broke and the ends of his fingers were bleeding and raw.

From the surrounding hills, smaller brooks flowed to join this rushing stream; through these quieter waters Gabriel was forced to wade, often nearly to his waist. The snow-melt streams chilled his legs to numbness, and when on the farther side he climbed out and the feeling returned to his thighs, he screamed in pain.

The woods enclosed him. On the low forest's floor clear films of dark water spread out in the stealthy quiet, trickling from higher to lower, seeping under roots and into sodden little hills of dead limbs and decaying leaves. Slimy red mushroom caps pushed up from obscene brown masses, and orange, wet folds of witches'-butter oozed from old rotten logs. The damp, heavy air smelled of mold.

Occasionally the path forked, sometimes leading up and away from the river, harder to climb but always open and clear, other times remaining near the rushing chasm, a level, easy route that required little effort but always stopped short in some impossible bog or dead end. Often at first Gabriel yielded to the ease of the lower path, but inevitably found himself in a cul-de-sac, forced to retrace his steps entirely, or to break his way directly up the steep slope through thick underbrush until he found again the clearer trail.

For a day and a night, without food and with little rest, Gabriel Dublanche drove himself, until he came at last to the foot of the great falls and gazed upward.

"So this," he said in a whisper that blended with the rush of the falls, "is the place where my hope comes to lie down and die."

High above his head, over a wide smooth lip of granite, the river poured in a broad, deep, liquid sheet. In silence the majestic cascade descended, then thundered and boomed into the rock-bound pool, hammering up a great cloud of spray marked by the noonday sun with a rainbow of greatest beauty.

On a spray-drenched promontory overreaching the pool, Gabriel's quest came to its end. At his feet, fresh green grasses and newly blooming flowers covered the sodden ground and reached up through last year's dead growth. Before him, just inches from

his feet, stood the promontory's tallest remnant of last year's verdant life: a single dry stalk tipped with a seed pod, now brittle
and empty. So transfixed was he by the overpowering wonder of
the falls that Gabriel paid the stalk no mind. Absently he placed
his hand about it, fingering its dry, rough stem, all the while
gazing steadfastly upward.

In abandoned desperation, he lifted up his voice and whispered,
"If you are there, speak to me now . . . or take my life away."

As he spoke his fingers tightened on the slender reed, and with
a sharpness that cut through the roar of the falls, it snapped in his
hand. With the same sharpness an unheard voice pierced the mist
of his mind. . . . "A bruised reed will I not break, and smoking
flax will I not quench."

At that instant, shocked as by lightning with long-forgotten
words suddenly remembered, Gabriel looked down at the dry
fragment of reed with its brittle pod in his hand. He dropped to
his knees as if shot, and amid the cascade's roar, the full power
of his lungs pressed a shout into the air, a shout of terrible sorrow
and exile. The sound of his cry joined with the roar of the falls,
climbed the hard, chiseled walls, and echoed into the surrounding
valleys.

It was a cry of anguish, but more, a cry raised to one whose
voice had spoken within; it was a cry of surrender.

When at last evening came, and the wondrous rainbow faded,
Gabriel descended from the promontory to a wide, level field of
dry grasses. Here, at a distance from the falls, all was quiet. He
sat down and, relieved of the falls' intense roar, lay back and
watched the sunset glowing above the trees.

His clothes were soaked and he was weary beyond expression,
but his frustration was gone, and the collected gall of many years
had drained from his mind. He had only strength to stretch out in
the grass and sleep.

Next morning, well rested, Gabriel struck a fire and speared a
fish in the stream. Refreshed by his first meal in three days, he
retraced the path along which he had come. Nightfall on the following day found him sitting on a broad ledge of flat rock overlooking the southeast edge of Wind Lake, gazing across at yellow
torchlights burning in the distant A-wish-in-aub-ay village.

There was no moon. The sky was dark and full of stars. A
breeze sprang up from across the water and touched his cheek.

From the farther shore the breeze bore the sound of evening drums mingled with faint laughter and song. He felt in their notes the mingled warmth of human life. The breeze murmured in the leaves above him, and he remembered how the trees spoke to Philepenca.

Philepenca.

He had loved her from the beginning. Though he felt a twinge of shame, he could at least admit it now that Celeste was gone. But it had been a chaste love, a special admiration of the sort one knows rarely in an entire lifetime.

He could also admit to himself now that he had sometimes felt bitterly toward Celeste for what she had become, though he knew the fault was not hers, but his. He had always loved Celeste tenderly, and had vowed faithfulness to her until death—his or hers.

Yesterday, at the foot of the falls, something had changed inside him, and was continuing to change. He could feel it. He would not return to his homeland; he knew that now. The door was closed, and yet he had peace, for he had relinquished stubborn control over his own destiny. Though he longed desperately for his son, he felt some contentment in knowing Michel was with Pierre and Emilie.

Celeste's death, Gabriel now saw, was the resolution of many problems, both for her and for him. She had been in misery, now she was at rest. Her condition had kept him in turmoil for years, now *he* could be at rest. Her continued life had left him without a companion. Now he could think again about the future and dare to believe that someone might share it with him.

Gabriel lay back and looked into the deep sky. He remembered that Celeste had loved the Milky Way and the Northern Cross and the Great Bear and he wondered where she was on that lovely night. He spoke her name, and somehow had faith she heard him.

He asked himself, and he asked Celeste, and he asked God if he might begin again. And something in the sounds around him— the raspy croak of frogs at the water's edge, the night bird's distant call, and most of all, something in the voices and laughter from the village, and something within himself seemed to say that he could. The shadows of his failed past must not be allowed to darken the future. He would go forward and build again.

CHAPTER 28

The Island

IN the shade of an old scarred birch that stood near the camp's eastern edge, Philepenca's grandmother sat outside the door of her summer lodge. Fifty good steps away the lake's clear water slapped lightly on the fine, clean sand. The morning sun passed through the old tree's heart-shaped translucent leaves so that each leaf glowed with a pleasant pale green light.

Quiet sounds of gentle industry whispered through the town: the bark of an ax, the distant happy cry of a fisherman with a new catch, the slow breathing of Gabriel's bellows, and the ring of his hammer against the anvil.

At the camp's highest point, where its north edge met the forest, a small child frightened three large crows from the newly planted corn. The villainous triad rose noisily and, with the tips of their glossy black wings inscribing rapid circles in the air, fled straight to the top of the tallest balsam fir. Here they lighted and from their perch scolded the little guardian with their annoyed, bold cries.

Wah-Wah-Taysee's old hands worked slowly and deliberately, pulling fine strands of linnwood fiber, weaving them in and out of a warp stretched on the upright loom staked into the ground before her. She was making a bag to be decorated with brightly dyed porcupine quills flattened and folded, woven among the fibers to form a wild rose with twining vines and leaves.

Wah-Wah-Taysee was an artist who worked in many forms. She had spent yesterday shaping fragments of white, iridescent mussel shell into tiny birds and squirrels, stringing them on nettle fiber cord for necklaces. Many of the Wind Lake people wore her intricate glass beadwork on their shirts and moccasins. She was honored and valued for her beautiful creations.

Many years ago, when Wah-Wah-Taysee was about sixty winters old, she had been forced to lay aside her work, for her eyes had failed her. But she had fasted and prayed for the return of her sight, and one morning after two years of near blindness, she woke and looked about with perfect clarity.

She was now somewhere beyond ninety, and every day worked as vigorously at her loom as any of the younger women. Whenever she gathered fibers from the fields, or plants and clays for her dyes, she prayed to Mother Earth for permission to take them, and cast the best of all she found to the winds as a thank offering for the return of her sight.

On this bright morning she had come to the end of a strand of thread and was twirling the end of another strand between her fingers, preparing to thread a new one, when she heard a sound and looked up. Gabriel Dublanche had left his forge and was coming toward her with an armload of wood for her firepit.

"Good morning, Grandmother," he said.

Rather than answer with her voice, she smiled, lifted her hand, and motioned him to come and sit on the other side of her loom. As he sat she reached across, took his hand in hers, and patted it warmly. The skin that sheathed the old bones, webbed sinew, and purple veins in her hands was a mottle of light and dark, dry like parchment, so dry that when it bent, one almost listened for it to crackle. Her hand was so thin as to seem translucent.

"How are you this morning, Grandmother?" he asked. Gabriel elevated his voice slightly as one does when speaking to the old, taking it for granted that they cannot hear.

Wah-Wah-Taysee could hear clearly, and she answered, "Very well, thank you." She smiled a pleasant, dignified smile. "When the damp winds blow and the leech sinks to the bottom of the jar, my bones ache, but otherwise I am well."

Gabriel wondered how old she really was. Eighty-five? One hundred and ten? Who could tell? Thousands of tiny rivulets ran in all directions across her face, the crevices forming miniature diamonds and squares drawn by the pen of elements and time. She had spent countless days working, exposed to sun in the rice shallows, to the winds in the berry fields, to the drying cold of winter, and to the acrid smoke of a cloudy lodge. She might look a hundred, he thought, and yet be seventy. But Wah-Wah-Taysee knew that she had indeed passed nearly a hundred winters.

Her upper teeth were all gone, and her lip had collapsed against its shrunken gum, while her lower jaw jutted forward to expose a row of deep yellow stumps of teeth, worn nearly away, their cutting edges ground down and their dark brown cores plainly visible. From their deep sockets, her eyes squinted and twinkled good-naturedly, and she grinned as though her age and condition were some enormous joke.

"And you, young man, you're looking well." Wah-Wah-Taysee's voice was thin, but each word was clear and distinct, spat out with emphasis in her ancient Chippewa tongue, fluid and musical. She continued. "The last year has been good to you. You didn't look so well when our young men carried you here, but now you're strong and healthy. The Master of Life has smiled on you. And not only so, our young women smile upon you, and they watch you closely." Her smile broadened and her impish eyes fixed on his as if to say, "Is it not so?"

Then her expression grew more serious. Her fingers picked up speed as they wove the fiber in and out of the warp. After a long pause she asked, "Gabriel Dublanche, do you see the love my granddaughter has for you?"

Gabriel was taken aback by the boldness of her question. For a moment he did not know what to say, but at last responded, "I have hoped, Grandmother, that she might love me, but I do not yet know all your customs and the meanings of some things."

The old woman waved off his answer as hardly significant. She knew Philepenca loved this young Frenchman and thought it foolish that customs should have anything to do with his knowing it also. She asked, "And do you love her?"

He sat in silence, watching her fingers skillfully slip the slender bone needle first to the right and then to her left, and at last he answered, "You see more clearly than I, Wah-Wah-Taysee. You know that I do . . . very much."

"Oh, how I envy you," the old woman said. "Both of you. You are so young. You don't know what it means to be young; that is something you cannot know until you are old. The flower of brightness is in your face. You can go where you want, when you want, and the flame of life burns bright within you.

"It is hard indeed for you to believe, but I was once a young woman. . . ." She turned her head to one side and looked at him out of the corners of her eyes, and continued, "Young. Yes, and beautiful, too. Perhaps lovely as Philepenca. Young men came on warm, dusky evenings and played the love flute outside my father's lodge." Her voice softened. "I would sit and listen as I combed and brushed my long hair." She fingered the braid that lay over her shoulder. "See," she said, "still long, but not fine anymore . . . old, coarse, and white, not a dark strand left.

"But then it was not so. They came and played, and I listened and brushed my hair and thought of the young men playing—fine of face and body some of them, dark eyes, fleet of foot, strong of form. Something stirred within me.

"Passion is good, Gabriel Dublanche, when it is controlled. Now I have no more passion. It is gone. I cannot call it back. But I remember passion, and I remember the pleasure it gave me.

"The young men came, and one day I decided between them and told the young man—not with my voice, mind you, but with my eyes. He went straight to my father and asked if he could visit me in our lodge. So that night he came, and in the yellow firelight he talked boldly to me of love.

"My father and mother and my old grandmother had lain down for the night, but grandmother was not asleep. No." Wah-Wah-Taysee chuckled. "Young passion must be kept in hand. So by her sighs she let us know she was awake and watching. Then the fire began to die and the *wigiwam* grew dark. We thought that now we would escape her eyes. But no.

"When the flames died down and only coals glowed in the firepit, just as he touched my hand, we heard her pull her covers aside. She gathered her robe about her shoulders, threw more wood on the fire, and sat down a little way from us, pretending not to see. She lit her pipe and sat smoking, and said nothing. She spent the rest of the night 'not seeing,' until my young man went home.

"In three days, by the hand of a friend, he sent a curl of white birchbark on which he had drawn two figures with joined hands. I sent my answer and that very day he brought my father gifts. We went away together, and when we returned my mother had built us a lodge near her own."

Wah-Wah-Taysee's fingers slowed and stopped. She lay her hands in her lap, looked out past the old birch to the blue lake, and sighed deeply. "There have been many winters since," she said, "and my husband traveled the Spirit Road longer ago than I want to remember, so long that my days without him are more than our days together." She looked directly into Gabriel's eyes and then down at her own body.

"Now look at me. Once my body was fine and shapely; there was no hump on my shoulders, my teeth were white as the down of a swan, my skin as smooth as the fur of an otter.'' She paused for a long while, drew a deep breath, and expelled it quickly. ''Now, even to myself I am a stranger.''

Gabriel sat without stirring, knowing instinctively that he must let her words sink down into his soul. Slowly he took in her meaning.

The shriveled hands and arms were not the hands and arms that had held her children. The white coarse hair had not the black softness from which the sun had shown and caught the young men's eyes. Her cheeks—once smooth, full of color, rich and blooming—were now sunken like the lodge wall's skin when the wind blows hard against it.

But she had not relinquished her youth willingly. She looked again full into his eyes, her head shook with a slight palsy, and she spoke intently. ''My body fails me. My bones are a cage, like the cages little boys make for the birds they snare. I am a bird, prisoner of my withering flesh.

''To grow old is to watch others die. Not only have I seen my own flesh wither and sag, I have seen my family and friends sicken and fail. This has pained me more than my own decay. The friends of my youth are all gone. I tell you, young man, I have many more friends in the Village to the West than I have here. One by one they have gone ahead of me. I will not have such friends again, not before I myself walk the Spirit Road.

''So you see, I have outlived my friends. I have outlived my children. Now I have outlived myself. Only memory assures me that I am indeed myself and not another. My people revere me for my age and for what they say is my wisdom, but I am through with the world.

''Soon I will walk on the Spirit Road, too. . . .'' Here a knowing smile crept across her face. ''And I shall be young again. The Master of Life tells me so.''

A look of deep calm came to her face. They sat quietly now, holding each other's gaze. His eyes were young and clear, hers cloudy with age, and yet in hers flamed a distant fire. ''Soon you will be old, too, all your past a handful of memories . . . and those only too poorly recalled. Gabriel Dublanche, hear what this old one speaks. Take your young woman and love her. Do it now while the blossom of youth still clings to the vine of life. Too soon the vine will tremble and rattle dry in the winter winds. The blossom will whirl away and you will see the petals only as lost tokens of a sweetness you cannot know again. Taste the ripe rich berry of youth before it falls to the ground and rots.

"At best life has much bitterness. Sweeten it with this girl who loves you. Rejoice in her raven hair and be enticed by her dark eyes. Let her softness fill you with peace.

"I tell you that if you do not, you punish yourself foolishly. The Master of Life permits you to remake your bed and lie down in sweetness. I pray He gives you the wisdom to do it. Wah-Wah-Taysee is done." She turned her eyes back to her loom, found the lost thread, picked it up, and bound it into place.

On the last day of June—the Moon of Strawberries—Gabriel and Philepenca were married.

Their wedding was both Christian and A-wish-in-aub-ay. Father Nathaniel led them in their vows and administered the Holy Eucharist. There-Is-Something-That-Knows lifted the pipe to the four winds and made an offering of sweet grasses and herbs. Afterward everyone feasted and danced to the drums.

The next day Gabriel and Philepenca floated their canoe on Wind Lake and paddled northward. At last, after two portages and a half day of river travel, they glided onto a smaller lake hidden in a vale of hills, where a tall forest of fir and pine lined its grass-covered shores.

This was in the evening on the first day of the Moon of Blueberries. The air was still and cool. The sun stood above the tops of the western trees and shone out from behind tall, white, gold-fringed clouds that billowed up from the horizon into the higher heavens like huge wind-filled sails.

Below their thin bark canoe, a fish as long as a man's arm, with eyes cloudy as milk, whipped its tail in long, slow arcs, leisurely exploring the white hull floating above it like an autumn leaf. Then, feeling in its dim brain a warning, it flicked its tail sharply and disappeared into the deep crystal twilight.

The couple talked quietly and their soft laughter floated to the surrounding shores. There was no hurry, for there was no place to be, no one to please. So, cradled in the small white canoe, Gabriel held Philepenca in his arms and breathed deep peace from her soft embrace. They lay in perfect tranquillity while the sun set, heard the echo of the loon's mad laughter skipping across the water, saw an owl flit and swoop low above them on silent wings. At last, with Philepenca reclining against him, Gabriel paddled gently to a small island darkly silhouetted against the evening's pale blue sky. Among the soft grasses on the island's crest, under the tall trees, they spread their marriage bed.

The next morning when Philepenca opened her eyes, she saw the sheltering arms of the stately firs above her. The day's first faint magenta reached across the dark sky, down through the trees' splayed needles, and cast its glow on the skin of her face. Beneath their luxuriant fur robe, she stirred and felt for Gabriel's arm. He was not there.

Startled by his absence, she quickly sat up to look about. Immediately the tension left her. He was sitting on the mossy rock a dozen steps away, where they had come ashore. His arms circled his drawn-up knees as he gazed toward the still faintly lighted horizon, watching for the first gold spark to herald sunrise.

The air was chill. She rose from her bed of boughs, took the fur robe, and went down to sit beside him. She pulled the robe close around their shoulders, and beneath its folds slipped her arm about his waist and nestled close.

He looked down at her. Her long black hair fell about her face and framed it wonderfully. So graceful was she in every part that her beauty overwhelmed him; so harmonious in form, in shade, in tone, that she seemed to him like some song, some melody of Pan rising from pristine forests before Adam fell, a harmony now forbidden lest man in his lostness become like a thing wild and sinfully free. Was it possible, he wondered as he looked upon her, for such ecstasy to be holy?

As for Philepenca, she had no such questions, though her passion was as great as his. She took pleasure in Gabriel's strength and form. In a spirit of perfect freedom she had abandoned herself to the sweetness of their love's consummation. Now she looked into his face, her softness filled him with joy, her dusky eyes reflected the nearing dawn.

"Nuco," she said—an A-wish-in-aub-ay word that meant dearest—"I love you with all my heart."

He held her tightly. "And I love you," he said, "with all that lies within me."

"I will tell you, *Nuco*," she said, "that last night was the most joyous of my life."

Her simple confession, her serene face made even lovelier in the subdued light of sunrise, her tender kindness—all after two long years in which he had known not one single intimate touch—moved him, and his eyes welled with tears. He thought of Milton's words written a hundred years before. "Loneliness is the first thing the eye of God named not good."

The tears broke over and ran down to the corners of his mouth. Philepenca took his face in her hands, drew him down, and kissed him, tasting the salt, making his joy her own.

He pulled her to himself tightly, as though afraid some terrible thing would come and snatch her away. For a long moment they held each other. He kissed her tenderly. Then warm, sweet passion rose as all the world disappeared and there was only Philepenca.

Abruptly, without warning, she was up and out of his arms, laughing and running. Daring him to chase her, she flung herself with a long graceful arch into the cold water.

Gabriel did not follow instantly, but stood on the shore for a moment and watched her. She slipped through the clear water as smoothly as a gliding otter, her body visible in broken rippling lines. He marveled at her grace, for it seemed to him she was to the liquid element born.

A short distance from shore she found a ledge beneath her feet. She stood and called out, "The water is warmer than the air. Come to me." And she gave a quick, convulsive shiver and dove again. Swirling little eddies and whirlpools played where she slipped beneath the surface.

Gabriel broke out with laughter and leaped forward into the water, swimming on her heels, bursting with frantic joy. He caught her, and together they sank beneath the water, then exploded again into the open air, gasping, laughing uncontrollably. Bright sunlight glistened in the droplets of spray flung from their thrashing arms and hair, and shone on their wet, smooth skin.

The sun was halfway to meridian before their frolic ended and they came up on the shore to dry.

"You're wonderful," he said breathlessly, "a nymph from the woods."

"Nymph?" she asked. "I have not heard that word before. What is it, 'nymph'?"

And Gabriel told her of the ancient Greeks, told their stories of gods and goddesses, centaurs, cyclopes, satyrs, and nymphs, none of which she had ever heard of before. Fascinated, she listened to every word, and when he was done, she said, "It's a good story. But I do not like it."

Surprised and slightly offended, he asked, "Why?"

"Because, the thing it speaks is not true. Rather than being your Greek nymph why can't I be your A-wish-in-aub-ay woman?"

"You're right," he said, laughing and leaning so close he felt her warm breath. "You are what you are, and that's very much better."

"And you can be my A-wish-in-aub-ay man," she concluded.

"No," he said. "I'm not A-wish-in-aub-ay, my home is France."

She shook her head. "No," she said. "You are no Frenchman. You are one of us, at home now among your own people—as A-wish-in-aub-ay as I."

They were dry now, but even so the sunlight glistened on her dark carmine skin. I was right, he thought. She is a melody, a perfect composition, a song that fell silent when the gates were closed on Eden, daughter of Eve, not once removed.

On the night when Gabriel and Philepenca had come to the island there had been no moon. The second night it was a slender silver bowl sitting upright in the western sky after sunset. Every night thereafter they watched the moon grow from a sliver to a crescent to a scythe, mounting higher each night at sundown. In a week it was a half sphere directly overhead. In two it had waxed until at last, just at set of sun, it rose a shimmering orange ball burning its way through the dusky firmament, and climbed slowly through the dark trees on the eastern horizon.

While the moon was full they canoed and swam and made love by its silver light. Then it waned, postponing its appearance longer every night until it was gone and stars alone lit the sky.

It was on such a dark, moonless night that the two lay looking into a sky black and clear, embedded with innumerable points of silver light. The loons had fallen silent and the whippoorwill had taken up his eerie song to the evening. Gabriel and Philepenca had swum and played to wash away the sweat and dust of the day, then climbed dripping and happy from the water to lie on the moss-covered rock.

The day had been hot, and now the heat lingered into night. The moss was like a thick towel that sponged the dripping water as they lay upon it. What the moss did not take, a warm pleasant breeze with deft fingers stole away.

"Have you ever seen the heavens so deep?" Philepenca asked.

"No, never," he answered. "My head whirls just to look. I feel I'm being pulled up among them, and yet I'm bound to this rock."

"I try to think of how far away they are," she said, "and how large. Father Nathaniel says they are many times bigger than the earth, and farther away than we can imagine or believe. When I try to think of how far, strange things happen in my mind. Distance loses its meaning, and it seems to me that my feet and hands are as far from my body as the stars are from the world."

He raised himself on his elbow and looked down into her dusky face, barely visible in the meager light. "What matters," he said, "is that you and I are so close we can touch one another."

She smiled in the starlight, clasped her hands behind his neck, and pulled him down. "Have I told you," she whispered, "that I am grateful you are my husband? You are more sensitive than the men of my people. You care more what I think and how I feel than others who played the love flute outside my lodge."

"And were there many?" he asked.

"Yes," she answered, hesitating modestly, "there were many."

Their lips were close to touching when in a hushed voice she said, "Gabriel, look," and pointed upward.

From the apex of heaven's black dome a white lace curtain of light was falling slowly across the face of the night, like a celestial net cast by the hand of an unseen fisherman gathering stars, or like a great white curtain blowing in the winds of boundless space, as though some vast window had opened and an immense breeze had come flowing in.

On the lake's bosom there was no wind; so still was it that one looking down into the water could see the stars as clearly as if looking up. Earth and heaven seemed one. The darkness, the land, the trees, the stars, the water, the night sounds, a man and a woman in harmony, lying together beneath the blowing curtain of light.

Perhaps, had there been no member of the race left but these two, they could have made a new and better beginning for the world. But they were not alone, and soon they had to return to their people.

PART FOUR

1748–1759

CHAPTER 29

The Road of Souls

It was night. Birchbark torches hanging from the trees spread an oily yellow light about the lodges.

It was again October, Moon of the Withering Leaf.

From the great lodge near the center of Wind Lake Village, the hollow voice of a drum spoke a steady unaccented beat that entered every lodge, laying a pall upon the people, then rolled unhampered outward across the lake's still waters.

A single plaintive voice, in rhythm with the drum, floated over and among the *wigiwams*. Tonight there was no shouting or merriment. Even the children were subdued, for old Wah-Wah-Taysee was dead.

In the center of the Mide lodge, her body freshly washed and clothed in her finest dress, her long white hair carefully braided, her neck and arms draped with fine beadwork, the product of her own hands, Wah-Wah-Taysee lay on a new bearskin robe. Under her right arm lay her own Mide bag of otter skin, containing medicinal herbs and a dozen cowry shells. Under her eyes, on each sunken cheek, a large round spot of brown fungus had been painted; from the middle of each spot, bright vermillion streaked back to her ears.

In a circle around the body, Wah-Wah-Taysee's friends and relations sat as Something-That-Knows assured them that the Great Spirit loved his people and had mercy upon them. While her spirit lingered near her body, one by one her friends spoke to Wah-Wah-Taysee, saying how they would miss her, warning her to watch for danger along the deep-beaten western road.

"Take care," said Something-That-Knows, "when you cross the wild river on the treacherous rolling bridge. On the fourth day you will find the Village of the West, where your husband and children will receive you with music and dancing. It is a country of clear lakes, tall forests, and prairies that abound in fruit and game. You will be happy there among your friends. You will make pouches and belts and necklaces with your hands, things even more beautiful than you made here.''

"Ke-go-way-se-kah," they said. "You are going homeward on the Che-ba-kun-ah, the road of souls.''

The next morning a wailing procession carried Wah-Wah-Taysee up the hill to her grave. Something-That-Knows cut a lock of her white hair and burned her Mide bag over clean ground. Then the people lowered Wah-Wah-Taysee into her grave, her upright body facing west and sitting among the things necessary for her journey—a fire steel, a copper kettle, and her favorite ax.

They filled the grave and lay a sheet of weighted birchbark over it, then drove a sharp stick into the ground at the grave's head, whittled flat and carved with an image of her clan animal, the loon. Beside the grave in a bundle her friends left enough food for a four-day journey, and then went away, wailing because Wah-Way-Taysee was gone.

Every evening Philepenca came back to the hill, her long hair loosed from its braid and tied back with a single thong, no ornaments adorning her neck or arms. But Philepenca no longer wailed, for even had it been in her power, she would not have wished Wah-Wah-Taysee's return. In the Village to the West, life was better.

It seemed to Gabriel a contradiction that Father Nathaniel allowed his people to mix their Mide and Christian beliefs. The old priest had baptized Wah-Way-Taysee many years before. He had heard her confessions, had given her last rites, and had said a requiem Mass over her remains.

Gabriel remained puzzled that Philepenca was a dreamer, a healer, a valued member of the Mide, and was at the same time Father Nathaniel's favorite disciple. Every day she prayed the rosary. He had heard her. Every day when the village bell sounded the Angelus, her voice softly intoned, "Pour forth, we beseech You, O Lord, your grace in our hearts. . . .''

In fact, it was Philepenca's certainty that had ended her wailing—certainty that as Christ had risen, so she herself would rise and old Wah-Wah-Taysee would rise.

* * *

Two days after the burial, Gabriel found Father Nathaniel sitting alone on a carpet of leaves, warming himself at the fire in front of his lodge. He sat down across from the old priest and came straight to the point.

"It's a good question, Gabriel," Dumarchais said. He shrugged deeper into the heavy blanket draped around his shoulders, rubbed his hands together vigorously, and held them out to the fire, then continued, "You probably know you're not the first one to struggle with it. When the Jesuit fathers came to Canada more than a hundred and thirty years ago, this was *not* allowed. We were as determined to make French Catholics of these people as the English are to make English Protestants of the peoples of Pennsylvania and New York. We called it 'Frenchifying.'

"But the people rebelled against it. We got nowhere with them. So, after a long time, the Jesuit fathers decided not to disturb the old beliefs, the ones that harmonized with the Gospels, but to use them to our advantage.

"The Algonquian people, such as the A-wish-in-aub-ay, believe in one God, maker of all things. They believe He loves them, that 'when the earth was new,' as they say, the red race offended Him by disobedience. I say 'red race' . . . until the first Europeans came, they had no idea that a race of any other color existed.

"But they angered Ke-ch-mun-e-do, and they say He sent a great flood upon the world, and then an intercessor from the world of spirits. This intercessor, Man-ab-o-sho they call him, is an uncle who reconciles them to the Master of Life. They make offerings of the best they have, the best tobacco, the best corn, the first fruits of the hunt, and they burn incense just as we do, except they burn it in their sacred red-stone pipes—red, they say, because it is mixed with blood."

The priest paused, thought for a moment, then challenged Gabriel. "See what you think of this one. One of their fireside stories is about a boy, the youngest of twelve brothers, the most favored of his father, a man who was a favorite of the Master of Life. The boy's name is Wa-jeeg-e-wa-kon-ay, 'Fisher Skin Coat.' In one of the stories Fisher Skin Coat helps his brothers by giving them corn."

"I had no idea," Gabriel responded thoughtfully.

"It's true," the priest replied. "It's also true that they believe in spirits other than the Master of Life. There is one great Evil Spirit, and lesser spirits, some good, some bad. I tell them that the great Evil Spirit we call the devil, and that the lesser ones we call good and evil angels, that the Master of Life we Europeans call 'God,' and that Man-ab-o-sho we call 'Christ.' They even have a cross in their ancient beliefs, and call it 'the sacred post.'

"I don't know where their beliefs came from," Dumarchais added. "I simply believe that God speaks to anyone who wants to hear.

"And you, Gabriel, you of all people, know they do have their visions. Before any European ever set foot on these shores, in a dream one of their chief men saw a man with the color washed from his skin. The man in the dream said, 'I've come to tell you more truth.' So," Father Nathaniel continued, "I believe I'm one of those with the color washed from his skin, come to show them the more truthful way.

"But," he went on, "there're many things the Wind Lake people have taught me. One of their wise men—dead many years now—once said to me, 'We will not forsake what we know to be true. We sustain our beliefs and our beliefs sustain us.'

"I tell you, Gabriel, that old man had more of the sun than the Sun King himself. Louis forsook what he believed, and forsaken, his beliefs could not sustain him, or the nation."

Gabriel was impressed, but not quite satisfied. "But Father, these people have killed women and children, roasted their captives alive, they've—"

"Like Europeans, Gabriel?"

Gabriel was silent, and Dumarchais continued, "We have periods of moral decline—deep ones. So do they. For example, down on the island of La Pointe several generations ago, the people ate their own children. But—as with the civilizations of Europe—a few of them stood firm, said it was murder, the work of the Evil Spirit. Finally the whole village saw the truth, punished the guilty, and as a symbol of their revulsion, abandoned the island."

Father Nathaniel filled his pipe, sucked on the stem to be sure it was clear, struck the tobacco to life, and when it was burning brightly, turned his eyes intently on Gabriel and said, "Now let me ask you something."

"Go ahead, Father. Anything you wish."

"You're so concerned about what these people believe. Unless my memory fails me, you're the young man who decided there's no God at all. What do you say now?"

Gabriel's forearms rested on his drawn-up knees, his fingers clasped together loosely. He looked at the ground and at last answered, "I've heard *some*thing, Father, something that changed me. At the foot of the falls someone spoke to me, not with a voice, but spoke to me nonetheless. And there's Philepenca. Her character, her beliefs are very persuasive.

"I can't account for the thing at the falls, nor for Philepenca's dreams, nor for her love . . . not unless I believe again."

"And so you do believe?"

"Yes, Father. I believe."

Long before dawn on a morning deep in December, Moon of the Little Spirit, Gabriel Dublanche awoke with a feeling of overwhelming peace. Outside the wind swept fiercely over the roof of his new earthen hunting lodge, but through its thickness he heard only its whisper. In the center of the small room a bed of coals glowed in the firepit and cast an orange glow on the mud-plastered dome.

Philepenca lay softly in his arms. She was sleeping on her side, facing away, the contours of her back nestled against him, his right arm a pillow under her head, the other embracing her waist. Even in sleep she loosely held his left hand in hers.

Gentle serenity filled his mind. He was at odds with no one, and Philepenca was near. Her long raven hair spread over his arm and reflected the fire's golden light. He pressed his face to the back of her neck, felt her hair against his lips and smelled its fresh clean fragrance.

What a wonder, he thought, that they had met. Had God arranged their meeting? If He had, why? Were they not from different worlds? Was she not better than he—more human, kinder, less selfish, more trusting?

Yet, for all their differences, they shared a certain tenderness of mind, a desire to do well, a reaching out to something—or someone—beyond. Each abhorred that quality that drove man to inflict pain upon man. Each understood that conflict arose from greed and jealousy, and from reluctance to forgive.

The wrist of his upper hand lay beneath her left breast. Her skin was warm, and her heart beat with a strong, slow, even beat. Her breath rose and fell with unhurried gentleness.

He reveled in the sweetness of her bouquet, a clean, subtle, feminine balm; he loved the pleasant musky redolence of her breath when their faces drew near in a kiss or when they nuzzled playfully.

All this and harmony, too. His heart swelled with thankfulness. Oh yes, of course there were moments when it wasn't so. There were even quick, sharp looks and chilled silence between them for a day, perhaps two. But always they forgave quickly and came together again with tearful confessions of stubbornness and mulish independence, and more importantly, with confessions of unrelenting love.

On those rare occasions when Gabriel's wisdom exceeded hers, Philepenca always saw it and acquiesced. When her wisdom or skill or courage went beyond his, eventually he saw it and yielded.

We're certainly not duplicates, he thought. When I'm weak, Philepenca is strong, and where she fails, there I shine more brightly. He looked at her in the fire's easy glow, and his heart overflowed with love.

Outside, the winter gale whistled among the trees and coated their waving limbs with ice. Inside, Gabriel remembered the past summer's days, when together they had explored the forest, searching for meadow mushrooms, bannock, dewberry, and sweet vernal grass.

He remembered how they had laughed and held hands, how they had run together like two carefree deer, luxuriating in the sheer wonder of two human beings born a world apart, come together in so unlikely a time and place.

He smiled to himself when he thought of how the old women had shaken their heads and smiled their own enigmatic smiles, clucking under their breath like mother hens at the couple's joyous work and love.

Love. Oh yes! How they did make love—joyous, spontaneous, unrestrained. Love on the rocky promontory of their island, love in their bed, on the needle-strewn floor of the forest in some hidden vale, or in the slow, cooling current of a deep river, on warm grasses, and on thick gold and crimson beds of fallen leaves.

He remembered the times when, passion spent, they had simply lain in the deep beds of fallen maple and sycamore leaves, holding hands, gazing at patches of blue sky through the yet unfallen foliage, talking away many happy hours.

It was true that their work was sometimes hard, that their very existence depended upon its success, but their work was not hurried, and being of one mind they made time for life to become Solomon's Song.

Now in the silent darkness, Gabriel's eyes welled with gratefulness, and warm, wet tears of joy mingled with the waves of Philepenca's fragrant black hair. His hand slipped from her sleeping grasp and caressed the soft skin of her belly. He ran his fingers in light, slow circles over its graceful swell, and his heart rose in a prayer of thanks. For amid all the joy that was his already, yesterday she had told him her secret. In the spring she would give birth to their child.

CHAPTER 30

The Bramble Briar Lodge

IT was now September, Moon of the Shining Leaf, 1752, four years after the death of Wah-Wah-Taysee. The formerly peaceful northern forests were astir with talk. From the northwestern Athabasca regions to Quebec, from Hudson Bay to Saint Ignace, around the cooking fires and in the councils, the name on every tongue was Langlade.

Charles Michel de Langlade, the son of a French trapper and an Ottawa woman, was only twenty-nine years old, a slender, dark young man with a keen mind, an intense Ottawa pride, a smooth personable way, strong energetic drive, and a wild thirst for living. His enthusiastic smile and quick understanding of men and situations made him a natural leader.

Beyond these forests tension was increasing between the English and French colonies. The strain between the two had not subsided with the end of King George's War and the Treaty of Aix-la-Chapelle.

Possession of land and trade of goods were bones of contention. The English wished to expand into the continent's interior, but many barriers stood firmly in their way: the rugged Allegheny Mountains, the deep forests, the ancestral hunting grounds of the

Cherokee, Shawnee, and Iroquois, and of course, the prior claim of France.

Only one highway led into the interior from the English colonies: the great waterway formed by the confluence of the Allegheny and Monongahela rivers, called the "Ohio" by the English, "Spay-lay-wi-theepi" by the Shawnee, and "La Belle Rivière" by the French. All three nations claimed it as theirs. Beyond question it was the southern border of New France.

Four years ago, Unemkemi, principal chief of the Miamis, had established a settlement north of the Ohio on the Great Miami River, that he called Pickawillany. Unemakemi favored the English in all their causes and even called himself "Old Britain." He had established his town deep in French territory as a favor to the English, who sought to win the goodwill of the people living there. English traders had set up business in Pickawillany, had outbid the French for furs, and had cut their prices for English-made goods. The town had grown rapidly until it numbered eight thousand native Americans of various nations, plus a host of English traders.

Less than a year ago, in November of 1751, Charles Michel de Langlade had brought furs to Pickawillany for trade. But on that night, while Langlade lay sleeping in the lodge of a friend, an English trader had stolen his furs.

The next morning Langlade had appealed to Old Britain for their recovery. Old Britain not only refused to give Langlade redress, but had ordered him to leave Pickawillany "here and now, lest I pluck the heart from your breast and feed it to my dogs." Langlade had left without another word, but he burned with rage and determined that he would have revenge.

Langlade spent the following winter and spring enlisting support for his cause. On the first day of summer, seven months and thirteen days after his encounter with Old Britain, Charles Michel de Langlade led over two hundred Ottawas and southern A-wish-in-aub-ay, along with Pontiac and fifty of his men, plus a dozen French regulars, in a flotilla of canoes to a point near Pickawillany.

The raiders came first upon women working in the cornfields. Panic and confusion followed. Children cried frantically, seasoned men of war ran aimlessly hither and yon. Walls of gunfire ripped into the milling crowds.

Old Britain himself ran headlong toward the fort, but while still a hundred yards from shelter, a musket ball in his shoulder slammed him to the ground. Langlade had cornered his enemy at last. Old Britain saw him coming and reached for his fallen weapon, but Langlade leaped upon him, straddled the chief's belly, and pinned Old Britain's arms under his knees. Langlade then drew his knife and plunged it into the chief's side just below his ribs and ripped across. Instantly he ran his hands into the wound, tore out the man's still-beating heart, and before his victim's eyes, sank his teeth into its blood-red muscle.

When the battle was done, Langlade held Old Britain's severed head high, scalped it, and kicked it into the helpless crowd of defeated villagers. It was an incredible act of barbarity and revenge.

Thereafter, the French and English border seethed with war.

It would be a long while before the conflict between England and France would touch Gabriel Dublanche. But in the spring of the year after Langlade raided Pickawillany, Gabriel began to feel an emptiness, not a tragic or profound feeling, simply a longing to go somewhere he had not been, to see what he had not seen.

It was not unusual for an A-wish-in-aub-ay man to leave summer encampment with his family and hunt alone in any part of the forest that he could reach by canoe or on foot. So in the Moon of Flowers, May of 1753, after nearly five years of marriage, Gabriel took his family and journeyed southwest toward the tip of Superior, to the village the French called Fond du Lac.

He and Philepenca now had two daughters. The oldest, nearly four, had been born in late spring of the first year of their marriage, and they had called her A-bo-wi-ghi-shi-g, "Warm Sky." The younger, now only eight months, was born in the Moon of the Falling Leaf, and her they had called Wi-ni-shi-ba-go-sin, "Evergreen." To accommodate Gabriel's awkward European tongue, they shortened A-bo-wi-ghi-shi-g to "A-bo-wi." He found he could manage Wi-ni-shi-ba-go-sin's name very well; even so, for convenience, they called her "Wi-ni."

Gabriel had been a nervous father, increasingly anxious as the time of each birth approached, afraid the child would be malformed or positioned wrongly in the womb. But in fact, each birth had been easy. Philepenca had worked at her usual tasks almost to the very hour, then entered her lodge, grasped the sapling secured horizontally above her head, and, hanging by her arms, delivered the child quickly into the hands of her attendant.

Both children were healthy, had round plump faces, large dark eyes, and lips that formed a bow.

Gabriel's doting made it hard for Philepenca to discipline the children. She often said to him, "Gabriel, the girls will be worth nothing if you have your way. You must help me make them strong."

After each rebuke he relented, but always returned to his softheartedness, pampering them until Philepenca threw up her hands in desperation. In truth, Gabriel loved his children beyond expression. They were his great consolation, and he could not bear to give them pain.

It was now seven years since Gabriel had seen his son. All that time, in a special place, he kept a short length of stick—half the thickness of his little finger, and about as long—he had cut from a sapling that grew in his favorite meadow at the east end of Little Vermillion. Every year on December 23, to mark the day of Michel's birth, Gabriel carved a new notch into this stick. Last December he had carved the thirteenth notch.

Sometimes Gabriel wondered how he might change the past if he had it to do over again, but he could not decide. When he said to himself, I wish I had not married Celeste, his next thought was, But then Michel would not have been born, and I don't wish that. If he said to himself, I should have returned to France at all costs, that was the same as willing Philepenca out of his life and wishing his daughters had never been born. He finally concluded that he would do it all over again just as he had, both his son and his daughters being worth all the terrible pain. Still, this confused him. It made him wonder if it was possible to really repent of his sins, when inside he felt his sins had produced some good—not only *some* good, but the good he held dearest to his heart.

Every summer evening as he sat in his willow-wand rest by the door of their lodge, little A-bo-wi would come, climb into his lap, and nestle down for a story. Philepenca would put Wi-ni-shi-ba-go-sin in her small hammock and, swinging her gently to and fro, sing a lullaby that repeated over and over again *"we-we-we,"* an A-wish-in-aub-ay word that meant "swinging." The melody was sweet and plaintive. Gabriel listened to her lovely voice, felt the nearness of his wife and children, and in his heart said that life was good.

* * *

The little family's journey to Fond du Lac was easy. They went by canoe and by foot to Superior, then followed its shores, traveling only on days when the wind was light or did not blow at all.

The Fond du Lac A-wish-in-aub-ay received them warmly into their lodges. But after seven days Gabriel wanted to go farther west and see for himself the headwaters of the continent's mightiest river, called by the A-wish-in-aub-ay "Chi-si-bi," and by their enemy, the Dakota, "Mississippi."

On the shores of Sandy Lake, only two miles from the Mississippi, they found a village of A-wish-in-aub-ay. The Sandy Lake village had been there only a few winters, for it was in the very heart of country where less than a generation ago had lived the Dakota, who, when driven out, had moved a hundred miles south to the banks of the Rum River. In spite of their nearness, the Dakota had made no raids on Sandy Lake. This led Gabriel and Philepenca to conclude that this was a place where they could live for a time without concern for war. So, feeling at home with the Sandy Lake people, they built a lodge, hunted, fished, and determined to winter among them.

In July, the Moon of Blueberries, the men of Sandy Lake prepared to canoe south on the Mississippi to patrol the boundaries between themselves and the Rum River Dakota. The leader of the contingent was a man of about forty winters, short and stocky with a wide face and a hairline receding almost to the middle of his crown. He was a forceful, likable man, a distinguished war chief who bore his nickname, "Bright Forehead," in good humor.

Bright Forehead extended an invitation to Gabriel to come with him and his party of sixty men. It was a distinct honor to be invited, and though Gabriel had no interest in war, he felt compelled to accept.

Philepenca woke late. The sun had already risen, and its first slanting rays, filtering through the guardian firs, cast a mottled pattern of bright gold mixed with soft shadow onto the black earth of the forest floor. Because the night had been stiflingly hot, about midnight she and the children had left the airless lodge and spread their bedding outside.

It was unlike Philepenca to let the sun clear the horizon before being up and about, but with Gabriel away and the children sleeping, there was no cause to hurry, so she took advantage of the unusual opportunity.

Now the morning was cool. With A-bo-wi on her left and Wi-ni-shi-ba-go-sin on her right, Philepenca lay for a long while and let wakefulness come slowly. As the morning's brightness gently cleared her mind of sleep's soft web, she began to reflect on the course of her life.

My life has followed gentle paths, she thought. My people have been good to me. Wah-Wah-Taysee taught me to work and gave me love . . . and even waited until I found a husband before going on the Spirit Road.

The friendly winds of the south have breathed on my life. I have a man who cherishes me, who helps me bear my tasks, and has given me children. Her thoughts went deep and she was full of gratitude.

Some said Philepenca was naïve, too kind, too trusting, that someday her gentleness would bring her to a bad end. Some, looking at her through inwardly tarnished eyes, accused her of false goodness. But what could one say to such accusations? She did not know, and so said nothing, treating her accusers as she wished to be treated.

Because she was gentle, wherever Philepenca looked, she saw gentleness, and so she was sure her antagonists simply did not know better. She looked on the world with compassion, construed the failure of others in the best possible light. Because she loved easily, she assumed others loved also. Some said she was too good for this world.

But Philepenca was also strong, and chose, inasmuch as she was able, to determine her own life rather than allow others to shape it for her.

Now she lay on her bed of boughs and looked up through the green lace of fir needles to the morning's clear blue sky, feeling very much at rest. Then, unexpectedly, like a low, slow-moving cloud, an uneasiness crept over her mind.

What is it? she wondered to herself.

At once Philepenca recalled from her night's sleep an almost forgotten dream. Always old Wah-Wah-Taysee had said to her, "Try to dream, and remember what you dream. It may have meaning." Philepenca reached down into the deep well of her mind, searched for the nighttime images, and slowly drew them out.

She recalled a meadow of tall green grass, motionless and quiet, so unstirring that she held her breath, heard her own heartbeat, and felt the stillness.

Then the scene changed. The grass was no longer green, but sere and dry as in the dead of winter when no snow has fallen. The meadow was empty now, but she heard soft weeping, the voices of men and women sobbing.

Again there was a change. In the midst of the meadow's dryness a green tree bloomed. Small, bright, blue birds with orange-red throats hopped and flitted among its branches, and called out beautifully with thin, melodious notes.

The weeping grew louder as from the dry grass rose a great black-winged bird that circled the meadow with long, slow beats. The sadness deepened. But the small green tree was yet green, and in its branches the birds still sang.

On the afternoon when Gabriel had been gone two weeks, a light glaze of high clouds moved across the sky. With it came blessedly cooler air that gave Sandy Lake Village new life. Children came out of the shade and played. Men and women worked with great vigor at their tasks. And the young girls, thinking it a perfect time to pick high bush blackberries, gathered their baskets and begged Philepenca to go with them.

Wi-ni-shi-ba-go-sin was small enough that Philepenca still kept her in the cradle board and carried her along wherever she went. The cradle board was a large pocket of heavy blue wool, on which Philepenca had embroidered a large red rose and twining green leaves. This pocket was fastened to a wood frame Gabriel had decorated with ornate carving. The baby fit snugly down inside, with only her face peeking out.

Philepenca had lined the pouch with moss gleaned from the cranberry bogs and dried over a fire, rubbed and pulled apart to make it soft and light. The moss cushioned the baby's ride and also absorbed her elimination. Several times each day Philepenca took Wi-ni-shi-ba-go-sin out, washed her, and replaced the soiled moss with moss that was fresh and new.

Today as Philepenca walked with the young girls to the berry bushes, Wi-ni rode happily, only her head visible above the blue wool. She laughed and cooed, her eyes following the dancing bead and cornhusk doll that swung to and fro from an encircling hoop above her head.

The berries that the young girls wanted to pick grew a half mile west of the village, in a low clearing surrounded by shadbark hickory and red oak, and filled with a luxuriant growth of different grasses. Philepenca stopped and gathered a sheaf of sweet flags to take home. Some she would dry, and in the winter burn in the lodge fire to purify and sweeten the air. The fresh ones she would cast about the lodge to make a sweet-smelling covering for the floor.

At last they came to the blackberry bushes. The bushes grew in a thick bramble all around the western side of a large clearing. They grew taller than the tallest man in the village, and their stalks and stems bore straight thorns, sharper than needles of steel. Small animal trails ran in an intricate network of low tunnels through the bushes, ending in little cavelike enclosures or winding in crazy circuits from side to side. Here and there in the briary maze were breaks so large that a small person might barely squeeze through without being pricked with the thorns. The children quickly spotted the low tunnels made by the animals and disappeared into the endless maze.

Today the berries were at their best. Some were still a hard pale yellow, and many were brilliant red, but most were a rich, deep, blackish purple, large and so ripe they left dark stains on the picker's fingers.

Philepenca had filled two birchbark handbaskets with berries and half-filled another when A-bo-wi appeared from the bushes and rushed to her.

"Mother, Mother," she said excitedly, "come into the briar and see what I've found!" She could not contain her glee. Philepenca, filling a third handbasket, answered, "Tell me about it, *Nuco*."

"No, Mother. Please come and see. Get down on your knees and follow me."

"I cannot, A-bo-wi," she said. "I'm too big for your little rabbit tunnels. Just tell me what you've found."

At last the child gave up her efforts to entice her mother into the briar and said, "Mother, it's a lodge, a *wigiwam*, a hollow place in the bramble with a roof and walls, a wonderful place to play." Motioning to her friend A-wa-sa-si, A-bo-wi continued, "We want to take Wi-ni with us and play camp. She'll be our baby."

"But, A-bo-wi, it's dark in there."

"No, Mother. It isn't dark. The sunlight comes through the leafy roof, all pretty in the green leaves, and the berries are as many as the stars. Oh please, let us take her. I'll tie her hammock to the strongest limbs and swing her and sing her lullabies, and I'll take baskets and pick berries from the walls. *Please.*"

Philepenca yielded to A-bo-wi's pleading, and soon the children were playing deep inside the blackberry bush in their bramble briar lodge. As she continued picking, Philepenca could hear A-bo-wi's small sweet voice chanting the lullaby of swinging. *"We, we, we . . ."* And Philepenca thought to herself, It's such a perfect day. If only Gabriel were here.

The Sandy Lake scouting party had gone south as far as the great rapids, to the very edge of Dakota country, without seeing any sign of intruders. They had turned homeward, and now labored against the powerful current at the place where the Mississippi is joined on the west by the Crow Wing. They were two days away from Sandy Lake Village.

It was evening. Bright Forehead ordered everyone ashore, and as the party set up camp on the low point between the Mississippi and the Crow Wing, they instantly saw that a large number of Dakota had camped there shortly before them. Immediately Bright Forehead sent out scouts, who found that the Dakota had gone up the Crow Wing to the Gull River and then north. The trail was a week old and there was no sign that the Dakota had returned.

This was a matter of deep concern. For it was likely that the Dakota were circling about to attack Sandy Lake Village from the north—and there were few men left to defend it.

A bitter taste rose in Gabriel's mouth. He wanted to leap to his feet, relaunch the canoes, and paddle desperately upriver.

But Bright Forehead restrained him. "It is not wise, Gabriel. The Dakota have probably already struck."

A scream cut through the clearing, severing Philepenca's thoughts. Screaming and yelling burst from everywhere. Berry pails fell to the ground and scattered fruit through the tall grass. Philepenca kept her senses, and like a clever animal sank low and hugged herself small.

For long, frantic moments she lay half-hidden in the grass, then dared to rise up a little and look about. A dozen men, bronzed and naked but for moccasins on their feet and black paint on their faces, were running from the meadow, each with a struggling woman in his grasp. Without warning, two men she had not seen stepped out of the trees and ran toward her. They caught her by the arms, lifted her kicking to their shoulders, and carried her away after the others.

Shortly downriver from the place where it is joined by the Crow Wing, the Mississippi suddenly bends eastward. Where it curves, its waters have cut the land until, on the south side of the bend, a hill is carved away and a high bluff overlooks the upward stream.

Along the top edge of this bluff, the Sandy Lake scouts had dug rifle pits and now waited for their unsuspecting enemy to pass by on their journey home.

The Dakota had left Sandy Lake in triumph and paddled through the night. They took with them the women and children they had captured in the meadow. Now, with the dawn's first light, their flotilla of twenty canoes rounded a curve in the river and headed directly toward the bluff on which the ambushing war party waited.

Just as the moment of rescue seemed at hand, the Dakota pulled their canoes to the western shore. They forced the kidnapped women to light fires, carry water, and prepare food. The Dakota seemed in no hurry.

Bright Forehead was hard-pressed to restrain the men who now lay on the bluffs watching their wives and sweethearts mocked and treated like dogs while the enemies ate, reveled, and danced the dance of scalps.

At last, with full bellies and high spirits, the Dakota again launched their canoes. Rather than paddling, each crew reached out for the gunnel of the neighboring canoe and drew it close, so that soon they were floating with the current in a compact mass, at ease, talking, laughing, lighting pipes and passing them one to the other.

The eyes of the captive women burned as their captors raised slender poles in the bow of each canoe bearing bloody flags of victory; the fresh scalps of their Sandy Lake victims. The scalp raised in the bow of Philepenca's canoe had hair that was long and fine, like a child's, blowing in the soft breeze. She was unable to take her eyes from it.

At the head of the flotilla, war ensigns flew in the breeze. The Dakota shouted and rejoiced as the current bore them nearer the overhanging cliff.

As the mass of canoes floated near the cliff's base, Philepenca heard a familiar sound—like a bird, yet not a bird. It was an A-wish-in-aub-ay war whistle. She quickly drew her shoulders forward and tucked her head low.

Suddenly heavy lead hit soft flesh beside her, and the distant concussion of a small explosion followed instantly. Geysers of water leaped high at the gunnel nearest her. Slivers of dry birch-bark and cedar splintered from the canoes. Flying bits of brittle pitch sprayed the skin of her face.

The piercing A-wish-in-aub-ay war cry tore through the air and changed the Dakotas' revelry to confusion.

The Sandy Lake women knew exactly what to do. Instantly each threw her weight to the right, upsetting the canoes, plunging captive and captor into the shockingly frigid water of the clear rushing river.

Two of the A-wish-in-aub-ay men died. All of the women and children were rescued.

The Dakota did not retreat, but fought on into the next day. The price they paid was high. During the night their heartbroken sobs of lamentation for dead brothers, fathers, and sons filled the heavy air.

At last it became clear to the Dakota that the Sandy Lake people held a clear advantage, and they began their sorrowful journey downriver, their song of triumph exchanged for the ashes of mourning.

Gabriel rejoiced at Philepenca's safety, but his joy was cut short when he learned that she did not know the fate of their children. The men and women from Sandy Lake turned upriver in a state of great anxiety.

When two days later they came in sight of their homes, the returning party began to wail, and in answer the surviving people of the village lifted a high, thin lament, like the cries of wolves, a sad, prolonged sound of many voices cutting through the morning air. The two groups ran to meet, and merged on the camp's south plain. They had sorrowful news for one another. The wails became louder, more bitter. They clasped each other tightly and wept until the power to weep deserted them. They would not be comforted.

Philepenca led Gabriel directly to Canodens, a young woman who often helped her with the children. "Canodens," she cried,

"A-bo-wi and Wi-ni, where are they? Do you have them in your lodge?"

Canodens stared blankly at Philepenca. "We thought they were with you," she said, tears rising again in her red-rimmed eyes.

"No, they were not captured with us," Philepenca answered.

"Then little A-wa-sa-si is missing, too," Canodens said, weeping. "They've all been slaughtered somewhere outside the camp."

Philepenca's mind went instantly back to the long pole raised in the bow of the canoe in which she had been captive.

Overcoming the paralysis of their sorrows, the people joined hands and in a long line combed the fields and woods, searching for the small bodies. They searched past noon, but found nothing.

By midafternoon all hope was gone. As the sun began its decline, Philepenca and Gabriel walked alone to the clearing where the raiders had surprised the party of girls picking berries. The searchers had covered the meadow twice, turning every blade of grass, pressing back every tuft, and no further hope of discovery remained in their hearts. But because this was the last place Philepenca had been with her children, she felt compelled to return. Perhaps one more time she could feel those final, fleeting moments of happiness.

All afternoon storm clouds had been building in the southwest. Now one gargantuan thunderhead stood due south, blotting out an entire quadrant of the sky, its heights spread in long, thin wisps by the cold winds that blew about its head. A declining sun lit the cloud's upper half, turned it milky white, and tinged it with gold.

Gabriel and Philepenca had always loved such beauty, but on this evening they were empty of joy. They sat together in the meadow, looking but not seeing as the sun sank below the horizon and the earth's shadow reached up to cover even the great thundercloud's towering crest. White lightning played beneath the thundercloud and winked from its deepest recesses.

Night fell, ominously still. Overhead the first stars came out to shine. Crickets began to sing in the grass. From the forest tree toads joined the gentle chorus, and then from the briar bushes a tiny sound blended among them. A small, melodious, high voice sang a mother's lullaby. "*We, we, we.* Hush little flower. *We, we, we . . .*"

Philepenca had trained A-bo-wi better than she knew. When A-bo-wi and her friend A-wa-sa-si had heard the terrible cries of the Dakota bursting into the meadow, their eyes had grown large, but instantly A-bo-wi had clasped her hand over the baby's mouth and held tightly.

"But, my little *Nuco*," Philepenca asked after their joyous reunion, "the long days and the dark nights. Weren't you afraid?"

"Yes, Mother," the small one answered. "But I prayed to the Master of Life, and my fears went away."

"And were you not hungry and thirsty?" Gabriel asked. Turning to Philepenca, he said, "*Nuco*, look at them. They are as fat and healthy as if they had eaten and drunk every day."

A-bo-wi answered, "But we *had* food. We ate the berries from our berry-bush lodge. In the morning, dew dropped down through the leaves of our ceiling and we caught it in our berry baskets. A-wa-sa-si and I were cold at night, and so we huddled together. But Wi-ni was warm in her cradle board.

"When she whimpered I was afraid someone would hear, and I sang to her as softly as I could. The worst thing of all was that on the second day she began to smell so bad."

That night Gabriel Dublanche walked alone in the grassy meadow. In the sky overhead one constellation, the Northern Cross, impressed its form on his mind. Tears ran freely down his cheeks; he lifted an offering of fine tobacco into the air and let the wind blow it away. Then with a full heart he raised his voice in thanks to the Master of Life.

The next morning as the four ate around the fire in front of their lodge, Gabriel told his family that he would never again take them to the borderlands of a warring people.

"I know we agreed to winter here," he said. "But the Dakota will be back for revenge. This war will go on. The winter nights will never be so cold or the snows so deep that they will not come.

"There is time enough to go back to Wind Lake if we leave now."

Their journey was good, and before first frost they were secure in their own village far from any frontier of conflict. Even so there was disconcerting news from the east. Three hunters from Wind Lake had met voyagers on the way to Rainy Lake Fort. The Frenchmen had told them that the Iroquois and English were joining hands to fight against the French and their allies.

Gabriel went to bed that night thinking all the world was insane.

CHAPTER 31

The Letter

THE following spring rumors ran wild. Just as devil's claw entangles itself in the fur of wild beasts to spread its podded seeds far and near, on the cuff of every trader came talk of war.

French and English troops far to the south along the Ohio were moving uneasily. It was said that in the month of May, Jumonville, a popular French officer, and his men had been ambushed and scalped by troops under a young British officer named Washington. By summer's end French soldiers had driven the English from the forks of the Ohio and there taken possession of a half-built fort that the French then completed and called Duquesne. Now, to help drive the English from the contested grounds, at the Ohio's forks gathered many nations—Pottawatomie, Ottawa, Delaware, Shawnee, and even a smattering of A-wish-in-aub-ay.

Indeed, the leather hand—the A-wish-in-aub-ay call to war—had been brought even to the Wind Lake people. Like other members of the A-wish-in-aub-ay, the Wind Lake people loved their French brothers, for in all the hundred years the French had been among them, never had they tried to provoke the A-wish-in-aub-ay to war, always they had treated them well, had even lived among them and adopted their ways, and never once had tried to take their land, wanting only to trade.

However, the English were exactly the opposite, always ready to fight, treacherous in treaty, rejecting the native Americans' ways, and stealing land at every opportunity. Truly, English triumph would be disaster.

But the Wind Lake council reflected upon it, and they were sure; the French could not be driven out. They had been there too long; nothing could dislodge them now. Besides, the Wind Lake people were peaceful. Long ago sated by war, they now wanted only to live quietly. Tucked away here among the forests in the northern pocket of Superior, were they not safe from the English?

"Yes," they said, "We are safe, and we do not wish to sacrifice our sons to some foreign cause."

Gabriel Dublanche was perfectly at ease with his people's decision not to enter the war. He, too, had personally shed enough blood to last him a lifetime and, having paid dearly for it, had learned his lesson. He needed nothing from the outside world. His family was everything to him. Especially since the birth of his daughters he had become increasingly devoted to a peaceful existence.

Once again he turned to his journal and wrote:

> September 16, Moon of the Shining Leaves, 1754
>
> Michel, I have concluded that men everywhere, for one reason or another, love war; some for gain, some for hate, some for glory, some for the thrill of danger, others for the love of killing. It is not just the Europeans. Whether they smear their bodies with bear grease and ashes or spray them with fine perfume and dress in silk shirts with ruffles at their throats, men are brutish and love to let blood!
>
> For me there is only one excuse for war: the protection of our homes and our people. The only glory possible in war is the glory of bravery in that defense. The Wind Lake people are brave, quite willing to defend themselves, but they refuse to make war on others. Therefore, among them I am happy.

Indeed, Gabriel had found an alcove of peace around which, at a distance, the rest of the world frantically danced. For four more years, while foment swept the world, he remained in the forest with his family, happily unaware.

In Europe, famous men advanced civilization, David Hume with his history, Rousseau with his theories about nature and the "noble savage," Edmund Burke with his statemanship and oratory, Voltaire with his plays and philosophy.

In Austria, Marie Antoinette, destined to rise to power, to earn the hatred of her adopted people, and to die under the falling blade, had just been born.

In Bohemia, Frederick the Great had won the first battle of the Seven Years' War.

In India, British soldiers were languishing and dying in the "Black Hole of Calcutta."

In England, Samuel Johnson published his *Dictionary of the English Language*.

In the English colonies, John Woolman was writing against slavery.

In Sweden, smallpox raged.

In Portugal, at nine-thirty in the morning on All Saints Day in 1755, with the churches filled to capacity, the earth convulsed beneath Lisbon. Falling walls and roofs killed fifteen thousand men, women, and children. Others fled to an open space by the seashore, where, with a tidal wave, the ocean rose up to greet them and drowned fifteen thousand more. Strangely selective, the cataclysm had chosen for death the city's worshipers and left untouched the brothel owners, their women, and all their patrons.

Voltaire wondered out loud how God could be good and let it happen, how he could countenance innocent children shattered on the breasts of their devout mothers, how he could exact payment from them, and for what crime.

But of these things Gabriel Dublanche knew nothing. He did not know the names of the great men and women, and of the great events he heard little. No longer did he struggle with the kind of agonizing questions Voltaire asked, for Gabriel himself had come to a point of resolution. Hope was now his prized possession. He prayed only to love his family and to be loved in return.

Gabriel reasoned that he was no defector from life, for he did his part. He provided for himself and for his own. He harmed no man. He prayed for the world's suffering peoples, and out of his own possessions helped those in his village who could not help themselves. He did not covet his neighbor's wife or his house. And he was content to live in this way, for if all men lived so, the whole world would be like the one he had found.

Outside of Gabriel's world, civilization plunged on toward war. In 1755 Charles Michel de Langlade again came on the scene and led eight hundred and ninety men to ambush British Major General Edward Braddock and his troops on the Wilderness Road.

The Ottawas were present that day and had taken prisoners. As they traveled north with their captives, they treated them savagely. One of their victims was a young Englishwoman in the final days of pregnancy. While she writhed fully conscious, the Ottawa cut the living babe from her belly and threw it into a caldron of boiling water, then methodically dismembered the wildly grieving mother and ate her piece by piece.

No one on the American frontier of Pennsylvania was safe. Wilderness families were burned out, tortured, shot, and tomahawked.

In 1756 the British declared war on France. Immediately France turned and drove every English ship from the Great Lakes.

In 1758 the English recaptured Fort Duquesne and fought battles on the shores of Lake George and at the Ticonderoga Narrows on the southern end of Champlain.

The Englishman Robert Rogers and his Rangers, a band of partisans specially trained in unconventional wilderness warfare, fought wild and bloody battles with the equally unconventional French-Canadian *coureur de bois*—runners in the woods. Victory and loss teetered to and fro.

With General Louis Joseph, Marquis de Montcalm, leading the French forces, it seemed for a time the French would retain every inch of their lands. The marquis, a man of great intelligence and high moral values, was a brilliant soldier.

But the government of New France was in the corrupt hands of Marquis Pierre François Rigaud de Vaudreuil, a vain, jealous man who coveted Montcalm's glory and sought to undermine his authority. Moreover, Vaudreuil was mastermind to a ring of profiteers who intercepted French supply ships while still at sea, bought their goods at normal prices, and resold them to the military for several times their true value. Vaudreuil's corruption ate away at the cause. French coffers dwindled, supplies ran low, and Vaudreuil grew rich.

Now, in the spring of 1759, English General James Wolfe and his fleet moved up in the Saint Lawrence to strike at the very heart of New France, Quebec herself. Wolfe's flotilla of sixty English vessels rounded Isle Royal on the twenty-fifth of June. Behind the fortress's great walls, Montcalm lay waiting.

That Quebec was superbly fortified gave Montcalm every reason to believe that he would emerge the victor. Nonetheless, when lookouts reported English ships ascending the river, Montcalm sent runners westward to rally support.

Along with Montcalm's war message, one of the coureurs carried word of a different kind—from a dark and beautiful woman of Quebec to a man she had not seen in twelve years, but whom she had never forgotten.

* * *

On the eighth day of the Blueberry moon, A-wish-in-aub-ay children splashing about on the sandy beach east of their village looked up and saw a light canoe closing rapidly from the north. The children ran naked and dripping up the slope to the lodges, clamoring loudly all the way.

One of the canoemen was a *coureur de bois*, French, but dressed in the Ottawa style, a repulsive man with a long scar that ran down his left brow across an empty, sunken eye socket and ended at the left corner of his mouth. The other was in fact an Ottawa, quiet and tall, who with a grand bearing stood aside while the grotesque man talked.

When Black Duck and other chief men of the village had gathered around, the Frenchman began to speak. "Quebec is under English siege," he said. "Pontiac and Langlade say come, help drive the English from our shores."

The Wind Lake people, determined not to be used by the whites to settle their conflicts, received this word with no more enthusiasm than past calls to war. That other A-wish-in-aub-ay and Huron, Ottawa, Shawnee, and Abnakis were going east to fight for the French meant nothing to them. Even the great A-wish-in-aub-ay chief Minirvanvana, whom the French called "Le Grand Saultier," felt exactly as they and had withdrawn from the conflict. So in council that night when the pipe was passed among them, the principal men agreed and said, "We will not come."

The next morning, the rising sun hidden by a slate-blue overcast and cool wind blowing from the southeast, the messengers righted their canoe and set it afloat on the uneasy breast of the lake. A crowd of men and women gathered about to see them off.

The big Ottawa had taken his place in the bow, sitting silently as ever, his paddle laid across the gunnels as he waited for his companion to push off from shore.

The one-eyed Frenchman lifted his pack from the sand, set it just forward of the back thwart, and was in the motion of launch when he hesitated, as though remembering something important. He looked back to Black Duck and asked, "You have a Frenchman living in the village? Name of Dublanche?"

Black Duck answered, "Yes. Dublanche is one of us. He and his wife and daughters crossed the lake yesterday to fish on the other side."

"Well, I nearly forgot," the man said, reopening his pack and pulling out a folded leather wallet. "Here. Give him this. It's all the way from Quebec."

He retied his packet and took hold of the gunnels. With two long steps he pushed the little craft out and with three deft paddle strokes set his course northward.

Gabriel Dublanche and his friend Two Babies paddled at a hard steady pace, pulling over the long rolls and hollows on the breast of the great Saganaga. They were one day east of Wind Lake.

Gabriel's rifle, one that had belonged to Huntermark, lay lengthwise with Two Babies' musket. In case of upset in a rapid, both were tied securely under the thwarts. Other than the guns, the two men had packed only a change of clothing and food for the long journey.

Gabriel calculated that they could make the twelve hundred miles in about twenty days. This would put them in Quebec on the thirtieth of July. It would be a prodigious task.

Gabriel's heart ached at leaving his wife and children, but as soon as he had read the letter he knew he must go. When he told Philepenca, tears swam in her large brown eyes, broke over and ran down her cheeks. She had held him in her arms and said, "Yes, *Nuco*. There is no question about it. You must go. I would never try to prevent it. But I will go with you."

"No, dearest. You can't," he had answered. "Quebec may be bloodier than the Crow Wing." He paused, tightened his arms about her shoulders, and continued, "I vowed I would never put you or the children in such danger again. You cannot go."

Philepenca had acquiesced. Gabriel hugged his daughters tightly. The younger, Wi-ni-shi-ba-go-sin, begged him not to go, saying she had heard there were high mountains there, and she was afraid he might fall off. A-bo-wi was old enough to understand that when fathers go to war, often they do not return. She, too, had pleaded with him not to go.

Gabriel pulled steadily in time with Two Babies, but his mind dwelt on the parting. Tears rose in his eyes, blinding him to the gray swelling water that rushed continually to meet him.

Then his mind went again to the leather wallet, and the letter inside. His memory was branded with the moment of its opening—the place where he had stood, the smells in the air, the noises about him, Philepenca's voice asking, "What is it, *Nuco*?" He felt again the great longing mixed with fear that had risen in his breast as he unfolded the fine, damp-wrinkled vellum and read the flawless feminine hand.

June 21, 1759
M. Gabriel Dublanche

Dearest Gabriel:

When I heard that messengers were going to the interior, I determined to write and tell you something you will want to know.

I have learned from Paul Robertson—who is still in service to M. Lefleur—that the last he knew, you were living in a village on the northwest side of Superior. He tells me you have married and now have children, and that my letter might reach you by the hand of a *coureur de bois*.

So it is that I have written.

By now you know that Quebec will soon be under siege. Even now many English ships lie just below Isle d'Orleans. Our spies tell us that their commander is General James Wolfe, and that he brings with him an army of nine thousand men.

For our part, we number fourteen thousand regulars, plus Quebec's usual garrison force of twelve hundred, and a thousand men under Pontiac and Langlade. All of this in a fort so strong that a thousand could hold ten thousand at bay forever. So, you see, we are secure. Yet we do suffer terribly for want of food.

General Montcalm, a good man and a father to us all, plans to risk nothing. His plan is to simply wait until Wolfe sees the futility of beating himself against our walls and goes home. Even if Wolfe is stubborn and waits for months, winter will drive him away.

So, you see, things are not going too badly for us here.

Now for the news that is most important to you.

A month ago a thousand fresh troops from Europe put ashore here—reinforcements for the Marquis de Montcalm. Since that time I have become acquainted with one of these, a bright promising young man who has risen to the rank of captain in spite of the fact that he is only twenty-one years old.

This young man—he is from Rouen—asked to be assigned to the North American theater of war because, he says, his father is somewhere on the continent.

His name is Michel Dublanche.

If I have judged you correctly, I will be seeing you before General Wolfe takes his leave of us. Until then, I am,

Affectionately yours,
Angelique Fontaine

C H A P T E R   3 2

Reunion

GABRIEL DUBLANCHE was afraid. Not of battle or of death, but of meeting Captain Michel Dublanche.

It was early morning, the fifth day of August. A crystal predawn light bathed the pristine landscape. Quebec was little more than five miles away. Gabriel and Two Babies had slept in the forest on the north bank of the Saint Lawrence, and now, unable to sleep longer, waited for the full light of day in which to cover the last distance and approach the fortified city. A night chill lingered in the air.

Within, Gabriel was like a tightly strung concert harp. Anxious beyond idle conversation, he paced back and forth along the river's high bank, gazing first into the gray silt-laden eddies below, and again into the tops of the trees about him. Often forgetting Two Babies was there, he burst out with some exclamation intended only for himself.

Through his mind ran pictures of a night more than twelve years ago when he had tucked a little boy with big, trusting eyes into bed. His last words to the child had been, ''Michel, I'll see you in the morning.''

Would they recognize each other? Why did Michel come searching? Perhaps he hated his father. Perhaps the boy would take one look, level his pistol, and shoot Gabriel on the spot.

In any case it was not death he feared. It was the uncertainty, not knowing whether this would be a beginning or an end. That was torture.

When the rim of the sun's orange ball broke over the eastern line of trees, Gabriel and Two Babies were up and away like a shot. Having hidden their canoe in a grove of wild cherry, they set out to cover the rest of the way on foot.

The woods ended a mile from the city. The men emerged from the forest into an open field of grass, then halted in their tracks at the sight that lay before them. On the far edge of the hilly, gently rising field, on a bluff that swelled out into the river, sat the city of Quebec. She was bound on three sides by water, and on her remaining quarter, a massive stone wall bellied outward toward the plain. The city's strength seemed unassailable. She sat on the hilltop like a queen on a throne, casting long, early-morning shadows toward them.

The open field that lay between them and the city was a vast meadow covered with tall, dew-pearled grass that glistened and sparkled in the early sun. On the meadow's south side the plain dropped suddenly into the Saint Lawrence. This grassy plateau belonged to a river pilot by the name of Abraham Martin, and everyone called it the "Plains of Abraham."

There was movement in the meadow. Cattle grazed at ease, children played, two teams of horses and wagons bringing food from Montreal clapped and rattled along the road that skirted the prairie's north edge.

It was a deceptive sight. Nothing seemed out of order, no one under the duress of siege. In fact the enemy camp lay wholly south of the river and downstream on the Isle d'Orleans. The meadow was a scene of perfect peace.

Gabriel and Two Babies walked with long strides directly through the dew-laden grass; their moccasins were quickly soaked through and their legs wet to the knees.

When they were halfway across the meadow, the distant groan of massive iron hinges announced the opening of the city gate nearest them. At that moment Gabriel and Two Babies caught their first glimpse of a fighting presence. Through the gate marched a military band toward the parade grounds that lay outside the city walls. A distant icy-clear ring of fifes cut the air. Quick drumsticks rattled, great bass drums rolled and boomed as the band stepped lively to its own rhythm. In time to the music, the two men quickened their pace.

Now, only an arm's length from the musicians themselves, Gabriel and Two Babies watched and listened in rapt fascination. The sound was deafening; the band marched in place, and the concussion of its united footfall ran through the ground into the soles of Gabriel's feet. Quivering excitement coursed in small tingling shocks over his skin, the bass drum vibrated into his belly, and the melody of the fifes lifted his spirits. Sharp, thin chimes tingled the base of his skull and ran down his spine. It was an exultation!

But a fearful impatience prodded Gabriel's memory. Somewhere very near this place he would find his son. He took a new grip on his rifle and walked toward the main westward gate. No one challenged their right to enter the city, for Two Babies was obviously a Great Lakes Chippewa and Gabriel appeared to be a *coureur de bois*.

Within the walls the city sprawled grandly in every direction, not on ground level, but upward here and downward there, sloping toward the river. Garrison soldiers on horse and afoot clapped and padded over the brown cobblestones. Women with baskets in their hands and children clinging to their skirts milled through the marketplace searching for some overlooked item of food.

As they made their way along the cobblestone street, Gabriel closely watched Two Babies' face. Never before had this Ojibway been out of the wilderness. This was the first city he had ever seen, the first buildings of sawn wood and cut stone, the first streets, the first pavements, the first walls. It was Ojibway custom to hide evidence of surprise, so as they walked along, Two Babies' face betrayed no emotion. Though his feelings were hidden, his eyes missed nothing, and later he would confide to Gabriel that he was awestruck by the grandeur, offended by this violation of the natural world, puzzled by this imposition of human industry and skill on the face of the sacred earth.

Now as they passed through the market the smell of day-old horse droppings rose from the pavement and mixed with the aroma of baking bread to permeate the air with strong pungency.

A large rawboned dog, his short reddish-gold coat stretched tightly over obscenely protuberant ribs, sauntered up, wagged his broomlike tail, and sniffed in a friendly way at Gabriel's frayed leggings. Gabriel looked down and shook his head. ''Poor fellow,'' Gabriel said, ''nothing but skin and bones. At least no-body'll serve him up for breakfast.''

Two Babies chuckled agreement.

Angelique Fontaine, her head cocked to her left and her eyes wide with uncertainty, looked up at the men standing directly before her.

Gabriel had thought that when they met again she might shout his name and throw her arms about him, but she did not. Instead she stood shocked and amazed, recognizing her old friend's voice, knowing who he was, but unable to adjust the image in her memory to fit the man who stood before her now.

Gabriel was now a man of forty-four years. His clean-shaven face was deeply tanned by long exposure to the sun. His dark eyes had exchanged their boyish uncertainty for a kind of calm, impossible-to-intimidate confidence that met her gaze with simple, unashamed ease.

His shoulders, she thought, were wider than before, as brown as his face, his arms thicker and smoothly muscled. Though dressed like his adopted people, his dark brown hair was the same as when she saw him last, and he still wore it in a queue down his neck. His only other concession to his former outward appearance was his mother's silver crucifix, shining brightly from its place at the end of a rosary, dangling squarely in the middle of his brown chest.

Gabriel stood on the stone threshold and looked down at his friend. She was no longer a young girl, but a woman of thirty-eight. He marveled that her beauty had not faded, that she appeared just as captivating as at their first meeting.

Playfully, in perfect Chippewa, he asked, ''Is this the house of Angelique Fontaine?''

Her eyes smiled, she shook her head from side to side in mock disgust, and began to laugh. Then she did throw her arms around him and welcomed him and his companion into her house.

Angelique's home stood at the end of one of the city's best streets, just below the eastern wall. The house, like Angelique, possessed beauty and character, both without and within. In the front room the drapes were open wide and a large south window admitted a flood of clear morning light that reflected brightly from a walnut table and cast little rainbows through a cut-glass pitcher that sat upon it.

Time had changed Angelique very little. She still held her chin high, and her eyes retained their bold blue. No matter how fine the furnishings about her, she was still the centerpiece of any setting.

Both men declined the chairs she offered, Gabriel saying he was too soiled by travel to sit in them and that he was no longer comfortable in chairs. So both he and Two Babies sat cross-legged on the polished parquet floor.

Gabriel did not ask how she lived so well. He knew her to be resourceful, that her parents in Boston were wealthy, and that if she wanted him to know, she would tell him.

As they sat, Angelique unfolded the events that had transpired since her letter. In spite of his interest, Gabriel's mind wandered, and he thought about the woman sitting before him rather than about what she was saying.

Quite unintentionally Angelique had been the catalyst of his ruin, and yet she had also been the salvation of his mortal life. But, he thought as he looked into her eyes, he had needed someone deeper than Angelique to be the salvation of his soul. What a contrast, he thought, between this woman and the one he left in the wilderness. Angelique wanted possessions, fine clothes, and power, not for the sake of vanity or ease, but for security. And given her difficult childhood, that was understandable.

Angelique was a true child of her experience. She had a morality of her own, even a spirituality of sorts. Of one thing Gabriel was sure: this woman would never go hungry and she would never wear rags.

What an experience it would be, he thought, if Angelique and Philepenca could meet. Each in her own way was strong and wise. Yet each had an approach to life that held them worlds apart.

Angelique's calm womanly voice floated back into his consciousness. "They've besieged us for more than a month now," she was saying. "This is the forty-first day. There hasn't been much fighting, just one skirmish downriver at the mouth of the Montmorency. Well, it was hardly a skirmish. Wolfe himself came up the slopes with three thousand men. We lost less than a dozen and they lost five hundred dead, wounded, and captured.

"They have managed to fight their way to Pointe Levi—that's east across the river—and set up batteries of cannon on the heights there. But Wolfe paid dearly for that piece of real estate. While they secured the point we cannonaded them, and Pontiac's men cut dozens of them down with guns and arrows. Scalped them. Dismembered them.

"Our biggest problem is still food. Everyone here is on the edge of real hunger. I'm afraid the men would weaken quickly if pressed to exertion.

"The irony of it is that it isn't Wolfe who cut off our food supplies." Her bright eyes grew brighter and bluer with anger. "Our own honorable governor is responsible for that. Everyone knows, but even Montcalm can do nothing. The hard evidence isn't there and the marquis is too good a man to bypass the law."

Angelique soon saw that Gabriel's mind was not on her narrative. "But you didn't come to hear this," she said. "Are you ready to see Michel?"

They were standing above her house now, overlooking the river from the easternmost point of the city's massive stone battlements. A hundred feet below, where the cliffs disappeared into the water, the broad stream glided on its gray, deep way toward the sea. Isle d'Orleans, fully twenty miles long and a forth as wide, loomed far downstream. Though it was nowhere in sight, Gabriel knew that Wolfe's army waited there for the right moment to advance on the city.

Southeast, across the river and nearly a mile distant on Pointe Levi, set firmly on the rock of eastern bluffs, Wolfe's cannon glinted in the sun. Occasionally rags of white smoke went up from a cannon's mouth, each puff followed shortly by a dull distant thud, and in moments by a whistling, rushing sound that grew until it ended in an explosion somewhere in or near the city.

"Damn Wolfe," Angelique said, and her eyes grew dark. The gable of a nearby house flew into splintering fragments, some of which struck the wall near their feet. "He can't breech the walls with those things. He keeps it up to let us know he's there and to kill our morale. He's blown apart a dozen houses, toppled the spire from the cathedral, and gutted its nave.

"Yesterday, just about this time, an old man was pushing his vegetable cart down the street in the very center of town. A shell struck close by and blew his legs from under him. He lay there in his own blood and died."

Angelique paused, then pointed. "Michel's camp is north-northeast—up there." She gestured across a great expanse of water where the Saint Lawrence's north side swept so far outward it formed something more like a bay than a river.

Gabriel followed her gaze to the north shore. All this land had an uncommon natural strength, and from the city itself to where the Montmorency entered the larger river eight miles away, French General Montcalm had thrown up earthworks and placed his men behind them. As far as one could see, until the northern shore disappeared around a bend far to the east, thousands of white French campaign tents dotted the tops of the bluffs.

The three descended the walls, left the city by its north gate, followed the road past the parade grounds, crossed the Saint Charles by bridge, and kept to the road as it ran east. Between the road and the river lay the French encampment.

Neither Gabriel nor Two Babies had ever seen so many men. French troops populated the mile-wide strip of land so thickly, and their guns and swords, pikes and carriages, wagons and horses, all appeared in such abundance, that both men fell into awed silence.

"Has the great father Montcalm emptied the land across the water to bring such numbers to this place?" Two Babies asked finally.

"No, my friend," answered Gabriel. "There are thousands of times as many yet in France."

Two Babies fell into a deeper silence, and then mused half to himself, "With so many, if ever they choose to come and fill our forests, how could we stop them?"

Gabriel answered, "If that's what they chose to do, we couldn't stop them. But you don't need to fear the French. They will never do it. For two hundred years their only wish has been to trade with you, not to take these lands. It will stay the same."

"But the English, are they as many in their land as the French are in yours?"

"No," Gabriel answered. "They are not so many. France is the largest of all the nations of Europe. There are twenty million of us."

Two Babies shook his head. "I cannot imagine it." He paused. "I am glad the English are not so many."

"No. Not so many," Gabriel said, "but nearly so."

"And they have come to take land, not to trade," Two Babies mused. "I am afraid for my people. If the French lose this battle . . ."

"If we lose," Gabriel picked up his thought, "my people may have to leave this country. And if they do, the English will do what they please with it."

Two Babies crossed himself and muttered, "I pray it will never be."

With an hour's walk they passed Vaudreuil's headquarters on the north, and in another half hour were close to their destination. Gabriel turned to Angelique and asked, "Angelique, you said in your letter that you know Michel. How did you meet him?"

"I came here one afternoon soon after the new troops had arrived," she answered. "The officers know me. You can see they do—else we could not pass through these lines so easily." She smiled slightly and continued. "Somehow Michel knew my name, knew that you and I had known each other, and that I live in Quebec. He asked around to see if any had heard of me, and happened on a lieutenant commander of the marines who knew me. The lieutenant commander introduced us that afternoon. We walked alone just over the earthworks there, and sat for a long time talking.

"He asked an unbelievable number of questions," she added. "Most especially, he wanted to know everything about you."

"What is he like?" Gabriel asked.

"You can soon see that for yourself," she said. "We're almost there."

It was now early afternoon. Angelique, Gabriel, and Two Babies turned down a deeply rutted wagon trail that ran among the row upon row of tents. Here and there men sat in circles of six or eight, playing cards or dice. Scattered among the French were dark-skinned Ottawa and Huron, teaching the soldiers games of chance unheard of on the European continent.

As they moved past the talkers and the gamers, none of the three spoke. Few times in his life had Gabriel felt such tension within.

At last they came to the final row of tents, the row that stood just beneath the earthworks, and to a tent near the end of the row. It seemed deserted, but the tent flap was untied. Angelique called out, "Captain Dublanche, are you home?" She stepped ahead of Gabriel and Two Babies and approached the tent alone.

Inside, there was a rustling, the sound of a table bumped, a brushing of the canvas wall. A man's voice answered, "Mademoiselle Fontaine?"

The flap lifted inward. Framed in the shadowy triangle of the tent door stood Michel Dublanche.

"Mademoiselle Fontaine," he said, "I'm surprised. No more than five minutes ago I was thinking of you, wishing you would come again. If you hadn't, I would have paid you a visit tomorrow." He paused, smiled, and held her hand warmly. "There are so many more questions I want to ask you about my father. But here, sit down. A camp stool isn't much to offer a lady but . . ." He reached into the tent and brought out a chair, unfolded it, spread its canvas bottom, and gestured toward it.

Angelique, momentarily disregarding the chair, motioned with her hand to her companions. "Captain Dublanche . . ."

"Please," he interrupted. Not 'Captain Dublanche,' just 'Michel.' "

"Very well . . . Michel. Michel, I have two friends with me. They want very much to meet you."

For the first time Michel noticed the men. He looked past Angelique and spoke directly to them. "I'm sorry. Please forgive me," he said. "It isn't every day I have a visitor like Mademoiselle Fontaine." His voice was strong for a man so young, and conveyed a calm, unpretentious assurance. He reached out, took Gabriel's hand, gripped it firmly, and looked directly into his eyes, trying to draw out the meaning of the visit.

Gabriel returned the gaze with an equal intensity.

Michel was both like and unlike his father. He was dark, and wore his hair in just the same way; he was a little taller than Gabriel, but he had Gabriel's eyes and the same pleasant way about his mouth. The nose was his mother's, as well as the strong cheekbones and the color of his skin.

Michel's eyes were warm and piercing, his jaw firm, his teeth white and even. A stray shock of hair, a full dark brown wave, fell over his forehead; this he kept brushing back. He wore knee breeches and a dark vest over a white shirt open at the throat. Cuffs turned back to the elbow exposed his muscular forearms. His hands were masculine and seemed large for his stature.

Gabriel felt a sudden irresistible swelling fill his breast. It was immediately obvious to him that both in body, face, and character, his son was worthy of a father's most extravagant pride. His breathing deepened, tears swam in his eyes, and his grip on the boy's hand became like iron.

When Michel saw the tears in the stranger's eyes and felt the strong grip of his hand, the first glimmer of understanding flickered in his soul.

For twelve years and more he had carried in his mind a picture of his father. The picture had once been strong and clear, but Michel had looked so often at the image that it was faded now, transformed first in one feature and then in another. He knew the image was no longer true, that he could not trust his distant memory, but the image was all he had.

Now he tried to see it again, to raise it from some hidden depth, to superimpose the image on the face before him. But he could not find the image at all. It was lost somewhere in the labyrinth of his emotions as the moment's light began to dawn.

Suddenly Michel was afraid. The mist his memory had cast about his father was silver. It had muted his faults and veiled the dark suspicions of his mother. But now he was old enough and wise enough to know that the real man might match neither the picture his mother had presented nor the image in his own mind.

He felt a sudden urge to draw back, to turn away.

Gabriel sensed the boy's uncertainty, and out of his own fear he took it for revulsion. Instantly he regretted having come. How foolish, he thought, to try and untangle the twisted roots knotted by time.

But their fears were absorbed into the larger emotion of reunion. Michel forgot he was a soldier and suddenly became a little boy with his arms bound tightly about his father's neck. "Papa," he breathed. "Papa. She took me away from you. I didn't want to go. I tried to stay. Please forgive me!"

"Forgive you?" Gabriel could not believe his ears. Not once in all the years of their separation had he dreamed that the boy might think himself to blame.

Clasped in each other's arms, they wept until they could weep no more.

CHAPTER 33

On the Plains of Abraham

ON the day after their meeting Gabriel and Michel Dublanche walked together alone on the city's stone ramparts.

"Fireboats?" Gabriel asked as he searched the river with his eyes.

"That's right," Michel replied. "Governor Vaudreuil's idea. He had them built upriver. What you see there is all that's left of them." A dozen charred hulks lay along the rocks on the south side of the river just west of Pointe Levi, angular shapes of black lying low in the gray water.

"French ships and log rafts chained together," Michel continued, "loaded down with tar, pitch, grenades, and shells. One dark night in June we brought them downriver as far as we dared, then set them afire and swam for shore, hoping the current would carry them into the English ships." Michel shook his head and chuckled. "Didn't touch one of them. They ran aground on the point and burned to the waterline.

"It wasn't Montcalm's idea," he repeated. "Vaudreuil gave the direct order. In fact he did it twice. It cost the English nothing, and it cost us money, ships, and humiliation. If Vaudreuil would get out of Montcalm's way we could *do* something here. But that's dreaming. The cause is lost."

"Lost?" Gabriel repeated incredulously. "Wolfe has lost hundreds. We've lost no one. His attacks have failed. How is it you think the cause is lost?"

"I think it, Papa, because south and west of here important forts have fallen. Five of them." Michel ticked them off on his fingers. "Niagara, Le Boeuf, Mauchault, Presque Isle, and Saint Frederick. Now we have bad news from Lake Champlain. Fort Carillon is weakening.

"Things are going well enough here. But everyone knows how they've gone elsewhere, and morale is low. Besides, many of our men are farmers and trappers—they've not fought before. If by some strange quirk Wolfe does break through—God forbid—I doubt we could hold him, much less drive him back. Vaudreuil has ordered deserters shot, but nearly every night another hundred men go over the wall.''

Gabriel was shaken. With a hollow look in his eyes, he stared toward the river, and then in an empty way said, ''So New France will fall, and the English will have their way with the whole continent.'' He shook his head sadly and added, ''Thank God my people don't live in the cities. We are far enough into the wilderness that it won't make much difference in my lifetime. But it makes me sorry for the others—the Chippewa and Ottawa and Hurons. Only God knows in the long run what will happen to them.''

The siege was now in its sixty-second day. Word filtered down that Montcalm believed it could not last more than another month. He was certain Wolfe would take his troops south before winter locked them in together.

Gabriel determined to wait it out. It was his hope that Michel would leave the army and come to the interior with him, but this was more than he could expect until danger to Quebec was past.

In spite of the threat, though Wolfe sat ready to spring at any moment of carelessness, and though life and limb could be lost in the next hour, for Gabriel Dublanche these twenty days had been among the finest of his life. They were fine because he was close to his son, fine because of questions laid to rest, questions that had for years squirmed about in his mind like maggots in a heap of rotting flesh.

His parents, did they hate him for what he had done? Did they really believe he had been unfaithful to Celeste? Were they still alive?

And Celeste, did she die despising him? How had she treated Michel? What had she told the boy about his father?

The answers were all there. Catherine had died two years ago; no one knew the cause. Abel had wakened one morning. She was lying beside him as always, but when he touched her she was cold. ''Grandfather died before the winter was out,'' Michel said. ''But Papa, they knew the truth. They trusted you in spite of all that Mama said. I overheard them talking once. They said that with what Mama had become, it was more than the best of men could endure."

Michel paused. "And Uncle Joseph, not once did he lose faith in you. 'A momentary slip of character,' I think he called it." He chuckled as he quoted his great-uncle's words.

Gabriel asked quietly, "And what *of* Uncle Joseph? Is he alive?"

"No. No," Michel answered. "Word came just before we embarked that he had died. Natural causes. But"—Michel brightened—"he was as ramrod straight at seventy-five as he ever was."

Gabriel smiled at the memory, then looked at the ground and sighed deeply. They were gone, all of those closest to him, all but Michel.

Although the death of his family was not a surprise to Gabriel, numbness and depression settled down on him. Still, this was no time to go into mourning; he took hold of himself, devoted every thought to Michel, and his cheerfulness returned.

On the night of August 12 the two men sat at Michel's fire. The boy reached forward to stir the kettle—their evening meal. As he leaned forward, a small silver medallion swung free from his shirt.

Gabriel saw it and asked, "Is that what I think it is?"

"What, Papa?" the young man answered.

"Around your neck, on the chain—the silver medallion."

"Yes, sir. It's the one you made for me when I was four. I slept with it under my pillow every night after you went away. Once when I was ten," he said, "I was spending the summer in Avranches and lost it. At supper Grandfather asked me why I wasn't wearing it. I looked down and saw it gone, and started to cry. I got up from the table and ran out into the twilight. The three of us crawled in the grass beneath the oak looking. I wouldn't let them go to bed until we found it. Somehow it made me feel close to you."

It was the next morning when Gabriel took a thick bundle from his pack and with loving hesitation handed it to his son. The bundle was leather-wrapped, securely tied with a soft deerskin thong. Michel slipped the knot and found within a thick sheaf of paper, the oldest sheets of which were yellow with age and exposure. All were inscribed closely in Gabriel's even, clear hand. Michel gazed at the sheets, then looked questioningly at his father.

"It's my journal," Gabriel said quietly. "I wrote it for you. I kept a record every day that we were apart. Every page shows that not one day did I forget you."

Michel's eyes clouded with tears, and tightly gripping this new-found evidence of his father's love, he wrapped his arms around Gabriel.

During these days, the two men excluded almost everything but each other from their minds. Angelique left them entirely to themselves. Two Babies spent his time among fellow Chippewa, and once was away for a week, far to the north, where game was yet undisturbed by hungry soldiers. He came back with the carcass of a young deer on his shoulders and a cornucopia of wild roots and herbs in his pouch.

Michel was excited at the prospect of staying on in New France after the siege was over. He questioned Gabriel about life on Wind Lake, what it was like to live there, how it felt to be cut off from all the world outside, how he bore up under the severe winters, what the people themselves were like.

"Tell me about your wife," he said. "Is she beautiful? Rousseau says these people are 'noble savages.' Is it true?

"I have *sisters*? No! I can't believe it. How old are they? Do they know about me? I can hardly wait to meet them."

When Gabriel learned of Michel's intention to come with him, he could not contain his joy.

On the evening of the twenty-eighth of August they sat together on a grassy knoll that jutted between the river and the encampment. The sun had just dipped from sight, but its remaining light turned the western edge of the earth to an undulating line of liquid gold beneath a dome of sunset blue.

Gabriel gazed west and thought of the happiness that awaited them on his return. In trying to describe Philepenca, he said to Michel, "She had never heard of a farthingale, has no idea what a palace of pink marble might be like, didn't know the Greeks ever lived, or that a sonnet exists. She has never seen a city. Sights that you take for granted back in Paris would throw her into a state of awe. Yet she's as lovely and intelligent a woman as you've ever seen."

"As lovely as Angelique?"

"As lovely as Angelique. A good mother, tender, compassionate. I can't wait for you to meet her!" He paused for a time and watched the darkening river flow by. "Michel, civilization is not finery or diction. Civilization isn't in buildings, not even in libraries or schools. Civilization is compassion, and understanding. Philepenca is as civilized as the finest European woman."

"Then Rousseau is right? The wilderness people, untouched by modern society, are more noble?"

"No. He's wrong about that. These people can be as cruel, even more cruel perhaps, than Europeans. But the better ones are as kind and as gentle as the best. The Wind Lake people are as peaceful as our old neighbors in Avranches. And I like their way. They stay close to the earth. Their lives are ruled by the seasons. They have only what the forest gives them and what they can make from it."

Michel sat between Gabriel and the setting sun, silhouetted against the pale sky. His profile was sharp and distinct. The outline of his intelligent, manly, well-formed face made Gabriel feel intensely proud.

"I can't tell you," Gabriel said, "what joy it is to be here with you now—what a joy to be talking to you like this, two men, father and son, who understand and feel so deeply that either would give his life for the other. It's been a long time. I've found peace of mind among the Wind Lake people, but this will always be one of the greatest joys of my life. I never dared to believe it would come, but now I have hope. God willing, soon all my treasures will be together on the shores of Wind Lake."

The earth's gold rim had grown thin, diminished to a delicately scribed line, and at that instant disappeared altogether.

"Papa, look at that," Michel said.

Gabriel turned and looked downriver, away from the setting sun, past the dark trees on Isle d'Orleans, past the vertical lines of tall masts and high yardarms of English ships anchored on its shores. "What is it?" he asked.

"There. The moon," Michel said, "just coming up. It's full tonight, and red. I've never seen it so red."

Two weeks later, on the tenth of September, it began to rain. Clouds swept up from the western horizon in the early morning, accompanied by a severe chill. By noon they covered the sky and the whole firmament began to lower. Big, dark puffs of cloud skimmed the spires and blended with the mist rising from the river.

The troops were in their tents, fully dressed as always, ready for any alarm. Montcalm's horse was saddled. He had not taken off his clothes since the twenty-third of June, seventy-nine days ago.

Montcalm was an exceptional man. He was forty-seven years old, possessed military skill of the highest order, and for two years had been commanding general of all French forces in America. He had won important victories in that time, but now he knew, even as his men knew, that the ultimate cause was lost. But duty to his king demanded that he press forward.

Now it was night. Rain spattered on the roof and against the windows of Montcalm's quarters. He paced back and forth, praying, hoping against hope that Wolfe would soon give up and leave. And why should he not, thought Montcalm, with his losses, and the absence of any strategic advantage?

Today, hoping to tempt Montcalm into the open, Wolfe had set fire to houses, barns, and fields up and down the valley. From Quebec the farmer-soldiers watched the gray smoke ascending, and now in the darkness went over the walls in even greater numbers.

Still, these desertions would make no real difference in the siege. For Wolfe to succeed, someone, Montcalm or his lieutenants, must commit some enormous blunder, and Montcalm prayed that nothing of the kind should happen.

Quebec had one vulnerable point, the southwest side from which Gabriel and Two Babies had first entered the city. There lay the undulating Plains of Abraham, a perfect battleground where either side might hope to gain the advantage. But two things prevented Wolfe from reaching the plains. First, the plains were on a high plateau, easily defended by three thousand troops under Montcalm's chief aide, Captain Louis Antoine de Bougainville. Second, the walled city itself sat overlooking the river's narrowest point and guarded those narrows with one hundred and six cannon. Any troop-carrying ships trying to reach the upriver side of the city could expect to be blown out of the water.

But on this rainy night, the tenth of September, the unexpected happened. Two French deserters, groping uncertainly through the rain and mud, blundered into the English lines. Under interrogation they yielded a single piece of vital information.

Two nights from now, on the twelfth, Bougainville's men, who now guarded the cliffs at the edge of the plains, would be diverted to bring a convoy of provisions from Montreal. During that time the bluffs would be left unguarded.

One question remained in Wolfe's mind. Would it be possible to bring troops up through the narrows under the city's guns? It might be, because on the night of the twelfth, there would be no moon.

A slice of morning sun cut through a crack in the tent flap, struck Gabriel in the eye, and woke him. He turned over, trying to escape the intruding brightness, but it was no use. He could not ease back into sleep.

From the sea of tents spread along the earthworks came the light tinkling of pans and iron dishes and the murmurs of soldiers moving about in the smoke of campfires preparing their rations for breakfast. Somewhere to the east two dogs were trading barks back and forth.

Good, Gabriel thought. The sky is clear. The ground's going to be wet, though. He thought of how his moccasins would feel after he walked a few feet through the wet grass. Damp and clammy, that's how they would feel.

The mornings were getting cooler. He lay on his back looking up at the tent's roof. His breath formed a small, misty cloud above him, silver where the narrow bit of sun scythed through it, light gray where it lay in shadow. He did not want to throw back the warm blanket, and so he lay there thinking of their plans for the day. He and Michel were going into the city to find Angelique. They had not seen her for several days—since Sunday, in fact—and this was Thursday . . . Thursday, September 13.

But there was no need to hurry. The sun was just minutes above the horizon, which meant it was just about six o'clock. He turned his head to the right to see if Michel was awake. He was not. Last night, just as they had every night since their reunion, Gabriel and Michel had talked until very late.

Suddenly a rhythmic concussion rose out of the ground into Gabriel's body. It was the rapid beat of hooves.

Seconds after he felt them, the hooves were thudding and scraping the ground only a few tents down the line, and a man's voice was shouting. The collage of sound came rapidly near; behind the rider's voice rose a roar of urgent voices and frantic activity.

The clamor broke into Michel's sleep and in a slurred voice he asked, "Papa, what's all the noise?" Then, sitting up straight as the barrel of his musket, he said quickly, "Something's happened!"

The horseman was in front of their tent now, shouting the message again and again. "Up! Up and out! To the bridge. They've broken through."

In an instant Michel was out, running headlong between the tents and toward the road. Gabriel, determined not to lose sight of his son in the scrambling crowd, ran close behind, his own rifle in hand.

The night before, when total darkness had fallen and the sentries on Quebec's walls could no longer see the river's face, men on the ships anchored by Isle d'Orleans had silently dropped heavy canvas from the stark, straight yardarms and spread it to the light upriver breeze. With cloth-swaddled longboat oars they pulled slow, deep, and hard, and the great ships moved against the Saint Lawrence's stiff current.

There was no sound but the creaking of timbers, the straining and stretching of taut rope, and the soft gurgle of water swirling past oar blades. On and below deck sat row upon row of tense Englishmen, huddled shoulder to shoulder, packs on their backs, bayonet-fixed muskets upright between their knees, not daring to speak, hardly daring to breathe or move lest the darkness become light about them. Yard by yard the warships stole beneath the wide mouths of the mute cannons.

In one breathless hour the ships slipped through the narrows and anchored beneath the plains. Then men at arms moved to the ships' smaller boats and rowed ashore.

Root by root, stone by stone, their boots slid and scraped up the wet bluffs. After two hours, five thousand men gathered on the edge of the plateau, spread across its flatness, and formed lines of battle. There the English awaited the moment when cannon fire would shatter the dawn.

Montcalm was not asleep. At sunrise, when the far thud of cannon came from across the Saint Charles, he mounted his horse and galloped toward the bridge. When yet two miles from the point of crossing, he saw on the rolling plain, formed up line upon line, Wolfe's five thousand redcoats.

Montcalm was no stranger to battle. His crisp uniform hid the scars of five bullets and the slash of a saber. Immediately he had recognized the gravity of the situation. Turning to his aide, he ordered troops from the center and left encampments to come on the run, lest, he said, Wolfe reach the road to Montreal and cut off the line of supply.

As for himself, he rode straight ahead, eyes fixed on the bridge.

When Montcalm reached the Saint Charles, he found the situation worse than he had supposed, for rather than a few hundred enemy on the plains, there were thousands, nearly all of Wolfe's army. French shore batteries were already pounding the British ships lying in the river. A few of Bougainville's contingent had already engaged the English, but they could not hope to win this battle alone.

Within minutes hundreds of Frenchmen reached their commander, and their numbers quickly grew into thousands boiling out of the camps and across the bridge.

From the back of his jittering mount, Montcalm looked down to his men. Faces leaped up at him, standing out even as a single wave might capture one's attention out of a choppy sea. A pair of eyes stared up, wide, waiting for orders, filled with fear; only moments before the same eyes had been closed in sleep, oblivious to approaching doom. But this was not the moment to think of the men, their individual fortunes and fates. Such thoughts would certainly shake his resolve, and his emotions would countermand decisions his mind had already made.

Yet he could not help but feel the deep undertone of sorrow, for many going out would not return. What a pity, he thought, that it was for a cause already lost.

Fear marched in tandem with calm determination. Officers barked quick orders to men who had run long and hard from their distant encampment and whose mouths were now open wide to gasp every breath of available air. Fife, drum, and bells rose up from the rear and moved forward of the milling thousands, and with the music Montcalm pressed through the mass and led them out to join the battle.

Michel and Gabriel were a hundred feet deep in the throng. The electricity of the moment wrenched at their innards. The young captain fretted at the upheaval and confusion, wondering how he would pull his own men together out of this diffuse mass. No one, not even Montcalm, had dreamed this would happen— and Wolfe was giving them no time to dwell upon it, for as they fell into orderly ranks and started to cross the bridge, dirt leaped up at their feet. At Michel's side a youth fell to his knees when splinters from the bridge rail flew up and buried themselves in his face. In front of him a soldier crumpled, and behind, another screamed out.

Once over the Saint Charles, Gabriel, not a part of any fighting unit, moved about independently, firing at long-range targets with his superior rifle. He was accustomed to shooting squirrels at that distance, so it was hard to miss a man. On the first shot he saw a man fall where he had aimed, but somehow the man's fall seemed disconnected from the pulling of the trigger and the fire that had bellowed from his gun. It had been a long while since he had killed another human being.

Gabriel knelt to reload. There was no cover here. All you did you did in the full light of day, hoping, praying that somehow in the confusion no one would notice and train his sights on you.

To his right knelt a man with a wide, friendly face. In his fifties, Gabriel guessed, probably a farmer from the valley. The man seemed undisturbed to be in the heat of battle; all his senses were about him, he was as cool as if he were at home tending his stock. As he ran the ramrod down the bore of his musket, his eye caught Gabriel's. He smiled, and above the report of guns hollered something about how uncommonly warm it was for an early September morning, and weren't the bees buzzing thick in the meadow today. Then, abruptly, his eyes lost their fire, the smile froze, and a spot of skin opened above his right eye and began to stream down blood.

The line directly across the meadow from Gabriel began to sag and the English fell back, but only so far. When they reloaded, back they came, knelt, and sent a withering fire into the defenders.

Where is Michel? Gabriel thought, remembering he had not seen him for . . . for how long? Who can count time in battle? He did not know how long. He only knew that suddenly he missed him.

The French were moving forward again. Acrid, bitter smoke covered the field. It lay in a dense white cloud over the ground, hiding men, living and dead, becoming thicker with every cannon blast, every musket explosion.

As Gabriel ran forward, bodies passed beneath his feet, some dead, some twisting in pain. Men cried and called out from where they lay in the tall grass. It was the saddest thing he had ever heard, men weeping, calling out for their mothers.

The Huron and Chippewa and Ottawa, their faces greasy black or pasty white, were everywhere, laying the edge of their razor-sharp knives to the crowns of dead men's heads or to the heads of men not dead. It made no difference.

Abruptly the French hit a wall of troops who turned them back. They reloaded on the run, dropped, and turned, firing into the oncoming hoard behind them.

The battle raged back and forth, first toward the city and then away. The tall September grass hid the black earth as its soil gradually turned deep red.

This was not Michel's first battle. He had seen men die about him before, had smelled their warm blood, had heard them scream; he had closed their eyes. He had written letters to mothers of dead men and men whose arms were cut away. Though war was no stranger to him, and though he had distinguished himself often in its roar and confusion, he always felt that he did not belong in the midst of it. Many nights he had lain awake wondering about the men he himself had killed. In a different time and place could they have been his good friends? Would they have been like brothers? Perhaps he would have courted their sisters.

What, he wondered, did they leave behind? Sons who would never know their fathers, just as he had not known his? How he hated death! Yet he was death's instrument. But there was duty to God and king and country. There was honor. Better to kill than to lose honor. Yet, deep within, he wondered if it was really so.

The battle was hand to hand now. Michel grabbed a pike from the ground, and with all his weight and force ran its dull end into the pit of a man's stomach. The downed man fought to rise, to suck air back into his deflated lungs. But before he could catch another breath, Michel twirled the pike about in his hands and drove its sharp point through the man's diaphragm and spine, pinning him to the ground.

Before he could take his eyes from the wide silent mouth of the man, Michel felt a dull, painless blow on his right side. He turned and was face-to-face with an Englishman. The soldier had just swung his sword and drawn it through the neck muscle of a young Ottawa. Completely by accident he had slapped Michel under the right arm with the flat of his bloody saber. The red blood of the dead Ottawa striped Michel's bright blue uniform.

Reflexively, Michel jerked the pike back into action and sent the man stumbling backward, but the Englishman regained his footing and flew back at his attacker with hatred in his eyes.

In war death comes calling in varied garb. Some soldiers die outright from a bullet or saber, shrapnel or cannon fire. Some drown. Others are beaten to death. Still others die of minor wounds that become infected and gangrenous.

In midbattle the Great Interrupter came close to Gabriel Dublanche in an uncommon way.

Montcalm had sent for twenty-five field pieces from the city's palace battery, but the commander of the city garrison, ignoring the order, had sent only three, and kept the remaining twenty-two for his own defense.

The three cannon he did send were twelve-pounders. As horses drew them on, the cannon bounced heavily, rumbled across the bridge, and emerged onto the field, their bronze barrels shining in the sun, their wood carriages boasting new paint as bright and blue as the sky. Montcalm ordered the three pieces into place at widely separated points; one at the center and one at each end of the battle's line.

Gabriel, finding himself near the middle piece at the moment when one of the gunners was shot down, stepped forward and volunteered to take his place. Immediately the remaining gunner put a long shaft in Gabriel's hand and set him to swabbing the bore between shots.

It was a poor time to take lessons in artillery. Fire leaped from the gun and its grapeshot ripped a wide hole in the enemy line. Immediately Gabriel stepped forward and swabbed the bore; the gunner rammed a new charge home and touched fire to its priming. The gun lifted its carriage from the ground and belched flame and shot far down field.

Gabriel, however, had not known, nor had the gunner presence of mind to tell him, that one must step behind an imaginary line running even with the gun's muzzle; for one standing to the left or right in front of that line, though untouched by shot, would likely be struck senseless or killed by the gun's concussion.

At the instant of fire, Gabriel was scarcely a step to the right of the cannon's mouth. He reeled as though hit by the shot itself, landed in a crumpled heap many feet away, and did not move again.

The two armies fought in a fury of desperation, but strength began to drain away, sucked out by bitter emotion and relentless physical exertion.

Montcalm, still mounted, rode up and down his lines, giving orders and directing the flow of battle. His Ottawa, Chippewa, and Huron allies fought with their usual fervor and wild abandon, shouting, raging for a long drink of the warm, red English "broth."

In the English lines Wolfe commanded his troops as courageously as Montcalm. With the sun blazing down, still two hours before noon, Wolfe led a company of charging grenadiers into the heart of the conflict. Suddenly his right wrist began to pour blood, shattered by a French bullet. He wrapped it with a handkerchief and pressed on. Almost immediately a musket ball caught him low in the right side, and then came a smashing jar to the center of his chest. The last ball whipped him backward, off his feet, and left him sitting upright, staring emptily ahead.

Immediately Wolfe sank into unconsciousness. Three men carried him to a place of greater safety and laid him down. Through the haze of pain and shock he heard the shout, "They run! Look how they run!"

Rousing from his stupor, Wolfe asked weakly, "Who runs?"

"The enemy, sir, the enemy. Everywhere they're running."

Wolfe smiled slightly, gave an order to cut off the retreat, closed his eyes, and said, "Now then, God be praised, I will die in peace." And he breathed his last.

Montcalm could not stem the spontaneous retreat. The great frantic mass pressed his horse back to the city walls. Montcalm was within a hundred yards of the open gates, sitting high in the saddle, when an English ball caught him squarely in the back just to the left of his spine.

A soldier in the press who saw his general slump reached up and steadied him in the saddle. Another took the horse's bridle and led the dying man through the Saint Louis gate. Within the city everything was chaos. From a group of weeping women just inside the gate came a scream, "Oh my God! My God! The marquis is killed!"

He looked down at her, smiled, and said quietly, "It is nothing.

Nothing. Don't be worried for me, my good friends.'' Gently his men lifted him from his horse, took him to the surgeon's chambers, and laid him down.

For the second time that day Gabriel Dublanche awoke to the sunlight, but this time its slanting rays were the tawny, polluted light of a doleful late afternoon. Between his first awakening and his second, a world of pain had intervened. The crystal-clear day that had begun with such bright prospect was now smeared and bespattered with blood.

The battle was over. Both armies were exhausted; the English now retired to the plains and the French shut themselves up inside the city walls.

Gabriel was in an open space within the city, the palace courtyard, he thought. The blue late-afternoon sky stretched out above him and the acrid smell of burned powder mingled with the white haze that still hung in the air. But another odor cut into his consciousness, the odor of burned flesh and hair.

He lifted his left arm and it trembled. When he flexed his hand, he felt the exposed flesh tear. With his right hand he reached around to feel the left side of his head. The hair was gone, the skin blistered and seeping, the pain horrible.

Why did the world seem so ethereal, he thought, why so silent? There should be groans of the wounded, shuffling feet, carts rattling on the cobblestones. A face moved into his circle of light, a dark face, beautiful, tearstained. Angelique's lips moved, but Gabriel heard no sound. He spoke to her, yet felt rather than heard his own voice.

He could not remember what had happened, and she could not tell him, for the concussion of the gun had both seared his flesh and burst the drums of his ears.

Angelique took Gabriel to her home, where she cared for him until his slow recovery was complete. Montcalm lived twelve hours after having been struck down, and then died peacefully. Two Babies survived untouched, accounting for the lives of six Englishmen, but unlike his Chippewa brothers, he had taken no scalps.

As for Michel Dublanche, when the lines had bolted in retreat, he had picked up a fallen soldier and was carrying him to safety when the mad, fleeing crowd trampled them under its feet, killing them both.

Adoring soldiers and civilians buried Montcalm in a shell crater within the walls of the shattered chapel of the Ursaline convent. For the most part French fighting dead were laid in a common grave; but Angelique, like Joseph of Arimathea, begged for young Captain Michel Dublanche's body, and like Mary of Magdala, prepared it for burial. In the rocky, porous soil atop a wooded hill northwest of the city, on a peaceful hill far away from the battle's site, overlooking a quiet, secluded bend in the Saint Charles, Two Babies dug the grave.

In spite of his pain, Gabriel accompanied Michel on his last journey. Two Babies and a friend of Michel's whose name Gabriel did not know carried Gabriel on a litter to the distant hilltop. There Angelique knelt beside him. A gray-robed priest spoke words Gabriel could not hear, and at the foot of a massive syca- more that was just now letting go its autumn leaves, they laid Gabriel's greatly longed-for son to rest.

When the priest was gone, and his friends had discreetly slipped away for a little while, Gabriel remained. There, beside the new grave, he lay on his litter, looking through the top of the sycamore at a patch of blue sky, a background against which the autumn leaves let go one by one and floated down. His desolation was unspeakable. He could not bear the finality, yet he had no choice but to bear it. The prayed-for days of joy had come, but so briefly, and now they were gone.

Gabriel wept alone.

PART FIVE

1760

CHAPTER 34

The Fruit of My Body

PHILEPENCA found it hard to wait for Gabriel; his absence was like having lost part of her own body. Every day, again and again, she looked up from her work to the northern waters for sign of his coming.

Last fall, before freeze-up, a trader on his way to Rainy Lake had brought word that Gabriel was wounded, that she should expect him in the spring. The traveler did not know the kind or extent of his injury, and though Philepenca was a dreamer, her dreams came of their own; she could not conjure the future or see distant things at will.

She had eased her loneliness by preparing for winter. She and her girls—who were quite as lonely as she—shelled maize, wove new mats for the winter lodge, set twice the usual number of rabbit snares, bartered for meat to dry, and otherwise made ready.

It all reminded Philepenca of her own childhood, and how she and old Wah-Wah-Taysee had struggled alone. But those days had toughened her, made her resilient, and had taught her that unless one gave up, loneliness was not fatal.

She had felt no rancor when Gabriel left for Quebec, no jealousy at the devotion that had held him there, and no bitterness at the hardship she now endured. But she missed her husband severely.

Now, winter was over, spring was nearly gone, and she waited. Today she longed tenderly for his coming, for no other reason than that she loved him.

It was the tenth of May, the Moon of Flowers, two months short of a year from the time of their leaving, when Gabriel and Two Babies returned. An old woman washing clothes on the shore saw the canoe coming and, when certain, called out, and a jubilation of welcome arose.

321

Gabriel's recovery had taken most of the winter. He could hear again, though in Two Babies' opinion, not as keenly as before. The hair on the left side of his head had grown, but the flames had carved deep into his left cheek and hand, wounds now covered by a tender network of pinkish-white skin.

Where the shirtsleeve had been incinerated from his arm and the blast had cut into the muscle underneath the skin, healing scars had woven ropelike tethers between elbow and forearm, so that now he could not straighten his left hand and his elbow was always slightly bent.

When she heard the shouts, Philepenca ran for the beach and, filled with joy, kept running until the water lapped about the swell of her thighs. With his good arm Gabriel drew her into the canoe, where she knelt between his knees, her face pressed against his scarred cheek, his arms folded tenderly about her. A-bo-wi and Wi-ni-sho-ba-go-sin joined them, and the reunion was complete.

It was Black Duck who, as he greeted Gabriel on the sands, examined his scarred arm and looked away. He shook his head and muttered, "Tangled wing." His words touched the imagination of the people, so that from that day they called him by this new name. Only to Philepenca and Two Babies was he yet Gabriel.

"Just give me time," he said to Philepenca.

"But time can kill the same as it can heal, *Nuco*," she answered.

It was a week after his return. The sun had set and the night birds were calling from the forest. Michel's death had left a dark, empty hole—though not so much a hole, for a hole is in one place, and this emptiness was everywhere.

Was his sorrow for Michel? Yes, but it was for himself as well—for his own mortality, for years that had missed their goal, for his life's rapid transit through time, and for so many wrecks left in its wake.

With the joy of reunion with Philepenca and his children past, Gabriel had withdrawn into some dark place in his own mind. Philepenca missed his touch, felt empty for herself and for their children. Before his arrival, she had tenderly imagined he would say to her, "Let's go away for a while, back to our little island, and redeem the year we've lost." But he had made no such invitation.

Tonight she took the initiative and said to him, "I've missed you so, Gabriel. Let's go away for a little while."

"I cannot go," he answered.

"Why not?" she asked.

"I've been away too long. There's much to do: fish to catch, meat to be hunted, work at the forge." He spoke in flat, emotionless tones that betrayed a kind of stupor, an absence of interest in life.

She tried again, "Then if not for days, just for tonight we'll go apart from the village. I want you near me, alone to myself. I need you to touch me." She reached out her lovely dark arms, but he looked away and made no answer.

When he turned toward her again, a tired, weary look clouded his face, and in the same flat tones he said, "Philepenca, a light has gone out. Something in me—I don't know what—is dead. I'm not the same. I don't know if ever . . . yes, I do know. I'll never be the same. You mustn't expect me to be."

Each month dragged into the next, and all he had said proved true. Gabriel's sadness deepened. He settled into a moribund state of mind, convinced that he soon would die. Not that he would take his own life—that would pain his family too deeply. Though, he thought, if it came to that, he could do it so no one would guess. He would not pull the trigger himself. Journey alone to Sandy Lake, fight in the border wars; sooner or later a bullet would find him. Or, more simply, he could let himself be sucked into the maw of some howling bizzard. Nothing would be easier. The old ones and the small ones would say the ice monster whose eyes are rolled in blood had devoured him, others would say it had simply been an unfortunate accident or a lapse of caution. Death by cold would be painless, he thought, just going to sleep, easing unknowingly out of life. But he feared that such an act might not be forgivable. He had an extreme fear of hell, of going to sleep cold and waking hot.

No. Suicide was not necessary, Gabriel reasoned. When a man's dreams are shattered, when he fails as bitterly as he had failed, he lives expecting to be struck again and again, to have the wind knocked out of him until he simply lies down and gives up. Without hope, a man will eventually die with no external cause.

So death became his expectation, something toward which he looked as a final release.

Many were the nights when he could not sleep, when he left

the lodge and went wandering along the water's edge, pondering the "if's," rehearsing his sins, flailing himself with the lash of misguided, outgrown conscience.

The weight on Philepenca's shoulders was oppressive. Though Gabriel was present, though they ate and worked together, his eyes were empty and his thoughts far away. Philepenca wept.

With the end of spring, rain ceased. Summer turned brown and sere. The leaves and grasses crisped and curled long before their time. Soon winter swept down hard, snowless. Without the redeeming beauty of soft white to cover the frozen land's obscene nakedness, the trees were bare, their black trunks dividing into black limbs that reached upward, like dried spiders that had laid on their backs and died, then more finely into webs across the desolate nickel sky.

Finally in January the heavens opened and the snows came. With a terrible fury they made up for their tardy arrival, so much so that their presence was as severe as had been their absence. In March and April the warm winds blew, giant drifts began to melt, and rivulets sent their winding coursers down the thawing hills to water the soil and fill the lakes.

Mild spring tints rose faintly on the face of black loam and, in May, buried the dead blackness in green life. Winter camp broke, sugaring was resumed. The cycle of life led the people back to Wind Lake, where again they farmed, fished, sang around their fires, played games in the warm nights, and to the fullest lived the months that made life worth living.

With the spring Gabriel returned to his forge where it stood alone on the hillock beneath the ancient oak.

After so many years the forge seemed grown out of the hill itself, something that had been there forever. On the side away from the sun, gray moss covered the greenstone blocks and there were dark gaps and cracks between the rocks where the mortar had broken out and fallen away. Yet the forge remained strong and useful.

A coat of heavy black soot creeped out of the chimney's throat and down over its edge. Directly above the chimney's mouth, where its smoke had for these dozen years passed upward through the overspreading tree limbs, leaves no longer grew, and a narrow passage extended through its naked arms on up to the blue sky.

The wide, old coal bed was black with use, and the thick leather of the great old bellows was worn and cracking.

Hanging around the hearth in their places were several pairs of worn iron tongs and hammers made tired by countless blows. After more than a year of disuse the big anvil's face was covered with rust. Now Gabriel's first chore at the forge was to rub the rust away until the face was bright again.

Gabriel had worked at this hearth for a dozen years now, and his fame as a smith in iron and copper had spread. From as far away as Rainy Lake people came to trade meat, corn, rice, skins, and woven articles for his work. Every man, woman, and child in the Wind Lake village dangled some copper piece about the neck—a cross of Lorraine, a fleury, Latin, or botonée cross, small bears, howling wolves, and swimming turtles—each of which Gabriel had shaped on his anvil or cast in a mold of clay.

Father Nathaniel lived among the Wind Lake people again that summer. He was now seventy-one years old. Decades of exposure to the elements and constant effort for his adopted people was marked deeply in his features. An intricate network of delicate furrows rippled in his face, but framed by dark olive skin, his even teeth still shone a brilliant white, and he was yet tall and pine-tree straight.

Now, on a bright morning toward the end of a luxuriant June, having taught morning lessons to a class of young catechumens, Father Nathaniel walked slowly and thoughtfully up the rise toward the forge where Gabriel was working. With his partly crippled left hand, Gabriel awkwardly grasped a bar of iron, one end of which he thrust into the burning coals; with his right he again and again pulled downward on a braided rope. In response to each pull, a stream of air from the leather lungs of the bellows rushed among the coals, making them leap and glow with intense heat.

After a time Gabriel pulled the rod from the fire and with his hammer began to draw out its cherry-red end. The priest came up beside him and stood watching, unnoticed. Dumarchais reached into the sash at his waist, pulled out a small pipe with terra-cotta clay bowl and a bamboo reed stem, and from a small, well-worn leather pouch filled the bowl with a mixture of leaves, dried, papery, reddish brown, shredded fine—his own concoction of bearberry, native tobacco, and spicebush. He picked a dry twig from the ground, laid its end in the coals until the twig broke into flames, and touched the fire to his pipe.

Till this moment he had said nothing, and the only sound was the hammer ringing on the face of the anvil. Gabriel thrust the rod back into the fire and pumped the bellows again for a second heat. The morning was warm and a sheen of perspiration covered his dark face. He had tied a light blue cotton cloth, folded narrow and smudged with soot, about his head for a sweatband. Already patches were soaked through.

Dumarchais leaned back against the rough bark of the oak, crossed his arms comfortably over his chest, drew on the pipe, and asked, "What's it to be? New trigger pan for that trap?" He nodded toward a small pile of iron pieces that lay on the edge of the forge bed.

"Yes, Father. That's what it's to be." Gabriel did not break his hammer's cadence. "It's Howling Wolf's," he added.

The priest picked up two iron fragments from the pile. "How in the world did he break a trigger pan?" he asked.

"Howling Wolf can break anything, Father. Just his nature. I wouldn't lend him this anvil."

Both men smiled. Howling Wolf's ineptitude was a standard village joke.

"Philepenca tells me this is your birthday," the older man said in a voice that showed his interest.

"Yes, I guess it is," Gabriel said, still not breaking the cadence of his hammer. "Twenty-third of June."

"Dare I ask how many?"

"Of course you can ask. Forty-six. I'm forty-six years old today." His last words were spoken with long pauses between them.

Father Nathaniel said nothing for a moment, and then, as though trying to reach something deeper, commented, "They've been a hard forty-six, haven't they, son?"

Gabriel kept hammering. His voice was taut with exertion. "Not all of them, Father. Some have been pretty good, and some couldn't have been any better." He flipped the iron over and worked its other side, then added, "If I weren't such a fool, all of them could've been good."

"That's saying too much, son." Father Nathaniel chuckled. "Nobody has a perfect life. Can't blame yourself for everything. In fact," he said, shifting and planting one foot flat against the tree behind him and leaning on its trunk, "it takes a sort of in-

verted pride to blame yourself for everything. If a man can blame
all his troubles on himself, it makes him feel like he's quite a
doer." Gabriel kept hammering.

Suddenly the priest lost patience. "Gabriel, lay that thing down!
I can't talk over that confounded din."

His friend's sudden vehemence shocked Gabriel, and, the hammer in midair, he looked around to see if the priest was serious.
Dumarchais' slate-blue eyes showed no hint of humor.

A breeze rustled the green spring leaves overhead. Father Nathaniel motioned to the forge. "Bank your fire, son," he said,
"and let's take a walk."

The two men ambled slowly in a westward direction away from
the lake and through the village, Gabriel following like a scolded
puppy, wondering. For half an hour they walked in silence,
through a deep growth of vaulted spruce, through a dell that lay
beneath a sudden hillock, past a grove of old scarred birches that
grew on the hillock's top, then unexpectedly—at least for Gabriel—they came into a hidden meadow.

The meadow spread out in the full bloom of lush, exuberant,
overgrown spring. Wild flowers of brilliant blue and six-petaled
blossoms of white with bright yellow hearts grew in prodigal profusion across its grassy undulating floor.

A sudden feeling of familiarity gripped Gabriel, a certainty he
had been here before. In the center, at the highest point of the
rising terrain, grew a perfectly shaped maple of great height and
breadth, a crown for the meadow's glory.

In a whisper Gabriel said, "Father, I know this place."

It was the clearing where he and Philepenca had come before
they were married, the place where the sun had broken through
leaden clouds and leaped to life in the variegated autumn leaves
of the wonderful tree, the place where she had told of having seen
his face in a dream before they met.

Now, with the sun high and beaming down from the cloudless
blue, the two men walked slowly, almost reverently, through the
green grass of the blooming field, and came to stand in the old
monarch's shade. With a startling whir a sudden barrage of small
wings flailed the air as a covey of quail exploded from hiding near
the trunk's base and flew away to taller grass on the clearing's
south edge. Father Nathaniel had as yet said nothing, and now

motioned toward the close-grown, matted tufts of grass from which the quail had flown.

Having sat, the two men faced each other. The priest's eyes narrowed and grew serious. "Gabriel," he said in an even voice, "don't you think it's time you came home?"

Gabriel, embarrassed and irritated by the confrontation, pretended not to understand. "Came home, Father?" he echoed. "What do you mean?"

Nathaniel Dumarchais' blue-gray eyes brightened with intensity. "Come home to your wife and children. It's time to pry the fingers of the past loose and let it slip back into the dark where it belongs."

Gabriel looked down to the ground, then at his crossed ankles. With his scarred, angular left hand, he ruffled the grass. "No, Father," he replied sadly, "I have years of penance yet to do."

"Penance!" The old priest spat out the word. Gabriel's eyes snapped into contact with his and Dumarchais continued, "Under God, Gabriel Dublanche, I don't know who you think you are! Atonement is the prerogative of God." He reached quickly toward Gabriel's collar, grasped the chain that held his mother's silver cross, and pulled so sharply that it bit into the back of Gabriel's neck. Dumarchais shook the cross under the younger man's eyes and said, "See this! *God's* prerogative! Not yours. You are *stupid*, and you are *arrogant*."

Never before had Gabriel heard Dumarchais speak so heatedly, and never had such words been directed at him. His anger began to rise. The priest kept on, "The suffering of God, *not* the suffering of Dublanche!"

"No," Gabriel shouted. "*His* death. *My* suffering." For a long moment tears brimmed in his eyes while emotion built in his breast. In a quieter, intense voice he added, "The fruit of my body for the sin of my soul."

Gabriel yanked the cross from Father Nathaniel's grasp and gripped it in his own fist. "Who are you to tell me about suffering, Father?" His voice was loud again. "I've a right to suffer. I loved my son more than I love life. And he's *dead*. Do you understand, Father? He's dead, and I killed him!"

Good! thought the priest, for the dam blocking Gabriel's emotion had finally burst. Gabriel breathed hard, and for the first time since his return, he wept.

At last he raised his eyes, gazed about in the branches spread above him, and subdued, asked sincerely, "Father, if God forgives from His heart, how is it that again and again I pay for my sins? How is it my wife and daughters suffer for what I've done?"

"Gabriel, son," the old priest said in a settled, firm tone, "you try to make forgiveness mean cancellation. Forgiveness, even God's, can't obliterate the past or deprive it of its consequences. Consequences go on like ripples in a lake when you throw a stone. You can't escape natural consequences by being sorry."

"Then I don't want forgiveness, Father. I've no right."

"We're not talking about 'right,' Gabriel. We're talking about mercy. And it's entirely up to you whether you want it or not."

Gabriel lifted his head, and finally, staring emptily into the branches above him, said, "I've never had such pain, Father. I loved him so. I can't bear it that he's gone."

"But," the old man said quietly, "that's the price."

"Price?"

"The price of meeting. The pain of parting is the price of meeting. Always, for everyone. Would you rather never have known him? Never have seen him? Never have held him? Never have called him your son?"

"Father, what are you *saying*?"

"I'm saying, Gabriel, that since your son was born, thousands of young men have died in war. You don't weep for them, because you never knew them. If Michel had never been, or if you had not known him, you would have no agony now."

Gabriel shifted his eyes uneasily. The priest went on.

"And you wouldn't have known the joy."

"But the joy didn't last long, Father. Mostly it's been misery."

"But it *was* joy, and it *does* last. The pain will fade. Oh, it won't ever all go away. But after a time the pain will fade until it's like a faint shadow on the wall, a dull pain in your side. But your memory of Michel—that's a different story. That memory will grow brighter. If you let him, he'll become a joy again, because of what you shared, and because you love him."

"So I have the joy of his memory. I have joy, and he has death."

"Gabriel, you're vain." The priest's tone was one of disgust.

"Vain!" Gabriel's anger sprang to life.

"Yes, vain. You can't see anyone but yourself. He had joy, too. Yes, you were apart for many years, but your absence didn't rob Michel of everything. You were not his entire world. There were people and places near to him. He had his God, his world, his dreams, his home. You're trying to turn your life into some grand piece of literature, some Greek tragedy. Trying to be the only good thing the boy ever knew.''

Gabriel said nothing. Nathaniel's last words were true and had cut deep.

Dumarchais spoke again, quietly this time. ''Gabriel, when you killed a man, you usurped the prerogative of God. 'Vengeance is mine,' said the Lord. You're trying to usurp it again, trying to buy Michel's atonement, and your own. You say you know beyond all question that you were the cause of his death.'' The priest paused to let his words sink in, then added, ''Is that not arrogance? Is it not vanity? And your vanity is killing you . . . and making your wife and children miserable.''

Then the old man unfolded his legs, put his hand to the trunk of the tree, and rose to his feet. ''I'm going back to the village now. You can come with me . . . or you can stay.'' He stood waiting for some sort of indication of what the younger man would do.

Gabriel sat staring at the ground. Finally, in a quiet voice, he said, ''I think I'll stay, Father. You go on ahead.''

Father Nathaniel stepped from the shelter of the big tree and started in the direction of the village, then stopped. Shading his eyes with his hand, he looked back at Gabriel and said, ''One more thing. I've noticed, Gabriel, that when we fail our trial, one day we face it again.''

Gabriel looked up and said quietly. ''That's not very comforting, Father.''

''No,'' the priest answered. ''It's not. But I'm not sure comfort is what you need.''

''What, then?''

''Fire.''

''Fire?''

''Fire to refine you. Fire to burn out the bitterness.''

''You make life sound dangerous, Father.''

''You should know, son. You should know.''

When Gabriel did not come home at nightfall, Father Nathaniel assured Philepenca that all would be well, that Gabriel had business to do alone.

On the morning of the third day, Gabriel did return, and immediately went to find Philepenca. He found her at last picking

blackberries in the bushes that grew between two stands of tam-
arack along an inlet southwest of the village. When Philepenca
saw him she felt ill at ease.

When he stood beside her, saying nothing, she did not look up,
but went on picking berries, dropping them into a cloth tied about
her waist, then spilling them to the half-full birch basket at her
feet. She wore a summer dress of light deerskin, the top of which
encircled her body below her arms and above her breast, suspended by narrow straps over her shoulders. The dark, soft skin
of her shoulders and arms glistened with a sheen of perspiration
caused not only by the day's heat but also by the moment's fearful
uncertainty.

"Philepenca," he said. She did not answer. *"Nuco."* He
spoke the word softly.

The intimacy of his tone shocked her pleasantly, and she looked
up into his face. Tears brimmed in his eyes and tenderness filled
his steady gaze.

He said nothing more, but lifted her berry basket from the
ground and handed it to the woman nearest by. He took his wife's
soft hand tightly in his own good hand, and without words led
her out of the blackberry bushes, away from the lake, up the hill,
and into the trees. Together they went without speaking to the
place where the old maple ruled.

The sun reflected in midmorning brightness from each of the
great tree's myriad green leaves, and each leaf added some unique
facet of glory to its splendor. To them it was more than a tree, it
was a symbol of their union, and now perhaps a tree whose leaves
would bring healing.

They sat again at the meadow's edge, and with tears he confessed—confessed his arrogance, confessed his vengeance, confessed his delusions of grandeur, confessed that he had forced her
to suffer. In the midst of his confession he pointed to the grass
where an ant was climbing a long blade that stood above all the
others. The ant reached the blade's tip, and with the sharp points
of black light that were his eyes, surveyed the Brobdingnagian
world about him.

"Nuco," Gabriel said, "I'm like that ant. I've tried to be wise,
but I've understood nothing that I've looked upon. But now, as
sometimes in the forest the sunlight suddenly burns away the thick
fog, I see." He paused and gazed into her big dark eyes, so full
of light. "It was your love that did it, and Nathaniel Dumarchais'

. . . and Michel's. Somehow I feel nearer than before to Michel—
as though the wall between us is paper thin. And there are our
children! And there is *you*, and the countless days we've been
together."

For a long moment he could not continue as tears of gratefulness made shining trails down his sun-darkened cheeks and fell
into the grass beside them. At last he was able to go on. "I see it
now, that my joys outweigh my sorrows, that your love has out-
weighed my bitterness. And more than all else, that God's grace
outweighs my guilt! *Nuco*, something has happened within me,"
he said, gazing deep into her brimming eyes, "and I feel Him
now as you seem always to have felt Him!"

The sun from behind shone on Philepenca's cheek and made a
silver halo for her face. Her heart was swimming in joy. She could
not conceal her unbounded love for Gabriel, and she reached out
with soft, strong arms, drew him to herself, and forgave him from
the heart.

The remainder of the day they spent in the meadow, in the shade
of the maple. A sweet, languorous peace filled them. Above them
a pair of doves, whose home was in the tree's branches, cooed a
delicate song. Once more the man and woman laughed together,
played beneath the tree's spreading branches like children, and
like children saw the world open to them again.

In the grass about them, the leaves of many autumns lay in a
mat of faded color and lifeless brown decay. But up from the
decay's ragged edges and through the mat's torn holes pushed all
that grew—the grasses, the flowers, the ferns and tender stalks.
Many rains had washed the particles of death into the soil, where
by some miracle of resurrection, death had once more become
life.

From a hidden crevice deep within the grasses and dead leaves,
Philepenca plucked a young, intricately formed fern, turned it
slowly between her fingers so that its sharp, clearly defined fronds
caught the light from every side and angle, and reveled in its
brightness. All around grew small clusters of bell-like flowers,
varied shades of blue, their mouths turned downward, quivering
at a touch, ringing a silent Angelus over the decaying, yet living
world at their feet.

AUTHOR'S AFTERWORD

It is an intriguing thing, trying to write a story about people who lived in another time. How does one discover the vantage point from which some man or woman who lived hundreds of years ago saw his or her world?

For Gabriel's story, I began with this premise: that in terms of relationships and human emotions and quests for truth, the things which we experience today are not different from what our forefathers experienced. In the most important sense, the things that happened to Gabriel Dublanche happen to twentieth-century Americans every day—the failed expectations, the accidents of time that thwart us all, the passions over which we ourselves stumble, the faith—or lack of faith—by which we live. Placing the account in an exotic period of history adds only color to any story that is truly human.

In my search for Gabriel's time, I had much help. In Charlevoix's *History and Description of New France*, published in 1744, I came across historical detail not readily found in modern texts. The wonderful books published by the Minnesota Historical Society were of great value to me; among them, Grace Lee Nute's works about the colorful, carefree voyageurs, Warren's *History of the Ojibway People*, and Ignatia Broker's *Night-Flying Woman: An Ojibway Narrative*. There was *Kitchi-Gami: Life Among the Lake Superior Ojibway* by Kohl (a German ethnologist who visited the Ojibway in about 1855), and *Chippewa Customs* by Francis Densmore. I studied the fascinating book from the University of Loyola Press, *Indian and Jesuit: A Seventeenth Century Encounter*, by James Moore. For general historic overview, I relied on Will Durant's *The Story of Civilization*, and gleaned much detail from Allan Eckert's works on the French and Indian War. There were books on plant and wildlife distribution, and Lopez's very popular book, *Of Wolves and Men*.

And in a different vein, the joy of being immersed in *Sigurd Olson's Wilderness Days* will never, ever leave me.

I dream that someday I might spend a full year on the shore of some "Wind Lake" or in a high mountain meadow, just to watch and absorb into my own heart the full cycle of the seasons as they come and go. But until that dream comes true, I'll be happy for every brief time that I may spend in our American wilderness—a place of quiet and calm that holds an enormously important key to our sanity—a wilderness that becomes more and more precious to us with every passing year.

ABOUT THE AUTHOR

Charles Durham is a free-lance writer, public speaker and Pastor of his local church. He lives on the harsh, barely populated High Plains in Western Kansas with his wife, Linda, who is part Native American. They have two sons and two daughters.

A student of the American Revolution and the westward migration, Durham participates in primitive encampments that replicate the Fur Trade Era of the late 1700s and early 1800s. He is a member of the American Mountain Men, a national brotherhood dedicated to re-creating this life, and as a Muzzleloader builds firearms styled to the period.

THE LAST EXILE is Charles Durham's first novel. His second, WALK IN THE LIGHT, is also being published by Ballantine.